Deborah Challinor has a PhD in history and is the author of ten bestselling novels. *Girl of Shadows* is the second in a series of four books set in 1830s Sydney, inspired by her ancestors — one of whom was a member of the First Fleet and another who was transported on the Floating Brothel. Deborah lives in New South Wales with her husband.

www.deborahchallinor.com

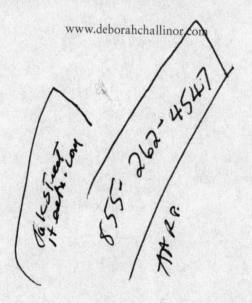

Also by Deborah Challinor

FICTION

Behind the Sun

Tamar
White Feathers
Blue Smoke

Kitty
Amber
Band of Gold

Union Belle

Fire

Isle of Tears

NON-FICTION

Grey Ghosts
Who'll Stop the Rain?

Deborah
CHALLINOR
Girl of Shadows

HarperCollinsPublishers

HarperCollins*Publishers*

First published in Australia in 2013
This edition published in 2014
by HarperCollins*Publishers* Australia Pty Limited
ABN 36 009 913 517
harpercollins.com.au

HarperCollins*Publishers*
Level 13, 201 Elizabeth Street, Sydney NSW 2000, Australia
Unit D, 63 Apollo Drive, Rosedale, Auckland 0632
A 53, Sector 57, Noida, UP, India
1 London Bridge Street, London SE1 9GF, United Kingdom
2 Bloor Street East, 20th floor, Toronto, Ontario M4W 1A8, Canada
195 Broadway, New York NY 10007, USA

National Library of Australia Cataloguing-in-Publication entry:

Challinor, Deborah, author.
  Girl of shadows / Deborah Challinor.
  2nd ed.
  ISBN: 978 0 7322 9300 0 (pbk.)
  Female friendship — Fiction.
  Women convicts — Australia — Fiction.
A823.3

Cover design by Nada Backovic Designs
Cover images: Woman © David et Myrtille/Trevillion Images; Street image from
State Records NSW:NRS 4481, Government Printing Office Glass Negatives,
items: Digital ID: 4481_a026_000205, Gloucester Street looking south from
little Essex Street, The Rocks (NSW) [Rocks Resumption photographic survey],
1901, Digital ID: 4481_a026_000206, Gloucester Street looking south from little
Essex Street, The Rocks (NSW) [Rocks Resumption photographic survey], 1901;
Women on street by shutterstock.com
Map on page vi uses detail from *Map of the town of Sydney 1836*, Dixson Library,
State Library of NSW — Ca 88/7; adapted by Laurie Whiddon, Map Illustrations
Typeset in Sabon by Kirby Jones
Printed and bound in Australia by McPhersons Printing Group
The papers used by HarperCollins in the manufacture of this book are a natural,
recyclable product made from wood grown in sustainable plantation forests.
The fibre source and manufacturing processes meet recognised international
environmental standards, and carry certification.

*This one is for my good mate Michelle Holman,
who always listens no matter how much I whinge*

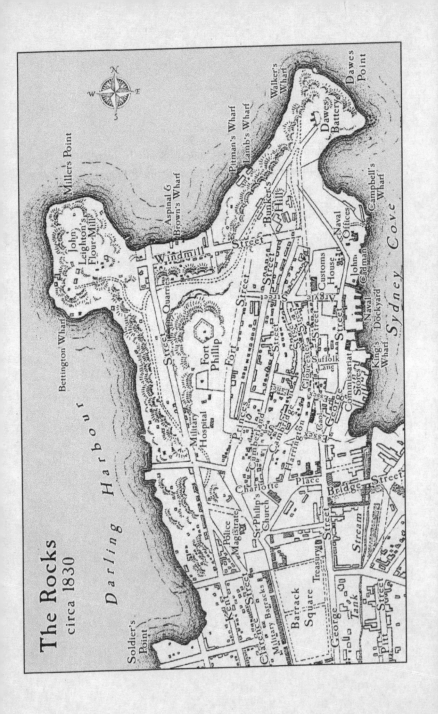

The Rocks
circa 1830

Part One

A Sense of Something Moving

Chapter One

September 1830, Sydney Town

As a lurid dawn broke over Sydney Harbour, the sun a slash of fire on the horizon, a handful of tardy bats straggled homewards across the shadowed land on a warm, salty breeze to seek dark shelter in trees and caves. Below them folk — free men and women and convicts alike — awoke, stirred blearily in their houses, and set about preparing for the day ahead.

The weather promised to be fair after a week of almost constant, pelting rain, and housewives and servants built fires beneath coppers for a long day of boiling mouldering laundry. Lags from Hyde Park Barracks looked forward to time outside the walls, even if it were only working on the roads or the tunnel from Lachlan Swamp, and ladies relished the prospect of time in the shops unhampered by heavy capes and umbrellas. In paddocks horses squelched morosely in steaming puddles, while their better bred, more highly strung counterparts kicked out at stalls and ostlers' boys. After a quick breakfast, market gardeners out towards Parramatta rushed to check that their recently planted vegetables hadn't been washed right out of the ground.

Sydney Town was finally beginning to dry out, but at least everyone's water barrels were full, and Tank Stream was perhaps cleansed of a fraction of its filth. The day that Mr Busby announced the completion of his water bore would be a day to celebrate indeed.

Those abroad by the time the sun hung free of the eastern horizon noted the change in the taste of the wind and agreed that spring had definitely arrived.

Sarah Morgan sat with her back against a sandstone wall, wrapped in a cloak of fear and gazing sightlessly at nothing, not even moving when she heard the rattle of keys.

There was little point. From outside came the clank and bang of the gallows being prepared: she knew very well who was coming for her.

The heavy door creaked open and the priest asked, 'Are you ready, Sarah?'

She didn't respond.

He tried again. 'Sarah, have you made your peace with God? Would you like to say a final prayer? It is not too late for redemption.'

Slowly, hearing her neck bones scrape as though her vertebrae had rusted, she moved her head to face him. 'I don't want redemption. I don't regret what I did. I'm glad I killed him.'

The turnkeys peering over the priest's shoulder stared at her.

As though he hadn't heard, the priest persisted, 'God will offer you forgiveness if you repent.'

'No. I refuse to. I hate spiders and that's what your God is.'

Shocked at her blasphemy, one of the turnkeys backed out of the cell, rapidly crossing himself. The other, evidently not so superstitious, fastened Sarah's hands behind her back with wrist-irons, then they were all in the corridor, their footsteps echoing hollowly off the flagstones. The passageway was cool and dim, and for several seconds a pair of sleek rats kept pace with them, scampering along the base of the wall, their pale faces those of the two girls belonging to the reverend on the convict ship *Isla*. What had been their names? Sarah struggled to remember: Eudora and Jennifer? No, Geneve, that was it. And then the rodents vanished.

She blinked rapidly.

'Those rats,' she said to the priest. 'Their faces, did you see them?'

'Yes, the Seaton girls,' he said. 'I know their father well.'

She stared at him in disbelief. Oh God, she was so frightened she was losing her mind.

Up ahead the door seemed to loom twelve feet tall. The priest, dwarfed, pulled it open and sunlight poured in, blinding Sarah. She squinted, shocked and confused by the noise until she realised it was the roar of the crowd gathered on Gallows Hill above the gaol, come to watch the day's hanging.

Beyond the door stood a column of soldiers, the scarlet and white of their jackets and trews glaringly bright. A drum began a slow, mournful beat as loud almost as her heart, and the troops set off towards the gallows across the yard. The turnkeys followed, gripping her elbows, while the priest trailed behind in his flapping black vestments, a tall, thin bat droning the funeral service under his breath: 'Jesus said unto her, I am the resurrection, and the life: he that believeth in me, though he were dead, yet he shall live. And whosoever liveth and believeth in me shall never die.'

A funeral service for *her*.

When her knees gave way the turnkeys simply jerked her upright again and dragged her along between them.

The good people of the Rocks cheered heartily.

She was hauled up the gallows's wooden steps and placed on a trapdoor beneath one of three rope nooses. Why were there three? She knew the number was profoundly important, but not *why* it was. If she closed her eyes and really concentrated it might come to her, but her terror and the drumming and the shouting and the rush of her own blood in her ears were all too much and it wouldn't. Surrendering, she let her need to know float away.

From the gallows she could see over the high stone wall and into the Harrington Street crowd, and all the way up the hill to the houses and shops and pubs perched along Gloucester, Cambridge, Cumberland and even Princes streets. In the mob she fancied she recognised familiar faces. There was her master Adam in his sober black coat and hat, hands cupped around his mouth, shouting and shouting and shouting. What was he trying to tell her? She'd never hear him from here. Mrs Dick from the Factory had come, too, and James Downey, and, oh God, Bella Jackson, and Mr Skelton from the pawnshop. And there was Rachel, her long pale hair falling free and catching the sun, turning everything around her to silver. No, that couldn't be right: Rachel was dead.

She couldn't see Friday and Harrie, but didn't blame them at all for not coming to watch.

The door to the gaol swung open again; more manacled figures emerged and suddenly there they both were, shuffling into the sharp light.

'*No!*' Sarah shouted in horror, her cry echoing around the yard. '*No, not them!*'

Harrie and Friday barely glanced up.

But no matter how loudly she screamed, Harrie and Friday were resolutely escorted across the yard and up the steps to stand beside her. The drum rattled on relentlessly, and overhead in the endless white sky crows wheeled and jeered.

Sarah blurted to Friday, 'But I confessed! I told them it was me!' Terror and panic conspired to make her feel dangerously light-headed, and she felt as though she might pass out. This was all horribly, horribly wrong.

Her copper hair shimmering in the sunlight, Friday shook her head sadly. 'You dobbed us in, Sarah.'

Sarah gasped. The shock almost stopped her heart and sent waves of confused dismay through her entire body. She hadn't, surely. Had she? She couldn't remember.

'It's for the best,' Harrie said in her lovely, kind voice. 'We'll be with Rachel soon. We'll all be together again.'

Sarah couldn't believe she could have done such a thing. 'I didn't! I know I didn't!'

But Friday and Harrie would no longer meet her eye.

Then a great howl rose from the crowd as the hangman arrived. Clomping up the steps in an absurdly large pair of heavy black boots, a top hat, and a coat reaching his ankles, he creaked his way across the gallows platform.

'Tell him!' Sarah pleaded. 'Tell him you're innocent!'

But Harrie and Friday said nothing, standing as still as statues, their hair lifting slightly in the light breeze, not even blinking. Refusing to help themselves.

Desperate, Sarah cast her gaze back out over the crowd. Adam had moved closer, his hands still raised, still trying to call out to her.

She opened her mouth and shouted as loudly as she could, but nothing at all came out this time. She tried again, straining until she thought her eyes might pop out of her head, and still nothing emerged, except perhaps for a tiny croak.

And the drum kept on beating, the crowd clapping in time now; a slow, gleeful, anticipatory cadence.

The hangman crouched, opened his leather case and removed three white hoods. He pulled one each over Harrie's and Friday's heads, and then Sarah's. The fabric smelt of lye soap and caught on her ear on the way down. The hangman then settled the noose around Sarah's neck, tightened it slightly and adjusted the knot so it sat just beneath her right ear.

She dragged in ragged, terrified breaths, the cloth of the hood drawing close against her mouth. 'Friday? Harrie?'

'Hush, girl.' The hangman stood back.

The drummer stopped drumming.

The priest intoned, 'For the wages of sin is death; but the gift of God is eternal life through Jesus Christ our Lord. Amen.'

The hangman yanked the trapdoor lever.

Sarah dropped like a stone.

She jerked upright, gasping, her shift plastered to her chest with sweat, her hand on her throat where she could still feel the rough scratch of rope. She sat for a few minutes, head bowed, until her heart slowed.

Her room was dark, though birds were starting up a racket in the tree in the backyard. She lit the candle on her nightstand and turned the miniature clock Adam had given her so Esther could never reprimand her for being late in the mornings. It was five-twenty — time to rise in a few minutes anyway.

Sarah threw back the bedclothes and set her feet on the floor. This was the fourth or fifth time she'd had the hanging dream, and every time she awoke feeling utterly hagridden, tormented — and riddled with cold, greasy fear. They had murdered Gabriel Keegan five months earlier and she had imagined the dread of being found out would have subsided a little by now, but it hadn't.

Thanks to Bella Jackson.

Sarah knelt and reached beneath the iron bed for the po and crouched over it, bunching her shift up around her waist and peeing for what felt like ages, then tossed the contents out of the open window. She crossed to the small chest of drawers and poured cold water from a jug into a bowl and scrubbed her face with a washcloth, then brushed most of the knots from her straight black hair and tied it up in a ponytail. Sniffing the armpits of the plain, sage-green dress she wore almost every day and deciding it would do, she shrugged it on over her head and fastened the buttons at the side.

She cleaned her teeth with bicarbonate of soda and, after a cursory glance in the tiny looking glass on the wall, took the candle and went downstairs.

Her mistress Esther Green was, as usual, already in the kitchen; coiffed and corseted and wearing yet another new dress. Sarah knew she wore stays because she'd crept into Esther's room one day and had a good poke around, discovering a drawer full of good-quality demi-corsets. Being slender, Esther didn't *need* to wear one, but all women of class did therefore Esther Green had to, even though, as an emancipated convict, she was hardly a toff. But rather than ask for Sarah's assistance she'd bought demi-corsets, which she could — just — fasten herself. This suited Sarah: she would rather walk a mile over broken glass in bare feet than consent to lace Esther Green's stays.

Sarah deduced from the way she was banging the porridge spoon around that Esther was in a bad mood. As a rule she often was, and usually at her worst at breakfast time. 'Morning,' Sarah muttered.

'Sarah,' Esther replied brusquely, without turning from the fire.

Esther Green believed that instead of residing in a series of small rooms above her husband Adam's jewellery shop on George Street, and daily cooking in a skillion kitchen — little more than a shed — attached to the house just beyond the back door, she should be living in much grander style. That the kitchen was so located to prevent heat and cooking smells permeating the house and shop, particularly in summer, was to her irrelevant, and so was the fact that the bricks forming both the large fire hearth and a barrier between the kitchen and house had cost a small fortune. Adam made good money as a manufacturing jeweller; if only he could be persuaded to work harder and sell more, then surely there must soon be the means to acquire a bigger and better-appointed house, perhaps on Woolloomooloo Hill on the other side of Hyde Park where the smarter set were building. If not there, up on Princes Street would possibly do, though it was rather too close to the rabble of the Rocks. Then she could have her modern indoor kitchen, with a big American cooking stove and room for enough sideboards to store her good crockery and cutlery and servingware. She loved to cook: Adam knew that. It was the least he could do for her, considering. She could also take on more servants — proper domestics from England, not sluttish convict girls — and get rid of sly, nasty, wanton Sarah Morgan.

She set the wooden spoon back into the pot and turned around, wiping her hands on her flower-sprigged calico apron. 'Have you emptied the chamber pots yet?'

Sarah shook her head: it was a chore she hated. In the mornings Esther always crapped in hers — on purpose, Sarah suspected, so she would have to clean it out. Esther could easily use the privy in the backyard. Adam did. And why couldn't Esther call it by one of its usual names? What was wrong with pisspot? Or thunder mug? Or even just po? No one called it a chamber pot.

'Well, go and do it then!' Esther demanded.

Sarah left the kitchen and went inside, passing through the small dining room where she would claw a sliver of revenge when she sat down to breakfast with Adam and Esther. Adam insisted on it and it drove Esther wild — probably *because* Adam insisted on it — otherwise she would have to eat in her room, or outside, or standing in the kitchen or parlour.

She met Adam on the first-floor landing.

'Good morning, Sarah. And how is everything today?'

'Same as usual.'

By 'everything' Sarah knew he meant Esther and her mood. There were two bedrooms on the first floor and Adam and Esther occupied one each, usually after a difference of opinion, which was a frequent occurrence. The following morning Adam always pretended nothing was amiss, as though Sarah couldn't possibly have heard Esther's carping demands and bitter accusations rising through the floorboards of her tiny second-floor attic room. Sarah couldn't decide whether the pretence was a product of his embarrassment, or because he didn't want to admit to himself the bellicose state of his marriage.

After a year as an assigned servant to Adam and Esther Green, Sarah understood that Adam did genuinely care for his lovely, bad-tempered wife; but she wasn't sure if he loved her. Mind you, who was she to say what form love took? She'd never been in love, and didn't care to be.

'Oh dear,' Adam said. 'What is it this morning?'

Sarah shrugged and thought, You should know — you were the one she was shouting at last night. He'd shaved already. The pale skin on his face was smooth and she could smell the toilet water he always wore, lightly fragranced with a hint of sandalwood and lime. This morning his dark hair, which had grown really rather long and well past his collar, was not tied back.

'Well, I expect I'll find out in due course,' he said.

Sarah nodded and went into Esther's bedroom. The pisspot sat on the floor near the bed draped with a piece of cloth, which was doing nothing to contain the stink. She picked up the pot by the handle and carried it downstairs, one hand pinching her nose shut, hoping she wouldn't meet Adam again. He knew Esther did this: it was embarrassing — for him and for Sarah. Obviously not for Esther, though, or she wouldn't do it. Dirty cow.

Outside Sarah tipped the turd down the privy and rinsed the po in the overflow from the rain barrel, then washed her hands thoroughly with carbolic soap.

At breakfast she set a covered dish containing sausage and an egg each on the table, ladled the beautifully prepared porridge into three bowls, poured the tea, then sat down.

Esther glared at her; Sarah glared back. Adam concentrated on his porridge.

Sarah knew that if Esther had her way, she would be sent back to the Parramatta Female Factory without delay. Esther had convinced herself that she, Sarah, was lifting her leg for Adam. She wasn't; she would never take such a pointless and unrewarding risk. Aside from having to endure Esther, she liked her assignment. Adam was a kind, intelligent and, at times, quite amusing boss, and she delighted in working with jewellery again. She was crafting her own designs now, as she'd learnt to do during her apprenticeship, and they were selling well, and her jewels were bringing new customers into the shop and increasing Adam's profits. Which was a good thing because she was still pilfering from him every chance she got.

And there was another reason she wanted to stay. When dear, precious Rachel had died six months before, Esther had deliberately denied her leave to visit Rachel's body or attend her funeral. Poor little Rachel, whom Sarah, Friday and Harrie had tried so hard to protect and care for, and whose baby, Charlotte, they were now all working to support. That had really hurt, and had lodged in her like the broken-off barb of an arrow, festering ever since.

Now Sarah wanted revenge.

That afternoon Sarah knocked on the back door of the house where Harrie Clarke lived and worked, towards the Essex Street end of Gloucester Street on the Rocks. When no one came, after a few minutes she let herself in, which she'd done before; it just meant everyone was busy.

The ground floor of the building was divided into four separate rooms, two of them shops. One was the premises of Harrie's boss, George Barrett, a tailor; another was his wife Nora's, a sempstress who made rather nice dresses for women with a bit of money to throw around. A third room was a very crowded little store where the Barretts kept their bolts of cloth and vast collections of thread and assorted sewing paraphernalia. In the fourth, a small foyer into which the back door opened, also cluttered with baskets and bales, were the stairs that led to the living quarters above, a parlour and two bedrooms. Mr and Mrs Barrett and the latest baby shared one bedroom, while the three older Barrett children slept in the other. As usual, the kitchen and the privy were outside in the backyard.

At the very top of the stairs was Harrie's attic room, which she'd made extremely cosy with the addition of rag rugs, drapes, cushions and a coverlet all cleverly fashioned from scraps of fabric. Angus, poor Rachel's odd-looking cat, also slept there, unknown to George Barrett who believed that at night he was outside chasing rats. Sarah would be envious of Harrie's comfortable little nest if Harrie hadn't plied her with all manner of handmade soft furnishings for her own room.

'Hello!' Sarah called up the stairs. 'It's Sarah Morgan. Is anyone home?'

Shrieking, '*Surprise!*' a little flaxen-haired girl burst out of an enormous wicker basket.

Sarah almost had a heart attack. 'Hannah! For God's sake! Didn't you hear me knocking?'

Hannah nodded. 'I was hiding.'

'You should answer the door when people knock, Hannah.' Sarah did her best mean scowl. 'It's rude to just ignore people when they knock.'

'But I was *hiding*!'

'Well, go and hide somewhere else. But first, tell me where Harrie is.'

'Upstairs with Mam and the baby. Lewis-spewus, that's his new name,' Hannah said, giggling wildly.

'Just go on up, Sarah,' Sarah heard George Barrett's disembodied voice say from the depths of his shop. George himself appeared a moment later. 'My apologies, I was busy with a customer. The things people expect you to do with a yard and a half of plain cloth and six buttons!' He shook his head in disbelief. 'And I thought I told you not to play down here, missy?' he said to Hannah, who stared at him defiantly, then scampered off up the stairs when he raised a warning hand to her.

George Barrett was of medium height, potbellied, dark-haired and pleasant-faced. Today mottled skin pouched beneath his eyes, testimony to the poor sleeping habits of his most recently arrived child, now almost two months old.

'Harrie's with the missus,' he went on. 'The babe had his worst night yet. Up, down, up, down. They're both exhausted, not to mention yours truly.'

Sarah nodded and sidled towards the stairs. She didn't particularly like George Barrett, though he'd never done anything specific to warrant her antipathy, and she most certainly didn't have any advice to offer regarding fractious infants.

She found Harrie in the parlour nursing the cause of all the trouble; a grizzly little bundle with a livid pink face and wispy hair the colour of treacle. From the doorway she said, 'I suppose this means you can't come out now?'

Harrie looked up. 'Good afternoon to you, too, Sarah.'

'Well, can you?'

'Mrs Barrett's just getting dressed. She and Lewis had a difficult night.'

'I heard.'

Nora Barrett appeared from the bedroom, trailed across the parlour floor and sank onto the sofa. She was still attired in her nightgown and a pale yellow cotton robe, the sash knotted loosely over the squashy mound of her post-confinement belly. From an untidy bun strands of blonde and grey hair fell across colourless, drawn cheeks, and the shadows beneath her eyes rivalled her husband's.

'I really can't be bothered struggling into my clothes,' she declared. 'Pass him here, Harrie. Go on, go out and have some fun.'

'Are you sure?'

Nora nodded. 'Go on. It's your afternoon off. There's no sense all of us being slaves to the little tyrant.'

Hannah ran into the parlour wearing one of her mother's bonnets. 'Can I come out with you, Harrie?'

'No,' her mother said. 'Certainly not. And take that off, it's not yours. Where are Abigail and Sam?'

'Sam's having a nap,' Harrie replied, 'which is what you should be doing, Hannah, and Abbie's next door with her friend.'

'Sam's napping 'cos he's a baby. I'm not a baby, I'm five,' Hannah said, and stamped her grubby bare foot.

Nora said, 'He isn't, he's three, but he still gets tired and so do you. Go and have your nap, Hannah. I'll not tell you again.'

Hannah glared at her mother for as long as she dared, then spun on her heel and stomped off into the children's bedroom.

'Little madam,' Nora muttered.

Harrie stood. 'Are you sure you don't need me this afternoon?'

Nora, her head bent over Lewis as she exposed a blue-veined breast for him, waved vaguely. 'I'm sure. Don't be late, though, will you?'

Outside, Sarah said, 'God knows why anyone would want to have one child, never mind four. That poor woman looks like she's been through a mangle.'

Harrie adjusted her bonnet. 'Oh, I don't know. Children can be very rewarding.'

'Not as rewarding as uninterrupted sleep, peace and quiet, a tidy house, and money in your purse.'

Harrie didn't respond: Sarah was frequently snide about the subject of children, but she was very good with baby Charlotte and Rosie whenever they went out to the Female Factory at Parramatta. Which had been quite often, lately. Thank God Esther Green had finally consented to allow Sarah more time off: until Mr Green had put his foot down and insisted his wife be a little more lenient, Harrie had been so worried Sarah would lose her temper and do something she would seriously regret.

They set off south along Gloucester Street, turned into Charlotte Place, then followed George Street until they came to their favourite tea shop. Unfortunately, it wasn't their original favourite tea shop — at which, several months ago, they'd been told their patronage was no longer appreciated because of complaints from customers about Friday's language — but the cakes and selection of teas available at this one were almost as inviting.

Today they were celebrating the passing of the first twelve months of their sentences as transported convicts. Harrie and Sarah now had six years left to serve, and Friday thirteen. Providing their behaviour was deemed 'good', they might apply to receive tickets of leave sooner than that and move independently into the community, at least partially free of the system that bonded them to masters and mistresses, working as servants for little more than food and board.

But the occasion today would also be tainted with a sadness that was still very raw. When they'd arrived in New South Wales after six months together in London's Newgate Gaol and almost four at sea, their number had been four. They had been as close as sisters, as much a family as it was possible to be without sharing blood. Now they were only three.

Friday, already seated at a table, waved.

'That's a very nice dress,' Harrie said as she pulled out a chair.

It was, and not the sort of thing Friday Woolfe usually favoured. Of glazed camlet in smoky blue and black stripes with black piping, the waist sat snugly and the neckline, for a change, displayed no hint of cleavage. The bodice, however, was very fitted thanks to cleverly placed darts, and in pleasing contrast to the fullness of the upper sleeves. The accompanying hat, a wide-brimmed straw, was devoid of the artificial flora and fauna that normally cluttered Friday's headwear. Instead, a black satin band held a simple fan of black ostrich feathers pinned with a jet brooch. The overall effect, especially against Friday's rich copper hair and pale skin, was one of well-tailored style.

'You don't think it's too plain?' she asked.

'No.' Sarah sat down. 'It's quite clever actually. Smart, but still shows off what you've got.'

'Mrs H is taking me in hand,' Friday grumbled, referring to the madam of the brothel where she worked. 'Apparently I dress like a tart.'

'Well, you do,' Sarah said.

'But I *am* a tart.'

'You don't look like one today,' Harrie said admiringly. 'You look like a proper lady.'

Friday snorted.

'You do!' Harrie insisted. 'Who made it?'

'Mrs H's dressmaker.'

'I could make you a couple more in that style, if you like,' Harrie offered. 'You'd only have to pay for the fabric and trims.'

Sarah made a disbelieving noise. 'Aren't you too busy running around after the Barretts to be sewing dresses for friends?'

'I could find the time. I miss sewing. I've barely done any since Lewis arrived, I've been that busy.'

'Didn't I just say that?' Sarah snapped.

Friday tut-tutted. 'You're grumpy today. What's the matter?'

'Nothing.'

The waitress arrived: the girls ordered tea and a selection of cakes and pastries. When she'd departed Friday and Harrie stared intently at Sarah, silently bullying her into confessing what was on her mind.

She sighed heavily. 'I had that dream again. The hanging one.'

Friday made a sympathetic face. She, too, had been suffering nightmares, except in hers Gabriel Keegan came back from the grave, stinking and slimy and ruptured with his guts spilling out everywhere, and chased her through the streets of the Rocks, shouting at her to give him back his money. Why he wanted money, she couldn't fathom: she, Sarah and Harrie had kicked him to death, yes, but they'd never robbed him. She also couldn't understand why she was dreaming about him; she'd hated the cove when he was alive and, though she still felt a little uneasy about what they'd done, she had no regrets. If anything, she'd expected to be having Sarah's nightmares about the gallows — which, after all, was the awful black shadow looming over them. Lucky Harrie. Usually the most susceptible to guilt, it seemed she only had to put up with Rachel floating in and out of her dreams. Though now that she thought about it, even perpetually good-natured Harrie had been subdued and ... distracted lately.

No one said anything for a minute.

'You haven't heard, then?' Harrie asked at last. 'From Bella?'

Friday shook her head.

'God,' Sarah said under her breath. 'It's driving me bloody mad, waiting.'

The waitress arrived with their order. She set down a two-tiered plate stand on which were arranged cakes and scones, poured three cups of tea, and asked, 'Will there be anything else?'

Harrie said, 'No, thank you.'

When the girl had gone Friday said, 'Don't think about it. She'll be biding her time, having the time of her life, thinking about us sweating.'

'It's not so bad during the day,' Sarah explained. 'It's at night when I'm asleep. I don't seem to be able to keep hold of what happens to my thoughts.'

'Could you not take a sleeping draught?' Harrie suggested.

Sarah shook her head. 'I might sleep too long in the morning. Esther would love that. It'd give her another reason to make my life a misery. *God* I hate that woman.'

Harrie reached for the sugar. 'Well, try not to think about Esther Green today. This is supposed to be a celebration. Come on, drink your tea before it gets cold.'

'Yes, here's to us.' Friday raised her cup. 'One year down.'

They clinked cups.

'It doesn't feel like we've been here a year already,' Harrie remarked. 'It's been bad, some of the time, hasn't it? But apart from that, it hasn't really been as awful as I imagined it would be. I actually *like* where I'm assigned now. I like the Barretts.'

Friday agreed. 'Look at me. An ordinary old whore, and I'm earning ten times more than I did in London.'

Sarah made a rude noise. 'You're barely twenty, and you're so popular the cullies have to book a week in advance.'

'Though you're not supposed to be doing that,' Harrie reminded her. She helped herself to a scone from the lower cake plate, inspected it, took a bite and said through it, 'Imagine how much less you'd be making if you really were a hotel housemaid.'

Friday waved her hand vaguely. She'd got away with it for nigh on a year now, and fully expected to continue to do so.

Harrie let the matter pass, as she always did. They needed the money and, if Friday weren't working as a prostitute and Sarah weren't stealing jewellery from Adam Green, there wouldn't be any.

'You should have a pastime,' she said to Sarah. 'Something to keep your mind occupied, so you don't worry so much. Then you might not have such awful nightmares.'

'A pastime? What a good idea,' Sarah said. 'If only I'd paid more attention to the straw-plaiting lessons at the Factory.'

Friday giggled. 'What about pin-prick pictures? Or you could press wild flowers. That'd be satisfying.'

Harrie frowned, but Sarah laughed. 'Paper-work or quilling?'

'Shell-work?' Friday suggested. 'You could have your own shell grotto.'

'What about papier-mâché?' Sarah added, getting into the swing of it. 'Or feather-work or wax flowers?'

'Knitting, knotting or tatting?'

'Butterfly collecting?'

'Playing the harp?'

'Stop it, you two,' Harrie said, laughing herself now. 'I mean it, though, Sarah. It wouldn't do you any harm to have a pastime. What about embroidery? I could draw some really nice patterns for you. Mr Barrett is thinking of sending some of my designs to England to calico-printers and lace workers he knows there.'

'Is he now? Well, you'd better make sure you get paid for them if he does,' Sarah cautioned.

'Well, of course I will,' Harrie said, who hadn't thought about that at all.

Sarah chose an Eccles cake and cut it in half, poking at the fruit inside with the tip of her knife. 'It's nice of you to think of me, Harrie, but I don't want a pastime. I'm too busy.'

Friday raised a sly eyebrow. 'Working out how to get your own back on Esther the Cow?'

'Something like that.'

'Oh, Sarah.' Harrie sighed heavily. 'She's just a bitter, spiteful woman. Try to ignore her.'

Friday suggested, 'Have you tried a horseshoe over your bedroom door?'

'To ward off Esther? I hadn't thought of that,' Sarah said.

Harrie tittered.

'No, though that's not a bad idea.' Friday poured herself more tea. 'I meant to keep the nightmares away. It's a pity you can't shift them onto her, isn't it? That would teach her.' Her face lit up. 'Actually, that *would* be a good idea! She could have mine as well, and be haunted by the gallows *and* Keegan.'

Sarah stared at Friday for a long, thoughtful moment. Then her mouth twitched in the beginnings of a rather unpleasant smile. 'Harrie, are you still dreaming about Rachel?'

'On and off.'

'Good dreams or bad dreams?'

Harrie took a long time to reply. 'Well, good, I suppose, because I still get to see her. But bad, too, because when I wake up I remember all over again she's gone.'

'Why don't you come calling and tell me about it?' Sarah suggested. 'When Esther's listening.'

Harrie frowned. 'What for? You already know. And why does Esther have to be listening?'

'Sarah Morgan,' Friday demanded. 'What are you scheming?'

20

Sarah pushed her cup and saucer away and crossed her arms defiantly. 'I *am* going to teach her a lesson. For stopping me from saying goodbye to Rachel, and for being such a bitch.'

'But what's that got to do with my dreams?' Harrie asked.

'While Esther's flapping her big ears, you can tell me that you think Rachel's haunting you in your sleep. Which isn't *really* a lie, is it? And I'll tell you it's the same for me. Then after a few weeks we'll tell each other she's haunting our daylight hours as well, and that Rachel must want ...' very slowly, Sarah leant forwards '... *vengeance*!'

Friday and Harrie both jumped: heads at nearby tables turned.

'Vengeance for what?' Friday said.

'For being left to die alone in the Factory. For having no one to mourn her when she was buried.'

'But that's not true,' Harrie protested.

'We know that, but Esther doesn't, and Esther's terrified of spirits. She's got hands and eyes and horseshoes and scroll whatsits all over the house. And crosses, and Jews don't even have crosses.'

Friday started to laugh. 'It's a bloody good idea and it would serve her right, but there is one tiny problem.'

'What?'

'Rachel *isn't* haunting you.'

'Ah, but I can make it *look* as though she is, can't I?' Sarah replied excitedly. 'A toppled vase here, a missing hairbrush there, odd unexplained noises. Don't forget I'm quite good at creeping around without people noticing.'

'And what's Adam going to think about you scaring his wife half to death?'

'Well, obviously I'll have to do it without him realising it's me.'

'What if you frighten the shit out of him as well?' Friday asked.

Sarah frowned: she hadn't thought of that.

Harrie shook her head. 'I don't think you should.'

'Why not?' Sarah said. 'You just said I should get myself a pastime.'

'It's disrespectful.' Harrie fiddled with her teaspoon and wouldn't look up. 'To Rachel's memory, I mean.'

'Oh, I don't know,' Friday said. 'I reckon she'd think it was a hoot.'

'Haunting, though,' Harrie replied. 'Spirits and the like. You should be very careful with that sort of thing.'

Especially, she thought, now that Rachel really *might* have come back.

Chapter Two

Friday hurried back to the Siren's Arms Hotel on Harrington Street down on the Rocks. It was supposed to be one of her days off but Rowena Harris had reluctantly admitted this morning she was too unwell to work in the attached brothel, so Friday had been rostered on in her place. She didn't really mind: it was all money in her pocket — and in the Charlotte fund, carefully hidden under the floorboards in Sarah's room.

Rowie, though, would have to do something about her bleeding: this wasn't the first time she'd cried off and she'd only been working for Elizabeth Hislop for four months. Rowie reckoned it didn't matter how many sponges she stuck up there it still leaked through. And she wasn't malingering either; you only had to look at the poor thing's pinched, white face to see the pain she suffered.

Friday smiled to herself as she thought of Sarah scaring the shite out of Esther Green. It certainly *would* serve her right. But the smile faded as she recalled the conversation that had given rise to Sarah's latest scheme — the dreams fuelled by the awful power Bella Jackson wielded over all three of them. Bella knew they'd killed Gabriel Keegan, and Friday hated Bella even more than she'd loathed Keegan — they'd both been directly responsible for Rachel's death — and the fact that Bella now controlled their fates made her blood boil every time she allowed herself to think about it. The worst of it was the waiting. Bella had shown her hand in May: it was now September and nothing more had happened except that Friday, Sarah and Harrie had become increasingly sick with worry, wondering when and how she would strike.

Friday walked down the carriageway at the side of the Siren's Arms and around the back to the cobbled courtyard, fanning flies from her face with her hat, and flicked a wave to the stable boy, thirteen-year-old Jimmy Johnson. He grinned and waved back. She poked her head into the kitchen, said hello to the girls working there, their cheeks red from the heat of the enormous cooking fire, then pushed open the hotel's back door. The light in the little foyer was dim but she could hear noise coming through from the bar at the front, and the sound of Jack Wilton swearing nearby.

'Jack?' she called. 'You need a hand?'

'Nah, I'm right.'

He came around the corner struggling to roll a large beer barrel along the corridor, cursing again as it veered and banged noisily into the wall. 'Shit, that'll put a bloody great head on it.'

Friday dropped her reticule and hat and grabbed one end of the barrel; between them they steered it across the flags in the right direction, towards the bar.

'You didn't heave this out of the cellar yourself, did you?' Friday asked, giving the barrel a shove with her palm to keep it going straight. 'Where's Al?'

Jack shook his head. 'Me and him hoisted it up, but the bar's flat out this afternoon. He had to nip back. I said I'd roll it along meself.' He stopped and whipped open a door. 'Quick, darlin', now's our chance.'

Friday laughed: it was the storeroom where Mrs H, who owned both the hotel and the brothel, kept the spare plates, cutlery and linen for the hotel dining room. She slapped Jack's arm playfully. 'You never give up, do you?'

'Nope.'

'I *told* you you'll be the first to know if I ever change my mind.'

'Not today, then?' Jack said, crestfallen.

'Not today.'

'You're missing the time of your life.'

'No doubt I am.'

'Ah well.' Jack closed the door again.

Friday smiled, more to herself this time, and turned back to the barrel. Jack Wilton was Mrs H's driver, handyman and part-time barman, very good-looking and a bit flash. He'd been after her for a shag ever since she'd arrived: she hadn't capitulated and was never likely to. She had no intention of doing it for nothing and he couldn't afford what she charged. Also, she suspected he genuinely fancied her and had high hopes, and she couldn't have that. On the other hand, she had a fair idea he put himself about, so she didn't feel too bad about constantly turning him down.

'Come on,' she said, 'let's get this where it belongs.'

Together they rolled the barrel into the noisy, crowded bar and up to the pumps behind the counter. Jack gave Friday a quick peck on the cheek by way of thanks and she left him and Al to it.

Upstairs in the hotel's accommodation wing Friday unlocked the door to the room she'd occupied since she'd been assigned to Elizabeth Hislop, sat on the bed, untied the ribbons on her delicate suede pumps, inspected the damage and tossed them into a corner. It was ridiculous: they were new on today to go with her striped blue dress and were ruined already from traipsing around streets full of potholes and stones and horseshit. Why she couldn't just wear her comfortable, black leather lace-up boots she didn't know. Being only six months old they were in reasonable nick, replacements for the pair she'd dropped in the cesspit behind the Bird-in-Hand after the incident with Keegan. She couldn't see what was wrong with her usual low-necked, purple and indigo and red and yellow dresses, either. She *liked* bright colours and lots of ventilation, especially when the weather was warm.

But Mrs H had decided the cullies would pay even more if Friday looked like she had class. Friday wasn't so sure about that. For a start she wasn't even *in* her street clothes when she was with her customers, but Mrs H insisted Sydney was such a small town that she could quite easily bump into them when she was out and about, which was probably true, actually. And for another start, Friday *knew* she didn't have any class, and never would. Also, in her experience, men most fancied the girls who were nothing like their dreary, prudish, dried-up — stripy-dressed — wives. But Mrs H was her boss, and her job was tolerable and she was making lots of money, so if she had to wear boring clothes and stupid footwear, then she supposed she would. And she did quite like her new hat.

She spent five fiddly minutes opening the covered buttons at the side of her dress so she could wriggle out of it, pulled off her stockings, and tugged down her half-petticoat and left it in a heap on top of her dress on the floor. She'd never worn drawers or a corset — she'd never known a female who did, outside of work hours — and couldn't see why she should start now. They were horrible things, stays; her waist was already neat enough, and she didn't need anything to push up her tits — they did perfectly well by themselves.

Collecting her pipe fixings from her reticule, she sat on her bed in her shift and tamped tobacco into the bowl, lit it, luxuriously puffed out clouds of blue, subtly flavoured smoke, then lay down. She had to get ready for work soon but before she did she'd grab a few minutes' rest.

This was the nicest room she'd ever had. The window faced east and welcomed the sun first thing, there was plenty of space, it was full of nice things and, best of all, there was only her in it. Harrie had made her dainty stuffed cushions for the chair and the bed, a quilted cover and a floor rug. As a thank-you present, Friday had bought her a very fancy sewing box — dark coromandel inlaid with mother-of-pearl with a bronze handle shaped like clasped hands, and filled with mother-of-pearl sewing implements, each in its own little compartment lined with red silk. She knew that when Harrie had decorated Sarah's room, Sarah had made her a delicate locket of silver and black enamel to hold Harrie's precious strands of Rachel's hair. Sarah had even paid Adam Green for the materials, albeit with chink she'd made from fencing bits and pieces she'd robbed off him. But it was lovely at last to be able to give each other nice things, after all the deprivations they'd endured.

It worried Friday, though, Sarah's stealing: surely her boss must have noticed things were going missing? She never took much; a pair of gold earrings here, a few small loose stones or some gold wire there, and she knew how to cover her tracks, but it had been going on for a year now. He *must* know, surely?

He certainly fancied her. Friday had seen the way he looked at her when he thought no one was watching, and it was pretty obvious. But what if he was biding his time and planning to blackmail her into doing something she didn't want to do, such as lifting her leg for him? Friday knew Sarah very well now, and it would really kill her to have to do that. It wasn't, Friday believed, that Sarah had taken against men; she just didn't want *anyone* that close to her. She was such a prickly little person.

On the other hand, Friday could definitely see the attraction for Adam Green. His wife Esther was a well-put-together woman but, God almighty, what a harpy! Mouth like a cat's arse, bitter as dandelion greens, *always* bitching and complaining. Sarah was quiet, very smart, witty when you took the time to listen to her, and really rather attractive herself with her shiny black hair, slanted glinting eyes that could mesmerise you if you weren't careful, and that mysterious scar on her face. No, she didn't blame Adam Green at all for fancying her. But if he ever did anything to hurt her, Christ, he'd better bloody well watch out!

Friday wriggled on the bed cover, relishing the feel of fresh, soft cotton against her bare calves and heels. She glanced at the little clock on her night table and started: bugger, she'd be late if she didn't hurry up. She pulled off her shift, poured water into a bowl and lathered fancy scented soap in her hands. After giving her face, armpits, groin and feet a quick wash, she dried herself and sat naked at her dressing table.

She opened a shallow drawer and fished out a bottle of gin and took a long swig, then put it to one side. Now, her face. First a dash of rice powder to cover the freckles on her nose and a dusting of Pear's White Imperial Powder everywhere else, including across the tops of her breasts, for a bit of a pearly glow, then a sweep of Bloom of Roses on her cheeks. Not too much, though, or it looked a bit much against her hair. She took another gulp of gin to steady her hand then opened a little pot of lampblack mixed with oil and, with a tiny sable brush, painted a thin black line above her upper eyelashes. Some girls applied it directly to their lashes but she didn't: it tended to end up all over your face by the end of the night, and anyway her lashes were quite dark and lush enough without it, despite her naturally red hair.

She put the lid back on the pot so it wouldn't dry out and contemplated her assortment of lip preparations. Which would it be tonight? Rose Lip Salve, Rigge's Liquid Bloom or the vermilion lip rouge? She never kissed her cullies under any circumstances, but despite that and no matter what she used it came off — how quickly depended on what she was being paid to do. The vermilion was her favourite because it was so bright; that would do. She outlined her lips with another little brush and filled them in, then blotted carefully with a square of cotton.

She knocked back another enormous swig of gin, shuddered as it went down, burped, dabbed oil of violets on her throat, breasts, belly and in her bush, and crunched a breath pastille.

'Ah, you look lovely,' she said solemnly to the glass. Grabbing her hairbrush — never a comb; a comb always got stuck, her hair was that thick — she worked on a section at a time to untangle the knots that seemed always to congregate at the nape of her neck, and twisted and pinned up a few fat, gleaming strands so it fell becomingly. Then she shrugged back into her striped dress, not bothering with her shift.

She opened all three doors of her clothes press and stood frowning at the shelves, then chose two corsets — one in pale green silk, which she didn't like wearing because it was itchy against her skin but looked nice, and one in finest white linen — and two pairs of fancy white lawn drawers you could almost see through. She always took at least two of everything as some cullies could be very messy. To go with them she selected a pair of green silk satin slippers, and from the hanging compartment of the press a lavender muslin robe with an embroidered border of indigo and white flowers and green leaves. Mrs Hislop owned everything, but the garments were at Friday's disposal for as long as she remained assigned to her and working in her brothel. As she would have to carry everything down the little alleyway that connected the Siren's Arms on Harrington to the brothel on adjacent Argyle Street, she folded the lot into a basket, grabbed her reticule and, jamming her feet into her comfy black boots, clomped out of her room into the corridor.

Two doors down she knocked loudly. 'Rowie? It's me, Friday.'

Without waiting for an answer she went in. Rowie lay dozing on her bed in a shift and robe, a cloth-wrapped hot-water bottle pressed against her belly.

'How are you feeling?'

Fatigue discoloured the skin beneath Rowie's wide grey eyes, her coal-dark hair looked lank and her skin was pale and slightly greasy. 'A lot better. I should be able to work tonight.'

Friday didn't think so. She rummaged in her bag and passed over a package. 'Here's your medicine.'

Rowie sat up, wincing, and opened the parcel. Inside was a bottle of laudanum, a paper twist of barley sugar and one of lemon drops.

'To cheer you up,' Friday said.

Rowie smiled. 'They're my favourites, too.' She eased the cork from the laudanum and drank straight from the bottle. The action reminded Friday so much of Rachel she had to look away. 'Has Mrs H said anything?' Rowie asked.

'Not to me.' And she hadn't, but Friday knew Rowie wouldn't last much longer in Elizabeth Hislop's house if her problems on the rag continued to interfere with her work. Mrs H was a fair employer and a decent-hearted woman, but she was running a business and wouldn't carry staff. 'Have you always had troubles down below?'

Rowie shrugged. 'Comes and goes. Before I started here I'd had five or six months when everything was good. I'm getting pretty sick of it, though. My mam says to have a baby. She says that'll fix it.'

'That's a bit drastic, just to stop a bit of bleeding. Is your mam here, in Sydney Town?' Friday knew Rowie had a ticket of leave, but hadn't heard she had family in New South Wales.

'No, but she sends me letters. Well, the neighbour does. Mam can't read or write. She's always telling me to marry a decent man, *not* like my father, mind, and settle down and have a family.'

'How does she think you're going to meet a decent cove when you're on the town?'

'She thinks I'm a maid of all work for a rich family in a big house. I'm sending money home to her and my little sisters. They depend on it. You've *no* idea how pleased I was to be taken on here.'

She leant over to set the bottle of laudanum on her night table, and Friday saw that blood had seeped through her rags, shift and robe, staining her bed cover.

'Don't move, love, you've sprung a leak.'

'What? Oh shite.'

Friday took a towel from a chair and slipped it beneath Rowie's bottom. 'Where do you keep your rags?'

Rowie pointed at her clothes press.

'Spare shift?'

Rowie gestured again and Friday fetched her what she needed.

'Look, I'm due at work in a minute but I'll send Annie up from the laundry with clean linen, all right?'

'Thanks, Friday. And thanks for my medicine and the sweets.'

'Any time.'

Friday turned to go but Rowie blurted, 'And Friday? *Please* don't tell Mrs H how bad I am. I'm desperate to keep this job. Please? I really can't afford to lose it.'

'I won't, don't worry. See you tomorrow.'

Friday knocked on the closed door of Elizabeth Hislop's office.

'Come in!'

Striding in and flopping down in the armchair beside her boss's desk, Friday stretched her long legs out in front of her. She'd sat there dozens of times over the past year chatting away to Mrs H, and over that time they'd become friends. Friday missed Harrie and Sarah desperately since they'd all been assigned to different jobs after being in the Female Factory together, and Elizabeth had become a substitute during the frequent times the other girls weren't available. She was older than Friday by almost thirty years, but she was wise and she was good. It had still taken Friday months, however, to tell her why she would have preferred not to work in a brothel.

One day she'd simply said, 'Mrs H, do you remember when I first started here and you asked me why I'd rather be on the streets?'

Elizabeth had nodded.

'Do you still want to know?'

'If you want to tell me.'

Friday had decided that she owed Elizabeth Hislop an explanation, and that it was time. 'I had a friend a few years ago, a very dear friend. Very pretty, she was. And sweet. I was fifteen, she was a year younger. We were working in a bawdyhouse on Long Acre

Street near Covent Garden for a madam called Ernestine Monk, a real bitch, flash as they come. And her crew! Bloody mongrels! We worked all hours of the day and night and she took sixty-five per cent. Sixty-five! Well, we were young and stupid and we just didn't know any better. One night a cully beat the shit out of my friend and cut her with a broken bottle. Everywhere. Nearly killed her. Monk said she'd asked for it and fired her. My friend couldn't live with looking the way she did and necked herself. I vowed then never to work for a madam again, or belong to a crew. And I never *have* worked in a brothel, until now. Never run with a crew, either.'

Elizabeth's eyes had filled with tears. 'Well, I can understand your reasons, Friday, but I hope you've realised I'm nothing like that woman.'

'I know,' Friday had said. 'I know you're not. That's why I've bothered to tell you.'

But Friday had never told Elizabeth Hislop how much she despised the men she had sex with day after day, how they made her sick with their pathetic, slobbering physical greed and inability to control their bodies and desires. Most days it required considerable will and gin before she could make herself do what was required to earn her pay, but she persevered because paradoxically she was good at it, she was in demand, and she made a lot of money, which she needed for the Charlotte fund, to help Harrie so she could send money home to her family, and to keep herself in drink.

'Friday, dear,' Elizabeth said. 'What can I do for you?' She glanced at the watch on the silver chatelaine she always wore around her plump waist. 'Shouldn't you be starting work?'

'I've got a few minutes.'

'I hope you don't plan to wear those dreadful boots?'

Friday smiled. 'No. Can I talk to you about Rowie?'

Sighing, Elizabeth closed the ledger in which she'd been writing, removed her gold-wire spectacles and sat back in her chair. 'How is she?'

'Bleeding all over her room,' Friday said without a shred of guilt, despite her assurance to Rowie only minutes earlier. She had a plan.

'My God, really? Should I send for Dr Chandler?'

'No, I just mean she's bleeding heavily.'

'That's unfortunate. It really is.' Elizabeth looked grim. 'I've thought hard about this and I'm sorry to say it but I'm going to have to let her go.'

Friday nodded.

'I really don't have much choice,' Elizabeth went on. 'I've had complaints from customers about availability, and mess and what have you, and it isn't as though she's only off a few days a month. We could have worked around that. She seems to be on the rag all the time. I *am* a bit cross she wasn't honest with me when I took her on.'

'She says she wasn't having trouble when she started here.'

Elizabeth rolled her eyes.

'What a shame,' Friday said, staring at the scuffed toes of her boots. 'The money she sends home to her mam and sisters will have to stop, I suppose. I hear they're only little girls, her sisters.'

Elizabeth sighed again, but much louder this time.

'Father's long gone, of course.'

Silence.

'Still, I suppose she can get work somewhere scrubbing floors. Christ,' Friday said, alarmed, 'I hope that doesn't make her troubles even worse!'

'Oh, for God's sake!' Elizabeth exclaimed. 'I'll see what I can do! Can she cook? I can probably put her in the kitchen until she finds something else. Not permanently, mind! And I expect I can spare the money for a few doctor's visits. What are you smirking at, young lady?'

Friday kissed Elizabeth's powdered cheek. 'Thank you, Mrs H. You're such a good person.' And she grabbed her things and hurried out, properly late now.

'So are you, Friday Woolfe,' Elizabeth said to the empty room. 'If only you would stand still long enough to realise it.'

October 1830, Sydney Town

Harrie perched on an upturned bucket and sipped her tea. Adam and Esther Green's backyard was really quite pleasant now that someone — Mr Green, probably, given that *she* apparently didn't like gardening — had planted shrubs and rose bushes along the tall fence and a flowerbed in each corner. They would all shrivel up to sad little sticks in summer because there would be no water to spare for them, but a few might struggle back in the autumn. There was also a new gate, installed at the behest of Mr Green, who likely didn't want Sarah's friends climbing over the fence and landing in the new plantings.

'Is your tea hot enough?' Sarah asked.

'Yes, thanks.' Harrie raised her cup. 'New tea service?'

'For my visitors. For you and Friday. I got sick of her telling me I had to use the old cracked cups, so I bought my own.'

'Very pretty.' It was, too, the pattern on the china a complicated arrangement of flowers and birds in dark blue against a white background.

'They're not actually new; they're from the pawnshop. I only got the cups and saucers and the teapot.'

'Mr Skelton?' Mr Skelton was the fence who bought everything Sarah stole from Adam Green.

Sarah nodded.

'Good price?'

'Reasonable. What's she doing now?'

Harrie squinted past Sarah into the house. 'Still looking through her magazine. Now she's ... no, now she's coming out.'

They'd positioned their buckets as close as possible to the kitchen without making it obvious. Esther Green emerged from the house, shot stony-faced disapproval at them and disappeared into the kitchen.

34

She popped back out a moment later. 'Sarah, I want you at work polishing the furniture in the parlour as soon as you've had your tea. Harriet, you'll have to leave. And when I've finished baking, Sarah, come out here and clean up.' With another pointed glare she vanished again.

'Ready?' Sarah whispered.

Harrie swallowed. Was she? She'd thought hard about this and still wasn't sure if it was the right thing to do. It was mean, but then Esther Green was mean herself, and really shouldn't be so unkind to Sarah. But it was more than that. Given what had been happening lately, she had an uneasy feeling that something may well be started that might not so readily be stopped again. Her friend needed help, though; Esther Green was wearing her down, that was plain. But it was all right for Sarah — she didn't believe ghosts were real.

Against her better judgment, she nodded.

Something clattered onto the table in the kitchen.

Sarah smiled and touched her hand. 'Good girl.' In a louder than normal voice she said, 'Are you still having those terrible dreams?'

'About Rachel?' Harrie replied squeakily. She cleared her throat. 'Yes. Have they gone away?'

The clattering next door ceased.

'No,' Harrie said. 'They haven't.'

'Mine haven't either,' Sarah admitted heartily. 'It's worrying, isn't it? What does she do in *your* dreams?'

For an awful second Harrie forgot what Sarah had coached her to say. 'She, um ... well. Oh! She appears and tells me she's all alone out at St John's Cemetery.'

'Yes!' Sarah exclaimed. 'That's what she does in *my* dreams. Except she seems *quite angry* in mine.'

'She's angry in mine, too.' Harrie agreed. 'Really angry.' From the corner of her eye she saw Esther appear at the kitchen window and peer out at them.

Sarah raised her eyebrows, silently asking Harrie if Esther had taken the bait. Harrie gave a barely perceptible nod.

'She stands at the foot of my bed, all pale but at the same time faintly *glowing*, like a lamp turned all the way down,' Sarah went on. 'At least, I *think* I'm dreaming when I see her. I was wondering if we should talk to a priest. What do you think, Harrie?'

'I don't know, Sarah. I *am* feeling quite frightened by it all.'

'So am I.' Sarah finished her tea and stood. 'I have to get back to work now. Do you mind if I come to church with you this Sunday? I don't really know any priests I can talk to.'

Harrie rose as well. 'I'm sure that will be fine. Father Davenport is a nice man.' She handed Sarah her cup and saucer. 'Thank you for the tea.' As she turned to go, she said through the kitchen window, 'Good day, Mrs Green.'

But Esther, eyes wide, only stared at her.

Harrie felt vaguely guilty on the way home to Gloucester Street, as if she'd let someone down, though certainly not Esther Green.

Rachel.

As she negotiated carriage traffic, potholes and piles of animal droppings on her way across George Street, she thought about how for her, in the end, it almost always came down to guilt.

She still felt guilty — every day, in fact — for the theft of the silk and embroidery thread for which she'd been arrested in London two years earlier. Not because she was now a convict — she'd actually made her peace with that — but because in those few seconds of terrible, misguided thinking she'd deprived her mother and her younger brother and sisters of both her presence and the regular wage she had earned. Robbie was ten now and, according to the letters she received from home, working for pennies as a barrow boy at Covent Garden, and Sophie at almost nine was bringing home piece work, much against her mother's wishes. And Harrie's: her sister would be blinded and hunchbacked by the age of twenty-five if she kept that up. Anna, the youngest, was still at home, but for how much longer?

She felt guilty, too, for not doing more to ensure that Gabriel Keegan had never gone near Rachel on the *Isla*. But she'd not done more because she'd assumed he was decent — just because he'd appeared to have good manners and could afford to pay for a cabin and wore a silk top hat. Oh, she'd been so *naive*, and look what had happened! It had been the same with Bella Jackson, whom she had initially considered so generous — kind, even — in spite of *everyone* saying what a nasty piece of work she was. And now they were at the horrible woman's mercy, waiting and waiting to see what she would do to them. The worry of it was dreadful and some days it built and built until Harrie felt like screaming so her throat bled.

And she hadn't done enough when the time had come for Rachel's lying-in, and their poor little sweetheart had slipped away. The damage Keegan had inflicted on her had killed her, of course, but surely she could have done something more to help her? And she hadn't even gone to Rachel's funeral — thank God Friday had.

Though they'd avenged her, the guilt over what they'd done to Gabriel Keegan was burning a hole in her. At first she hadn't really felt much at all and she'd stupidly thought she might have got away without any repercussions to her conscience. But that had changed and every day now she battled with herself: sometimes she was sure she would go to hell for the sin of taking a human life; at other times she believed they'd been right to kill Keegan. It was exhausting. She prayed for serenity and a sign she wasn't losing her mind, and at times it came. And sometimes it didn't.

And then of course she was responsible for the most awful betrayal of all.

She could have stopped James Downey, if only she'd known what he was going to do. She could have run after him and stood in front of the mortuary door and barred him from entering; she could have flung herself across poor Rachel's cold, still body and not let him near; she could have slapped the scalpels and drills and saws from his hands — anything so he couldn't have done what he did. But he *had* done it; he'd cut into her, horribly violating her even after death. And he'd done it without Harrie's permission.

She would *never* forgive him for that, no matter how much she had come to care for him; no matter what silly ideas had dared to blossom in her head about the two of them since his wife died. Rachel had been *hers*, she had belonged to her and Friday and Sarah, and James Downey hadn't asked. He had walked all over them in his shiny toff boots and his smart black mourning coat that *she* had repaired the button on, and he *hadn't* asked her permission.

And she was confused because she couldn't decide whether she felt guilty or angry about what he'd done. She was so accustomed to feeling guilt that whenever anger popped up it muddied everything. But she did know she wasn't ever going to speak to James Downey again.

Harrie entered the welcome shade of the new George Street market sheds and bought enough fruit to feed the Barretts for the next few days, then headed north down the sloping street towards the Rocks. On the way she stopped and peered into a shop window displaying lace and paper fans, gloves, embroidered and lace-trimmed pelerine collars, horn and tortoiseshell hair combs, fur muffs — as if anyone would need a muff during an Australian summer! — silk parasols, and fancy beaded and embroidered reticules.

Tapping her finger against her bottom lip she wondered: her own embroidery was, frankly, superior in both design and execution to that displayed here, even if it was imported from England. Could she make something that might compete? Handkerchiefs? Embroidered collars, perhaps? Not reticules — the beads were too expensive to buy. Would she have the time? Not really, especially if she was going to sew Friday some new dresses. But after that, perhaps? And if she actually made a profit she could make a genuine financial contribution to the Charlotte fund and stop feeling so useless. And perhaps even send a bit extra home to her mother.

She turned away from the window, full of ideas, and that's when she felt it: someone was watching her. But she walked on, eyes straight ahead. It could be anyone; it could even be a feral dog. She would be all right; there were dozens of people on the street.

She hurried along until she came to the plaza in front of St Philip's Church and turned into Charlotte Place. The being-watched feeling stayed with her. She went straight past the turning into Gloucester Street and at Cumberland turned right and walked quickly, her boots crunching in the powdered limestone gravel, until she came to Overton's grocery store. Risking a glance over her shoulder she glimpsed the shadow of someone ducking out of sight. So, not a dog, then.

Her heart knocking she entered the shop. Eleven-year-old Merry Overton stood behind the counter.

Her pretty face broke into a smile. 'Hello, Harrie!'

'Hello, Merry. How are you today?'

'Dandy, thank you. Can I help you?'

God, Harrie thought, was there anything Nora Barrett needed? 'Two pounds of crystallised white sugar, please.' Nora was always making jam.

While Merry measured out the sugar Harrie went to the door. There were half a dozen people abroad but no one sinister-looking. 'Merry, may I speak to your father, please?'

Merry nodded, twisted the package of sugar closed and disappeared into the back of the shop.

Harrie had been assigned to the Overtons for a few months but, after doing her deliberate best to behave incompetently, had been returned to the Factory, where she had cared for Rachel during the later months of her pregnancy. Harrie had liked the Overtons, except for the unpleasant older son Toby, and they seemed to have forgiven her for her earlier bumbling transgressions.

Merry reappeared. 'He'll just be a minute.'

'Thank you.' Harrie counted out the money for the sugar. 'How's Toby?'

Merry made a face. 'Same as usual.'

'Oh well. And baby Johanna?'

'Toddling all over the place and getting into everything.'

Harrie laughed.

Henry Overton came through from the back wiping his hands on his apron, his face even redder than usual from hefting bags of flour. 'Harrie Clarke, hello, girl!'

'Hello, Mr Overton. It's nice to see you.'

'You look well.'

'Thank you.'

'What can I do for you?'

Harrie felt her face grow warm. She put her packet of sugar in her basket. 'I'm on my way home and I was wondering ... actually, I think someone might be following me.'

Mr Overton's expression darkened. 'Some man, you think? Can you point him out?'

'Well, I'm not sure. I *might* have seen someone. I'd be very grateful if you could just watch from your door until I turn into Surrey Lane.'

Henry Overton came out from behind the counter. 'I can certainly do that. Better to be safe than sorry.'

'Thank you very much, Mr Overton.'

He waved away her thanks and planted himself in the shop doorway, a bastion of respectability and decency.

As Harrie scurried off down the street, he nodded to a couple strolling past, then to a pair of girls going the other way, then a smartly dressed gentleman who raised his hat and said, 'Good afternoon.'

There was no sinister man following her. She was a sweet girl, Harrie Clarke, marvellous with the children, but hopeless at everything else. Highly strung, too. Henry went back into his shop.

Harrie had almost reached home on Gloucester Street when, suddenly, she knew. She ducked down the side of the house, praying she reached the back door in time. Digging frantically around among the apples and pears in her basket for her key, her heart racing, she started violently when a hand settled on her arm.

'Dr Downey!' she burst out. 'Will you stop following me!'

'I wouldn't have to if you would just concede to speak to me!' James said equally passionately. 'And don't call me Dr Downey. Surely you can proceed to my Christian name after all the tribulations we've experienced?'

'*We* haven't experienced anything,' Harrie replied, yanking her arm away and spilling several pears.

'We *have*, Harrie. If you would only —'

The back door opened and Nora Barrett peered out, a swaddled Lewis clamped against her chest. 'Harrie, are you all right? Good afternoon, Dr Downey.'

'Good afternoon, Mrs Barrett. How are you?'

'Well, thank you.'

Harrie snatched up the pears and ran inside.

Nora Barrett and James Downey looked at each other.

'Well, good day then, Dr Downey,' Nora said.

'Good day, Mrs Barrett.'

Nora shut the door.

Chapter Three

The dining room of the Australian Hotel was quite grand, for Sydney Town. Swathes of velvet draped the windows, the carpets on the polished wooden floor were of above average quality, and the tables were set with silver and decent plate. One ordered *á la carte*, which was very modern, rather than dining *table d'hôte*, and the food was reasonably good. James liked it because it reminded him a little of his club in London, though of course sadly absent here were the extensive library of scientific tomes, the demandingly intellectual conversation, and the camaraderie and sense of purpose he'd so relished as a member of the Royal Society. Not that he'd attended a great many Royal Society dinners, as he'd been at sea so constantly. Perhaps someone would found a similar establishment here in Sydney. If so, he would seriously consider becoming a member.

He rearranged the napkin over his lap while he waited for Matthew to return. He'd ordered the cream of onion soup and roast beef with roast vegetables, and Matthew the soup and roast mutton, and James was looking forward to his meal.

He lived alone in a cottage in York Street, ten minutes' walk from his Pitt Street medical practice, and did his own cleaning and very mediocre cooking, so it was a treat to dine out. He'd declined to employ a live-in housemaid, or even a woman to come in during the day, as he didn't want gossip, something with which he'd not had to contend in the navy overseeing the welfare of tattooed, hairy-bottomed, foul-mouthed sailors, and a curse he'd more or less managed to avoid while superintending aboard emigrant and convict ships. Now that he worked among a land-bound civilian population he suspected he was much more likely to fall victim to wagging tongues.

When his wife Emily had died in England the previous year, and he had decided to retire from the navy and settle in New South Wales rather than return to his home in London, he'd taken a position as a general practitioner in Lawrence Chandler's medical practice. The position had initially been as an employee, but when Lawrence had offered him a partnership in May he'd accepted.

Lawrence was senior to James by twenty-four years and, at the age of fifty-five, was thinking more and more about retiring himself. He was quiet, mild-mannered, very decent and rather proper, and it had been quite a shock to James when he'd discovered that for the past thirteen years Lawrence had happily accepted as patients the prostitutes from the brothel where Harrie's friend Friday Woolfe now illegally worked.

He'd received yet another shock when he'd expressed his disapproval regarding this arrangement, and Lawrence had bluntly told him not to be hypocritical as most of the brothel's patrons were gentlemen just like him, and that no true Christian or humanitarian could deny medical assistance to the women employed there. Which had given James something to think about.

Matthew sat down at the table and took a sip of his claret. 'Still waiting? God, I'm starving.'

The dining room was very full this evening and they'd ordered almost half an hour earlier. James could feel his stomach rumbling. 'Can't be far away.'

He and Matthew Cutler, whom he'd first encountered on the voyage out from England on the *Isla* last year, had been meeting every fortnight for supper at the Australian for the past four months. He liked Matthew, and had done from the outset. He was an intelligent and cheerful young man of twenty-six with a bright future in the Office of the Colonial Architect, and of the two single gentlemen to have paid their passage aboard the *Isla*, he had been far and away the most personable. Of course, the other had been Gabriel Keegan.

'I only hope the mutton's not too … muttony,' Matthew said. 'It can be, sometimes.'

'Send it back, if it is,' James replied. 'Order the beef.'

Matthew shook his head. 'I'll still be sitting here at midnight.'

Their suppers finally arrived and Matthew pronounced his mutton thoroughly acceptable. To accompany it they ordered more claret.

'I spoke with Harrie this afternoon,' James said, raising his hand and, behind it, prising a morsel of meat from his teeth with an ivory toothpick.

'Did you?' Matthew kept his eyes on his plate. He always felt deeply uncomfortable when James talked about Harrie, having never summoned the nerve to confess that he had himself entertained thoughts of marrying her. And still would, given the tiniest chance. Though that was clearly out of the question now, with James so besotted with her and, even more unfortunately, his choice of Matthew as his confessor. Actually, it had been out of the question before: Harrie Clarke barely even knew he existed. And there was also the matter of his mother at home in England, who would rather die than allow her precious youngest son to marry a convict girl. Of course, he could have just done it, making it impossible for his mother to object. But it was too late now anyway, so he'd resigned himself to having to listen to James go on and on about Harrie once a fortnight across the supper table.

'Yes,' James said, placing the toothpick on his plate. 'Like a half-starved cur, I followed her all the way from George Street market to her house on Gloucester Street, then I frightened the life out of her just as she was opening her door.'

Matthew kept quiet: he knew James was annoyed with himself.

'Then I made a fool of myself,' James went on. 'An even *bigger* fool of myself, by attempting to speak to her, just before her employer told me I should leave.'

'Did he? That was rather rude.'

'It was Mrs Barrett. Actually, she didn't, not exactly. But I left anyway.' James sighed and dropped his napkin on the table. 'I'm at my wits' end, Matthew, I really am. It's been almost seven months and she still won't talk to me. And neither will her friends. God, she really is the most extraordinarily bloody-minded person.'

To be honest, Matthew wasn't sure if he'd be talking to James yet either, if he were Harrie. Although he liked James enormously, in Matthew's opinion what he'd done had been pretty awful. James was a man of science, it was true, and he supposed that went some way towards mitigating his behaviour, but still, to just wade in and hack up a girl's corpse like that. Especially that poor girl, after everything that had already happened to her. It really *was* almost unforgivable.

'And to round off the afternoon perfectly,' James said, 'do you know who I saw loitering on the corner of Bridge and George streets on my way back home?'

Matthew shook his head.

'That damned scoundrel Amos Furniss, that's who.'

Later that night, well after the bats had set forth and the moon had risen high in a cloud-tattered sky, Nora Barrett and Harrie sat in the parlour. After a day of colic Lewis had finally gone down, the older children were also in bed and Nora was enjoying a rare hour of peace and quiet.

'You know, Harrie,' she said through a mouthful of pins, 'most girls in your position would leap at the chance to be courted by the likes of Dr Downey. A *doctor*, Harrie, and a navy captain to boot.'

'He's not courting me, he's plaguing me.'

Nora removed the pins. 'Hark at you! A convict girl with six years to serve of a seven-year sentence, complaining because a gentleman's taken a fancy to you!'

'It isn't as though I can't take my pick, though, is it?' Harrie replied.

Which was true. The number of men in the colony of New South Wales, convicts and otherwise, so vastly outnumbered females that women really could choose with whom they took up, no matter their status.

'Don't be so ungrateful, Harrie. That's not like you. And you're so disrespectful to him. You want to be careful there.'

Harrie said nothing.

'Granted he doesn't quite have the looks to set a girl's heart racing, but that's a good fair head of hair on him and his eyes are kind. He's tall, too, and I'll bet there's more under that mourning suit than meets the eye.'

Harrie bristled: actually, James did set her heart racing. Still.

'And he obviously thinks a lot of you,' Nora went on, putting in the last pin. 'Otherwise he would've given up by now. He'd marry you, too. Not like my George — we were common-law for ten years and I'd had Abigail and Hannah before I could convince him to make it official. And don't forget, people will always sneer: you'll be a convict whore for life if you remain a spinster.'

'I'm not a whore!'

'Doesn't matter, love, you're still tainted.' Nora held up the inside-out bodice. 'Does this placket look straight? I haven't marked where the buttons are going yet.'

'Perfect,' Harrie said quickly, glad Nora had changed the subject.

'Good. I have to have it all tacked together by tomorrow dinnertime. She's coming in for a fitting.'

Noting Nora's tired, red eyes and the myriad needle pricks marking her swollen fingers, Harrie set down her embroidery frame.

'Mrs Barrett, I know this is none of my business, but do you not think you're trying to do too much? With Lewis and everything?'

Nora draped the bodice over the arm of the chair beside her and sighed. 'Well, yes, but what choice do I have? George in his wisdom has decided I'm to keep up my side of the business. But he's right, really. We need the money. That's why we employed you, to look after the children.'

I'm not employed, Harrie thought — I'm assigned. If I were employed I'd be receiving a wage. 'You'll have to sit up most of the night to get that dress tacked together in time,' she said.

'I know. But I have to be awake anyway to feed Lewis, so I might as well.' Nora reached for a sleeve. 'You get off, though, Harrie.'

'Are you sure?'

Nora nodded. 'Just leave your lamp here, would you?'

Harrie obliged, and lit a candle to guide her way upstairs. She washed quickly in her bowl, brushed out her hair and undressed. Then she climbed into bed, using her feet to shunt a complaining Angus to one side of the mattress.

She re-read a scrawled and misspelt letter from Janie Braine detailing Rosie's and baby Charlotte's latest little milestones, and listing what they needed the next time anyone planned to visit at the Parramatta Female Factory, then extinguished the bedside lamp and lay down. Thinking she would be awake for ages, her head was that full of thoughts, she fell asleep almost immediately, but woke again several hours before dawn with a crawling, prickling sensation that told her she wasn't alone.

Slowly, her stomach feeling fluttery and her heart beating a little faster, she sat up and peered into a dense blackness that had gathered around the little rocking chair in the corner of her attic room.

'Rachel? Is that you?'

* * *

Sarah licked her finger and touched it lightly against the flat iron: there'd be hell to pay if she singed Esther's best white damask tablecloth. No instant blister on her skin; the temperature was right. She wrapped an extra rag around the handle and ran the iron over the fabric until every tiny crease had been obliterated and the heavy cloth slid smoothly beneath her hands.

Some friend of Adam's was coming to supper; he must be worth impressing as Esther had been in the kitchen since morning cooking all sorts of complicated dishes. Adam didn't seem overly excited, though. He'd been in his workshop and the shop as usual, and had just received an earful from Esther for spilling sticky lemonade down the lapel of his good frock coat.

Sarah carefully carried the tablecloth through to the dining room and spread it over the table, then laid three place settings including enough different plates to sink a ship, four glasses per person for the wines, and a great clattering heap of silver she'd spent hours polishing. In the centre of the table she placed a silver and cut-glass epergne, now filled to bursting with rather a lot of rosemary and a lavish assortment of cut flowers Esther had sent her up the street to fetch from the market this morning. Then there were the ivory napkin rings and starched napkins that had taken ages to fold properly, and the fancy cruet set, the salts and all the other fripperies Esther had trotted out. Sarah thought it was absurd: what was wrong with a plate, a knife and fork and a mug? You'd think the new king was coming for supper.

Finally, everything was ready. Adam and Esther were both upstairs, Adam changing his coat and Esther dressing in her finery, when Sarah heard a loud rapping on the shop door. Wiping her hands on her apron as she hurried through from the dining room, she eased back the heavy bolt and opened it.

Before her stood a gentleman wearing a blue cutaway coat with fashionable raised shoulders, rolled collar and gilt buttons, a mint-green silk waistcoat over a white shirt with a pointed collar and a precisely tied cravat, pale trousers fastened over the instep of his gleaming boots, and a beaver felt top hat, which he didn't bother taking off to her. Good God, what a dandy. A heavy gold watch chain with a bloodstone fob peeked from beneath the waistcoat. Mmm, tempting, Sarah thought. He clutched a bouquet of flowers in one hand, a bottle in the other.

'Good evening, sir,' Sarah said.

'Evening. Jared Gellar. I believe I'm expected?'

He had a pleasing voice, though Sarah couldn't see his face clearly beneath the brim of his hat.

'Yes.' She stood back to let him in, then led him through to the parlour. While he wandered about having a good look at Esther's pricey furniture and bits and pieces, she turned up the wall lamps so she could see him properly. 'Mr Green shouldn't be long.'

Jared Gellar's face matched his voice — attractive. His dark features were regular and strong, his eyes shrewdly intelligent and, now he'd finally removed his hat, she saw his hair was a deep, glossy brown and curly enough to make most women jealous. He wore it in the slightly unruly style that she thought was effeminate, but which was all the rage among the wealthier classes.

'Jared, my good fellow!' Adam exclaimed, rushing into the parlour as though he'd been told to hurry up and get downstairs. 'Delighted you could come tonight!'

Sarah looked at him; she'd never heard him call anyone his 'good fellow' before and it didn't suit him. Adam wasn't one for toff banter; in fact he was dismissive of those who were, so why was he doing it now?

Gellar swept across the room and presented his bottle. 'Not much. Just off the ship but I hear it was a good year.'

Adam glanced at the label. 'Very nice. Thank you, Jared.'

Esther arrived then, pausing in the doorway so the two men would have ample opportunity to notice her.

She wore an extremely expensive gown in cream muslin with a full skirt, billowing sleeves, exquisite green and maroon floral embroidery at hem and elbow, elaborate shirring across the bodice, and a vandyke collar in satin silk that dipped to a deep point below her tiny waist. She'd pinned up her luxuriant blonde hair with an assortment of jewelled clips and looked, Sarah had to admit, not too bad.

'Mrs Green, may I say you are utterly charming!' Gellar said, and presented her with his bouquet of flowers. 'Please, do accept these unworthy blooms as a small token of my esteem.'

'Mr Gellar, how lovely! Thank you!' Esther simpered, and gave Sarah the impatient hand-flicking gesture that meant she was to go away and get on with whatever she was supposed to be doing.

So Sarah went out to the kitchen to prepare to serve the first course. When she heard the silver hand bell ring in the dining room, she carried in the tureen containing Esther's mock turtle soup. After that came the chicken pie, then the vol-au-vent of pears, then the curried beef.

It was during the game course, as Sarah was serving the stuffed roasted goose breasts, that it all started to unravel.

Adam, on his seventh glass of wine and peering intently at the epergne, said, 'Esther, why is there a rosemary bush on the table?'

Esther smiled tightly. 'I'm not sure there is, dear.'

'Yes. There is. I'm looking at it.' Adam pointed with his fork. 'See?'

'Oh, in the epergne?' Esther said, as though she hadn't realised what he'd meant. 'I often use rosemary in floral arrangements. You know that.'

'But there's almost an entire bush jammed in there,' Adam insisted.

Esther's laugh was brittle. 'Hardly, dear. A few sprigs, perhaps.'

'A few sprigs?' Adam echoed. 'Is there any left in the garden?'

Sarah stifled a smirk and placed Esther's roasted goose breast on her plate: this could be entertaining, especially as tonight Adam had imbibed far more alcohol than was usual for him.

'I think it looks absolutely charming,' Gellar said. 'Very festive.'

Smarmy bugger, Sarah thought.

Adam rather theatrically struck the back of the hand holding his fork against his forehead, causing a piece of curried beef caught on a tine to fly off over his shoulder. 'God, I've just realised. This is to do with the ghost business, isn't it?' He reached clumsily across the table and took Esther's hand in his free one. 'Darling, there's nothing to worry about, really there isn't.'

Esther snatched her hand away, colour shooting up her neck and face, and fixed him with a glare. 'Adam, not now!'

'Why not? Jared's a good friend.' Adam turned to Gellar and said a fraction sharply, 'Aren't you, Jared, old fellow?'

'Of course! At least, I've always hoped so,' Gellar boomed. He, too, had been knocking back the wine and his nose had gone quite red.

As Sarah bent to serve his goose, she felt for several terrifying seconds what she thought was an enormous spider crawling up her bare leg. She squeaked and jerked away from the table, but when Gellar smirked up at her she realised it had been his hand on the back of her knee. Gritting her teeth behind her smile, she set the food on his plate, managing rather satisfyingly to drip blobs of dark gravy on the shoulder of his coat.

'Adam, I'd rather we didn't discuss the matter this evening,' Esther said extremely frostily.

But Adam had apparently gone selectively deaf. 'You see, Jared,' he explained, leaning back in his chair so Sarah could get at his plate, 'Esther believes our home is at risk of intrusion from a ghostly presence.'

Sarah stole a quick glance at his face. What had Esther been saying to him? Whatever it was, from his casual tone it didn't sound as though he'd taken it too seriously.

'Really?' Gellar looked from Adam to Esther and back again. 'That *is* alarming! How terrifying!'

'It is, especially for Esther,' Adam agreed. He waved his hand around vaguely. 'Hence the rosemary and the amulets and the mezuzah all over the place. They ward off evil, you know. Esther has a very strong belief in the spirit world.'

'As I do myself,' Gellar said unexpectedly. 'In England I was once forced to sell a house I owned due to the fact it was haunted.'

'Is that right?' Adam reached for more wine.

'Yes, and it took months because everyone local knew. I ended up having to sell to someone from Cornwall.'

Esther suddenly burst out in a shrill voice, 'It's your fault!'

Sarah, in the act of removing the lid from the vegetable dish, felt her heart almost stop. 'Mine?' she said, as water from the lid dripped onto the tablecloth.

'Yes! That girl you knew, the one who died — I overheard you and that Harrie Clarke talking about her and now odd things are happening and I can sense something evil, here in this house. She's come back, the dead girl, I know she has!'

'Esther —' Adam attempted to stand but couldn't quite manage it.

Esther extended a shaking finger towards Sarah. 'She's following you and it's *your* fault and I want you *out of this house*!'

Adam had another go. He rose, moved around the table and laid a placating hand on Esther's arm. 'Esther, please, you're getting hysterical.'

She stood herself and slapped him. 'And you're drunk, so shut up!' Throwing her napkin on the table, she rushed out of the dining room.

They all heard her mount the stairs, a crash as she slammed her bedroom door, and her footsteps on the floor above. Then nothing.

Adam rubbed his stinging cheek. Gellar tut-tutted and helped himself to more wine.

'Would anyone care for broccoli or julienned carrots?' Sarah enquired.

Adam sat hunched over his workbench, rubbing his temples with his fingertips, a tumbler and an empty jug nearby. Sarah felt sorry for him; he seldom drank much and as a consequence of last night's overindulgence was suffering the horrors. Also, Esther had shouted at him over breakfast, and it was a warm day, the temperature in the workshop already unpleasantly high.

'Would you like some more lemonade?'

He sighed biliously and eased back his shoulders, shifting on his stool. 'Yes, I would, thank you, Sarah. Is Esther about?'

'Gone out,' Sarah replied.

She thought he was relieved. *She* certainly was, though Esther's filthy mood hadn't been helped by Sarah rising particularly early this morning to remove the porridge saucepan from the kitchen and leave it balanced incongruously on a tree-stump in the backyard. Not after last night's talk of ghosts and odd happenings.

She went out to the cool safe in the kitchen and poured some more lemonade. The house was so nice and peaceful without Esther. She was constantly stirring up agitation, although last night, when Sarah had fully expected a row between her and Adam, there'd been nothing. Adam had stayed up drinking with Gellar until all hours while she'd been stuck in the kitchen washing plates and pots until her hands had turned into prunes, but there hadn't been a peep out of Esther. When Gellar had finally staggered off into the night Sarah had braced herself for war, but Esther stayed shut in her room while Adam had crashed off to bed in his own chamber, bouncing off the walls and mumbling to himself like the village idiot. It was no wonder he felt poorly this morning.

She returned to the workshop and set the lemonade jug down on the workbench. With an eye on the shop in case a customer came in she perched on her own stool and watched what Adam was doing, which was filing into a bezel the grooves where claws would sit to secure a ring's central stone — in this case a large and rare pink topaz. He really was a very skilled jeweller, even if this morning his hands were shaking rather badly.

As he'd explained to Sarah when she'd first arrived, he'd had the workbench custom made, but she'd seen the like often enough in England and had worked at one herself for several years. This one had fittings and recesses for two craftsmen and when she'd finally been allowed to sit down at one she'd truly felt as though she'd come home.

The bench itself measured six feet long, two and a half deep and three high. On the side at which she and Adam worked were two curved recesses cut out to a depth of eleven inches and a width of twenty. Draped beneath each void was a pigskin to catch dropped gems and to prevent burns from hot metal. At the farthest extent of each recess was a drawer for small implements and a pigskin pouch to hold larger tools such as saws and files, to the left a rack for pliers, and above the drawer a tapered boxwood peg against which to work.

On the right of each recess — as Sarah and Adam were both right-handed — sat an oriental-style bronze oil lamp with a wick affixed to the spout. When the lamp was lit, a mouth-operated blowpipe was used to feed extra oxygen into the flame, increasing the heat, and the flame applied to whatever required soldering, the solder and flux to form the joint having been applied beforehand. It was a very fiddly and sweaty business, but a skill mastered by any jeweller worthy of the title. At one end of the bench was fixed an engraver's ball, with an accompanying padded case of the burins used to engrave jewellery, and to shape and carve gold and silver, and to assist with the setting of stones.

The bench was situated so that Adam and Sarah faced an unusually large window as they worked, overlooking part of the backyard. The window had been made and fitted by glaziers specially, its mullions solid iron to deter burglars, which Sarah thought poignantly amusing as the thief was already on the wrong side of it. At night or on badly overcast days they worked under the light of half a dozen Sinumbra oil lamps, which cast no shadow, burning in them only the best sperm oil so smoke didn't pollute the air and irritate eyes.

Against the walls of the workshop were a bench on which sat the rolling-mill for rolling out sheets of precious metal, a draw-bench for drawing down gold and silver wire from those sheets, and a table on which were arrayed various, less frequently used, tools. Also in the room were the safe — whose lock Sarah had picked during her third week with the Greens — where the metals and gems were kept and the most expensive pieces were stored at night, and a small charcoal furnace to heat alloys of gold and silver and form them into ingots for rolling or drawing.

On days when the furnace was operating the room was unbearably hot, especially in summer when the house's ground floor was stifling anyway, but when opened the windows admitted hordes of mosquitoes and other insects, not to mention the stink from the Tank Stream just beyond Adam's back fence. To date he hadn't found a fabric fine yet robust enough to stretch over the window frame that would exclude pests but still admit light and any breeze, so they sat at their workbench and suffered, sweat pouring down their faces, wiping their damp hands every few minutes. But Sarah was once again doing what she loved, so the discomfort was something she was more than willing to tolerate.

Adam had chosen her to work for him because of her skills as a jeweller, but initially she'd been limited to housework until she'd demonstrated her trustworthiness. Esther had protested against Sarah serving in the shop, believing she would steal the stock, which of course she did, but Adam reasoned that if he already trusted her in the workshop, he might as well trust her to serve behind the counter as well. Now she and Adam shared the duty, Esther only rarely consenting to help when business was very brisk.

For Sarah, stealing from Adam Green had at first been like stealing from anyone else — easy and completely unencumbered by the complication of guilt. But as the months passed and Adam had shown her increasing respect, allowed her more privileges, and stoutly defended her against his wife's endless harassment, she'd grown steadily more uncomfortable. She couldn't stop her pilfering, however, as she had no other means of contributing to Charlotte's welfare. Rachel had gone, but now there was Charlotte, seven months old. She relied on them completely for that money to pay for her care and it cost a fortune because of the corruption in the Female Factory, even with wily, tough Janie Braine as her foster mother.

There were other considerations, too. If Sarah stopped stealing from Adam and didn't put anything into the fund, Friday would be the sole contributor. Sarah loved Friday and would do anything for her, but she couldn't bear that prospect. It would alter the balance of power among the three of them in a way that could harm their friendship. Friday, being the generous soul she was, wouldn't mind, but Sarah certainly would. She, Sarah, frequently told Harrie it was of no concern that Harrie wasn't in a position to put money into the fund, and it wasn't, because Harrie gave so much in other ways, but it was a different matter when it came to herself. Also, of the three of them, Sarah knew she had the skills and intellectual ability most suited to generating money, and it would drive her to distraction if she couldn't use either to contribute to the fund. Finally, the idea of not being able to honour her commitment to their vow to take care of Charlotte was something she could not — and *would* not — live with. It smacked of the mercenary, disloyal and dishonourable behaviour so typical of Tom Ratcliffe, the boss of the crew in which she had worked in London, and whom she had loathed. The last she'd heard he was rotting on a prison hulk in the Thames, and a bloody good job, too. Her belief that men could not be trusted had only been reinforced by Ratcliffe's double-crossing ways, and her resolution to maintain her own version of honourable behaviour was further entrenched as a result.

So she continued to steal from Adam, though growing increasingly ill at ease with her conscience as time passed. Occasionally she picked pockets on the street but this rarely netted more than a few pounds; it took time to set up a potentially lucrative mark and she hardly ever had that luxury, even after Adam ordered Esther to allow her more freedom.

'How long have you known Jared Gellar?' she asked, hoping Adam wouldn't tell her it was none of her business, which it wasn't.

He didn't look up, intent on what he was doing. 'Why do you want to know?'

Because he gave me the shits, Sarah thought. 'You seem to be good friends,' she replied.

He did glance at her then. 'Six or seven years.'

'Is he in the trade?'

'No, originally he was a book-keeper. Owns a schooner now and has moved into imports. He also buys up ailing businesses just before they go bankrupt, then injects his own money and resurrects them.'

'He *is* doing well then, for one of us.'

Adam reached for his flat-nosed pliers. 'He's not a convict. He immigrated here about eight years ago.'

'Is that when you met him?'

'A year later, perhaps. Why the interest?'

'He did rather get the royal treatment last night. I just wondered why.'

Sighing, Adam said, 'Jared Gellar is very wealthy. Esther thinks *my* business could benefit from an injection of his cash. Which really isn't your affair, Sarah.'

She knew then it was time to let the subject drop. 'I couldn't help noticing she wasn't very happy this morning.'

'No, she wasn't.' Adam put down the pliers, removed his

magnifying spectacles, pushed his stool back and turned to face her. 'Sarah, what exactly did she overhear you and Harrie talking about? This business about a ghost?'

'Did she not mention it to you?' Sarah said innocently.

'Yes, she did, and she seems very distressed by it. I want to know exactly what was said.'

'Well, Harrie was here one day and we were talking about the dreams we've both been having, about Rachel. Our friend who died.' Sarah felt awkward lying to his face. It was uncomfortably like stealing from him. 'Mrs Green must have overheard us.'

'Yes, but what did you say about her?'

'Mrs Green?'

'No, *Rachel*.'

'Oh. Well, we said that in our dreams Rachel told us she's all alone out at the cemetery, at St John's. And just that we had the impression she was angry at us. That's all.'

'And this is all true? You've both been having the same dreams?'

Sarah nodded, willing herself not to look away from him.

Adam's dark brows went up. 'How bizarre. Well, Esther's got it into her head that there actually is a ghost, that the spirit of your friend is here and causing mischief.' He reached for a cloth, wiped his pale, sweating forehead and poured himself a tumbler of lemonade. 'She's always had an unhealthy interest in the supernatural. She thought the last house we lived in was haunted, too. This won't do her nerves any good at all.'

Dearie me, Sarah thought, that's terrible news.

Adam sipped his drink. 'She told me you planned to consult a cleric. Did you?'

What? Then Sarah remembered her remark to Harrie about accompanying her to church: she'd actually gone on a picnic with Friday to Hyde Park. 'Yes, we did, the priest at Harrie's church. He told us to pray.'

'I think Esther was hoping he might come here.' Adam swept his hair back off his face. He looked tired and a bit defeated. 'What do you think, Sarah? Has the spirit of your friend really come back?'

'I'm not entirely sure. I've never encountered a real ghost before.'

'No, neither have I,' Adam admitted. 'I'm not at all convinced there are such things. And if there are, I'm reasonably confident the only place they're residing around here is in Esther's mind.'

'I'm sad to hear that,' Sarah replied.

Adam gave her a sceptical look.

Hurriedly, Sarah said, 'Last night she said she wanted me gone.'

'I know. However, you're assigned to me, not Esther. *My* signature is required on any documents pertaining to your return to the Factory, not Esther's, and I have no intention of sending you back. You're far too valuable to me.'

Equal measures of relief, gratitude and self-reproach washed over Sarah. 'Thank you.'

The relief was at least partly due to Adam's admission that he didn't think ghosts existed. If he did, she would have to rethink her plan regarding Esther's haunting: it would be too much, even for her, to scare Adam silly as well as rob him blind. She had considerable respect for him, although obviously not enough to keep her hands off his property. She appreciated his intelligence and kindness, his sense of humour and his skill as a jeweller. He was attractive, too, though whenever she caught herself appraising him physically she put an immediate stop to it. Any thoughts in that direction could only lead to danger, trouble and, ultimately, misery — hers.

There had never been a man in her life, not in the romantic sense, and while she didn't object to the *idea*, she knew the reality would be altogether different, without doubt fraught with difficulty and disappointment, and inevitably tainted by those brutal girlhood memories she seemed incapable of erasing — always there, like bloodstains on a snow-white cloth. She was plain, already set in her ways, viciously independent, mistrustful and generally sour-natured; all attributes she knew men did not find appealing. Also, she was an extremely competent dip, screwsman and cracksman — again not attractive qualities in a potential mate. And as she had no intention of changing any of those things, that was that. It was much safer to stay the way she was.

'I'd like Esther to see a doctor about her nerves,' Adam confided. 'But she won't. I'm sure you've noticed she can be quite irrational at times. And … I think she's getting worse.'

Sarah stared at her hands. It was quite useful hearing about Esther's precarious state of mind, but embarrassing as well.

'Does she have any lady friends?'

'She has friends she meets when she goes out, to take tea with and what have you.'

'Why doesn't anyone come here in the evenings?' Since Sarah had been assigned to the Greens, Jared Gellar had been the first visitor they'd entertained at home.

'We used to have supper parties. But, well, now we don't.'

The bell over the shop door rang.

'I'll get that,' Sarah said.

Relieved, Adam turned back to his work. He wiped his hands on his cloth and put his spectacles back on. Talking to Sarah was the highlight of his day, *every* day, but he did wish she wouldn't ask so many difficult questions. Other people might consider her overly curious, impertinent even, but he saw her for what she really was; a girl with a shrewdly intelligent and deeply enquiring mind.

The reason he and Esther no longer hosted social functions at their home was that two and a half years earlier he'd had a brief affair with the wife of an associate after they'd met at one of Esther's suppers. Esther's rationale since then had been that if no women came into the house, he wouldn't be tempted. It had been the beginning of why she disliked Sarah so much and wanted him to send her back to the Factory — though since then antipathy had certainly grown between the two women, and now there was this ghost business. But there had been no jewellers among the male convicts at Hyde Park Barracks for some time — he had specifically enquired — and anyway Esther needed someone to help her with the housework, given that she refused to lift a hand to do anything at all except cook.

He'd had the affair for purely selfish reasons. Esther was a beautiful woman and he loved her. Or, more truthfully, he loved the memory of the woman she'd been when he'd first met her. Now he cared about how she felt and for her welfare, but that essential spark of passion that drives lovers to be together had died well before his affair, extinguished by Esther's ever-increasing demands on him to make more money. He'd felt belittled by her, and her apparent inability to stop spending what he did make created a never-ending treadmill about which she constantly chastised him, withholding sex as punishment when he flagged and maintaining stony silences and foul moods for weeks on end.

So when pretty Cynthia had offered the promise of a few stolen hours of uncomplicated fun and sexual relief, he'd accepted. He hadn't loved her, and she'd been a little noodle-headed and quite possibly fairly annoying in large doses, but she'd had lovely breasts, smooth white skin and the most deliciously perfumed quim, and he had enjoyed himself. But she'd told a friend, who had told someone else and Esther had found out. Whether or not Cynthia's husband had ever realised, Adam never knew; he'd seen the man often enough since with no unpleasantness.

There had been very unpleasant repercussions with Esther, however. While many women might have looked the other way, she hadn't, and he hadn't expected her to. There certainly had been no sexual relations whatsoever since, and no let-up in her drive to ruin him; he was beginning to view her spending as an obsession if not an actual form of sickness. The fact that she was also ruining herself seemed not to deter her at all. So he'd done the only thing he could do and that was to work harder and make more money, which ironically was what Esther had wanted in the first place. And to do that he'd had to take on an appropriately trained assistant, who was Sarah, another constant irritation to Esther. To appease her he'd agreed to go to Hyde Park Barracks whenever a new shipment of convicts arrived, on the off chance one might be a jeweller, but whenever that occurred he would simply wander down to the Rocks and have a cup of tea somewhere for an hour or so, come home and say there wasn't anyone.

Because he didn't want to replace Sarah.

She was an excellent jeweller but, more than that, he thought he might be in love with her.

Chapter Four

Wilting in the sun and swatting at flies, Harrie and Friday stood outside the tall wooden gates of Parramatta Female Factory.

'Jesus, hurry up, will you?' Friday muttered. 'It's bloody hot out here.' She raised a fist and pounded on the wicket. *'Visitors! Open up!'*

Finally, the wicket swung open and the porter peered out. 'Hold your horses.'

'You hold yours, we're bloody melting out here,' Friday replied as she barged her way through.

'Just as hot in here, you know,' the porter grumbled, mopping his brow with an enormous celery-green handkerchief.

But Friday and Harrie had already set off towards the second set of gates in the inner wall. The portress, peeping through the slot in the wicket from the other side, opened it and let them in.

'Ta, Glad,' Friday said.

'Thank you, Gladys,' Harrie echoed.

Gladys asked, 'How are yis?'

'Good,' Harrie replied. 'Yourself?'

'Can't complain. Janie and the kids've been waiting for yis. Wait here an' I'll get 'em.'

'Hold on.' Friday surreptitiously passed Gladys a decent-sized block of tobacco. 'Don't smoke it all at once.'

'Oooh, very nice.' Gladys sniffed it appreciatively. 'Ta.'

She hurried away across the yard and disappeared into the entrance of the three-storey dormitory building dominating the Factory compound; a few pale faces could be seen staring down from the windows. It was past midday so Sunday services and dinner would be over by now. Neither the matron, Mrs Ann Gordon, nor her assistant, Mrs Letitia Dick, were anywhere to be seen, which was fortunate as Friday and Harrie were smuggling in a large bag of contraband.

Gladys returned minutes later accompanied by Janie Braine carrying baby Charlotte on her hip and leading her daughter Rosie, a toddler, by the hand. Janie wore the regulation Factory skirt and blouse, plus a bright blue waistcoat, a red kerchief at her throat, black boots and a straw bonnet that made her large pink ears stick out even more than they normally did. Her light brown hair was pulled back in a tidy bun and her good eye was healthy and bright, though the left one, as usual, stared forwards sightlessly. Behind her trailed a tall and very solidly built girl.

Janie embraced Harrie and Friday and presented both babies for kisses.

'Afternoon, Pearl,' Friday said to the big girl.

Pearl nodded pleasantly.

Gladys said, 'Visitors' room's empty.'

The group trudged across the yard and settled themselves in the airless visitors' room, Charlotte on Harrie's knee and Rosie on Friday's, though Pearl stayed outside, sitting on the step, smoking her pipe.

'Have they been well?' Harrie asked. 'Have you?'

'We been good, haven't we, chickens?' Janie smiled fondly at the children. 'Rosie fell down the other day,' she said, indicating a scab on the toddler's knee, 'but she'll mend.'

'No coughs or nasty rashes, no runny bottoms?' Harrie persisted.

'For God's sake, Harrie,' Friday said, 'Janie's a grown woman. Don't talk to her like she's a child. Runny bottoms! It's called the shits.'

'No, none of that,' Janie confirmed. 'They been good. Well, Charlotte had a touch of the runs a week ago but it didn't last long. Everyone did. Hospital's full of folk with dysentery at the moment.'

Friday handed over the cloth bag packed with supplies: Janie opened it and looked inside.

'Oooh, lovely. I'm nearly out of decent clouts.'

There was also clothing for the girls made by Harrie, and soap and skin cream, and the nipple salve and bottles of tonic Janie had asked for in her letter as she was still breast-feeding both children, plus playing cards and trinkets for trading, plenty of fresh and preserved food, and money. Most of the money was for Pearl, whom Janie paid to look out for her. After Harrie had left the Factory for good it hadn't taken Janie long to realise she couldn't watch over two babies *and* keep an eye on the contraband the others brought in for her. Without Pearl, who was extremely loyal providing she was paid on time, she'd be robbed in a minute.

Harrie gazed fondly down at Charlotte, and flicked a fat, lazy fly off her arm. 'She looks more and more like Rachel every day, doesn't she?'

'Thank God,' Friday said grimly. 'Imagine if she favoured her rotten bloody father.'

Charlotte's hair had been the colour of wheat when she'd been born and had grown paler since, strands catching the sun and turning silver the way her mother's had. Her eyes, however, had not lightened and were a very dark brown, clearly inherited from Gabriel Keegan, as Rachel's eyes had been a startling cornflower blue. In her round baby face there were hints she may grow into a beauty, but this young such a prediction was too early to make with confidence. At least she no longer resembled the scrawny-necked little creature she'd been when born, though even then Harrie had thought she was beautiful.

Rosie was a sweet child but, based solely on the size and angle of her ears, it was clear who her mother was. She was happy and managing to thrive even in the misery and filthy conditions of the Factory, unlike most of the children there, many of whom died before their first birthday. But then they didn't have the benefits that Friday, Harry and Sarah made sure Charlotte and Rosie received.

'Lotta,' Rosie said, laying a proprietary little hand on Charlotte's chubby bare foot.

'Yes! That's Charlotte, isn't it?' Harrie said, delighted. 'When did she start talking, Janie?'

'Said her first proper word two weeks ago,' Janie replied proudly.

'Really? What was it?'

'Bugger.'

Friday roared with laughter, startling Charlotte so her little hands flew out.

Janie laughed, too, when she heard about Sarah's plan to haunt Esther Green, but shook her head reproachfully as Harrie told her about James Downey's latest attempt to get her to talk to him.

'You know, Harrie, you been playing this silly game for ages. Don't you think it's time you got off your high horse? He'll get sick of it and find himself a lass who *will* talk to him, *and* warm his bed. Then you'll be sorry.'

'James isn't like that,' Harrie said stiffly.

Janie and Friday looked at each other and laughed. 'He's a man, isn't he?' Friday said. ''Course he is.'

'You don't understand what he did,' Harrie insisted.

Janie said, 'I do so, I were there, remember?'

'Well, I can't forgive him.'

'You mean you won't.' Friday rolled her eyes.

Janie shrugged. 'Suit yourself. But sure as eggs you'll lose him.

Some pretty little thing'll come along and —' She clicked her fingers. 'Just like that he'll be gone.'

Harrie said nothing. She ran her fingers over the silky softness of Charlotte's hair and down her plump pink cheek. The thought had occurred to her, of course; James could well give up his pursuit of her, tired at last of her constant rebuttals, and find himself someone else. And then what would she do? But she could not bring herself to forgive him, she just couldn't.

'I don't want him, anyway,' she said.

Friday and Janie exchanged a knowing glance but remained silent. The remainder of the visit passed pleasantly, filled with gossip, Janie's sharply witty character assassinations of her fellow Factory inmates, and the removal of a half-chewed piece of nougat from Rosie's hair. But soon it was time to leave.

Outside the visitors' room someone other than Pearl was waiting for them.

'Look what the cat's dragged in,' Friday remarked.

'Afternoon, Miss Harrie, Miss Friday,' Matilda Bain said, giving a wobbly half-curtsy.

Matilda had been transported on the same convict ship as Sarah, Rachel, Friday and Harrie, but at the age of seventy was too old to be assigned and had languished in the Factory ever since. She was frail, suffering from dementia related to tertiary syphilis, partially blind and missing most of her teeth. Today her sparse white hair, stained ochre in places by tobacco smoke, lifted in the slight breeze like liberated dandelion spoors and her ragged Factory slops hung crookedly off her skinny, bent frame, exposing one bruised and bony shoulder.

Friday rummaged in her reticule and handed her a good-sized bottle of gin. 'Here you go.'

'Thank you, Miss Friday. Much 'preciated.'

It was Friday's atonement for shoving, shouting at and insulting Matilda on the voyage out from England. There had been no real reason for her behaviour other than she'd needed a punching bag, and whining, irritating old Matilda had been it. So every time Friday visited the Factory now she gave Matilda something. Neither had discussed the matter — that would be too embarrassing for both of them — but each knew exactly why Matilda was getting gifts when Friday came to see Janie and the children.

But this time, instead of scurrying off across the yard, Matilda turned to Harrie.

'I got something to tell you, Miss Harrie.'

Joggling Charlotte up and down to make her giggle, Harrie raised her eyebrows. 'What's that, Matilda?'

'I seen her,' Matilda said.

Harrie stopped joggling. The hairs on her arms rose and her skin broke out in goose bumps, because she knew: she knew without Matilda having to say a single word more.

'Who?' Friday demanded.

'That young lass Rachel. Standing by winder where she used to wait, watching them bats go by.' A fly landed on Matilda's nostril; she didn't seem to notice.

Janie, seeing the look on Harrie's face, took Charlotte from her and said, 'You're mad, Matilda. Rachel's gone, remember?'

Matilda shook her head vehemently; the fly hung on. 'I got up to use bucket and there she were, plain as day.'

'You must have been dreaming,' Friday said, and turned to Harrie. 'Like you have, eh?'

Harrie nodded, but she knew Matilda hadn't been dreaming.

'James?' Lawrence Chandler called out as James passed his office door. 'Do you have a minute? I'd like a word.'

James, bag in hand, was about to leave for the night but he did have a minute, several in fact: no one was waiting for him at home and all he had to look forward to were two pork chops he would more than likely carbonise over his fire.

'Sit down,' Lawrence said, indicating the chair beside his desk.

James sat, his bag on the floor at his feet, hat balanced on top.

'Whisky?' Lawrence offered.

'Just a small one, thank you.'

Lawrence poured two drinks from the cut-crystal decanter on his desk. 'I had a patient in here today, someone I've known in a professional capacity for some years. A very kind-hearted woman.'

James nodded politely.

'She currently has working for her a girl who, for medical reasons, is no longer able to continue in her present capacity and is therefore looking for more suitable employment. Apart from this one particular matter concerning her health, which is not generally limiting, she is a fit young woman.' Lawrence pulled at his greying beard as if deep in thought. 'How are you getting on at home, James?'

'At home?'

'Yes. With your meals and housework and what have you?'

James suspected he knew where this was heading. 'I believe I'm managing.'

'Are you? Is that why you've come to work in the same coat with egg on its sleeve every day this week?'

James grasped his sleeve and twisted it; there was indeed egg on it — quite old egg.

'I really do think it's time you got someone in to look after you,' Lawrence said. 'No, don't start on about wagging tongues. Virtually every bachelor with means in this town has a domestic servant of some sort.'

'Yes, and they're all gossiped about,' James protested. On the rare occasions he attended social events it seemed that gossiping was all people damned well did.

'Are they? I don't listen to gossip myself. If that really is what's troubling you, James, I think you're probably fairly safe. There are far more interesting people than you in this town to talk about.'

Lawrence took a sip of his whisky. 'It has also occurred to me that something else may be bothering you. I realise you're still in mourning for a wife whom I do understand was deeply beloved to you, and forgive me for being blunt, James, but could it be that you're allowing your memory of her to prevent you from having a female servant in your house? And, in effect, dictate that you must eat appallingly prepared meals and go about looking like some grubby alms-hunter, for that matter? You need nourishing food, and at the very least clean clothes.'

James rubbed at the dried smear of egg on his arm.

'Am I correct in understanding your period of full mourning has come to an end? Yes? Will you be going on to half-mourning?'

James had thought about it, but had decided a year had been long enough. To be honest he felt an absolute hypocrite chasing Harrie Clarke around the streets dressed head to toe in widower's weeds.

'No, I think not.'

'Good man. Then I can see no excuse for you to continue to deny yourself, and it sounds to me as though Elizabeth has just the girl you need.'

An unpleasant suspicion stole over James. 'Elizabeth who?'

'Elizabeth Hislop.'

'Lawrence! I can't have a *prostitute* in my house!'

'James, this is a marvellous opportunity for you both.' Lawrence leant forwards in his chair to emphasise his point. 'The girl will be placed in decent and wholesome employment, and you'll get a perfectly adequate servant. Where's your Christian charity, man?'

James squirmed, recalling having employed similar tactics himself not so long ago. 'It's out of the question. What would my patients say?'

'Why would they say anything? Why would they need to know of your domestic arrangements at all?'

'Because things get around. This is a small town, Lawrence. It's hardly London.'

'But who's to know where she worked before she came to you? It's my understanding that Elizabeth Hislop operates a very discreet business.'

Thinking of Friday Woolfe, James wondered about that. He took a large gulp of his whisky, feeling very much cornered. 'Well, can she even cook?'

'Elizabeth says she can. She's also lent a very competent hand in the hotel laundry.'

'Then why can't she stay on in Mrs Hislop's employ?'

Lawrence frowned, his wiry brows meeting in the middle. 'Elizabeth doesn't require another cook or laundress. I'm sad to say she needs a girl with a different set of skills.'

James felt himself blush. 'Oh God, Lawrence, I don't know. Is she a convict?'

'I understand she has a ticket of leave. And a family she supports in England. So she desperately needs employment.'

James sighed deeply. 'What exactly is ailing her?'

Lawrence finished his whisky. 'I have examined her and my diagnosis is excessive menstrual bleeding caused possibly by a tumour, though I found no evidence of one. No metritis, either, or lues venerea. Elizabeth has always been very meticulous about that.'

'Is there mania associated with the episodes of bleeding?' James asked, envisioning a lunatic servant running riot through his cottage.

'No, just pain requiring rest, and an inability to perform her, er, intimate duties, according to Elizabeth.'

James thought he could possibly tolerate that. 'What treatment have you prescribed?'

'Tonic for blood loss, laudanum for discomfort and light domestic duties during heavy bleeding. I've asked her to come back and see me in two months' time. I'm not convinced she isn't harbouring a tumour of some sort, though as I said I saw no evidence.'

'Well, I suppose I could at least interview her,' James said reluctantly. If the poor girl was suffering women's problems she'd hardly be likely to hurl herself at him. 'What's her name?'

Lawrence looked delighted. 'Good man, James! Her name is Rowena Harris.'

'Sit down, Rowie,' Elizabeth Hislop said.

Reluctantly, Rowie perched on the edge of the chair beside Mrs H's desk, knees together, spine bent, rocking slightly. She'd cut herself peeling potatoes in the hotel kitchen; a rose of blood was slowly blossoming through the strip of muslin she'd wrapped around her finger. But Elizabeth knew that wasn't the reason for her despondency; she was expecting to be told she would shortly be without employment altogether.

'Do you need another bandage for that?' Elizabeth asked. 'It looks nasty.'

'I'll be all right.'

Elizabeth sat down herself. 'I have some good news, though I do regret having to let you go. You do know that, don't you?'

Rowie nodded, refusing to meet Elizabeth's eyes, her own gaze darting about the room. In fact she looked more than despondent, she looked desperate, and Elizabeth wondered why. 'I like it here. I'm very good at what I do.'

'I know you are, but I just can't afford to pay someone who isn't pulling her weight. And I realise it's not your fault, but I do have the business to consider. Now, I understand you have family in England who rely on you for financial support? Is that right?'

Rowie nodded again, and looked as though she might burst into tears. 'I don't know *what* they'll do without the money. Can't I *please* stay?'

'It wouldn't work, dear. It *isn't* working.'

'The kitchen, then? Can't I work there? Or even the laundry?' Rowie was sounding panicked now.

'No, Rowie. I don't need anyone in the kitchen or the laundry.'

'But —'

'I said *no*,' Elizabeth replied sharply. 'But I've spoken to Dr Chandler, who you saw about your troubles the other day, and he's very kindly arranged alternative employment for you. The position is with Dr Downey, the other doctor at the surgery, as his live-in domestic servant.' She paused, relieved to see a smile transforming Rowie's features. 'It will be the usual, cooking, cleaning and what have you. Dr Downey is fairly new to Sydney, and recently widowed. Are you interested?'

'Would that be Dr James Downey?'

'It would.'

'The surgeon who was on Friday's transport?'

'Do you know him?' Elizabeth was surprised.

'No, but she's mentioned him. He's her friend Harrie's beau, isn't he?'

'I gather that's a touchy subject. And don't you go getting any ideas in that direction, miss.'

'I won't! Thank you *so* much, Mrs H. I'm that grateful!'

Elizabeth waved away the thanks. 'Yes, well, mind you do a good job. You're there on my recommendation, remember.'

'I'll do a *wonderful* job, I promise,' Rowie said. 'It's perfect.'

Harrie gaped at Friday in appalled disbelief.

'You'll swallow a fly if you're not careful,' Friday remarked.

'And he's taken her on? A *prostitute*?'

Friday nodded. 'Well, she's not now. She's a maid of all work.'

'But *why*?' Harrie demanded. 'Why would he employ a servant now, when he's been perfectly happy by himself for a whole year?'

'How should I know? Maybe he's sick of eating in the pub and sleeping in filthy linen.'

Harrie continued to stare at Friday; in a single minute, disbelief had progressed to dismay, then jealousy and now anger. 'Was this *your* idea?'

''Course not. It was Mrs H's.'

'But why *James*?' He'd done this on purpose, Harrie knew he had, just to spite her for refusing to speak to him.

'I suppose because he works with Chandler and Chandler is Mrs H's doctor, and Mrs H has been keeping an eye out for another job for Rowie, seeing as she can't work in the brothel any more. And James didn't have a servant and needed one.'

'Sounds a likely story,' Harrie said, her lip curling.

Friday laughed. 'That's because it is.'

Harrie switched back to feeling jealous. 'What does she look like?'

Friday hesitated, then sighed. Even though Harrie's reaction was quite funny because she'd been swearing black and blue for months she wanted nothing to do with James Downey, she knew the news had upset her, and this was only going to make it worse. 'She's pretty. Black hair, grey eyes. Quite a nice figure, I suppose.'

Harrie immediately compared that to her own mouse-brown hair, ordinary brown eyes and rounded shape, and felt a surge of resentment so sour she could taste it. And she hadn't even met this Rowie Harris.

'And she's been there a week?'

'Give or take.'

'Have you been to visit her?' Harrie demanded. 'What does James think of her? How does he behave around her?'

A long moment passed during which Friday and Harrie stared at each other. Slowly, Harrie's hands came up to cover her ears, something that only happened when she was under considerable duress. She forced herself to lower them again.

Friday said, 'Harrie, stop it. Will you listen to yourself? No, I haven't been to see her. It's just a job she's got. Christ, he probably barely says good morning to her. You know how boring and proper he is.'

Actually, Harrie didn't. What she knew was that he was kind and clever, amusing, courteous and generous. And she had *thought* he was considerate, until he'd done what he had to Rachel. If it hadn't been for that, it might have been *her* cooking James's meals and laundering his linen and sweeping his floors — and yes, perhaps even sharing his bed. But now, it seemed, it was some tuppenny-uprighter called Rowie.

She sat very still, aware Friday was watching her, and all the worry and anger and guilt and fear she'd felt since Rachel had died converged into a cold ball of dread just below her breastbone. Everything around her became very bright and she thought for a moment she was falling, though she knew she wasn't. Her hands felt suddenly icy, her lips numb, and her heart thumped furiously. The sensation was terrifying and she understood with dreadful clarity that if she didn't move, if she didn't haul herself out of the pit of despair and confusion into which she knew herself to be sliding she would be lost.

She had to do something, and she knew what it was. James could have his other woman; it didn't matter, because she had an admirer, too.

She touched Friday's knee. 'Thanks for coming to tell me.'

Friday nodded. 'Will you be all right? You don't look very happy.'

'It was just a shock. As you say, he probably doesn't even notice her.'

'Probably,' Friday agreed. 'But it might be time to stop ignoring him, eh?'

Harrie slept badly that night. At four o'clock, well before the sun had even begun to rise, she got up, lit the lamp and sat on her bed to compose a note. After three attempts, finally happy with what she'd written, she folded the single sheet of paper and sealed it with wax, then hid it in her drawer.

She washed, dressed and went downstairs early to tackle a pile of ironing before she started breakfast, her nerves jangling and her determination to carry out her plan coursing through her veins so vigorously she almost tore one of Abigail's shifts with the point of the iron. As the early morning sun crept across the parlour floor, the Barretts appeared one by one, George first, attired for work, then the older children still in their nightclothes.

Having finished the ironing and folded it into neat piles, Harrie prepared and served breakfast, waited until George had dawdled frustratingly over his cup of tea and pipe and gone downstairs, shooed the children off to get dressed, then carried the dirty breakfast things down to the kitchen and washed them.

Finally, she knocked on Nora's open bedroom door and popped her head around: Nora was reclining on the bed nursing Lewis.

'Do you mind if I go out for half an hour, Mrs Barrett?'

Nora frowned and adjusted Lewis's position on her breast. 'Must you, Harrie? Samuel needs his bath and Hannah could do with a good wash as well. I don't know what she was doing yesterday but she's rather whiffy. And we've that cloak to finish for Mrs Cowley, don't forget.'

'I won't be long, I promise. Perhaps not even half an hour.'

Nora checked the clock on the mantel. 'Oh, well, all right, then. But please don't be long.'

'I won't, I really won't.'

Now Harrie felt guilty on top of everything else. She ran up the stairs to her room, ripped off her apron, jammed her bonnet on her head and snatched the note from the drawer.

Minutes later she was hurrying north along Gloucester Street, walking so quickly she almost turned her ankle in a pothole. It wasn't until she passed the delicious smell of fresh bread drifting from the open door of a bakehouse that she realised she hadn't eaten any breakfast herself, and farther along the stink from a slaughter yard behind a butcher's, combined with the lack of food and the state of her nerves, nearly made her vomit.

She turned left at Argyle and toiled up the hill to Princes Street where she stopped, patted her pocket to make sure the letter was still there, and thought for a moment. Friday had passed on the address last year and she'd never forgotten it, but would he still be living here?

The houses at the northern end of Princes Street were elegant and very comfortable. Not grand, not by London standards, and not small mansions like the residences at the Bunker's Hill end of Cumberland Street, but very nice all the same. They were detached or semi-detached, and one- or two-storey with several chimneys each, plenty of windows, verandahs and low picket fences, and some had lovely, luscious gardens. This far up the hill they escaped the worst of the smells emanating from the jammed-together little houses, lanes, closed-in yards, privies, cesspits and open drains down nearer the water.

These homes were owned mainly by artisans, well-to-do merchants and slightly lesser professionals such as solicitors and surveyors, many of whom insisted they resided in Millers Point, not the Rocks. And possibly they did as from the tallest of the Princes Street residences a view could be had of not only Sydney Cove and South Head, but also glimpses of Darling Harbour to the west and the rolling, scrub-cloaked hills beyond.

Nice people would live here, Harrie decided. Husbands who worked hard and honestly for their money, of which they would have a comfortable amount, but not in a job where they got sweaty or their hands dirty, and they would have nice, kind wives who donated their time to worthy causes and their children would be polite and wipe their bottoms properly and not pick their noses. She knew if she looked closely there would be cats sunning themselves in the gardens, and probably even a well-trained dog or two on chains in backyards — beloved family pets, not the feral sort that terrorised people as they went about their business in town. There might be a goat, too, for milk, and chickens for fresh breakfast eggs.

She sighed without even realising it; she would love to live in a house like one of these. Determination driving her forwards, she followed the line of smartly painted fences along the street in the direction of Dawes Battery, looking for the right address. It was embarrassing enough handing a note to a servant; it would be *awful* if she delivered it to the wrong house.

The creak and jingle of a carriage rattling along the road made her turn, and when she did her heart leapt so violently that for a second her breath snagged painfully in her chest. Bella Jackson! The midnight-blue curricle and those black horses were unmistakable. Then the air burst out of Harrie's lungs accompanied by a terrified squeak and she looked around wildly for somewhere to hide. She snatched up her skirts, darted through the nearest gate, kicked it shut behind her and ducked behind an oleander bush.

The driver of the curricle, which Harrie now saw was empty, executed a turn and came to a halt before the very front yard in which she was hiding, the horses snorting and stamping impatiently. Heart racing madly, she pushed herself further into the bush, praying her feet weren't visible below the foliage.

The front door of the house opened and out came Bella Jackson and another woman.

Bella looked subtly different and it took a moment for Harrie to realise why: her style of dress had changed. Gone were the expensive and well-made but rather garish skirts and bodices she'd worn on the *Isla*. Today her outfit consisted of an elegant, summery day dress with a pattern of — Harrie had to squint to make this out — purple irises and red lilies against a lemon background, with a bodice perfectly fitted to Bella's thin torso and modest bust, puffed sleeves and a gathered skirt with a frilled hem. Her wide-brimmed straw hat was trimmed with artificial irises and lilies *exactly* the same shades as those on her dress, and she wore a yellow silk scarf at her throat, the ends of which trailed down her back. Her strong, striking face looked, as usual, heavily made up and the dark curls beneath the hat gleamed.

Even while jammed in an oleander bush sweating with terror, Harrie felt envious. Bella Jackson was an evil, evil woman, *and* a bonded convict, and here she was swanning about Sydney Town virtually free, wearing beautiful clothes no doubt paid for by her new rich husband. She noted with satisfaction, however, that Bella's scarf lent the outfit a slightly common air.

The other woman — pleasant-looking, smartly dressed and somewhere in her forties — said, 'Thank you so much, Mrs Shand. I'm so sorry my husband couldn't be here today, but I know he'll be *delighted* when he returns. It's been a pleasure to do business with you.'

Harrie stifled a gasp. But Bella Jackson was a whoremonger! Was this woman condoning her husband's infidelity? Or, even worse, facilitating it?

Bella replied graciously, 'The pleasure has been all mine, Mrs Clayton. And I'm sure Dr Clayton will be satisfied. As you know, I procure only the very highest quality. Thank you for the tea and cake. Most delicious. I'll be in contact when the time comes.'

They smiled, exchanged limp handshakes, the woman went inside again and Bella walked down the little path, opened the gate and passed through, closed it behind her, and climbed into her curricle. And just sat there.

Harrie grimaced and closed her eyes.

'You can come out now,' Bella said loudly, 'you cowering little squirrel.'

Harrie stayed where she was, face on fire, blood pounding in her head, so frightened she thought she might be sick.

A moment later the driver cracked his whip and the curricle clattered off.

Harrie waited until the sound had faded completely, then, branch by branch, disentangled herself from the oleander and crept out of Mrs Clayton's yard. Bloody, *bloody* hell. She lived in complete terror of encountering the rotten woman, she really did, but why did it have to be today? And would seeing Harrie remind Bella of what she knew about them? Of course it would. Would there be a demand soon? Or would it be the police knocking on the Barretts' door early one morning?

God, she couldn't *bear* this! Her mind felt so tormented and jagged and ... *brittle*. Once again her hands suddenly felt like ice, she couldn't feel her mouth, and the sensation of falling swept over her. Her arms flew out, but she was fine, it was only in her head. Then she bent over, hands on knees, and vomited. Not much came up and it wrenched at her belly, but she felt better. She spat, wiped her mouth on the hem of her skirt and started walking again.

The house called 'Swansea' was fourth from the end, one of the last houses on Princes Street. It was two-storey, with three dormer windows, three chimneys and a verandah. Harrie went around the back and knocked on the door.

When Matthew Cutler himself opened it she wanted to weep. It was so unfair; in a proper house the servant always answered the door!

'Harriet!' he exclaimed: the first word he'd ever spoken to her.

Despite the hour he was still wearing his nightclothes and a robe belted at the waist, a woollen scarf around his neck and leather slippers. His eyes were bleary and his nose bright pink, his sandy hair stuck up at the back, and he had a scabbed-over canker in one corner of his mouth. He looked awful.

'The Vincents aren't home. And neither's Dolly, our girl. Just me. I'm indisposed with an early summer ague,' he wittered on apologetically.

Wishing she could disappear into a hole in the ground, Harrie knew if she didn't do it now, she never would. She thrust her note at him.

'For me?'

She nodded.

He opened and read it, and a grin spread across his face, cracking the canker on his mouth. He winced and dabbed at it with a finger.

'Thank you very much, Harrie. May I call you Harrie? Or would you prefer Miss Clarke?'

'Harrie, please.' What did it matter?

'I'm truly honoured. I would love to attend afternoon tea with you next Saturday. Thank you.'

Harrie finally allowed herself to relax slightly. 'Thank you, Mr Cutler.'

Matthew waved his hand dismissively. 'Oh, please, it's Matthew, if I'm to call you Harrie.'

'Thank you, Matthew,' Harrie said.

They were quiet for a minute. Uncomfortably so.

'You've some sort of stick in your hair,' Matthew said. 'Under your brim.'

Harrie felt around for it, found it and pulled it out.

'And pardon me for saying so, but have you recently been unwell?' Matthew pointed to a dribble of vomit on Harrie's front.

She rubbed at it with her sleeve, her face burning.

'Would you like something to drink?' Matthew asked.

'No, thank you. I have to go back to work. I'm in service on Gloucester Street.'

'Yes, I know where you are,' Matthew said, then winced again in case it occurred to Harrie to ask how he knew that. James had told him, of course. 'Well, until Saturday, then? I'll call for you if I may?'

Harrie nodded. 'Thank you.'

As she hurried off, Matthew gently closed the door. What a tremendous shock; what a wonderful, marvellous surprise! God, what was James going to say? Should he tell him? And would this hideous sore on his mouth be healed by Saturday?

Two minutes along Princes Street Harrie started to giggle. Lord, that had been a shambles; her covered in vomit and him full of snot and with that awful sore on his face!

And then her giggles turned into hiccups and she began to cry.

Chapter Five

James leant back so Rowie could set his breakfast plate on the table. Today she'd prepared scrambled eggs — pale yellow and fluffy and with a sprinkle of chives, just the way he liked them — accompanied by toasted bread and slices of black pudding; a far cry from the rubbery, incinerated fare he'd been consuming before she'd arrived.

This morning, having risen from a bed made up with recently laundered and lavender-scented linen, he would be setting out for the surgery wearing a pristine shirt starched and ironed only yesterday and a coat bearing not a trace of egg, leaving behind him a cottage that would be cleaned, swept, polished and dusted to within an inch of its life, and returning home this evening to be served another filling and beautifully cooked meal.

He had to admit that in the beginning he'd been very wary of taking on Rowie Harris, particularly with regard to her previous vocation, but she'd turned out to be a Godsend. He didn't know how she did it but no longer were there cockroaches running roughshod through his pantry or giant spiders squatting in his clothes press, and of late he'd not seen a single skink or lizard darting across his parlour floor.

Ironically, however, it had been he who had upset *her* during their initial interview, and he cringed at the thought of what he would have missed, had she declined the position. She possessed a ticket of leave, which meant that although she was still legally a convict she was entitled to live and work as a private individual. After a certain period of time, providing she behaved, she would be in a position to apply for a conditional pardon. In his opinion she had been risking her very future working in Elizabeth Hislop's brothel, and he'd told her so in no uncertain terms. It was at that point she had tearfully informed him of the destitute family members she financially supported in England, explaining that her position with Mrs Hislop had been the most expedient way of earning the income she so desperately needed. However, she'd said, if he couldn't reconcile himself with her employment record she would understand, and take her recipes for Yorkshire and Devonshire pies, lamb cutlets, beefsteak and oyster pudding, apple charlotte and pear tart somewhere else.

The interview had been all the more disturbing for him because she was a very attractive girl, which had made him feel uncomfortably on edge and even more conscious of potential rumours regarding any relationship between them. He had been unable to stop himself envisioning the graceful lines of her ripe body rising naked from his bed each morning, and had had to cross his legs to conceal the evidence. It had been sixteen months since Emily had passed away, seventeen since he had seen and been intimate with her. Or any woman.

But it wasn't Rowie Harris he wanted, it was Harrie Clarke, and it had been since before he'd learnt of Emily's death, if he were to be truly honest with himself. Harrie, however, was refusing even to speak to him, never mind demonstrate an inclination to share his cottage. So, feeling guilty because his libido had betrayed him, he'd apologised to Rowie for lecturing her, then surprised himself by hiring her. She'd driven a hard remunerative bargain, his position somewhat undermined by the tale of woe she'd spun about her family in England because it had resonated so closely with Harrie's, and he strongly suspected he was paying her over the odds, but what did that matter? He could afford it.

The room Rowie occupied was external, a skilling built on to one side of the cottage and not accessible from within. The day after she'd moved in she'd asked him to have a lock fitted to the door. He'd assumed she was concerned about her personal safety and had obliged, but it had taken several more days for him to realise, with considerable shock, that it might be *him* she was worried about. He'd very awkwardly broached the subject and had been relieved — and vaguely insulted — when she'd admitted that an advance from him had been the *last* thing on her mind. But she confessed she was concerned about her safety, and that she had friends with whom she wanted to spend private time, which he could hardly prohibit on moral grounds, given her previous job.

So the tension that clearly only he had been experiencing had abated, and they were now getting along together very well. He couldn't imagine how he had managed before without her. She was very capable in terms of domestic affairs, cheerful, somewhat cheeky, and seemed to know a fair number of Sydney's townsfolk. And if people were gossiping about the fact he had a live-in servant, James no longer cared. It was worth it, even if just for Rowie's scrambled eggs.

'Will you be here for supper?' she asked as she set the teapot down near his plate.

'I'm not sure yet. We've been very busy this week. Outbreak of dysentery again. Is there any black pudding left?'

'Two slices or three?'

'Three, please.'

Rowie served them and James ate them in four minutes flat, stifled a burp, blotted his mouth with his napkin, then checked his watch. 'Excellent breakfast as usual, thank you, Rowie. What are your plans for today?'

She glanced around the cosy dining room-cum-parlour. 'Cleaning up, I've those shirts of yours to starch, a bit of ironing, the windows, some shopping. Then I'll be back to get the supper on, just in case you are home on time.'

James took a last hurried sip of tea, rose from the table and collected his bag from the floor next to a fireside armchair. He walked to the door, Rowie behind him. He turned and ... only just stopped himself from kissing her goodbye. Good God! He must be feeling a *lot* more settled these days!

Seeing the tiny smile on her lips and feeling himself reddening, he said, 'I'll see you this evening.'

Sarah waited until Esther had slammed the shop door on her way out, told Adam in the workshop she was going 'down the yard', but instead crept upstairs to the best bedroom. Harrie was visiting this afternoon and Sarah wanted her mistress in a suitably precarious state of nerves.

She gazed around, brow furrowed, lower lip caught between her teeth, searching for something that would cause the biggest impact for just a small amount of effort, as she didn't have much time.

What if she emptied Esther's rice powder jar and put a dead mouse in it? Would a ghost do something like that? More to the point, was Esther likely to powder her face this afternoon? Because if she didn't, she wouldn't see it.

Perhaps if she pulled all the bedclothes off the bed? No, that wouldn't work; she wasn't sure if Esther had been up to her room between breakfast and leaving the house. If she hadn't, she would just accuse Sarah of not making her bed today.

Foot tapping, she thought about it, letting her mind wander wherever it wanted to go.

And then she had it.

From the clothes press she lifted out the cream muslin dress Esther had worn the evening Jared Spider-Fingers Gellar had come to supper. Placing her feet carefully to avoid creaky floorboards, and working quickly because she knew Esther had only gone to the chemist's, she laid the dress on the floor and spread out the sleeves and skirt. Then she arranged Esther's best satin slippers below the skirt, the toes turned out slightly, and took a pair of lavender kidskin gloves from the dressing table and placed one at the end of each sleeve.

They weren't really suitable for evening wear, though, were they, kidskin gloves? Sarah opened a drawer of the press and discovered at least two dozen more pairs. Christ, no wonder Adam was always scolding Esther for spending money. She grabbed a white lace pair and swapped them for the kidskin, then cast a critical eye over her handiwork. Not bad, but she needed something else. What, what, what?

Then her gaze fell on the perfect finishing touch; Esther's hairpiece, a collection of long blonde ringlets she occasionally pinned into her hair. Sarah artistically spread them on the floor above the bodice of the dress, leaving a gap that would accommodate a neck and a face, and tucked a tortoiseshell comb ornamented with paste diamonds into the ringlets. Perfect.

The whole ensemble looked really quite grotesque, as though a woman not even a second earlier had been wearing the costume but had suddenly vanished. Which was exactly the effect Sarah intended.

She crept downstairs, banged the back door, went through the shop to the workshop and took her place beside Adam.

'Warm, isn't it?' she commented. 'I nearly fainted in the privy.'

'That,' Adam said as he polished the shank of a newly repaired ring, 'could more likely be attributed to the state of the privy. It's time I paid someone to dig a new pit and move it.'

Sarah grunted. They worked companionably together for some minutes, though she sensed Adam had something on his mind. At last he came out with it.

'Sarah, I need to go to Van Diemen's Land soon. I'll be away for perhaps three weeks. I know Esther pushes you to the limit at times, but while I'm gone do you think you and she can get along without too much aggravation?'

Bloody unlikely. 'I can't see why not,' Sarah said.

'She's rather unsettled at the moment.'

'I had noticed.'

'I might even be home in less than three weeks, if I can complete my business quickly.'

'What will happen with the shop?' Sarah asked. 'We've been busy lately. I can't be in the workshop and behind the counter at the same time.'

'I've arranged for another jeweller to step in while I'm away, a friend and colleague of mine, Bernard Cole,' Adam said. 'He has premises on Pitt Street, but his wife is perfectly capable of managing the shop by herself. And willing,' he added a little sourly.

Sarah experienced a vague pang she recognised as disappointment, though to feel that, she knew, was ridiculous. What might she do were she to be left unsupervised? Pile the safe and the entire contents of the shop onto a handcart, push it along to Mr Skelton's and pawn the lot? Surely even Adam would notice that. Or was she disappointed because he didn't trust her?

'Won't your colleague be short someone in *his* workshop?'

'He doesn't manufacture, he's retail only. And he'll only be here during opening hours. I think you'll like him, Sarah.'

Not if he was as odious as Jared Gellar, she wouldn't. Mentally she crossed her fingers, but without much hope.

The shop door opened then closed with such a bang Sarah knew Esther had returned. With a pleasant sense of anticipation she settled more comfortably onto her stool and waited for the explosion. Footsteps could be heard on the stairs, a door squeaked overhead, then a very rewarding shriek echoed down the stairwell.

Adam started, fumbling his pliers, and stared wide-eyed at Sarah. 'Christ, was that Esther?'

'Was it?'

But Adam was already rushing out of the workshop.

Sarah thought Harrie was doing an excellent job of pretending to be upset. Her normally rosy face was almost haggard and she looked as though she hadn't slept properly in days.

They were in the dining room this time, taking advantage of the fact that Esther had taken to her bed after her dreadful shock that morning. Or rather, she'd taken to Adam's bed as she'd refused to go back into her own chamber.

'You should have seen her,' Sarah said, her voice low but full of glee. 'Her hair was almost standing on end. It was my best trick yet!'

'She's not going to want to hear any more ghost stories, then, is she?' Harrie said.

'She won't be able to help herself. Wait and see.'

Sarah went upstairs and knocked gently on Adam's bedroom door.

'Who is it?'

'Just me, Mrs Green,' Sarah called out softly. 'Do you need anything at the moment? Tea? Brandy?'

'No. Go away.'

'It's just that Harrie's here. She's in a bit of a state and needs my help. It's about our friend. The one who died.'

There was a long silence. Then Esther said, 'You can have ten minutes with her. That's all.'

'Thank you, Mrs Green.' Sarah smirked and returned to the dining room.

She poured tea for herself and Harrie and when she heard Esther step off the bottom stair and come to a rustling halt in the short hallway, she started talking.

'Have you actually *seen* her, though, Harrie? Properly? When you're not dreaming, I mean.'

'Yes. Yes, I have,' Harrie replied. 'Standing at the end of my bed. Or sometimes sitting in the rocking chair in my room.'

Sarah thought that was an inspired touch. 'Yes, I've seen her, too, though I haven't told anyone. And she's been moving my things around. And Mrs Green came home this morning and found her clothes all over her bedroom floor!'

Harrie hesitated; she'd forgotten what to say again. Sarah gently kicked her shin and mouthed the words.

'Well, I wonder why Rachel would be bothering Mrs Green?' Harrie parroted woodenly.

'I don't know. Perhaps she's angry at her because she wouldn't permit me time off to go to her funeral.'

A muffled gasp came from the hallway.

'I hope she goes away soon,' Harrie said.

'So do I. God knows how far Rachel will go to get her revenge.'

Harrie burst into tears.

Sarah nodded in approval: this wasn't in the script but it was good. She jumped as she heard Adam's voice.

'Esther, shouldn't you be resting?'

'Get your hands *off* me!' Esther hissed.

There was a scuffling noise, then hurried footsteps retreating up the stairs.

Adam appeared in the dining-room doorway. 'Oh, I beg your pardon. I thought you were in the yard.'

Sarah stood. 'We can go out there if you'd prefer.' Bugger; he'd ruined everything.

'No, stay where you are.' Adam glanced at Harrie, who was surreptitiously dabbing at her eyes with a handkerchief. 'Is everything all right?'

'Yes,' Sarah said.

Adam eyed them a moment longer, then nodded and disappeared back down the hallway.

'Shite,' Sarah said. But Harrie was still crying. 'What's the matter?'

'I don't know.' Harrie blew her nose. 'I just feel ... I don't know.'

Overhead the floorboards creaked.

'Is it James and that girl he's hired?' Sarah asked shrewdly.

Friday had told her about James Downey getting himself a maid of all work, and Sarah had been wondering how Harrie felt about it. A prostitute, too. Actually, an ex-prostitute according to Friday, but Sarah expected the news wasn't sitting comfortably with Harrie. Well, she'd been warning Harrie for months Downey would lose interest if she continued to spurn him, and obviously now he had, because what bachelor paid an attractive girl to live in and just starch his collars?

Harrie flapped her hand in a half-hearted attempt at dismissal, then nodded and choked out another sob. 'That, and Matthew Cutler.'

Sarah frowned; the name was familiar. 'Who?'

Upstairs raised but muffled voices could be heard.

'Matthew Cutler, the other gentleman on the *Isla*. Remember, he gave Friday his address to give to me?'

'Oh yes, your admirer. What about him?'

Harrie's face, already pink from weeping, flushed a deep red. 'I've invited him to afternoon tea. This Saturday.'

Sarah gasped and laughed at the same time. 'Harrie Clarke, you hussy! How forward of you! And you, of all people, Miss Prissy-Skirts!'

'Oh, don't,' Harrie pleaded.

'Will you actually go?' Sarah knew what it must have cost Harrie to ask Matthew Cutler, and what measure it was of her jealousy regarding James.

'Yes. Why shouldn't I?'

'That'll teach him, won't it?' Sarah said.

'Who?'

'You know very well who. You can't fool me, Harrie.'

Harrie stared at her, opened her mouth to say something, then shut it again and concentrated on folding her handkerchief into a neat, ever-diminishing square. On the floor above something thumped, and a door slammed.

Finally she said, 'Well, he should have thought twice before taking on a whore as a house girl.'

Sarah shook her head. 'Harrie, this isn't like you. You don't even know this girl. She might be perfectly nice.'

Harrie's sour expression clearly conveyed her appraisal of that likelihood. 'And there's another thing. I saw Bella Jackson in Princes Street, when I went to see Matthew. And she saw me. It ... it unsettled me.'

'God, really? That must have given you a fright.'

'If she knows what we did,' Harrie said, her voice rising, 'why doesn't she damn well *do* something? This waiting and waiting for something to happen is sending me *insane*.'

Sarah moved around the table and gave Harrie a quick hug. 'Hush, love. And I know. I think that's the point. It's supposed to.'

Eyes filling with tears again, Harrie looked up at her. 'But I don't know how much longer I can stand it, Sarah. I really don't.'

'Leave the clearing up for a minute, Harrie,' George Barrett said. 'Sit down. I'd like a word. Go away, kids. Shoo.'

Harrie glanced at Nora, who raised her eyebrows, mystified, and sat down again at the small dining table around which the Barrett family and Harrie squeezed themselves at meal times.

'I've had an idea,' George announced.

Oh no, Harrie thought; George often had ideas, frequently to do with making money, and they weren't always good ones. The most recent had involved using the skins from rats caught by Angus the cat to manufacture gloves, hat-bands and purses, and passing them off as articles made from 'genuine' tree-bear hides to a vendor in George Street market. Being of inferior quality they'd quickly disintegrated and the stallholder was still vigorously pursuing a refund of his investment.

'What is it this time?' Nora asked warily.

'It's regarding Harrie's remarkable talents as a pattern-drawer,' George said. 'Hannah, I said go *away*! I can see you over there!'

Harrie knew it couldn't be to do with her designs he'd said he was sending to England — they would take four months to get there by ship, and any potential response at least another four months to arrive back.

'I was down on the waterfront today, near the Commissariat Stores,' George went on, deliberately not looking at his wife, whose face had taken on a very pinched expression, her mouth a straight, white line. 'And I happened to run into a friend.'

'Really?' Nora said contemptuously. 'What was her name?'

Harrie felt herself reddening. According to Friday, there was a brothel of very ill repute on lower George Street near the Stores; surely Nora couldn't be alluding to that?

'It was Leonard Dundas, actually, Nora,' George replied, though his own face had gone pink. 'He was telling me he's so busy at the moment he doesn't know what to do with himself. He's getting more and more coming into the shop and can barely keep up, and was saying he'd like to offer more variety but doesn't have the time to develop that side of the business. So *I* thought, well, we've got the perfect remedy to that problem right here, haven't we?' He beamed, thrilled by his own cleverness. 'I had a word and he's willing to pay, and given how good Harrie is at what she does, we'll be quids in. We're going to see him this afternoon.'

Harrie was alarmed; and Nora didn't seem any happier.

'That's all very well, but what am *I* supposed to do if Harrie's off working somewhere else? What about the children? What about *my* business?'

'Well, you'll just have to work harder, won't you?' George shrugged. 'Lewis is almost three months old now — surely he doesn't need your attention *all* the time?'

Harrie leant back in her chair, ready to dive out of the way if necessary. She'd seen Nora Barrett lose her temper before; it was a rare occurrence, but always spectacular.

Nora's face was white, except for a vivid red patch on each cheek. She took a deep, controlled breath, her nostrils flaring. 'No, George, if you expect me to continue with my business, *and* manage the children and the household without Harrie, *you* will have to help look after Lewis.'

George gave an incredulous laugh. 'Me?'

'Yes. You can have him on *your* side of the shop. *I'll* feed him because I'm the one with the tits, but you can burp him and put him down for his naps and when he shits his clout, *you* can change it. And *you* can do all his bloody laundry as well.'

Harrie was astounded. Surely Nora didn't mean that? George didn't know the first thing about looking after an infant.

George shoved back his chair and stood up. 'I've never heard anything so bloody ridiculous in all my life!' Grabbing his hat, he marched across the parlour, kicked the wall for good measure, and stamped downstairs.

Nora and Harrie stared after him.

Eventually Nora said, 'I'm sorry, Harrie. That's been coming for a while.'

'It's all right.' Harrie rubbed pointlessly at a jam stain on the tablecloth. 'What exactly does Leonard Dundas do, Nora?'

'Leo? Well, I believe he was a sailor for about thirty years, but these days he's a tattooist.'

The lower end of George Street, terminating just prior to Dawes Point, was Sydney's maritime heart. In recent years new wharves had appeared, extending like rigidly accusing fingers into Darling

Harbour at the end of Market Street and near Campbell and Goulburn streets, but the area below the Rocks continued to bustle with industry connected to the sea — warehouses, chandlers and provisioners, sail- and rope-makers, sailors' lodging houses, pubs and brothels — and sheltered Sydney Cove bristled with ships at anchor.

Near the Commissariat Stores on George Street stood one-, two- and three-storey buildings, including the fire station and those that until not long before had housed the town's first post office and the *Sydney Gazette*. The Stores themselves sat right on the water's edge, waves breaking against the barnacle-encrusted pilings of the wooden walkway fronting the severe, triple-storey brick edifice. Nearby King's Wharf reached a short distance out into the cove and, a little farther north towards Dawes Point, lay the dockyard and busy Campbell's Wharf.

Leonard Dundas's tattoo shop was on the west side of George Street, down an alley wide enough only for foot traffic, tucked into the side of a hotel named the Sailors' Grave. According to George, who hadn't stopped talking since they'd left Gloucester Street, Leo had been leasing the trio of small rooms for the past ten years.

The shop door was open but beside it, hooked over a nail driven into the mortar between the bricks, was a sign saying *CLOSED*. Across the doorway hung a curtain of dried bamboo reeds rattling gently in the afternoon breeze. Painted on the curtain was the most stunning image of a flower in colours of flame orange, bright yellow, indigo blue, purple and sage green. Harrie slowed to admire it but George barged straight through, sending the reeds skittering in all directions.

Harrie followed, preparing to adjust to dim light inside, but the interior was unexpectedly well lit. She turned in a circle and saw that a ledge had been built right around the wall at a height of about four feet, and on the ledge sat six Sinumbra lamps, three of which were blazing brightly.

The room was just large enough to comfortably accommodate an odd-looking Windsor chair with flat, wide arms, a waist-height wooden bench, a small cabinet, a full-length looking glass, two stools and, incongruously, an elegant wheeled tea trolley. On this were arrayed a collection of long needles, pots of colour pigment, squares of lint, paper, several drawing pencils and a bottle of what looked suspiciously like smelling salts. On the white-washed brick walls were displayed floor to ceiling an overwhelming selection of designs rendered on parchment, paper and fabric, including: hearts and daggers; anchors and sailing ships; pigs and roosters; mermaids and stars; swallows, bluebirds and eagles; sharks and whales; snakes and dragons; skulls and crossbones; turtles and octopuses; crossed cannon; flags of many nations; religious insignia; beautiful exotic designs made up of lines and swirls; and the words *HOLD FAST* in at least a dozen styles of script.

But there was no sign of Leonard Dundas.

George took off his hat, ducked through a doorway and called, 'Leo? Leo, it's George Barrett!'

Something stirred overhead. Harrie heard feet creaking down wooden stairs and a moment later a man followed George into the room.

He was tall, perhaps five feet ten or eleven inches, wiry, muscled and old. His long hair — tied back in a cue — was silver-grey, as were his moustache and short beard. The skin on his face, hands and arms, revealed by the rolled sleeves of his grey shirt, was so weathered it resembled tanned leather and deep creases lined his face and surrounded his pale grey eyes. He wore a small gold hoop in each ear just below a miniature tattoo of a star, and on one forearm was a very faded image of a turtle. His long feet were bare; on one was tattooed a pig and on the other a rooster.

'Leo, this is Harrie Clarke,' George announced.

Leonard Dundas eyed Harrie disapprovingly. He wiped his hands on his faded duck trousers and grudgingly offered her the right one. Across the tops of his fingers were tattooed the letters *FAST*; on the fingers of his left hand she glimpsed *HOLD*. She shook the hand gingerly; already she didn't like him.

'This is a lass,' he barked at George.

'I know,' George replied cheerfully.

'You said it'd be a lad.'

'I'm not sure I made mention either way,' George said quickly. 'But think of the advantages, Leo. She'd be a drawcard, don't you think? A pretty face like hers?'

Harrie cringed inwardly; she felt like a cow George Barrett might be attempting to sell in Campbell Street's new cattle market.

'I couldn't have a lass here.' Leo looked Harrie up and down again. 'Not one like her — not with my customers. Too rough.'

'But you could advertise the designs as having been drawn by a girl, though, couldn't you? Think of the novelty!'

'Can't see that helping,' Leo snapped. 'Women are unlucky at sea.'

Harrie noted George's smile getting more and more strained.

'Well, could you at least give her a trial?' he said.

'No.'

'Could she not even do just one tiny sketch? She's very good.'

Leo crossed his arms, eyes narrowed. 'If I let her draw something, will you leave me alone to get on with my work?'

George was already at the tea trolley gathering up paper and a pencil. He thrust them at Harrie. 'What do you want her to draw?' he asked Leonard.

'What the hell does it matter? I don't know. A mermaid will do.'

Offended by the rudeness of both men, Harrie said, 'I'm sorry, I can't.'

'Why not?' George demanded, his voice squeaking slightly as the easy profit he'd envisioned from this venture fluttered ever closer to the window.

'Because I've never seen one.'

The corners of Leo's mouth twitched.

'What *have* you seen, then?' George asked in desperation. 'A goat? You must have seen one of those. Yes, draw a goat.'

'No.' Leo shook his head. 'What sailor would want a bloody goat tattooed on his arm? Be reasonable, man.'

'An angel?' Harrie suggested. 'I could draw one of those.'

Leo's interest was finally piqued. 'Oh, you've seen an angel, have you?'

'I might have.'

'Is that right? Well, away you go, then.'

Harrie sat in the wooden chair and, resting the paper on the wide arm, worked for five or six minutes. She drew Rachel's lovely face, long silky hair and lithe body, but when she came to the wings she found herself sketching an enormous pair of bat wings rather than those you would expect to see on an angel. The effect, however, was somehow right. She handed the finished image to Leo Dundas.

He studied it for some moments. 'Have you ever seen something called the *Book of Kells*?'

Harrie said no.

Opening the little cabinet, he ferreted around among the books and papers inside then passed her an illustration. Harrie gasped; it was possibly the most breathtaking image she'd ever seen.

Leonard said, 'The *Book of Kells* is the most beautifully illuminated manuscript in the history of man. This is a hand-painted reproduction of a single page. Do you see the triple spiral at the bottom there on the left? Can you copy that?'

The large central motif was the letter P, filled with and surrounded by interlaced and extremely intricate spiral and geometrical designs, and the entire page glowed with colour. If this was only a copy, Harrie thought, what must the original be like? She knew, though, that of course she could copy the spiral, and extended her hand for another piece of blank paper.

Leo examined the finished sketch with the same indifference he'd accorded the angel. Again he went to the cabinet. This time he retrieved a leather tube about two feet long from which he withdrew a roll of oiled parchment. Carefully spreading it flat on the wooden bench, he beckoned to Harrie to approach. This close she could smell him: a mix of fresh sweat and a hint of the sea, not unpleasant.

The parchment was quite brown, and very delicate, and on it was an image of a ferocious oriental dragon with bristling whiskers and yellowing teeth, eyes and claws, and a sinuously scaled body and tail. The beast was wrestling with a cherubic child against a background of stormy skies and wild seas, and maple leaves and chrysanthemums were interspersed across the crowded, colourful scene.

'It's irezumi,' Leo said. 'Japanese. Just copy the dragon's head.'

Harrie looked at George, who, transported by greedy anticipation, was almost hopping on one foot. She glanced back at Leo and, for an instant, was sure he'd rolled his eyes.

She'd just finished the outline when she realised, with a deeply unpleasant jolt, that the parchment was very possibly tattooed human skin.

'You *are* quite good, aren't you?' Leo said as he viewed her completed drawing. 'George said you do original designs. That's actually what I'm after.'

Harrie remained silent: she didn't want to work here at all.

Leo said, 'And sometimes my customers have their own ideas. Do you think you can interpret what a man tells you he wants on his skin, and put it into a drawing?'

Thinking about it, Harrie replied, 'Well, in what way would that be any different from sketching a pattern of what a lady would like in a gown?' Then wished she'd kept her mouth shut, because she knew it was a good answer.

Carefully Leo rolled up the tattooed parchment, slid it back into its tube and put it away. 'All right. I'll give you a three-month trial.'

George actually clapped, then immediately began haggling with Leo over the rate at which he would hire out Harrie, while she sat on the chair feeling humiliated.

'Moo,' she said.

George stared at her as though she'd lost her mind. 'What?'

'Nothing.'

When they'd eventually agreed on a fee the men shook hands, then Leo told George to be on his way.

'What do you mean?' George narrowed his eyes suspiciously. 'I'll have to escort Harrie home. It's not safe around here for a girl.'

'It's safe enough,' Leo replied benignly. 'The lass and I have matters to discuss. Good day to you, George.'

George lingered in the doorway, sensing — correctly — that he was about to be excluded from something. Reluctantly, however, he finally departed.

Harrie edged towards the door herself; she was *not* remaining here alone with Leo Dundas.

'Stay where you are, lass,' he growled. 'You're working for me now, so let's get one thing clear.'

Harrie could only stare at him, transfixed with rapidly escalating alarm.

'The tea things — they're kept next door on the shelf beside the hearth.' Leo suddenly grinned, revealing several gaps between his teeth. Of those that remained, one appeared to be made of dull gold. 'Put the kettle on, there's a good lass, and I'll go up to the baker's and get us something nice. Raisin buns? Will that do you?'

Oh Lord, which was the real Leonard Dundas? Harrie felt paralysed by doubt. Could she trust him? She closed her eyes, praying for guidance, and when she opened them again Leo was staring right at her.

He tut-tutted. 'Aye, I can see I was a bit hard on you, but you can't let a coney-catcher like George Barrett get the upper hand now, can you? There'd be no end to it.'

When he'd gone off up the alleyway in his bare feet, Harrie returned to the chair, sank onto it gratefully and waited until her heartbeat had returned to something approaching its normal rhythm. For a hideous second she really had thought Leonard Dundas had been going to force himself on her.

Tea: that would help. The other room contained a small table, three mismatched chairs, a hearth with a camp oven and cooking implements — it must get so hot in here during the height of summer — a tin bath on its end in a corner, a narrow cot made up with a blanket and pillow under a small window, and shelves holding boxes and various bits and pieces. Against one wall steep wooden stairs rose to the next floor.

The kettle was already filled and hanging on the sway, so she stabbed at the fire with a poker and blew hard on the flames to invigorate them. She found the tea caddy — an unexpectedly beautiful one in rosewood with a sailing ship rendered in intricate marquetry on the lid — and set out two cups and saucers and the teapot. Leo's good taste apparently didn't extend to china — the cups didn't match and were of an inferior blue and white pattern, and cracked and stained. Does he take sugar? she wondered.

'Who are you?' a voice demanded.

Harrie spun around so fast her skirt flicked into the fire; the fabric caught just for a second and she slapped out the tiny flame, leaving behind a brown singe mark.

The speaker was a boy of eleven or twelve, standing in the doorway between the two rooms. He looked familiar. A small scruffy dog with a black snout and ears sprouting ridiculous tufts of hair crouched at his feet, growling menacingly.

'Where's Leo?' the boy said, giving the dog a nudge with a dirty bare foot to quieten it.

'Gone out for a minute,' Harrie replied. 'I know you, don't I?'

The boy shook his head, shaggy hair flopping across his forehead. The dog trotted into the room on short, bandy legs, growled again and bared its teeth at Harrie, jumped onto the cot, turned around several times and lay down.

'I'm sure I do. What's your name?'

'John Smith.'

'No, that's not it.' Harrie suddenly remembered. 'It's Walter, isn't it? You were on the *Isla*, the ship's boy! I was the one who needed two sets of slops, remember, one for my friend?'

The boy shook his head adamantly. 'It's John Smith.'

It was Walter, though, and she could see he did recall the incident.

'Oh. All right, then. Would you like a cup of tea? Leo's gone to the bakery.'

At the mention of the bakery, the boy's eyes lit up. Then Leo himself silently reappeared and laid a hand on his shoulder; the boy jumped and cried out.

Leo shook his head ruefully. 'I told you, boy, keep your back against the wall.' He took a plate from a shelf and arranged on it half a dozen fancy buns and several small cakes. 'Not much left. Bit late in the day. Walter, you having a cup?'

Smiling to herself, Harrie wrapped a cloth around her hand, removed the kettle from the fire and set it down on the hearth ledge. Opening the lovely caddy, she carefully measured tea into the pot and replaced the lid.

'It's Walter Cobley, isn't it?' she tried again. 'I do remember you, you know.'

Looking miserable, Walter said nothing and took a seat at the table.

'You already acquainted?' Leo remarked. 'I'll be blowed.'

'He was ship's boy on the transport I came out on,' Harrie said. 'The *Isla*. Although he's saying he wasn't.'

'He's lying low,' Leo explained. 'He jumped ship.'

Harrie poured the tea then sat down herself. 'But that was a year ago. Why are you pretending to be someone else? You're not in trouble with the law, are you?'

'Not the law, no.' Leo offered Walter a bun. 'It's up to you how much you want to say, boy. It's your story, not mine.'

Walter took the bun, tore a piece off and tossed it to the dog, who caught it neatly in its mouth and swallowed it whole. 'Sorry I were rude, missus.'

'Oh Walter, it's Harrie. My name is Harrie.'

His eyes were big and haunted and she wondered when he'd last seen his mother.

'And you don't have to tell me anything if you don't want to,' she added.

'I couldn't stay on. I *hated* him,' he blurted and crammed half the bun into his mouth.

'Who?'

Walter chewed and chewed, and finally swallowed. 'Amos Furniss. The *devil*.'

Harrie glanced at Leo, but Leo was resolutely stirring his tea, clearly letting Walter tell his story the way he wanted to tell it.

'He *was* a very unpleasant man, wasn't he?' Harrie agreed.

Walter nodded, his skin flushing from neck to temples. 'He ... he hurt me and I couldn't stop him.' He put down his bun and pressed his hand over his mouth, as though holding back vomit.

Leo patted his thin shoulder. 'Hold fast, boy.'

And Harrie realised then that Rachel hadn't been the only one to have suffered horribly during the voyage out from England. She felt sick and her eyes burnt with sudden, hot tears for Walter.

The boy stared down at the wooden table top, his shaking finger tracing a long, weathered gouge. At last he said, 'So I jumped ship and made meself scarce until the *Isla* left port. And then a few days after that I bloody *seen* him. I seen Furniss, on the street. I hadn't got away from him after all.'

Leo took a noisy sip of tea. 'I found him hiding behind a pile of barrels at the back of one of the pubs on Harrington Street.'

Just like Angus when he'd been a tiny, helpless kitten, Harrie thought.

'Him and the dog,' Leo added. 'Bad-tempered bloody article. Won't be separated from it. So I brought them both here and they've been with me ever since.'

'Can you not go home?' Harrie asked. 'To England?'

'I could.' Walter's finger stopped moving and he raised his eyes to meet Harrie's. The frightened boy in them had gone, replaced now by a persecuted and angry youth on the cusp of manhood. A vein began to throb in his temple. 'But I want him to pay.'

Harrie understood all too well how Walter felt, but she also knew where such bitter desires could lead. 'Be very careful, Walter. He's an evil man, Furniss. And we think he's working for someone just as nasty as he is. Do you remember Bella Jackson?'

'The abbess?' Walter asked. 'Her on the ship? With the big beak and the fancy clothes?'

Harrie nodded. 'Bella Shand she is now. She got married.'

'I know who *she* is,' Leo said, startled. 'Bitchy old Clarence Shand's new missus. He's an importer. Owns warehouses on Sussex and Market streets. And one on Phillip, too, apparently.'

Harrie stared at him, the hand holding her cup frozen in mid-air. 'Where, exactly, on Phillip?'

'Near the lumber yard, I think. Damned dangerous piece of work, her,' Leo went on. 'Clarence, too. You want to steer clear of them, boy.'

'How do you know Bella?' Harrie whispered, a glimmer of dreadful realisation almost robbing her of her voice.

Leo's furrowed brow wrinkled even further. 'Something wrong, lass?'

'No, I ... I just really don't like Bella Jackson,' Harrie obfuscated. 'How *do* you know her?'

'I don't, personally.' Leo tapped the side of his own considerable nose. 'But I get all sorts in here. There's not much I don't know about this town, especially its stinking underbelly. And who's this "we" you're talking about?'

Harrie swallowed and cleared her throat forcefully. She felt as though she'd swallowed a bucket of mouldy chaff, her mouth had gone that dry. 'Me and my friends, Friday and Sarah.'

'I remember Friday,' Walter said. 'She gave me the willies. Weren't there four of yous? The little blonde girl, how's she? I liked her.'

'We liked her, too. Very much,' Harrie said tonelessly. 'She died.'

Walter's eyes widened, then he stared down at his hands. 'Were it ...?' He touched the back of his head.

'In the end, yes.'

'The crew thought he should of been keel-hauled, that Keegan cove,' Walter said. 'Well, some did.'

Leo watched the interchange with interest. 'You do have some tales to tell, don't you, the pair of you?'

'Another day, though,' Harrie said. 'I should be getting home. Mrs Barrett will be wondering where I am.'

She wanted to leave now. The news about Clarence Shand owning a warehouse in Phillip Street — in the exact location where she, Sarah and Friday had murdered Keegan — had come as a horrible shock.

But she had decided to trust Leo. Friday and Sarah would no doubt chide her yet again for being gullible, but any man who would give a frightened, lost boy shelter must have a decent heart. Clearly nothing untoward was going on here — poor, abused Walter wouldn't stay if there were.

'Before Mr Barrett left, Mr Dundas, you said to him we had matters to discuss. What did you mean?'

'Well, what hours do you want to work?' Leo asked. 'How much do you want to be paid? That sort of thing.'

'But ... you're paying Mr Barrett, aren't you?'

'Aye, I am, a finder's fee, if you like. But you're doing the actual work.'

Harrie didn't know what to say. What was Leo suggesting?

He looked at her expectantly. 'In terms of hours, I thought that given you're already assigned to the Barretts, and obviously busy helping that poor missus of George's in the house, you might just want to work on ideas for flash whenever you can fit it in.'

'Flash' was a word Harrie usually associated with the criminal world, and again she wondered what she was letting herself in for. 'I'm sorry, but I'm not sure I know what you mean.'

Leo inclined his head. 'Come with me.'

He ushered Harrie through to the other room and gestured at the drawings all over the walls. '*These* are what you call flash — designs for tattoos. I want new ones, original designs that no tar will see anywhere else. Unless it's on another sailor I've tattooed, of course. But they have to appeal to men who love the sea, and to other folk who've a mind to have their skin inked. I do get a few. There's a real art to the designs, and quite specific fashions. You've got your traditional Jack Tar motifs, your dragons for those who've sailed to China, and your Jolly Rogers and the like. Also, the New Zealand and other Polynesian designs, these ones over here, have been getting popular lately.'

Harrie nearly laughed; Leo sounded just like a society woman prattling on about the merits of the new fichu-pelerine. 'Who drew these?'

'I did most of them. But I don't have the time these days. As I said, what I pay George will be a sort of retainer for your services. What I'll pay *you* will be your commission, due on delivery of every flash. And if I have a customer with a specific design in mind, I'll get you down here to draw the flash on the spot while I'm getting the gear ready. Providing Mrs Barrett doesn't object. How does that sound?'

'I think it sounds wonderful!' Harrie was delighted; now she could send her own money home instead of Friday's and, at last, make a real financial contribution to the Charlotte fund! 'But I can't let it get in the way of my normal work. Mrs Barrett needs me.'

'Fair enough. I wasn't joking when I said they're a rough crowd who come in here, though, lass,' Leo warned. 'You'll not find much rougher.'

'Mr Dundas, I spent six months in Newgate Gaol and another four locked on the prison deck of a female convict ship. I think I'll manage.'

Leo rubbed his chin. 'Aye, well, when you put it like that, perhaps you will.'

Chapter Six

November 1830, Sydney Town

Adam said, 'Sarah, this is my good friend and colleague, Mr Bernard Cole.'

Sarah shook the proffered hand. It was plump and matched the rest of Bernard Cole. At barely five feet two inches he wasn't much taller than her, but was considerably wider, with a beaming pink face and hair that looked desperate to curl, if only it could break free from its liberal dressing of Macassar oil. He wore straining fawn trousers and his loud, kingfisher blue cutaway coat revealed a bulging belly. Every finger sported a ring, and an extremely handsome gold watch chain in the byzantine style disappeared into his emerald waistcoat.

'Good day to you, Sarah,' he said in a distinctly East End accent. 'Very nice to meet you.'

'And you, Mr Cole.'

Sarah suspected that originally Bernard Cole hadn't come to New South Wales as a free immigrant, but clearly he'd done very well for himself during the years since, as so many convicts had.

'So, you and I will be working together, will we?' He regarded her with unexpectedly shrewd and piercing eyes. 'Adam's told me much about you.'

Sarah studied him back. He certainly didn't strike her as stupid;

she might have to curtail her extracurricular activities while Adam was away. 'It seems so,' she replied.

'I hear you're actually a qualified jeweller.'

'Yes, I trained in London under Tobiah Cohen.'

'Adam told me. Old Toby Cohen, eh?'

Startled, Sarah said, 'Did you know him?'

'Had dealings with him. A long time ago, though. Miserable bugger. I'm surprised he let you complete your apprenticeship. In my day he had a habit of sacking his apprentices just before they finished. Saved him money, you see.'

Sarah hadn't known that. Perhaps she'd been luckier than she'd realised: Cohen hadn't fired her until after she'd qualified, and that had only been because of his son's advances towards her, for which *she'd* been blamed. 'But you're not a jeweller yourself?' she asked.

He held up his pudgy hands. 'Not built for it. The good Lord gave me sausages for fingers and they're fit for wielding nothing but a knife and fork. And counting money, of course. I've an eye for a good jewel, though. We do well enough, the missus and me.'

'Would you like to look around, Bernard?' Adam asked.

'Already have. Found the nearest bakery. Very tasty Eccles cakes.'

Adam smiled. 'No, I mean here.'

Bernard gave the shop a cursory glance. 'What's to see? I know my way around a money drawer, I can talk any fool with too much money into parting with it, and the workshop's Sarah's domain, isn't it? I only came today to meet her, and now I have. Did I hear an offer of morning tea? I know what a damn good cook your missus is.'

As Adam led him down the hall towards the parlour, Sarah caught herself smiling. He wasn't what she'd been expecting, but she thought she might quite like working with him.

* * *

Friday moaned seductively as her customer pulled the long satin ribbon all the way out of her corset and lifted it away from her, glad he couldn't see the annoyed expression on her face. It really was a bugger when they wanted to take it off; it took ages to do up again afterwards. All those bloody eyelets. He ran his (cold) hands down her back and she felt him kiss her all the way along her spine from her neck to the crack of her bum. She moaned again and thought, for Christ's sake get on with it, you'll run out of time soon and end up having to go like a bat out of hell.

She was sitting, naked now, on a stool in her 'boudoir', the afternoon sun streaming through the gauze curtains at the window and turning the hair on her head and between her legs into a glorious blaze of copper and bronze. She glanced at the rough and ugly tattoos on her pale arms, rendered stark in the pure light, and thought again about Harrie's new part-time job. The week before she'd gone with her to Leo Dundas's little tattoo shop on George Street and been utterly bewitched by what she'd seen there. She'd known many tars whose bodies had been tattooed, of course, but Leo Dundas's work was in a different category altogether. His designs were stunning, bold and precise, his colours vibrant and mesmerising. She hated most of her old tattoos now, and desperately wanted them covered with something new and beautiful.

'I'm ready now,' her cully whispered, his voice made husky by lust.

Friday rose from her stool, crossed to the bed and pushed him onto it. Some men didn't enjoy being shoved around, but this one did. Expertly she flicked open the buttons at the sides of his trousers and yanked them down, grinning wickedly at him as his cock sprang up.

'No drawers,' she purred. 'You naughty man.'

She rucked up his shirt to his armpits and mounted him, making sure her nipples brushed his face tantalisingly. He groaned helplessly as she sank onto him, and closed his eyes. Fascinated,

Friday studied him as she bobbed up and down. He wasn't an ugly man but he had a disgustingly large blackhead at the end of his right eyebrow; it had been there for as long as he'd been coming to see her and her fingers itched to dig it out.

He began to thrust harder, screwing up his face in approaching ecstasy, while she contracted the muscles in her vagina to encourage him. Squeeze, relax, squeeze, relax.

Squeeeeeeze.

Letting out a strangled moan, he grabbed her shoulders and pulled her against his chest as his hips bucked wildly, then he climaxed with a sharp cry before subsiding back onto the mattress. Surreptitiously she turned her head to look at the clock.

She gave him two minutes to get his breath back then climbed off him. His cock, which had fallen out of her as soon as he'd rung his chimes, lay limp and shrivelled on its thatch of pubic hair, like a little blind sea creature left behind on the rocks by the tide. She passed him a towel.

'Oooh, that was lovely,' she said, patting his sweaty thigh.

And he *was* quite nice, she supposed, compared to some of them. He didn't expect acrobatics, he didn't shove her around or curse at her, and he didn't go on for hours, wearing her insides out and boring her shitless. Not that Mrs H tolerated outright abuse from any of the cullies in her house; she'd have Jack and Al over in a minute flat if that ever happened.

'Was it?' he asked, struggling to pull his trousers back up. 'I do hope so. I like to think I know how to please a girl.'

'Oh, definitely.'

He swung his legs over the side of the bed, stood, tucked in his shirt and did up the buttons on his smart vest. Crossing to the looking glass, he retied his cravat and smoothed his hair, then reached for his coat.

'Here you are.' He handed her the requisite fiver plus a sovereign. 'Something a little extra for yourself.'

'Thank you, sir, that's very generous,' Friday said, still lounging naked on the bed.

'Same time next week?'

'That would be lovely.'

He lifted her hand and kissed it, and Friday gave him a genuine smile.

As soon as he'd gone, she opened the window and tipped out the bowl of water in which he'd washed himself when he'd arrived, refilled it, then squatted over the used towel. She slid her index finger into her vagina and probed around until she felt the sea sponge, hooked her finger behind it, drew it out and dropped it into the bowl, where it floated around dispersing milky semen. Giving it a good swish about, she squeezed the sponge a few times and set it on the windowsill behind the curtain to dry.

As she was expecting another cully shortly, she took a jar of fresh lemon juice from the night table, poured a little into a small bowl, added a pipette of quinine suspension, and dropped in a new sponge. After a minute she compressed it to remove some of the juice, then inserted it high into her vagina. There would be no more accidental babies for Friday Woolfe; she — and Sarah and Harrie — had Charlotte to look after now.

Finally she had a quick wash with some of the lovely Pears soap Mrs H provided in the rooms, threaded the ribbon loosely back into her corset and wriggled it up her legs and over her hips, put her drawers, muslin robe and silly dainty slippers back on, and went downstairs for a quick drink.

Nine other girls worked for Mrs Hislop, and three — Hazel, Constance, and the new girl Lou — were at present in the parlour, two were upstairs and the rest weren't on duty.

'Connie,' Friday said, 'be a sweetie and do up these bloody stays for me, will you?'

'Stephen Davies again?' Connie remarked.

Connie, whose real name was Aggie Mitchell, was a very buxom, flaxen-haired girl with huge brown eyes, a lovely smile and a patient and generous nature.

Friday nodded as she slipped off her robe and turned her back. 'Can't do it with it on. Has to have the bloody thing off.'

'Then why don't you *start* with it off?' Lou asked.

'Because he likes to start with it *on*. And it's his money,' Friday said.

She eyed Lou, whom she didn't like. Loulou Lacroix had replaced Rowie. Apparently she had a French grandmother or something, hence her fancy working name, though her actual name was Effie Tuttle. She'd told them she was descended from a long line of courtesans accustomed to consorting with the aristocracy — though, in Friday's opinion, she was about as French as Friday's arse. What a disappointment it must be, Friday had said to her, to find herself in a bawdyhouse on the Rocks servicing businessmen, government officials and the odd sailor with a pocketful of money.

To give her her due, though, Lou was an attractive girl — raven-haired, fine-boned, and poised and elegant in a way Friday knew she would never be. Except she wore too much scent. Tuberose; a cully had given it to her. Lou had thought herself so special until she'd discovered the man had also given Rowie some in an even prettier bottle when she'd been in residence. And Esmerelda, one of the other girls. He must have got a job lot from somewhere.

In a way Lou reminded Friday of Sarah — they were both small, neat and dark — but without Sarah's quick intelligence and wit, and certainly none of her loyalty. Lou was a free immigrant to New South Wales, whereas Connie had a ticket of leave and Hazel, whose full name was Hazel Wicks, had originally been assigned to Mrs Hislop as a domestic, as had Friday.

'Breathe in,' Connie ordered.

Friday did and Connie yanked vigorously on the laces, causing Friday inadvertently to fart.

Connie, Hazel and Friday exploded in almighty fits of the giggles.

Not Lou, though. '*Must* you be so vulgar?' she said, ostentatiously fanning her face with her hand.

'That's good, coming from you!' Connie said. 'I heard you the other day out in the privy. I thought it was the guns going off at the battery.'

Shrieks of laughter from Friday and Hazel.

'Girls!' Elizabeth Hislop exclaimed, appearing in the parlour doorway. 'What's going on in here? Keep it down, please. The customers will hear you.'

When she'd gone Friday slipped her robe back on and helped herself to a tumbler of brandy from the drinks trolley. Her tipple was gin but there wasn't any; Mrs H's well-heeled customers would rather die than drink common gin, preferring spirits or port.

'I thought we weren't supposed to touch that,' Lou protested.

'Oh, fuck off, Lou.'

Hazel and Connie exchanged a gleeful glance; they didn't like Lou either, and were eagerly waiting for her and Friday to finally come to blows. Or at least slaps. Lou was sharp-tongued, self-serving and had a very high opinion of herself. She was also mean and last week had suggested to Hazel — who was fractionally slow and could never formulate suitably acerbic rejoinders — that she do something about the little roll of fat on her belly, and consider applying henna to her hair to improve its 'stockyard' brown colour. The former hadn't mattered to Hazel as men adored her full figure, but the latter had stung as she was very proud of her luxuriant, cocoa-coloured hair.

'What did you say?' Lou demanded.

Collapsing onto the sofa and tucking her slippered feet beneath her, Friday replied, slowly and clearly so there could be no mistake, 'I *said*, fuck off.'

'Don't you speak to me like that!'

The bell in the hall rang; on her way past the parlour Elizabeth warned sharply, 'Girls, that's enough.'

She opened the front door, spoke briefly and closed it again. Entering the parlour, she handed Friday a letter.

Friday turned it over but there was no indication of the sender. 'Who's it from?'

Elizabeth shook her head. 'I don't know. A lad delivered it.'

As Friday broke the seal and read the short message, her face went as white as bleached cotton.

Wearing her best bonnet and dress, one she'd recently made herself, Harrie felt extremely self-conscious sitting across the little table from Matthew. She suspected everyone in the tea shop was looking at them because she was unchaperoned, and though there was no reason she should be chaperoned — she was only a convict girl after all — no one else knew that. They probably thought she was a tart. She wondered if Matthew was aware of the attention they were attracting.

'These are jolly nice little cakes, aren't they?' he said, offering her the plate.

She shook her head. 'No, thank you.'

She'd had one already, which had been a mistake; she was nervous and her mouth was dry and it had taken most of a cup of tea to wash it down. Now that they were here she was wondering whether this had been such a good idea after all, and couldn't think of anything to say to him. And yesterday she'd realised that having afternoon tea with Matthew Cutler wouldn't teach James a lesson for hiring Rowie Harris, if he didn't even know she'd *had* afternoon tea with Matthew. Because how was she going to tell him if she wasn't speaking to him?

'Do you have family at home?' Matthew asked.

'My ma, and my brother Robbie, who is ten, and my sisters Sophie and Anna, who are nine and eight.'

'And what does your father do?'

'He died when I was quite young.'

Matthew's brow furrowed as he attempted to work out the Clarke family structure.

Taking pity on him, Harrie explained, 'After my father died my ma took another husband, my brother and sisters' father.' Though they'd never been legally married. Neither had her mother and father.

'And what line of work is your stepfather in?'

Why on earth did it matter? Harrie wondered. 'I don't know, now. He left us before Anna was born.'

'Oh.' Matthew's ears went pink. 'Well, are you enjoying being with the Barretts?'

'Most of the time. The children are very sweet, and so is Mrs Barrett. Mr Barrett has his moments.'

'And did you have much trouble finding somewhere suitable to work?'

Harrie stared at him, speechless. He gazed back, blood suffusing his face, his mouth slack with embarrassment. 'I am *so* sorry, Harrie. Truly. I ... for a second I forgot.'

And she realised then that he very possibly felt just as nervous as she did. How odd. She'd assumed that because of his superior background he would be practised at all sorts of social situations.

Feeling his discomfort acutely, and prattling to cover the awkward moment, she said, 'Actually I have another job as well, now. I've just been commissioned by a tattooist called Leo Dundas to draw some designs. Flash, they're called.'

Matthew didn't respond. Oh dear, she thought, perhaps that had been the wrong thing to tell him.

She ploughed ahead anyway. 'Usually Mr Dundas draws the designs himself but he's too busy these days, there's that many sailors wanting tattooing. So I'll be drawing them. He's done some lovely work, really quite beautiful. I was surprised. He's a friend of George Barrett's, well, an acquaintance really, or should I say Mr Barrett is an acquaintance of *his*. I suspect that's more likely. And you'll —'

'A *tattooist*!?' Matthew interrupted.

'Yes. You know. They draw pictures on the skin with needles and ink.'

'Yes, I do know what a tattoo is. It's just that …' He trailed off, looking extremely uncomfortable.

'You didn't think I was that rough?' Harrie said bluntly. It was written all over his face.

He shifted slightly on his chair, refusing to meet her eyes. 'I'm sorry, Harrie, really I am. You must think I've the most awful airs.'

'Stop saying sorry all the time, Matthew.' Harrie smiled to herself; it was such a novelty for her to be saying that to someone else. 'It was Mr Barrett's doing. He arranged it. And obviously I don't know the first thing about tattooing — I'm a sempstress and I design and sew embroidery patterns. But Mr Dundas considers my design skills to be just what he's looking for. And he's going to pay me, Matthew! At last, after nearly two years, I'm going to be earning my own money again. Imagine that!'

Matthew blinked; he hadn't realised assigned convicts weren't paid a wage of any sort. He'd always assumed that Dolly, the Vincents' girl, was getting *something*. 'Well, that part's good news. But will you have to actually go to where this Dundas fellow works, to deliver these … what did you call them?'

'Flash. I've already been. And it's only ten minutes' walk from your lodgings, Matthew, not in some den of vice somewhere.'

'Not by yourself, I hope!'

Matthew was actually quite scandalised, but told himself he really shouldn't be, given who Harrie was — he couldn't afford to be if he didn't want to offend her. The way she must have lived her life in England, and certainly the way she was living it now, were markedly inconsistent with the manner in which he lived his, and he was just going to have to accept that, if he hoped to win her. Sydney was not London and, while some rules of society were actually exaggerated in the colony, others, of necessity, were quite different. He was reasonably confident he could use the latter to his advantage if he wanted to court her, which he most certainly did. A number of men with social standing far superior to his own had married convict girls; he'd seen that already.

However, there was also James, whom he liked and admired very much, and to whom he'd listened for hours over recent months plotting to win her back. He felt deeply disloyal being here today, but considered it would have been the height of bad manners to decline Harrie's invitation … and, frankly, he hadn't wanted to. If things progressed in the direction in which he hoped they might, he'd worry about James's reaction, and his own guilty conscience, later.

'No, I went with Mr Barrett,' Harrie said. 'He's a very nice man, Mr Dundas. His shop is on George Street near the Stores, down the side of the Sailors' Grave Hotel.'

'Will you have to go back there? They can be pretty unsavoury characters, sailors.'

Harrie smiled. 'Yes, I did spend four months on a ship, you know.' Which reminded her. 'You'll never guess who else I saw at Mr Dundas's. From the *Isla*?'

Matthew couldn't imagine who it might be. Of the people they both might recall from the ship, Gabriel Keegan was of course dead, and he hadn't exactly been a friend of Harrie's — or, in the end, Matthew's — and the Church Missionary Society family, the rather irritating Seatons, would hardly go to an establishment like this Leo Dundas's. Similarly James, Matthew was sure, wouldn't be seen dead in a tattoo shop. Or would he? He *had* been in the navy, after all. And Matthew hadn't known most of the other convict women, except for Friday and poor Rachel Winter.

'I expect you're right. You'll have to tell me.'

'Walter Cobley, the ship's boy.'

'The poor lad who had his head shaved when we crossed the line?'

'Yes. He jumped ship before Captain Holland set sail again for England. Mr Dundas found him and took him in. Poor love. He was terrified of that evil, rotten Amos Furniss,' Harrie explained, deciding to keep the rest of Walter's story to herself.

'But Amos Furniss is here, in Sydney. James told me he saw him.'

'So has Friday. Apparently he's working for Bella Jackson.'

'Is he? Well, I can't say I'm surprised,' Matthew remarked. 'If what I heard some of the crew saying about her is true, they'll be well suited as partners in crime.' He frowned. 'What do you mean, working for her? Hasn't she been assigned?'

'She made arrangements to marry a man barely three weeks after we arrived. A very wealthy, older man. She's more or less free to do as she pleases.'

'Good God,' Matthew said. 'The fellow must have been desperate!' He turned his teacup around so the handle lined up exactly with the pattern on the saucer. 'Harrie, what do you think happened to Gabriel Keegan?'

She froze, but only for the shortest of seconds. 'I thought he was murdered. Wasn't he?'

'Yes, but why? And by whom?'

'I don't know. I'm not the police.'

'I read in the papers it was a very vicious beating.'

Harrie suddenly felt too hot. She asked cautiously, 'What do *you* think happened to him?'

After a moment, Matthew said, 'I think he was up to his old tricks again but this time he picked the wrong victim. I think this time he went after a girl who had brothers, or perhaps a father with a couple of staunch friends. Who else could beat a big man like that to death?'

Harrie felt at least some of the tension ease out of her. 'Yes. Yes, that could have been it, couldn't it?'

'I don't particularly *care*,' Matthew said harshly, 'because I think he deserved it. But I do wonder.'

'I don't. I really don't. I think it's best forgotten.'

'I expect you're right.' Matthew sat back in his chair and relaxed into a smile. 'I've enjoyed myself this afternoon. Well, apart from the most recent topic of conversation. To tell you the truth I was quite nervous to begin with. And I did make an awful gaff earlier, didn't I? I do apologise for that.' Ignoring another pang of guilt as he thought again of James, he asked, 'Do you think we might do it again? Have afternoon tea, I mean?'

To her surprise Harrie realised that, eventually, she'd quite enjoyed *her*self. 'Yes, please, Matthew. That would be very nice.' Take that, James Downey.

'And Harrie, promise me that if you ever need to go to this Dundas fellow's shop, do send word to me first. I'd be delighted to escort you. Truly, you can't go there on your own, especially at night. Also, I'd rather like to say hello to young Walter Cobley myself.'

That's kind of you, Harrie thought. Really impractical, especially if you're at work, but kind.

Friday strode along the gravelled street, barely noticing the buffeting wind that was already fat with heat. By midday it would be uncomfortably hot and all abroad would long for shelter from the baking antipodean sun. She glanced at the wisps of cloud scudding overhead; later on there may even be one of the violent spring storms she usually enjoyed so much. But not today — she was still too angry. Bloody a hundred and fifty pounds! That was close to half of everything they'd saved.

She'd almost marched straight up here to confront Bella as soon as she'd received the note, but her gut had told her to leave it a day or so until her temper cooled a little. Instead, she'd gone to see Leo Dundas and made a start on covering her ugly old tattoos. The new one was an improvement already, though it wasn't even finished, but it was sore, and not helping her mood.

She slowed as she approached Bella's brothel, an inoffensive-looking two-storey house between the smaller cottages on south Princes Street, and the more expensive residences to the north. In fact, it looked a lot like Elizabeth's premises, with heavy curtains at the windows and, from the street, an air of desertion about it, only this house was built from wood, not stone, and had a tidy verandah at the front.

Friday knew the servants' door was more likely to be answered than the front, so she opened the gate in the tall fence surrounding the property, marched around the house to the back verandah and knocked.

A girl wearing a lace robe and pink silk slippers came to the door.

'Yes?' she said, looking Friday up and down.

'Bella Jackson, please. I want to talk to her.'

'Do you mean Mrs Shand?'

'Yes,' Friday said impatiently.

'Why? Who are you?'

'Never mind that,' Friday snapped. 'Just go and get her.'

'Can't. She's not here.'

'What do you mean?' What sort of madam would let her girls work unsupervised?

'I mean, she's somewhere else,' the girl said.

Cheeky cow. 'Well, where?'

'I'm not allowed to tell. She can't be here *all* the time. She's got other businesses, you know. She's a very busy woman.'

'You can tell me. I'm her cousin. I've just emigrated and she wrote and told me to contact her when I arrived. She said she'd have work for me.'

'Her cousin?'

'On my mother's side.'

'Well, I suppose that's all right. She's at home this morning.' The girl moved to close the door.

Thick as well. Friday put her boot in the way. 'Hang on. How do I get to her house?'

The girl frowned. 'Don't you have her address? I thought you said she wrote to you?'

'She did but I just got here. I don't know my way around.'

'Oh. Well, just keep going that way until you get to Argyle Street, go down the hill to Cumberland, then turn left and follow the road until you come to a big house facing out over the harbour. It's actually the back of the house you'll see, but there's a fancy garden with a pond and a statue.'

'Much obliged,' Friday said, and took her foot out of the door, which closed smartly in her face.

She traipsed down to Bunker's Hill, and knew Bella's house — or rather Clarence Shand's house — immediately she saw it as the midnight-blue curricle was parked in the carriageway on the far side of a gated, wrought-iron fence. The pond and statue were also in evidence, the statue a fat little boy with no clothes on playing a trumpet, his tiny willy sticking out. No doubt Clarence thought that was lovely. The gardens were manicured to within an inch of their lives, though there was hardly any grass — just shrubs, flowers and a few shady trees.

Being mucked about had made Friday even angrier and she thought she might just surprise Bella — to hell with knocking on the door. The elegance of the house also irritated her. What had Bella done to deserve to live in a grand place like this, except for being in the right place at the right time and having enough dosh to pay a marriage broker? Who cared that her husband was a molly who preferred men not women and that the whole marriage was a sham? Bella obviously didn't.

Keeping close to the side of the house she walked along the carriageway, leaving open a tall hand gate, until she arrived at the front, which afforded a truly breathtaking view of the blue, diamond-scattered harbour.

She crept along the verandah, hugging the sandstone wall, and stole a look through the first French door she came to, her heart leaping when she saw that Bella was in the room, alone. This was going to be easier than she'd expected.

She was sitting at a desk, writing in a ledger. Friday could see her profile; the strong, slightly hooked nose and well-defined, not quite sharp chin. Even now, when there was no one else to see, she wore her trademark heavy white face powder, kohl and lip rouge. Her glossy crow's wing hair was arranged in ringlets and caught at the back of her head with a comb, and she wore a beautifully cut dress of deep purple, black slippers, and dangling jet earrings. Friday wondered who had died. No one probably, the witch just knew the dark colours suited her.

She was undeniably attractive, in her own skinny way, but her beauty was hard and artificial. Friday suspected she was a lot older than she looked, and went to great lengths to hide the fact.

Suddenly, with a horrible sinking sensation, Friday became aware she wasn't alone on the verandah. Slowly, she turned; behind her crouched a pair of enormous brindle dogs, open maws drooling long strings of spit. As she made to sidle off, they emitted twin, bowel-churning growls.

Amos Furniss appeared behind them. 'Tsk, tsk, tsk. Always sticking your nose in where it ent wanted, that's you.'

'Call them off, Furniss,' Friday ordered, barely moving her lips. Loathing for him reared up inside her and her skin crawled. He was just as revolting as he'd been on the *Isla*, sneery smirk and broken, tobacco-stained teeth and everything.

'All in good time.'

He stepped around the dogs and tapped on the French door. Friday was too scared to take her eyes off the animals, but heard it open.

'Well, well,' Bella Jackson said, her voice close. 'What have Ikey and Solomon caught? More vermin? Bring her in.'

Furniss signalled to the dogs and, to Friday's immense relief, they trotted off. He grasped her arm and marched her inside, then left her and Bella alone.

Bella sat back down at her desk, the many yards of expensive silk in her skirt rustling. 'Did you want to speak with me, or have you always been a Peeping Tom?'

On the back foot now, Friday felt even more riled. 'You can forget about your pathetic attempt at blackmail.'

'Can I? Why?'

'Because I can dob you in for running a brothel. I'm sure your girls will sing if they're paid enough.'

Bella gave an elegant shrug. 'So? I'd do six months in third class in the Factory, a year perhaps. You and your motley little crew will swing for Keegan. I think you've more to lose than I have, don't you?'

'And I can prove you were the one running the brothel on the *Isla*. Plenty of those girls are still roaring about the money you took off them.'

'Prove to whom?'

'The governor.'

Bella laughed, revealing large, yellowish teeth. 'Why would he care about a few randy sailors on a transport well over a year ago?'

Friday played her best card. 'And speaking of what happened on the *Isla*, there's also the matter of who murdered Liz Parker. I know it was you.'

'Prove it,' Bella shot back. She wasn't laughing now.

'I'd love to know what she did to you that was so bad it got her killed.'

'She was a stupid, fat, greedy old fool. And a troublemaker. But you can't prove it was me.'

'I can pay someone to say it was.'

'And I can pay someone to say it wasn't.'

They glared at each other. At last Bella said, 'I win, Woolfe. You don't have anything over me. Nothing that matters. I want that money paid by the end of the week. You're an idiot if you thought you could come here snivelling and whining and hoping to appeal to my better nature, because I don't have one. And be warned — I'm not going to stop until I've bled you dry and all three of you are in the gutter, where you belong.'

Friday felt her vision narrow and blood pound in her ears. Her fists clenched, but giving Bella a thoroughly good dewskitch wasn't going to achieve anything, especially not with Amos Furniss and those filthy animals lurking outside. She might have lost this round, but she wouldn't lose the next.

She had a question for Bella, however, before she left.

'Why do you hate us so much?'

Bella drew in a sharp breath, her startled gaze fixed on Friday's face, and for a second she looked as though she might answer. She picked up her pen and stared intently at her ledger. 'By the end of the week,' she ordered. 'Now get out.'

Friday retreated through the French doors, and saw that Furniss was still outside with the dogs. As she stepped off the verandah, she gave him two fingers. This was a mistake as he immediately set the animals loose. Barking explosively, they launched themselves at her. She snatched up her skirts and sprinted around the corner of the house and along the carriageway, boots slipping in the gravel.

To her utter dismay she saw that the hand gate had been closed, but she threw herself at it anyway, intending to hurl herself up and over. When the first dog to reach her sank its fangs into her left boot, all her weight was balanced on her arms, her hands resting between the pointed finials along the top of the gate; if she collapsed, the finials would plunge through her abdomen. She kicked her left leg furiously, but couldn't dislodge the growling, slobbering dog, whose teeth she could feel piercing her foot. Her arms trembling madly, she swung her leg, causing the dog to move right, then viciously stamped down on its head with her other foot. It let go but the second dog immediately tore at her right calf. The pain was extreme and she shrieked. Knowing her arms were about to give way, she kicked back at the animal as hard as she could with her free leg, and the moment the dog's jaws slackened she heaved herself over the gate, tearing her skirt from waist to hem, and landed in a heap on the other side. Barking wildly, the dogs shoved their blunt snouts through the rails at her as she scrambled away, staggering to her feet.

Blood was pouring down her right leg into her boot — she could feel it — but there was no time to stop and look. She ran limpingly up the remainder of the carriageway and out onto Cumberland Street. She would probably need the doctor, but home was closer. She would go there.

'Dare I ask how this happened?' James said as he readied his instruments. Normally Lawrence Chandler would have seen a patient from Elizabeth Hislop's brothel, but Lawrence was busy attending to an emergency and it had fallen to James to treat Friday Woolfe when she'd arrived at the surgery. And, of course, he knew Friday.

'Well, obviously a bloody dog bit me,' Friday said, lying on her stomach with her bloodied boots and stockings off and her ruined skirt rucked up to her knees.

'Yes, I can see that,' James remarked mildly. 'What I meant was, what were you doing to make it bite you?'

'Nothing! Walking down the street. It was a couple of those feral dogs.'

'Mmm.' James squinted as he threaded his surgical needle. 'That's what I was afraid of.'

'It's a worry, isn't it?' Elizabeth said, who knew exactly what Friday had been doing when she'd been attacked. She'd got the story out of Friday not long after she staggered into the brothel, leaving a gory trail of blood along the polished floorboards in the hallway, and announced she'd been savaged by dogs.

'It is. As you will no doubt be aware, a dog bite is never good news. There is always the potential for hydrophobia.'

'Shite,' Friday muttered, and covered her head with her hands. She hadn't thought of rabies. Until now.

'What did they look like?' James asked as he wiped away the blood still oozing from the deep, ragged wound in Friday's calf.

'Big, and sort of brindle.'

'I think what he means, dear, is in what way were they behaving?' Elizabeth prompted.

'Yes, were either of them agitated? Or slavering or foaming at the mouth?'

Friday suddenly found it difficult to swallow. 'Sort of. Yes.'

There was a long and uneasy moment of silence.

James bent over her leg. 'I can stitch this fairly tidily but it will still leave an obvious scar. Is the tincture of opium having any effect yet?'

Nodding, Friday said yes; she felt drowsy and not unpleasantly disconnected. 'When will I know?'

'Know what?'

'If I've got rabies?'

'Symptoms usually manifest in thirty to forty days, but occasionally not for as long as three months.'

'What exactly are the symptoms?' Elizabeth asked. If Friday was going to turn into a raving lunatic some time over the next few months, she definitely wanted to know what to watch out for.

'Agitation, chills, fever, a stiff neck, spasms and a build-up of thick mucus in the throat, difficulty swallowing water, uncontrollable and violent bodily movements, delusions, and eventual death.'

Elizabeth scowled at him. 'Don't pull your punches, will you, doctor? Is there no cure?'

James frowned down at Friday's calf. 'Well, that's the other thing. The accepted treatment is to excise the wounded tissue, taking a liberal amount of unaffected flesh with it. In this case that would mean removing almost all the calf muscle, leaving the patient quite likely crippled and most definitely disfigured.'

'No,' Friday said abruptly. 'No, I won't have that. I'll take my chances.'

'I was hoping you might say that,' James said. 'I personally don't altogether agree with the treatment. Although it's often employed, it doesn't seem to be particularly effective. Patients still die.'

'Fuck that, then,' Friday muttered, then giggled. 'If I'm going to die, I'm doing it with nice legs.'

James turned to Elizabeth. 'I think the opium is working nicely. Would you care to hold her hand? This procedure will still be somewhat painful.'

Elizabeth moved her chair to the examination table and gripped Friday's hand, while James got to work. Friday swore the air blue, but James was quick and very efficient and in no time had cleaned out the L-shaped wound the dog had torn in the meaty part of her calf with a solution of diluted carbolic acid, and sutured it so neatly even Harrie would have been impressed. He then smeared on an ointment containing collodion and a hint of mercuric chloride, a savage antiseptic, and bandaged Friday's entire lower leg. Turning to the puncture wounds on her left foot, he swabbed them with carbolic acid, applied the ointment and covered them with gauze.

'I'd like you to come back in four days to have the dressings changed,' he said as Friday sat up. 'And keep that leg elevated, please. Also, try to limit your walking. I don't want those sutures to burst.'

'Can I still work?' Friday asked, tittering again. 'My legs will be up.'

Elizabeth hid a smile.

'No, you can't,' James said, going red.

'Really? Damn,' Elizabeth said, not smiling now. 'How long will she need off? I've a business to run.'

'She can't return to work until I've removed the sutures and I'm satisfied that the healing process is well under way. I'm not sure you comprehend the gravity of the situation, either of you. If the wound doesn't close satisfactorily gangrene will almost certainly develop. Friday, please take your predicament seriously. Mrs Hislop, will you please ensure she follows my instructions?'

'Of course, Dr Downey.'

Friday slid off the table and wobbled precariously; James grabbed her arm. 'Did you come by carriage?' he asked Elizabeth.

'Clip clop, clip clop,' Friday sang.

'You did? Good. Perhaps, while you're *not working* for the next few days, Friday, you might like to visit Rowie. By vehicle, of course, not on foot. She speaks of you often. I expect she's accustomed to far more congenial company than I can provide.'

'I could, couldn't I?' Friday said, quite taken with the idea.

'Only if you behave,' Elizabeth threatened. 'Or I won't lend you the gig. The sooner you mend and get back to work the better.'

'Now go home and go to bed,' James ordered. 'Or at least lie down. You've had a very unpleasant experience.'

'Yes, I have,' Friday agreed soberly. 'I wasn't keen on those dogs, either.'

129

Chapter Seven

Friday passed the letter to Sarah. It read:

> *To Friday Wolfe, Sarah Morgan, Harrie Clark*
>   *I know what you did.*
>   *If you value your lives, prepare to pay my price. This*
> *time it is one hundred and fifty pounds.*
>   *My man will be in the Black Rat at midnight next*
> *Sunday. Give the money to him.*
>   *B*

Sarah asked, 'Have you shown this to anyone else?'

'Of course I bloody haven't,' Friday snapped. Her leg was throbbing even though it was propped up on the laundry basket, and the more she thought about what had happened yesterday the more humiliated she felt.

'Not even Harrie?'

'Not yet. Look, the bitch couldn't even spell my name right. Or Harrie's.'

'And it was delivered to Mrs Hislop's?'

'Yes, I *said* that.'

'And did people notice?'

'They couldn't help it. I just about shat myself.'

'So what did you say?'

Friday dug angrily in her reticule for her pipe and tobacco. 'Stop asking me questions, Sarah. *I* didn't send the bloody thing.'

'No, but *we're* going to have to pay the money, aren't we?'

Sarah's voice had risen and she glanced over her shoulder at the open back door in case Adam or Esther might have heard. But Adam was packing for his trip to Van Diemen's Land, and Esther was no doubt too busy chastising him about leaving her while her nerves were in such a terrible state to be eavesdropping.

Regardless, she lowered her voice and indicated Friday's leg. 'Didn't anyone want to know how that happened? Did they connect it with the letter?'

'What does it matter if they did?'

'But does anyone know you went to see Bella?'

Friday sucked on her pipe. 'Mrs H does. She wouldn't take me to the doctor unless I told her how I got mauled.'

Sarah looked alarmed. 'Christ, you didn't tell her why, did you?'

'What do you think? I just said I had a bone to pick.'

'Why *did* you go? You know she isn't going to let us off.'

'I don't know.' Friday shrugged. 'I thought we might have done a deal.'

'What sort of deal?' Sarah persisted.

'I don't *know*. I just wanted … to have a go at her, I suppose.'

'So there's no chance of her letting us off?'

'None. I got the impression she'd rather die.'

'Did you … feel a fool?'

Friday nodded reluctantly. 'She enjoyed it, too. I think she'd have been disappointed if I hadn't gone to see her.'

'Well,' Sarah said, 'much as it sticks in my craw to say it, we've got the money. We can afford it.'

'Yes, but that's supposed to be Charlotte's nest egg, and to support her and Rosie and Janie in the Factory. We'll have to double our savings schedule to replace it. Then the bitch'll just demand more and it'll be gone again.' Friday's voice was going up and up. 'It'll be a never-ending bloody cycle. Ow, *God* my leg hurts.'

Sarah eyed Friday's bandaged leg as though it might suddenly develop a life of its own, leap up and attack her. 'When will you know if you actually have been infected?'

'James Downey said a month or so.'

'Christ, Friday, it's a worry.'

'Maybe. I'm not going to think about it till I have to.'

Sarah gave Friday's hand a comforting squeeze. 'Did Bella say anything about when the next demand would be?'

'No. If we knew that it'd spoil the game, wouldn't it? Christ, she's a bitch.' Friday fired a tobacco-stained gob at the ground. 'God, who'll tell Harrie, you or me? She's already in a state over Rowie and James. She's in a state *anyway*, Sarah. I'm worried.'

'I know. So am I. But I'll be lucky if Esther lets me over the doorstep once Adam's gone, so can you tell her?'

Friday nodded a second time. 'When's he back?' She pushed herself stiffly to her feet, the bucket beneath her backside scraping on the cobbles, and reached for her wooden crutch.

'Three weeks, less if everything goes well.'

'Why's he going?'

Sarah shrugged. 'Something to do with the business. Haven't asked.'

'And this Cole cove is all right?'

'Seems to be.'

'Well, good luck with Her Majesty,' Friday said.

She pecked Sarah on the cheek and departed through the shop to Elizabeth's carriage waiting outside, leaving a trail of pungent pipe smoke to befoul Esther's hallway.

After she'd gone, Sarah spread several sheets of newspaper across the dining table and sat down to polish Esther's precious silver cutlery. When she'd finished here she had plenty to get on with in the workshop, which was good; she'd be much too busy to brood over Bella's note.

Bella would never stop, and Sarah knew it. After they'd paid once, demonstrating that they in fact could, she would delight in wielding her power over them, demanding more and more, making them suffer, bleeding them dry. And what would happen to Charlotte, Janie and Rosie, if she and Friday and Harrie could no longer provide them with the money and supplies they needed in the Factory? What would become of the vow they'd all so solemnly sworn to keep Rachel's child safe?

In a fit of frustration and anger Sarah hurled the silver-cleaning cloth across the dining room. Stinking of a solution of chalk, alcohol and ammonia, it had made her eyes water and she dabbed at them furiously with the hem of her apron.

'Don't cry, Sarah, he'll be back in a few weeks,' Esther said as she bustled into the room, a coat of Adam's over her arm.

Sarah didn't even bother to look up.

'There's a button missing from this, and one loose on the cuff. I'd like you to make the requisite repairs. I believe there's a button that will do in the button box. And hurry up. He's due to leave shortly.'

Sarah fetched the button box, stored with the rest of the sewing things in a drawer of the 'chiffonier', as Esther called it. Everyone else Sarah knew who owned such a piece of furniture called it a sideboard; Esther was the first person she'd ever met to possess a 'chiffonier'. She opened the box and sorted through it until she found the appropriate button. In fact, she reflected, in the last five years most of the people she'd associated with hadn't even owned enough spare buttons to put in a box. They weren't cheap, good buttons. What was it about Esther's life that made her think it was so bloody terrible, anyway? She was constantly complaining and doing her best to make everyone else miserable; most women would consider themselves extremely lucky to be married to someone like Adam and living in a comfortable, well-appointed home like this.

She really does deserve to have the life frightened out of her, Sarah thought. She threaded a needle and jabbed it roughly into the fabric of Adam's coat. While he was away she was going to bloody well scare Esther shitless.

When a loud knocking came at the shop door she jumped, pricking herself. Swearing, she dumped the coat on the table and hurried through to the shop.

It was Bernard Cole, sweating already in the morning's heat, beaming from ear to ear and carrying a basket packed with goods from the nearby bakery.

'Good morning, Sarah. Not too early, am I? Provisions,' he explained, presenting the basket.

'Oh. Thank you. Well, we don't actually open until nine o'clock, but please, come in.'

She stood aside and he waddled past, reeking from a fresh application of his ylang-ylang-scented Macassar oil.

'Adam still here, is he?' Bernard asked over his shoulder.

'Upstairs packing.'

'Bernard!' Adam called from the top of the stairs. 'You're just in time. I'm about to leave for the quay!'

Esther appeared behind him dressed for the street, her handsome face creased in its perpetual frown. 'Sarah, where's that coat?'

Shit. 'Won't be a moment, Mrs Green.' Sarah rushed back to the dining room, put a few more stitches through the button's shank, then cut the thread.

Esther marched in and snatched the coat from her. 'You'd better hope that doesn't come off!'

Sarah thought Adam would probably manage if it did.

'Esther, the gig's arrived,' Adam said from the hallway.

Sarah and Bernard followed Adam and Esther outside, watching as the driver loaded Adam's suitcases into the luggage compartment at the rear of the gig. Before he and Esther climbed aboard, Adam shook Bernard's hand.

'Shouldn't imagine I'll be any longer than three weeks at the most. You're in good hands with Sarah. I trust her implicitly.'

This prompted an even less attractive scowl from Esther, who said, 'I'll be back by midday, Sarah, and I'm not expecting to see a *single* smudge or speck of dirt on that silver, do you understand?'

'Yes, Mrs Green,' Sarah replied.

Ignoring Esther, Adam deliberately caught Sarah's gaze. She expected him to say something but instead he gave the slightest shake of his head and narrowed his eyes at her. It was a message of some sort, a warning, but she didn't understand it. Then he climbed onto the gig beside Esther; the driver gave the reins a gentle flick and the horses headed off, leaving behind a great steaming pile of manure directly outside the entrance to the shop.

Sarah frowned at it.

'That Esther's a piece of work, isn't she?' Bernard remarked as the horses turned, causing a slight traffic jam, and plodded off down George Street. 'I don't know how Adam puts up with her. Don't know how *I'm* going to put up with her.' He stepped into the shop out of the light breeze and retrieved a silver snuff box from his coat pocket, tapped the lid twice and opened it. Taking a small pinch between thumb and forefinger he rolled it for a few seconds to release the aromatic oils, then sniffed it into each nostril. 'Still, it's only for three weeks, I suppose. And it's for Adam. If she was anyone else's missus I'd tell them — sorry, too busy.'

Sarah gave a polite little smile. He *sounded* as though he genuinely disliked Esther, but he might not. This could all be a trick cooked up by Adam — or, even worse, Esther — to test her loyalty to them. You never knew how fickle people could be; she'd learnt *that* lesson some time ago.

'Mrs Green has her good points.'

'Well, she can cook, that's true,' Bernard said. 'That's one. And she's a fine-looking woman, there's no denying that. When she's not scowling, that is. Face like a smashed crab otherwise.' He sighed.

135

'Damn shame, really. Good man, Adam. Don't know why he took up with her.'

Sarah thought she did; he must have loved her. It was the only reason she could think of. Having come to know him over the past year, she'd decided, contrary to what she'd initially assumed, that he wasn't the sort of man to marry a woman for her money, and anyway she doubted Esther had had much, being an ex-convict. On the other hand, Bella Jackson had arrived in New South Wales with plenty of dosh, so perhaps Esther had, too. But she still couldn't see Adam as an opportunist of that ilk. And Bernard was right — Esther was an attractive woman, and capable of considerable charm when she felt like it. Adam had fallen in love with her, it was probably as simple as that. He cared a lot for her now, Sarah knew, but did he still love her? And more to the point, why should she care whether he did or not?

'And by the way, Sarah,' Bernard added, 'you don't have to watch your tongue. There's no love lost between me and Esther Green, and even less between Esther and my missus. They hate each other's guts. Esther thinks we're common. So we are, and we're proud of it. And truth be told there's not a lot of difference between my Ruthie and Adam's Esther, bar about three stone in weight and a put-on toffy accent. They're both East End lasses and they're both emancipists.'

East End? She's doing a good job of hiding that, Sarah thought.

'I was transported for receiving, same as Adam, in case you're wondering,' Bernard went on, 'and he's told me about you. A cracksman? You don't see many lasses doing that. I have to say I'm impressed.'

'I wasn't transported for that,' Sarah said.

'No, but still. He's been very trusting with you, hasn't he?'

'Yes, he has.' Why was he saying this to her?

'He must think a lot of you.'

That's none of your business, Sarah thought. Shut up.

Bernard beamed. 'Anyway, that's between you and Adam. Now, what's this I hear about a ghost?'

Feeling on far less dangerous ground, Sarah said, 'Did Adam tell you?'

Pulling his watch from his waistcoat and checking the time, Bernard said, 'Why don't you tell *me* over a nice cup of tea? We don't have to open for half an hour and Esther won't be back for a while. I always say a good story goes best with a nice cup of char.'

So Sarah made him tea, which he rounded out with three of the buns he'd brought, and told him how the ghost of Rachel Winter was haunting both herself and her friend Harrie, as well as this house and now, apparently, Esther Green. She spoke earnestly, and Bernard received the account as though it were the most reasonable thing he'd ever heard.

'We had a ghost once, Ruthie and me, in a house we had in Suffolk Lane. This was a few years ago now, when our kids were still small. Our youngest, Albert, would have been about six or seven. The ghost was the spirit of a little girl, drowned in a cesspit in the yard.'

'Really?' Sarah said. 'How did you know that?'

'Ruthie felt sorry for the poor thing wandering around caught betwixt one world and the next, and the kids were getting sick of having their bedclothes pulled off in the middle of the night and what have you, so we got a spiritist to come in. This woman, you should have seen her, she was only in the house twenty minutes and managed to come up with all this history about our ghost. Apparently her name was Pansy — the ghost, not the spiritist, *her* name was Mrs Savage — and she was nine years old and she'd slipped into the cesspit reaching for a doll she'd dropped, and drowned. What a terrible way for a kiddie to die. Well, for anyone, really. But it's marvellous what they can do, these spiritual people.'

'It certainly is,' Sarah said. 'And so altruistic of them to work for nothing.'

'Actually, it cost me a tenner,' Bernard said, frowning.

'And did Pansy go away?'

'No. We ended up moving ourselves. Ruthie had another baby and we needed a bigger house. Well, we could afford it. Pansy might still be there, for all I know. So you actually know this ghost of yours?'

'Yes, Rachel was a very close friend of ours.'

'And what does she want, do you know?'

Sarah said, 'I don't know if she wants anything at all from me or Harrie, but I think she might be angry at Esther because Esther wouldn't let me attend her burial.'

'How do you know that?'

'She told me one night, in a dream.' Sarah almost cringed because it sounded so silly.

'Mmm. Well, it certainly seems to be scaring the stuffing out of her ladyship,' Bernard said cheerfully. He dug a knife into the butter and plastered his bun with it. 'That'll teach her for being so heartless, won't it? I wonder if I'll see her? Your ghost, I mean.'

Highly unlikely, Sarah thought. She looked at the clock. 'Time to open up.'

Friday lurched her way up the Barretts' stairs, swearing, tripping and clattering her crutch against the wall. This wasn't exactly keeping her leg elevated.

Nora Barrett appeared at the top of the stairwell holding the baby, her little boy Sam clutching at her skirts.

'Mr Barrett said Harrie's in?' Friday said.

Nora nodded. 'What have you done to your leg?'

'A dog bit it.'

The little boy went, 'Woof woof!'

'Woof's right,' Friday muttered.

'Do you need help?' Nora asked, coming down.

'No, I'm good, thanks. But could you fetch Harrie, please? If she's not busy?'

Nora retreated, and by the time Friday reached the top of the stairs Harrie had appeared. Beside her hovered Hannah Barrett, looking unusually clean, her wet hair stuck to her head.

'Friday!' Harrie exclaimed. 'What happened?!'

'A dog bit me,' Friday said, hobbling to the sofa and collapsing on it. 'Can I sit down, please?'

'Of course.' Nora waved her free hand.

Hannah asked, 'Can I see the hole?'

'No, you can't,' Harrie said.

'Oh, pleease! Is there pus?'

'Hannah!' Nora reprimanded.

'I just wondered!'

'Well, go to your room and wonder.'

'Can't. My hair's wet.'

Harrie attacked Hannah's head with a towel, rubbing her hair so energetically the little girl lost her balance.

'Have you got rabies?' Hannah asked when she'd regained her bearings.

Nora's face paled.

'I don't know,' Friday said. 'Shall I bite you and see?'

Hannah shrieked and tore off to the children's room.

'There's no sign of it,' Friday said to Nora. 'I'm under a doctor's care.' She swore, apologised, and shifted on the sofa to ease her leg.

'Fuck fuck,' Samuel said.

Nora took his hand. 'We'll be hanging out the washing, Harrie. Not too long, now. We've that gown to cut out.'

Harrie nodded. When Nora and the children had gone, Friday said, 'Where's the oldest girl?'

'Abigail? With her father in the shop, I think. Why? How on earth did you get bitten by a dog?' Carefully, Harrie sat next to Friday.

'I don't want anyone to hear us. It's about Bella. I finally got a note.' Harrie's hands crept towards her ears, but Friday caught

139

and held them. 'You need to listen to this, love. She's demanded a hundred and fifty pounds, and we're going to pay it. We have to. We don't have a choice.'

Harrie stared at her, eyes slowly filling with tears.

'It's not that bad,' Friday said, though it was. 'She could have asked for a lot more.'

'I can't do it,' Harrie whispered. 'I can't be the one who gives it to her.'

'I know. Don't worry, I'll do that.'

'Will that be the end of it?'

Friday so desperately wanted to lie. 'No, it won't. She'll keep making demands so we'll have to save twice as hard now.'

Harrie looked stricken. 'It'll *never* end, will it? It'll go on and on and on.'

'Don't worry, Harrie, please. We'll find a way to stop her.'

'But *how*, Friday? How?'

And Friday could only stare at her, because she had no idea.

Matthew loitered in the shadow of the Commissariat Stores on George Street, mustering the courage to go ahead with what had initially seemed to be such a wonderful idea. He'd taken the day off work, sending Dolly with a note citing a recurrence of the ague he'd suffered several weeks earlier, and had already ducked into the pub for several stiff whiskies, retiring to the dimmest corner lest he be seen by someone he knew, so now he was feeling half drunk — at ten in the morning! — as well as nervous.

Taking a deep, steadying breath, he crossed the busy street and strode briskly along the footway, trying to look as though he had somewhere vitally important to be, then dodged quickly into the alleyway beside the Sailors' Grave. Expecting to encounter reeking piles of rubbish and possibly a dead dog or two, not to mention prostitutes and lurking pickpockets, he was pleasantly surprised to note that the alley was free of detritus and no more smelly than the rest of the Rocks. Halfway along he came to an open doorway, across which hung a brightly painted bamboo curtain. A sign declared the premises to be *OPEN FOR BUSINESS*. He knocked before he could change his mind.

'Enter!' came a gruff voice.

Matthew parted the bamboo reeds and stepped into the little shop, blinking at the bright light within.

A shirtless, heavily muscled man sat on a waist-high wooden bench, dabbing salve onto what was clearly a new tattoo over his right pectoral area. It wasn't his first, either; his arms were covered with them and there were already two on his chest. Beside him an older man, his hair, moustache and beard all very grey, sat bent over a tea trolley laden with implements, wiping off a handful of wicked-looking needles with what smelt, even from the doorway, like raw alcohol.

The old man said without raising his head, 'Can do you something very small, or maybe an outline. You'll have to come back if you want anything bigger. I've a booking at one o'clock.'

'Er,' Matthew said.

The old man turned around.

'Are you Mr Leonard Dundas?' Matthew asked.

'Who wants to know?' the grey-haired man said, his voice heavy with suspicion.

'Oh, no one, just me. My friend recommended you. Harrie Clarke.'

'Did she now? And who might you be?'

'Matthew Cutler,' Matthew offered a hand.

The man looked at it but didn't take it. 'Aye, I'm Leo Dundas. What do you want?'

Matthew hesitated; this Mr Dundas didn't seem anything like the 'very nice man' Harrie had described. 'Well, actually, I'd like a tattoo.'

Leo exchanged glances with the fellow on the bench; they both burst into snorts of laughter.

'You do know what a tattoo is?' Leo said. 'Once it's on it'll never come off again.'

'Yes, I do realise that.'

'You don't look like a sailor.'

'That's because I'm not,' Matthew said patiently. 'I'm a civil servant.'

Grinning and shaking his head, the newly tattooed man got off the bench and shrugged into his shirt. 'How much do I owe you, Leo?'

Leo told him and the man left the money on the trolley.

'Mind you keep up with the salve, Bill. And don't ruddy well pick the scab this time!' When Bill had gone, Leo said to Matthew, 'You'll have to pardon my bad manners, lad. I've a certain reputation to maintain. I am busy, but if you're a friend of Harrie's I've got time to listen.'

Leo had only met Harrie three times, but already he was growing fond of her. He'd seen how gentle she was with Walter, and he was grateful to her for it. He was a rough old bugger himself and knew it. Walter was still young, he'd had a shocking time with that Furniss bastard, and could benefit from the kindness and gentle ways only a woman could provide. She was pretty, too, Harrie, and round in all the right places; Walter shouldn't have to put up with an ugly, weathered old sailor's face *all* the time.

'All the same,' he added, 'I don't think you do want a tattoo.'

'Yes, I do,' Matthew said firmly. 'Though obviously I don't want it right in the middle of my forehead or anywhere like that.'

The corners of Leo's mouth twitched.

'And I'd like something that has ... resonance.'

'Such as?'

'Well, I don't know. What about one of Harrie's, er ... flashes? Is that what they're called?'

Leo suddenly realised what had brought this young man to his shop. 'Flash. She hasn't produced any yet. Not had the time.

142

Look, lad, if you want to impress her, why don't you just buy her an extravagant gift?'

Matthew shook his head. 'I've made up my mind. I want a tattoo. She said —' she thinks your work is beautiful, he finished to himself. 'Never mind. I can't afford to buy extravagant gifts, and anyway it's not that straightforward.'

'Isn't it?'

'Unfortunately, no, it isn't.'

'Well,' Leo said, 'if you've set your heart on getting inked I won't stop you. And I admit you wouldn't be the first gentleman to do it. But I meant what I said, once a tattoo's been done there's no getting rid of it. Unless you flay it off, and to do that you have to go fairly deep.' He winced. 'Not nice, lad. And it leaves a bloody great scar.'

Matthew crossed his arms but said nothing.

Leo gave a half-hearted shrug. 'Right then, what did you have in mind? I am booked up this afternoon, so if you want a map of the globe across your back you'll have to come back another day.'

'Just something smallish,' Matthew said. 'And nothing too, well, vulgar.'

'Nothing a sailor'd want, you mean?'

'I wasn't going to say that. But nothing too … effeminate, either.'

'Where do you want it?'

'Well, not on public view.'

'Then how's she going to know you've got it?' Leo asked slyly. 'Or are you planning on strutting around in front of her in the nud?'

'Certainly not!' Matthew said, his face heating up.

Good, Leo thought, I don't think I like that idea. 'Well, does anything on the wall take your fancy?'

Matthew spent about ten minutes having a really good look. 'Nearly,' he said at last. 'I like some of these oriental ones. This lion thing here is quite appealing. Or is it a dog? It's a bit hard to tell, isn't it? Would it have to be that big, though? I was thinking of my upper arm.'

Leo opened his cabinet and took out a book. 'Some of those are Chinese lions and some are Korean temple dogs. That one you're looking at is a lion, or a kara shishi. Strictly speaking they're all actually Japanese designs. You often get both in Japanese work. It's part of their mythology. There are more images in here.'

Matthew thumbed through the beautifully illustrated book, full of colour plates. 'This is marvellous. Where did you get it?'

'I studied the art of irezumi for some years. That's Japanese tattoo, to you.'

'Not in Japan, surely?'

Leo nodded. 'That book was given to me as a gift by my tutor.'

Matthew eyed him with new respect. 'How on earth did you get into Japan?'

'In my younger years I was a sailor. I jumped ship, didn't I?'

'But it's been closed to other nations for two hundred years, hasn't it?'

'Big jump, very quiet splash. It's not *that* closed.'

'So how long were you there?'

'Long enough,' Leo said in a tone that suggested he'd finished talking about his time in Japan. 'If you want the lion you have to have a peony as well.'

'Peony as in the flower?'

Leo pointed with an ink-stained finger at an image of a particularly luscious-looking bloom. 'Aye, one of these. The lion is all-powerful and all-protective, a symbol of guardianship —'

'Oh, I like that,' Matthew interrupted.

'Thought you might,' Leo said dryly. 'And guardianship is yin. To balance that you have to have something that is yang. The peony, symbolic of good fortune, a hint of risk-taking and high honour is yang. You can't —'

'Sorry, I'm getting confused.'

'Yin and yang, very complex oriental concepts. Two opposing forces and what matters is the balance. I'll not go into it or we'll be here all day. The lion always appears with the peony, and I won't do the lion without it. Up to you.'

Actually, Matthew really rather liked the peony; the way its rich red petals curled delicately at their edges was quite sensuous and the packed profusion of smaller petals unfurling at the centre of the bloom evoked in him a sense of something ... spurting out, an idea that stirred his loins with embarrassing effect. He turned slightly away from Mr Dundas. What a funny idea to get from a drawing of a tattooed flower. Hell, he *was* getting desperate.

'Right then, the lion and the peony, on my upper right arm? Would that be appropriate, do you think?'

'It's your arm, lad,' Leo said. 'But, aye, it's a good choice. We'll start on the outline today. I'm warning you, though, it can get painful.'

Matthew nodded, having expected it would. 'What colours do you have?'

'A good range. I use pigment, mixed with oil.'

Removing his coat and draping it across the end of the bench, Matthew asked, 'Where shall I sit? Or should I recline?'

Leo pointed to the chair. 'You need to sit for an arm.' He glanced at the small clock on the cabinet. 'And I'll probably only do the kara shishi outline today. We're running out of time.'

Matthew sat and reached for the book of illustrations again. 'They are ferocious-looking, the lions, aren't they?'

They were, too, with their heavy brows, glaring eyes and wide, wide mouths filled with sharp, curved fangs. He flicked through several more pages until he came to a drawing of a man tattooed from knees to neck, including all over his apparently semi-erect penis. Hastily Matthew closed the book and put it down.

'You'll need to take your shirt off,' Leo said, amused.

'What? Oh yes, of course.'

Matthew removed his waistcoat and shirt and laid them on top of his coat. Half naked and feeling decidedly vulnerable, he sat down again. Good God, the door was still open; anyone could walk in. He crossed his legs, then uncrossed them and planted the soles of his boots firmly on the flagged floor in as manly a fashion as possible.

'Comfy?' Leo asked.

'Yes, thank you.'

Leo worked very quickly drawing the outline onto Matthew's skin, and a few minutes later sat back and said, 'Go and have a look in the glass. Tell me if you're happy with it.'

Matthew was, and returned to his seat.

'Ready to start, then?' Leo asked.

'I think so.'

Leo chose from his tray a small brush, which he held between the smallest and ring fingers of his left hand and loaded with pigment — a viscous black ink smelling sharply and incongruously of fish. With his right hand he selected a tool consisting of several fine steel needles bound to a wooden handle with silk thread. He turned to Matthew, touched the needles to the ink-loaded brush, and made the first rapid but vigorous insertions.

They felt, to Matthew, like mild bee stings, the sensation not as uncomfortable as he'd expected.

'All right?' Leo asked after a few minutes.

'Yes, thank you. It's not as bad as I'd thought it might be.'

'Not yet, it isn't.'

As the minutes became a half hour and then an hour, and then ninety minutes, during which Leo seemed barely to pause to reload his brush and occasionally stretch, the sensation blossomed from mild discomfort to a throbbing, burning pain that spread down to Matthew's elbow and as far up as his shoulder joint. His neck, too, was becoming stiff and sore from bracing himself against the needles' onslaught. Glancing down, he saw that the flesh around the new black lines was red and raised, and that the gauze cloth on Leo's tray was heavily spotted with blood. It wasn't the worst pain he'd ever endured but he was certainly looking forward to one o'clock when Leo's next customer arrived. Finally, just as he was contemplating confessing he'd had enough for one day, Leo gave his arm a final wipe and sat back.

'I think that'll do for today, lad. Go and have another look.'

Matthew pushed himself creakily out of the chair and stood before the long glass, his torso at an angle to better admire the startling addition to his pale skin. He flexed his arms for effect, thinking it was fortunate he already had reasonably good muscle definition, otherwise he really would look ridiculous with an oriental lion on his upper arm.

'Bravo!' someone called from the doorway, and applauded energetically.

Mortified, Matthew whirled and made a dash for his shirt.

'Hang on a minute, lad,' Leo said, a broad smirk accentuating the creases in his face. 'You'll be needing a bit of salve on that.'

'Good afternoon, Miss Woolfe,' Matthew said stiffly, and sidled towards Leo, his shirt clamped against his chest.

Friday said, 'I'm impressed, Mr Cutler. I had no idea you were hiding all that under your sensibly tailored clothes.'

Matthew's face positively scorched as he accepted the little pot of salve Leo offered him. In an attempt to keep a grip on his shirt and open the pot at the same time he dropped the lid, which rolled at a leisurely pace all the way across the floor past Friday until it came to rest at the base of Leo's cabinet. Friday limped over, retrieved it, picked a bit of fluff off it, and returned it to Matthew.

'Here you are, Mr Cutler. Would you like me to rub your salve on for you?'

'No thank you,' Matthew said in a rush, 'that won't be necessary.'

Awkwardly draping his shirt across his chest and tucking it beneath his arms, he poked a finger into the salve, smeared some onto his new tattoo, then turned his back and put the shirt on before grabbing his waistcoat and coat from the bench.

'Thank you, Mr Dundas. I shall make another appointment. Good day to you both.'

Friday and Leo listened to the sound of his boots rapping away up the alleyway.

Leo said conversationally, 'Do you often have that effect on gentlemen?'

'No, usually they're getting their clobber off, not putting it on.'

'I don't believe he paid me.'

Friday removed her hat and dumped both it and her reticule on the bench. 'He will. I doubt there's a dishonest bone in that one's body.'

'Decent sort, is he?' Leo asked, wiping down his needles.

'Seems to be. Don't know him that well. Have I got the whole afternoon?'

'If you're up for it. Is he courting Harrie?'

'He'd like to. He's escorted her to afternoon tea once, at her invitation. At the moment she's using him to get back at someone, another cove who's made her *really* angry.'

Leo was startled. 'Harrie? I'd never have picked that.'

'Then you don't know Harrie very well, do you?'

'I know she's been good with Walter.' Leo's wily old eyes narrowed. 'How do I know you're not just jealous of her? You say you and Harrie and this girl Sarah are the best of mates, but I don't know you very well either, do I?'

'No, you don't,' Friday said, her voice deceptively light. She began to undo the buttons on her bodice. 'And it's up to you what you believe. I don't actually give a shit. Harrie and Sarah, and Rachel before she died, are the best friends I've ever had, and I know Harrie far better than you ever will. And I love her. And I know she's not happy right now. If you can be a friend to her as well, that's good, but you have to be loyal. You can't let her down.

She's had enough of that already. And that's a warning, Mr Tattoo Man, not a piece of advice.' She shrugged out of her bodice revealing a sleeveless shift underneath. 'And don't go thinking you know something about her, or *us*, when you don't.'

Leo, four inches taller than Friday, and standing only two or three feet away now, stared at the dark nipples pressing against the white cotton of her shift. He sighed wearily and lifted his gaze to her face. 'I'm not interested in interfering, lass. I like Harrie, and so does Walter. She's a kind, trusting soul.'

'Yes, she is. It's been a worry.'

'Unlike yourself,' Leo added.

'You should meet Sarah.'

'I hope I do.'

Friday sat on the chair. Leo took hold of her left wrist and turned her arm, studying it closely.

'That's healing nicely. What have you done to your leg?'

'Dog bite,' Friday said flatly.

'I hope you saw a doctor. Dog bites can be very nasty. Do you want the shading finished on the roses today, or will I start on the name?'

Friday was starting with the unevenly inked word *MARIA* on her left forearm, the name of the child she'd borne five years before, when she herself had only been fourteen, and who had died at the age of three months. That was being disguised with three red rosebuds, the darkest aspect of their shading covering the old ink, above a banner featuring a much more elegantly rendered version of her daughter's name. After that Leo would tackle the very amateur dagger plunging through a heart above a set of initials on the outer aspect of her upper left arm. Friday had chosen a peacock to cover those, which would extend in all its gaudy magnificence from the top of her shoulder all the way down to her elbow. As for the anchor and initials on her upper right arm, she hadn't decided. Perhaps a spiky-looking dragon, as depicted in the flash on Leo's wall, or maybe a phoenix bird to represent her and Harrie and Sarah rising from the ashes of their time as convicts. Secretly, she harboured an ambition to have an enormous version of a phoenix tattooed across her entire back, though she hadn't mentioned that to Leo yet.

There were also the three outlined stars on her right hand between the thumb and forefinger — her first tattoos, executed when she was thirteen. She still rather liked them, as lately she'd come to think of them as representing herself, Sarah and Harrie; she planned to have Leo simply colour them green and add another in purple to symbolise Rachel.

Most folk assumed the initials on her arms were those of past lovers but they weren't; they belonged to the tattooists who had inked the heart and dagger, and the anchor — fairly incompetent artists who had operated out of verminous little corners in pubs down near the docks in London's East End. She couldn't even remember getting the tattoos, she'd been that drunk. The word MARIA she'd scratched into herself with a shard of glass, over and over until the blood had run freely, giving her some — but not much — relief from her monstrous grief and gut-wrenching guilt. Then she'd rubbed lampblack into the raw wounds so she could never forget the terrible thing she'd done.

But Leo's tattoos were very different. Not only was his work extremely beautiful, she'd discovered that the process of getting tattooed by a master was ... mesmerising; there was no other word for it. Yes, it hurt, and yes, her arm was sore afterwards and some clumsy cully always knocked it while he was grinding away on top of her, but the sensation of Leo's needles jabbing into her skin so rapidly and rhythmically seemed to send her into a delicious sort of trance. The feeling was very close to sexual, but not quite. Her mind almost disconnected from her body, the only thing holding the two together the bright thread of pain generated by Leo's needles, and when that happened she was free to go wherever she pleased. Being in the place where Leo's needles took her was as good as being blind drunk, only better, because there were no horrors the next day, and she got a lovely new tattoo out of it as well. It took Leo many hours to complete a good-sized tattoo, though he was a very quick worker, so there was plenty of time in the good place, but it also meant she had to wait to see the finished work, and she didn't like to wait. For anything.

'We've got all afternoon. Can't you do both?'

'Probably not. Let's see how we go with the shading.' Leo sat on his stool and pulled his tea trolley closer.

Friday didn't actually dislike Leo, regardless of what she'd just said to him concerning Harrie, though she was a little jealous of the fact that she seemed to have taken such an instant shine to him. As usual, Harrie had made a decision to trust someone without taking the time to assess his character, a habit of hers which in the past had not stood her in good stead. Friday didn't *think* she was making a mistake befriending Leo Dundas — he did seem a decent, reasonable sort of cove — but she did wish Harrie would occasionally follow her head more than she did her heart.

She asked, 'Has Harrie told you anything about Matthew Cutler?'

'Don't know her *that* well yet,' Leo said as he dipped his brush into a pot of dark red pigment.

'Do you want to know?'

'Is it any of my business?'

'Not really. But you did ask about him before.'

'That's true.'

Friday recounted the basic details about Harrie and James Downey falling out after Rachel's death, James's acquisition of Rowie Harris as a servant, and Harrie's retaliatory afternoon-tea invitation to Matthew. She told Leo as a way of explaining that Harrie was currently not her usual calm, sensible, rational self. Then it occurred to her that Harrie might sound like nothing more than a girl who'd been spurned. She certainly hadn't said anything about Bella or Keegan, so Leo didn't know how terribly frightened and worried and guilty Harrie was feeling because of that. How bloody worried they were *all* feeling. But then, Harrie *was* jealous of Rowie, that was plain.

'Like I said, none of my business,' Leo remarked. Though he thought it did sound like this James Downey could do with a good box around the ears. Uppity bloody ex-navy doctors, accustomed to ruling the roost and too arrogant to adjust when their boots touched dry land. And clearly *this* one didn't know an honest, generous, clever, pretty lass when he saw her.

Chapter Eight

Like a number of Sydney's streets, York was long and reasonably straight, and home to close to a dozen licensed hotels. By the time Friday arrived at James's cottage to visit Rowie Harris, she'd been into the Green Man, the Flower Pot and the Warwick, and was pleasantly muzzy. So was Jack Wilton, who was driving Elizabeth's gig, and at present dozing on the seat with the hood raised.

'You don't have anything stronger?' Friday asked as Rowie served tea. A drop more wouldn't hurt.

'Oh. Well, I've a bit of gin in my room, and James has some good brandy. But we shouldn't really drink that.'

'"James"? That sounds cosy. Gin, thanks. Getting along well then, the two of you?'

'Not in the way you think,' Rowie replied.

'Do you call him James to his face? Wouldn't have thought he'd stand for that. Too proper.'

'Do I hell,' Rowie said, grinning.

While she was fetching the gin, Friday had a good look around. The parlour, with its big open hearth — where Rowie obviously did the cooking — was clean, comfortable and welcoming. The windows sparkled, not a speck of dirt besmirched the patterned oilcloth or the rugs on the floor, a pile of precisely folded linen waited on a chair to be put away, and a vase of flowers sat exactly in the centre of the recently polished dining table.

Rowie returned and poured Friday a decent-sized gin. 'He said you might visit.' She sat and helped herself to tea. 'So what were you doing when the dog bit you?'

'Walking down the street, minding my own business,' Friday said. 'It was one of those bloody feral dogs.'

'Really? My God,' Rowie said. 'That's shocking. You really have to keep an eye out, don't you?'

'So it's working out here all right?' Friday was quick to change the subject.

'It's been good. I've been so lucky. He's a nice man, James. Decent.'

'Yes, well, just remember he's spoken for.'

Rolling her eyes, Rowie said, 'How could I forget? He's always mentioning one or other of them. "Emily always did that", or "Harrie says this". Especially Harrie. I don't think he knows he's doing it, half the time. I think he must be quite lonely.'

'Very likely, but it's not your job to keep him company. Not in bed, anyway,' Friday warned.

'Half the chance,' Rowie grumbled. 'I'm still having trouble down below. James has given me some draughts, and plasters to use at night, and they're helping. But, well, it's just lucky I'm doing this now, and not still on the town.'

'You'll be missing the extra chink.'

'I am, but James pays well enough. There'll be enough to send a bit home, but I won't be able to put money aside the way you do. You must have a fortune saved by now, with all your regular cullies. You'll be able to retire soon!'

'I wouldn't call it a fortune,' Friday said, but couldn't resist adding, 'but we are talking a good few hundred. It's earmarked, but, and not for me.'

'Is it? Who's it for, then?'

Friday shook her head. 'Any chance of another drink?'

Rowie poured. 'I keep expecting Harrie to turn up here, but she hasn't. Mind you, I wouldn't know her if she did. You should bring her. I know James would love to see her.'

'She's not that thrilled you're here doing for him.' Loyalty stopped Friday from saying any more.

'Well, what does she look like, in case she does turn up? Or will she be the one with the axe in her hand?' Rowie laughed.

Friday didn't. 'She won't have an axe. She's far more mature than that.'

'Sorry. I didn't really mean that.' Rowie sipped her cooling tea.

'She has beautiful, thick nutmeggy hair, a very pretty face with lovely rosebud lips, and a gorgeous curvy figure with fantastic tits.'

'Really? Well, it's obvious why James fancies her, then.'

'No, he admires her for her brains and her bubbly character,' Friday corrected.

They paused, then shared a snort of laughter.

'And she fancies him?' Rowie asked.

'She does.'

'Then why aren't they together?'

Friday sighed. 'Oh, it's a bloody long story, Rowie. He pissed her off and she won't forgive him.'

'Is that it?'

'That's it.'

'Some people,' Rowie said.

'I know.'

'Well, he can't have Emily back, can he?' Rowie said. 'She's rotting in her grave back home. Shall I see what I can do about Harrie? Drop hints about, oh, I don't know, the joy of raising a family or something.'

'No. He'll think you mean you and him.'

Rowie winced. 'God, he will, too. Well, I don't know. Any ideas?'

'I'll think about it.' Friday gulped the last of her gin and used her crutch to push herself to her feet. 'Christ, this bloody leg is driving me insane.'

Rowie accompanied her outside and they woke up Jack, who, for a moment, didn't know where he was. He helped Friday up into the gig, where they sat crunching liquorice-flavoured cachous to disguise the alcohol on their breaths before they headed for home.

On the eastern side of George Street down near the waterfront crouched the Black Rat Hotel, one of the roughest and least salubrious pubs on the Rocks. It was a favourite with sailors on shore leave looking for a wild time, and with those who had brought to Sydney the culture of England's underworld, which was a significant number of the town's inhabitants, no matter that they might now have earned tickets of leave, been granted pardons or otherwise served their sentences. While many ex-convicts were content to put down roots and build new, law-abiding lives in the colony, others were just as happy to carry on as they had in the old world, living off their wits and criminal endeavour, and for them the Black Rat was the place to go.

The night was warm and Friday hadn't bothered with a jacket or a shawl. Her left foot had healed enough now for her to wear both boots and, even hobbling on a crutch, the Black Rat was only a few minutes' walk from the Siren's Arms. She'd asked Jack to come with her but wouldn't tell him the full story, and he was sulking because of it, which only made her filthy mood even filthier. All she could tell him was she owed someone money and had to pay it back, and she wanted him with her in case she was robbed on the way to the Black Rat, which was true.

At five to midnight she made him promise to stay outside and wait for her, then went in. The pub was noisy, choked with smoke, badly lit, and crowded with the usual assortment of shady characters, low-rent whores, drunken tars and misfits, and she spied Bella's 'man' slouched in a dark nook not far from the door. As expected, it was Amos Furniss.

'Very wise, girlie,' he said as she hop-skipped up to him on her crutch.

He slid a bag off his shoulder and held it open; gritting her teeth, Friday took a small leather pouch containing one hundred and fifty pounds in notes from her own reticule and jammed it in.

'I hope someone murders you for that on the way home,' she said so viciously she spat on him.

Furniss cackled. 'Better start saving for the next lot.'

'Fuck you.' Friday swung around and hobbled away.

'Unless,' Furniss called after her, 'she decides to tell the pigs, that is.'

Friday ignored him, but his words sent an icy spear of fear into her belly — as, of course, he'd intended them to.

Outside the Black Rat, in the sharp sea air and the glimmering moonlight, she raised her crutch, whacked it against the ground so hard it broke, and screamed, *'Fuck, fuck, fuck!'*

'Hey, hey,' Jack said, grabbing her arm. 'Settle down!'

'*You* fucking settle down!' Friday said, aiming a slap at him.

'*I'm* not upset. Come on, calm down. Come on, that's it.'

Friday couldn't stop the tears of rage spilling down her cheeks.

Jack took her hand. 'Come on, let's go home and open the gin and you can tell me about it.'

'I *can't* tell you, Jack. I just can't.'

'Well, let's open the gin anyway.'

Adam had been away for eleven days, and Sarah was running out of things to do to frighten Esther. She'd heated the milk very early one morning so it curdled, and replaced all the fresh produce in Esther's pantry with rotten fruit and vegetables bought for a penny from a costermonger very happy to offload it; she'd laboriously and very quietly moved all the furniture she could around in the parlour, which had taken half the night; she'd left one of Esther's own turds in a dish tucked overnight into a recess above a beam in Esther's bedroom so that the smell permeated the whole chamber; and she'd spent several hours another night walking ponderously up and down the stairs, making sure every tread creaked as she trod on it. It was all having the desired effect, however, as Esther was beside herself. The bags beneath her eyes were enormous and a dreadful purple colour, and her skin had gone pasty and spotty.

Fortunately, Sarah was up so often and so late at night perpetrating the 'haunting' that she looked just as awful, and was able to commiserate regarding their shared fatigue without lying, though her fear of the 'ghost' was of course pure fabrication. It clearly pained Esther to have to discuss even her fear with her, but Adam had gone and there was no one else. She would not talk to Bernard about it, sensing perhaps, Sarah thought, that he didn't like her, though he was eager every morning to hear from Sarah about the ghost's latest escapade.

'Have you consulted a clergyman?' he'd suggested on the fifth day of Adam's absence. 'The missus and I did. Came and said a few prayers and sprinkled some holy water around. Didn't work, mind you.'

But this morning he didn't have any useful suggestions, or even a smile. He'd been in the dining room with Esther, having his morning tea, but now he'd come into the workroom where Sarah was putting the finishing touches to a gold chain-link bracelet.

'Sarah, lass. I've some bad news.'

Sarah glanced up, her heart beating just a little bit faster.

'I'm sorry, love, there's no easy way for me to say this.' He indicated a document in his hand. 'These are papers to return you to the Factory.'

Sarah dropped the bracelet; it slithered into the middle of the pigskin apron. 'What? But she can't! Only Adam can sign that!'

Bernard's voice was very gentle. 'Love, he has signed it.'

Sarah's heart hammered violently, she couldn't catch her breath and a wave of dizziness washed over her. 'But …'

Bernard stepped forwards, a hand out as though to placate her, but she leapt up from the stool and backed away from him.

'Often an assignment doesn't work out, Sarah. Who you end up working for is a very arbitrary thing. It's a lottery. I was assigned twice before I settled somewhere.'

'But I've been here for over a year! We work well together! I thought …'

But clearly it didn't matter what the fuck *she* thought, did it? Adam didn't want her working with him any more, and that was that. He'd signed the papers and left it to Bernard to tell her while he was away. Gutless *bastard*.

'Did you know about this?' she demanded.

Bernard's head jerked back. 'Me? I had no idea. Esther only just gave me the papers.'

'Give me a look at that,' Sarah said, snatching it out of his hand.

But there it was, Adam's distinctive signature at the bottom of the page. She marched over to the cabinet where the records of all the materials that came into the workshop were kept, yanked out a drawer and pulled out a receipt she knew he'd signed only a fortnight ago. The signatures were exactly the same.

She waved the Factory papers at Bernard. 'She's a screever, you know. That's why she was transported, for forgery.'

Bernard nodded. 'That has occurred to me. But to all intents and purposes what she's given me are papers signed by Adam to return you to the Factory. And she insists he wants you gone by the time he gets back. She wants you to leave today, in fact.'

'I'll bet she bloody does.'

'Between you and me,' Bernard said, lowering his voice, 'I think she thinks that if you leave, so will our supernatural visitor.'

Or had Esther realised *she* was behind Rachel's ghost? Sarah wondered. 'No, Bernard,' she said, her initial shock subsumed now by a rapidly escalating sense of outrage. 'There's a lot more to it than that. She's *jealous*. She's jealous because Adam spends so much of his time with *me*. *That's* why she wants me gone.'

Bernard's brows went up. 'And does she have reason to be jealous?'

'I'm not sharing his bed, if that's what you're asking.'

Sighing, Bernard said, 'Well, I'll put in a good word for you at the Factory. I'll tell Ann Gordon I've been supervising you and I've been very happy with your behaviour. And I'll talk to Ruthie. Perhaps we could manage another servant ourselves.'

'Thank you,' Sarah mumbled, trying to sound grateful.

Although she strongly suspected Esther had forged Adam's signature on the papers, she couldn't banish the baneful thought that Adam might have signed them himself, and the idea made her feel horrible — humiliated and sick.

Was her work not up to standard? Was she not clever or amusing enough? Or was he just bored with looking at her plain, scarred face and thin little body? Then it suddenly occurred to her that he might finally have realised she'd been stealing from him all these months, and that the warning he'd given her before he'd left was not to assist her in any way, but to tell her off. Her stomach clenched as unaccustomed shame surged through her. And if he was aware of that, then perhaps he knew she was also responsible for the 'ghost'.

'What is it?' Bernard asked.

'Nothing.' Sarah strode around the workshop gathering up her personal possessions. Bugger Adam Green; if he didn't want her here, then she was happy to leave. He was spineless anyway — spineless, hen-pecked and a milksop. 'How am I supposed to get out to Parramatta?'

'I'm to deliver you.'

Sarah thought quickly. 'Will you take me to my friend's house first? Please? I need to give her some things I can't take to the Factory.'

Bernard nodded.

'No,' Esther said from the doorway. 'Mr Cole, I want you to take her straight to the Female Factory.'

Sarah wondered how long she'd been listening. Bloody *cow*.

'If that's what you'd prefer, Mrs Green,' Bernard said impassively.

'It is. And Sarah, I want every single thing of yours out of that room upstairs, do you understand? And leave your house keys.'

'I'll take everything that's mine,' Sarah said. 'Except perhaps for Rachel. It's *you* she's so angry at, Esther, not me.'

Esther blanched but glared at her. 'Just get packed and get out.'

It didn't take Sarah long to gather her things, including her satchel containing her set of skeleton keys and safe-breaking tools, and the Charlotte fund hidden beneath the attic floorboards. She had her own canvas bag that held her clothes and Bernard found her a box for her cups, saucers and teapot. They left through the shop door, which Esther refrained from slamming after them; perhaps, Sarah thought, too conscious of the neighbours' scrutiny.

'We'll walk to my house and collect my gig,' Bernard said. Sarah's beautiful cushions made by Harrie were jammed under one arm, a rug was rolled under the other and a pair of curtains printed with birds and flowers fluttered gaily from his shoulders. 'Where did you say your friend lives?'

'She'll be at work by now, on Argyle Street. She's at Elizabeth Hislop's establishment.'

'Bette Hislop! I've known Bette for years. Magnificent woman. And your friend ...?'

'Is a prostitute, yes.'

'Well, we'll collect the gig first. My poor legs won't carry me as far as Argyle Street. Not carting all this.'

'Bernie Cole, as I live and breathe!' Elizabeth Hislop opened the door wider to let him in.

'Hello, Bette, love. It's been a few years, hasn't it? You're still a picture, though, I see.'

'Oh, get away with you. And Sarah Morgan. Hello, dear.' Elizabeth frowned at the odd pair standing in her foyer.

'I'm on my way back to the Factory,' Sarah explained. 'It's a bit sudden and I was wondering, could I speak with Friday, please?'

'Actually, she's with a customer at the moment.'

'No, I'm not,' Friday called from the stairs. 'Just finished.' Looking worried, she hurried down and gave Sarah a hug. 'What are you doing here? What's happened?'

'Esther bloody Green's sending me back to the Factory. Or Adam is, I'm not sure. Anyway, that's where I'm going. Bernard's taking me.'

'The Factory? Right *now*?'

Sarah nodded grimly.

'But ... when did all this happen?'

'About an hour ago.'

'Bloody hell, Sarah. Did he finally wake up?'

Elizabeth and Bernard exchanged uneasy glances.

'Don't know and don't give a bugger,' Sarah snapped. 'It was time to move on anyway. I've had a bloody gutsful of the pair of them.'

Friday knew that wasn't true, not as far as Adam was concerned at least, but wisely kept her mouth shut.

Sarah turned to Elizabeth. 'Do you mind if I speak with Friday in private for a few minutes, please?'

'Not at all. Use my office.'

Friday led Sarah into Elizabeth's private room and closed the door. 'Fucking hell, Sarah, what's all this about?'

Sarah sat in Elizabeth's chair. 'I *think* that bitch Esther forged Adam's signature on the papers to send me back to the Factory. Either that or Adam really did sign them and left Bernard to tell me while he was away.'

Friday could see from Sarah's pale, pinched face, stiff posture and repeated blinking that her contemplation of the latter possibility was hurting her very much.

'But why?'

'Wasn't told a reason.'

'But you were doing so well there. Adam said so. He said his profits had improved no end because of you, didn't he?'

Sarah nodded. Then she shrugged.

'Well, how do you feel about it?' Friday asked.

'Too bad. His loss.'

But Friday knew this for what it was.

'Anyway,' Sarah said, 'you'll have to look after the Charlotte fund. Well, what's bloody well left of it. I can't have it in the Factory. It'll be nicked in five minutes.'

'It'll be nicked in five minutes here, too. I'll ask Mrs H if I can keep it in the safe.'

'There's something else. If Esther *did* forge Adam's signature, it could be because she suspects I'm behind the ghost business.' Sarah looked Friday in the eye. 'So, what if the haunting continues while I'm not there?'

'Well, how can it, if you're out at Parramatta stuck in the Factory? Oh.'

Esther sat at her dressing table applying Gowland's Lotion to her face with hands that would not stop shaking. At six shillings a quart the lotion was very pricey and one had to pay the cost of importing it on top of that, but her complexion lately had been so dreadful — lifeless and with tiny pimples erupting across her chin and nose — it was definitely worth the expense.

She had checked the locks on her bedroom door, and the shop and back doors twice, and been around to every window to ensure that they, too, were all firmly closed, despite the warmth of the night. There were lamps burning downstairs with enough oil to last until morning, another on the landing outside, and two here in her chamber. Sarah Morgan had been gone five nights now, and although she didn't miss the sly bitch at all during the day, she did wish there was someone with her in the house after dark. Someone ... alive.

The first two nights that Sarah was gone had been heaven. She'd not heard a sound. There had been no ominous footsteps on the stairs, no chilling dragging noises from the parlour, no foul stenches straight from the grave, and she'd ventured downstairs in the mornings to find everything exactly as she'd it left the previous evening, which reinforced a private suspicion she'd harboured for several weeks. What if the ghost hadn't been real? What if someone had been trying to drive her insane? Adam, perhaps, so he could lock her away in the lunatic asylum and have his way with Sarah Morgan, or even Sarah herself?

But, oh God, the night before last, it had all started up again, and her fear and the extent of her dismay had rendered her physically sick. It was real, all of it — the spirit of the dead girl Rachel was back from the grave and in this house.

First had been the *tack, tack, tack* of something hitting her bedroom window. She'd opened it and leant out, but the moonlit yard had been still and empty. It had gone on all night accompanied by the sound of a girl sobbing — first outside, then seemingly from within the house, a low muffled sound that had risen to a desperate, high keening, which had tapered away just when Esther had thought her nerves couldn't bear it a moment longer. Then it had begun its torturing ascent all over again.

Last night the tapping had begun in her very bedroom, making its way across the floor, then, an hour or so later, across the ceiling where it had turned into aggressive thumping, knocking off little flakes of plaster and dislodging a large spider that had dropped onto her bedclothes. She'd squashed it, then pulled the blanket over her head and lay there quivering with terror to await sunrise.

The dragging sounds had also started up once more in the parlour, and when she'd gone down this morning the furniture had all been jammed into the hallway. *All* of it. Bernard Cole, when he'd arrived for work just before nine o'clock, had been amazed, and far too entertained by the spectacle for Esther's liking.

But he'd waddled off and returned with someone to help put all her pieces of furniture back where they belonged, and had also offered to have his wife spend the night in the house with Esther if she so wished. No, she did not wish; she would rather be dragged by the hair through the gates of hell than spend a night under the same roof as Ruthie Cole, the common baggage.

Surely Adam would be home in a few days. She really did not know how much longer she could tolerate this. They would have to sell the lease to the shop and house and move to other premises immediately: there was no other thing to be done. Adam would just have to work harder to compensate for any drop in their income.

She took the pins from her hair and began to brush it, listening as she always did these days — these *nights* — for strange and untoward sounds. But it wasn't just noises, she could *feel* the dead girl's spirit, a cold hollowness that drifted through the house, lowering the temperature in doorways and in the hall and on the stairs. Twice she thought she'd even caught glimpses of her floating up near the ceiling, her vindictive and accusing face surrounded by a tangle of wafting hair, her ghostly presence rendering the lamplight a bilious green colour, the pattern on the expensive new wallpaper visible through her grave-thin limbs and wasted body.

But no spirit would dare appear tonight, not in here. She'd taken all the crosses and amulets and mezuzah from downstairs and arranged them around her bedroom, bar one large cross she'd nailed to the outside of her bedroom door, and filled eight preserving jars with rosemary cuttings and set them on the floor against the walls. As further insurance, she'd sprinkled around and over the bed a vial of holy water a Catholic acquaintance had obtained for her, just in case the girl Rachel had been a Catholic.

Esther finished brushing then quickly plaited her hair. She checked yet again that her bedroom door was locked — not that a lock would stop a spirit, she knew that — and at last climbed into bed, leaving the two lamps burning. She pulled the sheet and blanket up to her chin and lay sweating in the night's heat, staring up at the ceiling, listening to the house as it creaked and ticked. Somewhere not far away a couple of dogs exploded into savage barking, the sound echoing up the gully forged by Tank Stream.

Minutes passed. Next door the neighbour's cat started its nightly yowling. If Esther could operate a gun she would have shot it by now.

But there was no tapping, and there were no footsteps.

Sweat trickled down her temples and pasted her nightgown to her chest; unable to bear it, she threw off the blanket.

An hour passed.

Her eyelids were so heavy. Nothing had happened. Perhaps, tonight, it wouldn't. Perhaps the amulets were working.

She drifted off to sleep.

Two hours later she jerked awake.

What was that? It came again; something bumping against the underside of the bed. And a dreadful, low, demonic growling. She leapt up onto her knees and stared down at the mattress.

For a moment everything was silent and still, then came a barrage of such violent thumping and banging the bed itself shifted across the floor.

She shrieked, scrambled off it and lunged for the door, which wouldn't open. Remembering she'd locked it, she fumbled wildly with the bolt until it shot back, and ran out and down the stairs. Screaming her head off, she hurtled through the shop, wrestled with the front door and burst out into the street.

Upstairs, Friday rolled out from beneath Esther's bed, barely recognisable in a shirt and trousers, the seat stretched rather tightly across her backside, with burnt cork rubbed all over her face and cobwebs festooning her tied-back hair. Giggling madly, Jimmy Johnson appeared on the other side looking equally dishevelled.

Friday urged, 'Hurry up, we'll only have a minute!'

They pelted down the stairs, Friday still favouring her healing leg, and escaped the house through the back door, stopping for a moment to retrieve Sarah's skeleton keys from their hiding place behind a bush.

'This is a flaming nice set of screws,' Jimmy remarked, his teeth flashing in the moonlight. 'Do you think she'll notice if we don't give them back?'

'Yes, I bloody do,' Friday replied. 'Now hurry up and get over that fence.'

There was no time to open the gate; Friday gave Jimmy such an energetic leg up he landed flat on his back on the other side. It didn't stop him giggling, though; he hadn't had such a lark since his London days.

When Adam arrived back in Sydney, it was to a household in complete disarray.

He was sorry that Esther had relocated to a ladies' lodging house, and concerned for her wellbeing, but profoundly angered by her dismissal of Sarah.

'So you didn't sign the papers?' Bernard asked.

'No, I did not. It's never once crossed my mind.'

'Well, that lass has an idea you did. If you want my advice, if you want her back you'd better get out to Parramatta fairly smartly.'

'Christ.' Adam ran his hand through his hair. He was tired from travelling, and hadn't had a decent wash in days. 'What on earth possessed her to do it?'

'Your esteemed good woman?' Bernard gave an eloquent shrug: who knew why women did the things they did? 'You can probably answer that better than I can.'

But Adam wasn't really listening. He looked at his watch. 'If I hired a mount and left now I could get there by early evening.'

'I'm surprised to hear myself saying this,' Bernard said, sounding it, 'but hadn't you better attend to Esther first? She's in the most terrible state, particularly after being alone here at night.'

'For God's sake,' Adam said, biting off the words one by one. 'If she hadn't sent Sarah back to the Factory she wouldn't have *been* alone, would she?'

'Go and see her, Adam. Get that sorted out first.'

'No. At least, not until tonight. I have to think first. This time she has absolutely gone too far.'

Adam and Esther walked back from the lodging house on upper Castlereagh Street in frosty silence, their discussion having petered out by the time they'd reached Market Street. Esther had complained bitterly about the terrifying experiences that had driven her out of her own home, and the dreadful conditions she'd had to endure in the lodging house; the cheap, mismatched furniture and hideous rag rugs and the like. And the women there! She wouldn't be surprised to learn they were all on the town. She hadn't needed too much persuading to return to George Street, despite its unearthly intruder, now that Adam was back. They would only be there a day or two anyway, she informed him, because he was to set about finding new premises immediately. She would not live in that house a moment longer than she had to.

Adam had lit all the lamps before he'd gone to fetch her; he was extremely annoyed and disappointed with Esther, but there was no sense in frightening her unnecessarily. He deposited her travelling case in the hall, then sat her down at the dining-room table.

'What?' she said. 'I've to see to supper.'

'No, supper can wait. I want to talk to you.'

'About what?'

'You know very well, Esther. You forged my signature, didn't you?'

For a moment she looked as though she might lie about it, which would be pointless and they both knew it, because who else could have done it?

'What if I did?'

'Well, why? Why did you send her back?'

'God have mercy, you are so stupid sometimes, Adam. Because I don't *want* her here.'

'But why not?'

Esther banged her hands on the table. 'Because she brought the ghost of that girl with her! You have *no* idea what it's been like for me! I've been terrorised *day and night*! It's driving me *insane*!'

Again, Adam thought wearily. 'Is that all?'

'What do you mean, is that *all*? That's enough, isn't it?'

'I do know you've been very frightened by all this … activity, and I agree, it has been rather puzzling.'

'*Puzzling?* It's been *horrific*!'

'And I do understand how badly it's affected your nerves. But Esther, you'd taken against Sarah before any of that had even started. This is all still to do with Cynthia, isn't it?'

Esther's face screwed up in fury and she shouted, 'Cynthia, Cynthia, *bloody* Cynthia! *Why* is it whenever you say her name it sounds like you *really* want a fuck?'

Adam stared at her incredulously. 'What? What the hell does that mean?'

'You just *can't* let her go, can you? And now there's Sarah. I've seen the lewd way you look at her. Oh, you think you're hiding it, but you're not. I know.'

Adam felt himself go red because she was entirely accurate about his attraction to Sarah, though he would never act on his desire. He'd learnt his lesson.

'Oh God, I'm right, aren't I?' Horrified that she'd proved herself correct, Esther grabbed a salt bowl and hurled it at Adam's head, the contents scattering everywhere. He dodged and it missed. 'She's a whore, Adam, a common whore! *That's* why I got rid of her!'

Brushing salt out of his hair, Adam said, 'I'm fetching her back tomorrow.'

'You are not! If you do, I'll take matters into my own hands. I swear I will.'

Abruptly, Adam stood. 'I'll speak to you in the morning.'

As he walked past the end of the table, Esther leapt up and punched him on the arm. He ignored it. She followed him down the hall, hitting his back and slapping at his head; at the foot of the stairs he turned and in silence pushed her away.

When he reached his room he locked his door.

Part Two

With Feet that Make No Sound

Chapter Nine

Sarah had only been back at the Factory a little over a week but already it felt like months. When Mrs Dick had asked her what she'd done to ruin such a good assignment, Sarah had had to walk away before she hit her.

Nothing much had changed. The food was still deeply unappetising and the servings miserable, the living conditions were awful and the hospital remained a dire place to be. There were a few old faces, perhaps the oldest being Matilda Bain's. Janie and the children were well, however, and Sarah had to admit it was very nice to spend time with them, even if it was within the confines of the Factory.

She had been returned as a first-class inmate, which meant she could be reassigned at any time. She'd worried that as a returnee she would be relegated to second class, separated from Janie and the babies, and therefore on probation, which would mean she would have to earn her way back into first class, but perhaps Bernard had bunged someone a bribe. If he had, she'd find a way to repay him because he'd done her a very big favour; she had to make money and the best place to do that was in town, and the only way to get into town was to be assigned there.

Sarah had been thinking about the past fifteen months and realised now she'd become too comfortable working for Adam

Green; far too comfortable, lazy and really quite dangerously deluded. She'd allowed herself to believe that while he admired her skills as a jeweller he also liked her for herself, and obviously she'd been mistaken. He thought no more of her personally than he did of the cove who came every six months to dig a new hole for the crapper. She'd lost her finely honed edge, and because of that her instinct had failed and she hadn't seen this coming. This was her own fault and she must never let it happen again.

'Penny for your thoughts?' Janie said.

'Not worth that much.' Sarah wiped Charlotte's mouth with the hem of her apron. She'd done a particularly long dribble, stretching all the way from her plump bottom lip to her fist.

'Bet they are.'

'I don't know. I'm just thinking that sometimes I need to kick my own arse.'

Janie snorted. 'We all need to do that.'

'How's it been here? Really?' Sarah asked. 'Be honest. Wouldn't you much rather be somewhere else?'

'What, working for some bossy old bag running me ragged every day? No thanks. Me and the kids are fine here.'

'You sure? Two babies are a lot to look after.'

'Not for me.'

That was probably true, Sarah thought; Janie was a born mother.

'I don't mind,' Janie went on. 'I know I moan about it here but Pearl looks after me. I got plenty of money and supplies thanks to you lot, and most of the girls aren't so bad. They're my sort. Mrs Gordon's all right. Letitia Dick's a bitch but, well, I know how to stay out of her way.'

'Don't you ever want to see what's outside the wall?'

'Yeah, one day. But right now me job's being a ma, isn't it? You'll know what it's like when your turn comes.'

'Don't know if it will.' Sarah couldn't think of much that might be worse; she'd never really fancied the idea of having children of her own.

'Get away. You're fond of these two, aren't you?'

They looked down at Charlotte and Rosie sitting on the ground in their nappies and nothing else, tossing handfuls of dirt at each other's legs and squealing with delight.

'Very, as long as I can hand them back to you.'

A shadow fell over them. 'Are you Sarah Morgan?' a girl asked.

Sarah squinted up at her. 'Who wants to know?'

'If you are, there's a visitor for you in the visitors' room,' the girl declared.

'Harrie or Friday?' Janie guessed.

'Not Harrie, she'll be at work,' Sarah said. 'It's not visiting day, either. It could be Bernard Cole. He did say he'd think about getting me assigned to him.' Which wouldn't be so bad, she supposed. Except she'd feel a bit low stealing from him, especially if he had paid a bribe to get her into first class. Bloody guilt — it really was playing havoc with the way she worked.

She stood, brushed the dirt off her skirt and made her way to the visitors' room. The door was closed so she knocked and opened it.

Adam Green sat alone in the austere little room, his hat and gloves on the table. He looked tired and exasperated.

He nodded at her tersely. 'Sarah.'

Startled into silence and instantly alert, her thoughts racing, she stayed where she was, a hand gripping the door knob for support. Was this about the missing jewellery? Was he going to tell her he'd reported her to the police?

He half rose, then sat down again. 'I'm so sorry about Esther.'

She remained quiet, waiting.

'I had no idea she was going to do that,' he said. 'I would never have agreed to it. I'd like you to come back. Please.'

Sarah's heart soared and she struggled mightily to squash her elation. 'Is that what Esther wants?' she said, not bothering with 'Mrs Green'.

'It doesn't matter what Esther wants. I've told her I'm bringing you back. Today.'

'She doesn't want me in the house, does she?'

Adam sighed. 'No.'

'Well, then I can't come back.'

Sounding as irritable as he looked, Adam said, 'For God's sake, Sarah, will you come in? And close that door.'

Sarah shut the door behind her, chose the chair farthest from Adam's, and sat down. 'I don't understand why she hates me so much.'

'She's jealous of you, and she thinks you brought the ghost.' Adam's eyes narrowed, just a little. 'It isn't real, is it, the ghost.' A statement, not a question.

Sarah cast about for a way to agree, without actually admitting to him that she was responsible for orchestrating all of it. 'It's as real as she thinks it is.'

'You've expended quite a lot of effort, haven't you?'

'I don't know what you mean.'

Adam's gaze bored into her: she could see he was angry — really *quite* angry — but she wasn't at all sure now it was directed at her. Still, she glared back, refusing to lower her eyes.

'I suppose I should ask you why,' he said.

'Why what?'

'Why you bothered with the whole charade.'

'It's to do with loyalty, Adam, which is something Esther wouldn't know the first thing about. And loyalty to friends continues even after they die. She should have let me go to the cemetery when Rachel was buried. It serves her right. And, yes, I know she's jealous of me, but God knows why. That's just ridiculous.'

And Adam thought, Oh God no, it isn't, not at all. If I could only tell you, Sarah. If I could only touch you.

Instead he said, 'Will you come back?'

'No. I won't. Not if she's there.'

So Adam did something he'd been hoping to avoid, and which Sarah had clearly forgotten was within his power.

'Well, you haven't been physically mistreated during your assignment to me, you're given enough food, you're well-housed and not particularly overworked. You can lay no valid claim against me. I've explained to the superintendent here that my signature was forged on those papers and that you were returned without my permission. I'm your master, Sarah, and I'm telling you that you *will* come back to Sydney Town with me.'

Utterly shocked, Sarah stared at him. 'You rotten —'

'That's enough! Now go and pack your things.'

It was dark by the time they arrived at George Street, neither having said a single word during the long, rain-filled journey back. The house was silent, though the lamps were burning downstairs. On the dining-room table was a basket piled with Bernard's ubiquitous buns, a note folded between the top two, sticky with jam. Adam opened it and read:

> *My Dear Adam,*
>
> *Supper for you and the lass. The day's takings are in the Safe. Her Ladyship was abroad before Midday, but I didn't see her at all after that. Wouldn't be surprised if Something was astir there. Come by if you need anything.*
>
> *Your Friend,*
> *Bernard Cole*

'Wait here, I'll just check on Esther,' Adam said to Sarah, a worm of dread stirring in his belly.

He climbed the stairs with legs that felt as heavy as lead and approached her closed bedroom door. She hadn't taken that cross off it, he noted.

'Esther?'

No response. But was that busy flies he could hear buzzing? Or just his imagination?

His heart hammering, he turned the knob and pushed but nothing happened. Oh God, she'd locked it. He put his shoulder to the door; it resisted, grown tight in the frame with the damp warmth of the day, then burst open. Stepping in, he immediately looked up, squinting against what he might have to witness, but to his immense relief there was no purple-faced monstrosity dangling slackly from the beam. And there was no limp, staring corpse slumped across the bed, dead from laudanum or from the razor, slashed white forearms atop huge roses of blood staining the quilt. Feeling dizzy and aware his pulse was galloping, he bent over and breathed deeply in and out. His worst nightmare — his single, greatest fear — had been that she would one day actually do what she had for years been threatening.

When he felt slightly recovered he crossed to Esther's dressing table. Her lotions and jars and her silver-backed hairbrush had gone; her drawers were empty. So was her clothes press, except for a single sheet of her personalised notepaper left conspicuously on a shelf.

The note read:

Adam
    I have left you. You will never find me. I wish you and
that whore nothing but bad luck and misery.
    Esther

He stared at the note for several minutes, then put it back on the shelf and went downstairs.

'She's gone,' he said.

'Esther has?' Sarah said, startled into speaking to him.

'Yes.'

'Gone where?'

'I don't know. She left a note. She says she's left me.'

'Oh.' Sarah shut her mouth; it would be hypocritical of her to say she was sorry.

Adam picked up her bag and the box containing her china.

'What are you doing?' she said quickly.

'Taking your things up to your old room. Or would you rather have Esther's room now?'

Sarah suppressed a shudder. 'No, my old one's fine, thank you.'

She could easily have carried her belongings herself, but let him do it. Lighting a taper candle from a lamp she followed him up the stairs, the realisation sinking in that it would just be the two of them living in the house now. The prospect was both liberating and daunting. They would be free to get on with their work uninterrupted by Esther's endless carping and tantrums, but on the other hand she had no intention of becoming Adam's substitute wife. Even if she happened to be in love with him — which she *wasn't* — that would require trusting him. The only people she'd ever fully trusted were Friday, Harrie and Rachel. She still had Friday and Harrie, and they were enough. Look at the way she'd felt when she'd thought Adam had sent her back to the Factory; she certainly wasn't going to put herself in that position again. Even now, was she really certain he *hadn't* signed those papers?

On the landing, Adam stopped. 'Er, can you cook?'

'Nothing fancy. Just basic meals.'

'That sounds excellent. Would you mind taking care of that side of things?' He looked embarrassed. 'I don't expect you to clean the house the way Esther made you do it.'

Good, she thought. I wasn't going to.

He stepped aside so she could climb the narrow stairs to her attic room ahead of him.

'I don't know if there's any linen on the bed,' he said.

'It's all right. I know where it's kept.'

She opened the door, crossed to the lamp and lit it; as expected Esther had stripped the bed, obliterating any trace of Sarah ever having been there. She would have to go around to Friday's and collect her nice furnishings.

Adam put her things down. 'Well, I'll leave you to it, then. I think I'll turn in.'

'It's been a long day,' Sarah agreed.

'I take it we won't be seeing any more supernatural activity?'

'If we do it won't be anything to do with me.'

Adam stood in the doorway, the lamplight illuminating only half his face. He looked very tired, but some time during the last hour his anger had ebbed away. The news about Esther barely seemed to have registered with him yet.

'Sarah?'

She waited, watching him. His eyes glittered in the honeyed light and he appeared to be collecting his thoughts.

But all he said was, 'Sleep well.'

He'd left her alone in the shop for an hour or so while he went to the bank, which was a perfect opportunity for her to steal whatever she liked — a watch chain, a bracelet, perhaps some earrings, though she couldn't take loose stones today as she would have to crack the safe because Adam had the key and Friday still had her tools.

However, a terrible thing was happening; she couldn't do it. She drifted around the shop looking into all the display cabinets, her fingers almost physically itching, but unable to actually take anything. It was the most bizarre sensation. And while her head was busy assessing what Mr Skelton might give her for various items, some other part of her — some combination of her heart and gut — was *loudly* insisting that what she was doing was wrong and to desist. This had never before happened to her, and she didn't quite know what to do. In the end she gave up and retreated behind the counter empty-handed, wondering what on earth was going on.

She served several customers, and was still wondering, when Adam returned looking very grim-faced.

He waited until the shop was empty, then said, 'I'm afraid I have some bad news, Sarah.'

This time it'll be about my thieving, she thought, only half aware that as usual she was thinking about herself. Thank God I haven't got anything in my pockets or tucked down my front.

'Esther's cleaned me out,' Adam said. 'She's been to the bank, forged my signature and withdrawn every penny I had.'

'*Both* accounts?' Sarah exclaimed. He'd be ruined!

'How do you know I have two bank accounts?' He leant into the shop window and turned the sign so it read *CLOSED*.

Shite; she could hardly admit she'd picked the lock on his desk and gone through his private papers. 'Every businessman has two bank accounts. Don't they? Surely the bank is liable, for handing it over to her.'

'My signature appeared to be on the withdrawal note. Evidently she told them I'd sent her to collect the money.' Adam gave a humourless laugh. 'They even offered to escort her home as she was carrying such a lot of money, but she declined. And do you know why?'

Sarah shook her head.

'She wasn't coming home. She went straight down to the quay and boarded a ship an hour before it sailed for England.'

Sarah stifled a gasp. The cunning bitch! 'And this was yesterday, while you were out at Parramatta getting me?'

'Yes.'

'Oh, Adam, I really am sorry. Just a minute, she can't leave New South Wales, can she? Not if she only has a conditional pardon.'

'Esther has a full pardon. She can go anywhere. My pardon's the conditional one. I even had to get permission to go to Van Diemen's Land.'

'So you can't follow her?'

'What would be the point? Chances are I wouldn't find her. She could disembark at any port her ship puts into between here and England, and just disappear once she arrives home. The thing is, Sarah, seven years ago I took out a ten-year lease on this shop. I pay the rent twice a year, in February and July. It's a lot of money, even over two payments. Almost all the February payment was in the bank waiting to be paid —'

'And Esther's taken off with it?'

'Yes. Along with the working capital, some of which was earmarked to pay for that last shipment of bullion we bought. There wasn't much to speak of in my savings account, but that's gone, too, of course.'

Sarah had already realised that if Adam broke his lease agreement he would lose the shop, his income and his home, and would have to pay a heavy financial penalty. 'What will you do?'

'I really don't know. I could possibly scrape up the rent payment if we sell what we currently have in store at a steep discount, but then I wouldn't have the money to restock.' Adam thrust his hands into his coat pockets and stared down at his boots. 'I really don't know, Sarah.'

That evening Sarah served Adam an uninspiring supper of sausages, mashed potato and green beans. It was nothing like as fancy as the meals Esther had prepared but he barely seemed to notice and ate everything, wiping his plate clean of gravy with a bread roll.

'I'm sorry but there's no dessert,' she said. 'I didn't have time.'

'Of course not. You've been in the workshop all afternoon.'

And so she had, repairing an aquamarine and gold cannetille and meshwork choker belonging to some old trout whose fat neck had burst the clasp, but she'd been even busier thinking. A memory of something she'd said to Friday nearly a year earlier, about replacing the gems in the expensive pieces in Adam's shop with good paste and fencing the genuine stones, had been revived by the sparkling aquamarines in the broken choker. What if they had a regular supply of quality jewellery coming into the shop just long enough for the stones to be swapped? The sort of gems owned by well-heeled, fashionable, middle- and upper-class ladies who might perhaps appreciate having their jewels cleaned and valued free of charge? This was such an exciting possibility she'd squeaked, which she had to turn into a cough when Adam had looked at her.

'Yes?' he'd said.

'What?'

'You've that look on your face.'

'No I don't.'

But how crooked was he prepared to be, to keep his shop and business? Clearly he'd been on the wrong side of the law in the past, but he'd never demonstrated any dodgy inclinations since she'd worked for him. So what was he prepared to risk? She hadn't a clue.

She collected the supper plates, took them out to the kitchen, and put the kettle over the fire.

'Tea's coming,' she said as she sat down at the table again. There was no time to waste; she had to talk to him about it now if they hoped to have the rent money by February. Well, if *he* hoped to; it wasn't *her* business.

'You were quiet this afternoon,' Adam said softly.

'I was thinking.'

'So was I.'

He'd been contemplating Esther, and wondering why he didn't feel devastated, or at least bereft, because she'd deserted him. The night before as he'd lain in his lumpy bed, on top of the blanket because of the heat, he'd considered everything he'd felt on discovering she'd gone. There had been anger, embarrassment, frustration and regret, but overwhelmingly, relief. He'd expected to feel at least some degree of melancholy today as the truth of the situation had sunk in, but it simply hadn't happened. Instead there'd been a hollowness as though *something* had gone, but he couldn't define exactly what. Finally, at around midday, he'd realised what it was: his constant expectation that Esther was about to nag at or criticise him for some reason, and that was all.

It had occurred to him then he'd already done his grieving for their failed union, and that there was little left for him to feel except gratitude now he no longer had to worry about her tyrannical moods, her jealousies and tantrums and manic behaviour, and whether one day she really would take her own life. He was still bloody angry, though; she hadn't had to rob him of every single bloody penny. But then, being Esther, he supposed she had. She'd always been obsessed with money.

'What was occupying your mind?' he asked.

'Well, your predicament with the rent.' God, Sarah thought, if she wasn't careful how she did this, she really could be out on her ear. 'I've been trying to think of ways to come up with the money.'

'Well, that's very thoughtful of you, but it's not something you need to be concerned with. This is my burden, not yours.' Adam drew Esther's fancy cruet set towards him, rucking the tablecloth, and lined up its four condiment bottles together with the salt bowl, the mustard pot and the pepper shaker, then sat back, shoulders slumped. 'To be blunt, Sarah, I think I'm going to have to go on the flash again, just for a while. I can't think of any other way around it.'

'I'll just check the kettle,' Sarah said and rushed outside.

In the kitchen the kettle was steaming madly; she removed it from the fire and poured water into the teapot, shaking hands slopping boiling water onto the table. Leaning against it, she waited until her heartbeat found its normal rhythm again. That had been unexpected! She'd been so sure Adam's crooked days were behind him. If she happily went along with his plans, however, whatever they were, thereby demonstrating her own dishonesty, would he suspect her of stealing from him for more than a year? Christ, she'd only this second thought of that, and here she was about to suggest he operate a scam! And if she pretended she disapproved of what he had in mind, she'd have to leave. Though she might as well go; she seemed to have lost her will for stealing here, which meant the place was useless to her as a source of money. But she didn't *want* to leave. Shite!

She loaded up the tea tray and carried it into the dining room, set out the cups and saucers, sat and turned the teapot a couple of times.

Adam slid a piece of paper across the table.

Sarah glanced at it. It was a list arranged in two columns; jewellery, mostly small pieces, and loose stones, with dates beside them. She turned the paper over to see the same on the reverse side. An icy hand closed around her heart and her stomach plummeted. She recognised every piece.

He knew, and he must always have known.

She swallowed, her mouth suddenly as dry as chalk, and stared across the table at him.

Utterly dismayed, she whispered, 'What do you want?'

He sat with his arms crossed and his head slightly back, the lamplight making even deeper pools of his dark eyes. He wasn't smiling, but neither did he seem particularly angry. 'I would like us to be honest with each other, Sarah.'

'You haven't ...' Her voice cracked and she roughly cleared her throat.

He reached for the teapot, poured a cup and pushed it gently towards her. Some slopped into the saucer and Sarah thought irrelevantly that Esther would have told him off for that.

She sipped, burning her tongue. Her eyes watered. 'Why haven't you reported me to the police?'

Adam poured himself a cup. 'I'll tell you that one day, but not tonight.' He added sugar. 'You're as crooked as a dog's hind leg, aren't you?'

Why deny it? It was true. Sarah nodded.

'Does your conscience not bother you? Or don't you have one?'

Sarah shrugged. 'It didn't to start with. It does now.'

'And you fenced everything?'

'Yes.' The shock was subsiding, replaced now by fear and mounting anger. He knew about her stealing and with that knowledge he could blackmail her. She shouldn't have come back with him; she should have lied, accused him of rape and brutality, anything to stay in the Factory. Her first instinct had been right — she should never have allowed herself to trust him.

'What do you do with the proceeds?' he asked. 'I know you don't spend them on yourself.'

'That's my business.'

He sighed exasperatedly. 'You hold your cards so close, don't you?'

Sarah remained stiffly silent.

Gesturing at the list of stolen jewellery, he said, 'Keep it. Tear it up. Throw it on the fire, I don't care. I didn't show it to you to intimidate you.'

'Why, then? There'll be a copy anyway.'

'There isn't. And I showed you because I wanted you to see that I knew, and that I *haven't* done anything about it. I wanted you to see that I have faith in you and that I —' Abruptly, he stopped himself.

'How do I *know* there isn't a copy?' Sarah demanded.

Adam exploded. 'For fuck's sake, there just isn't, all right! You'll just have to trust me!'

Sarah blinked; she'd never heard him say fuck before.

He swept his hand through his hair. 'There's no copy, I'm not telling the police and I don't care about what you've pinched. My business is in trouble and I would very much like your help to rectify that. You're clearly rather practised at rackets and what have you, whereas all I know about is receiving. I'd like us to work together, Sarah, and we can't do that if we're hiding things from each other.'

'Well, you obviously know what my sins are,' Sarah snapped, but reminded herself that actually, he didn't, thank God. 'What are *you* hiding from me?' There was something, and she bloody well knew it.

Adam met her gaze, but couldn't hold it and gutlessly focused on the horseradish sauce bottle instead. Only that I love you, he thought, and that I'd give everything — my business, all the glittering, precious gems in my safe, even my freedom — to lie with you even for just a single night.

'Someone's tampered with the safe,' Elizabeth Hislop said, hands on ample hips, peering down at the solid, upright chest in her office and turning her two chins into three. 'See, around the lock? Someone's been at it with a chisel.'

The safe, made of heavy wooden slabs secured with iron hoops, remained closed, but it was clear an attempt had been made to prise open the door.

'Anything missing?' Friday asked nervously.

Elizabeth selected a key from the rattling collection on her chatelaine, stooped and unlocked the safe. The door opened with a squeak, revealing an interior divided by wooden partitions. Assorted cloth bags and a few small boxes sat on various shelves and five or six ledger books took up the rest of the space.

'Doesn't seem to be,' Elizabeth said, relieved.

Friday retrieved the bag containing the Charlotte fund and emptied it onto Elizabeth's desk. Paper money fluttered out and coins rolled everywhere.

'Hell's bells, Friday, is that all yours?' Elizabeth exclaimed, impressed. 'I hope you locked the door. The thief could be anyone.'

Friday quickly counted the money. 'It's all here.'

'Perhaps they were interrupted.'

Friday examined the safe door. 'Nah, this is a crap effort. They just couldn't get in. I'd say they weren't professionals, which makes me suspect someone here. Unless you've taken on a cracksman?' Friday knew of one who occasionally visited, but she certainly wouldn't leave a mess like this. Or a full safe.

'Not to my knowledge.'

'You're hardly ever out of your office, so it would have to be someone who could keep an eye on your door.'

'One of the girls?'

'Maybe.'

'Who?'

'Well, not Connie, it's just not in her nature. And not Hazel: she can barely open the sash on her robe she's that daffy, never mind a safe. Vivien, I'm not so sure. Same with Sophie. I'd think it unlikely of Esmerelda, Molly or Rose. Or Jane.'

'I don't know about Molly,' Elizabeth interrupted. 'I'm not convinced I totally trust her.'

'Really?'

Elizabeth made a rueful face.

'Well, I definitely wouldn't put it past Lou,' Friday said. 'She's always griping about not getting paid enough and the terrible prices she forks out for her work clothes.'

'Yes, well, she could wear the costumes I provide here,' Elizabeth said.

'Ooooh, I can't *abide* wearing second-hand clothes,' Friday mimicked in a silly falsetto. 'All that dirty skin.'

'They're laundered regularly. It's a funny attitude from someone happy to have entire dirty bodies all over them. Do you think it could have been her?'

Friday shrugged. 'Don't know. But then I'm biased. I don't like her.'

'Yes, I had noticed. Why not?'

'She's a bitch, and she's mean to some of the girls, especially Hazel.'

'Well, I'll keep an eye on her. In the meantime I'll get Jack to put an extra lock on the safe. Most of the money from the house and the hotel gets banked in the mornings, but I do keep my jewellery in there.' Elizabeth hesitated. 'Er, you don't think it could have been Jack, do you?'

'No. He's a bit flash, but he's loyal to you. He's a good man, Jack. You could put the safe somewhere else. What about in your room?'

'I'm hardly ever in my room. And I don't actually want it over in the hotel, I want it here where I can see it.'

'You didn't see it being broken into, though, did you?' Friday said. 'Does this house have a cellar?'

'No. It's built on solid rock.'

'Then where does that little wooden door by the back steps go to?'

Elizabeth sat down at her desk and bent her head over a ledger. 'That's not really a cellar. More of a coal hole.'

'But there isn't any coal. We have wood fires.'

Evidently concentrating on her columns, Elizabeth remained silent.

'Mrs H?'

Sighing, Elizabeth turned to face Friday. 'I've some old bits and pieces of furniture stored down there, a few trunks and the like. But the steps are steep and there are huge spiders everywhere. I don't like to go down there. It would be a ridiculous place to put the safe.'

'Just a thought,' Friday said. 'Keep your wig on.'

'Don't you be so cheeky.'

'Sorry.' Friday hesitated, then said, 'The banking, is it *your* bank account?'

'No, it isn't. I'm a woman — obviously. I'm not allowed to open an account. My husband had to open it in his name.'

Which started Friday thinking.

Matthew's arm was on fire. Leo had finished shading the lion two days previously and, as it usually did, the whole area had puffed up and become inflamed, causing considerable discomfort.

After his first session he'd had nightmares about his arm becoming horrifically infected and requiring amputation at the shoulder, which had frightened him so badly he'd gone to Dolly, the Vincents' house girl, and asked for a suitable ointment. She'd produced one but explained it was very greasy and would stain his clothing, so he'd let her dress the tattoo, the sight of which had almost caused her eyes to pop out of her head. Now, apparently and rather tiresomely, it was 'their little secret'. Since then he'd been through half a pot of the stinky unguent, consisting of hog's lard, white lead, red lead, bees' wax, black resin and common turpentine. Leo told him he could use it 'if you feel you really have to, lad, but it'll get better by itself, you know', but to leave the bandage off so a decent scab could form. Matthew had done as instructed, but as his shirts were indeed ruined and his arm didn't require amputation as he'd feared, he'd recently stopped using the ointment altogether.

Soon they would start on the peony, and Matthew thanked God he hadn't chosen some ridiculously huge and complicated design that would take months and months to complete.

Harrie was late. He had offered to escort her but she'd returned her acceptance of his invitation with a message to the effect that she would meet him here at the appointed time. It was quite a long way for her to walk. He hoped that explained her failure to so far materialise; far better that than she'd changed her mind. He'd thought last time she'd looked a little uncomfortable in the tearooms, so this time, as he was extending the invitation, he'd suggested they share a picnic in Hyde Park. It was after all the fashionable thing to do, and he'd noted on his invitation that she need only bring herself, as he would provide absolutely everything else. And he had, including a rug on which to sit, a very nice cold dinner, a pricey bottle of wine, a cheaper spare, and one of non-alcoholic cordial in case she was teetotal.

It was hot and he would have preferred to do without his coat, but one did not go out courting in one's shirtsleeves. His mother would faint at the very thought. It was a real pity there were no trees in the park. Oh well, he supposed it was better he appear tidy than too informal.

He raised his hand against the sun as he saw Harrie crossing Hyde Park towards him, accompanied by her friend, Friday Woolfe. Damn. He hoped she wasn't expecting to share their picnic; there was really only enough for two. With an acidic stab of disappointment he realised that Friday had probably already told Harrie about his tattoo, which was deeply annoying as, after it was completed and nicely healed, he'd been hoping to casually mention that he happened to have one, and yes, it was in fact the work of Leo Dundas. And perhaps Harrie would ask to see it, which would necessitate him having to remove his shirt, which might just lead to …

'Hello, Mr Cutler,' Friday said, towering above him. 'How's things?'

He squinted up at her, peering straight up her nose. She laughed and moved sideways.

He scrambled to his feet. 'Good afternoon, Harrie,' he said. And to Friday, the tiniest bit sourly, 'Why don't you call me Matthew? We've met often enough now.'

'Have you?' Harrie said, surprised.

'Well, we haven't really,' Friday replied, turning slightly and giving Matthew an exaggerated wink that Harrie couldn't see. 'But I'll call you Matthew. I'll call you anything you fancy. And you can call me Friday.'

Matthew perked up; perhaps she hadn't said anything after all. 'Would you like to join us?'

'No, thanks, I'm off visiting.' She pecked Harrie on the cheek. 'Have a nice time, love. Goodbye, Matthew.'

Harrie accepted Matthew's hand as he helped her settle on the rug, and they watched Friday sail off across the park, a vision in low-cut violet velvet that clashed with her hair, her wide-brimmed straw hat covered with a profusion of fake velvet hydrangeas. Now that the weather was warmer, she'd relegated her 'classy' gowns to the back of her clothes press and happily resurrected her more revealing costumes, much to Mrs H's frustration.

'I'm so sorry I'm late,' Harrie said.

'It's a long way to walk from the Rocks, isn't it?'

'Not really. I was held up.'

'Would you like some wine? Or perhaps cordial? You must be rather hot.'

'What sort of wine?' Harrie asked, who didn't know one from another.

'It's quite a nice French champagne by a house called Moët & Chandon,' Matthew said casually, showing her the label.

'Goodness, that looks expensive.'

I'll say it was, he thought, recalling the pergola plans he'd promised to draw for a colleague's private garden in exchange for the purchase of the wine at half its import price.

'A little,' he said modestly, setting out two champagne flutes he'd borrowed from Mrs Vincent. He wrestled with the wire collar around the bottle's cork, praying it wouldn't explode and the contents spew forth all over the rug. To his relief, he managed the task without incident and poured them each a glass, raising his in a toast. 'To happiness and good fortune.'

'Yes,' Harrie agreed. 'Happiness and good fortune.'

He watched as she lifted the flute to her lips and hesitantly sipped, looking for all the world as though she'd never tasted wine before.

Friday rapped on Adam Green's back door and sang out, 'Anybody home?'

'Hang on,' came Sarah's disembodied voice.

She appeared a moment later hurrying down the hallway, her sleeves pushed to her elbows and her hair falling out of its normally neat, low ponytail. Under one arm was a bundled sheet and a pair of pillowslips were draped over one shoulder.

'Still doing all the drudge work?' Friday observed disapprovingly. 'And on a Sunday.'

'Well, who else is going to do it?'

'Is Adam home?'

'Gone to see Bernard Cole.'

'When are you coming to pick up your things? Or should I send Jimmy up with them?'

Sarah dumped the linen on the dining-room floor. 'Could you send Jimmy? I'm just not going to get the time.'

'You've got time for tea, though, surely. Or ...' Friday whipped a bottle of gin out of her reticule. 'A drink?'

Sarah eyed the bottle, and took two tumblers from the 'chiffonier'. 'Perhaps just a small one. There's some lemons in the pantry.'

'Bugger off. I'm not ruining mine with lemon.'

Friday sat, opened the bottle and poured: a little for Sarah, lots for her. She'd seen Sarah twice since Adam had brought her home from the Factory. Esther sending her back had shocked the shit out of Friday; she'd realised Esther was a mad bitch, of course, but that had been *nasty*. She knew all about her leaving — bloody good riddance — Adam's consequent money woes, and him being aware all along of Sarah's thieving. She had to say she wasn't really surprised about the latter; Sarah was as cunning as a shithouse rat, but a man would have to be really stupid, or completely blind, not to notice all those bits and pieces disappearing from the shop. But it was as obvious as the nose on your face — to everyone, that was, except Sarah — that Adam was bursting to give her a good seeing-to.

Actually, it was a lot more than that, as Friday was well aware. It was in his voice when he spoke to her, and the way he looked at her, and how his body tensed whenever he went within five feet of her. And now that Esther had slung her hook Sarah could help herself, if only she didn't always insist on being such a prickly, mistrustful, independent little article. For which Friday refused to chastise her, because how the hell else were they supposed to survive in the world?

'Did you talk to Harrie about the bank?' Sarah asked.

Friday took a large sip of her drink, shuddered, and nodded. The gin was a bit rough. 'She's having a picnic with Matthew today. She said she'll ask him about it.'

'A picnic? Whose idea was that?'

'Matthew's, apparently.'

'I hope she knows what she's doing,' Sarah said. 'There'll be tears if she's not careful.'

'There're tears now, Sarah.'

They looked at each other.

'You don't seem that chirpy yourself,' Friday said.

'Neither do you. Have you been back to James Downey?'

'What for?'

'Well, it's been more than thirty days, hasn't it? Have you ... noticed anything?'

'I have been chasing the odd rabbit and barking at the full moon.'

'It's not funny, Friday. Don't joke about it.'

'Sorry, love. No, I've not noticed anything. I doubt those dogs were rabid. Just trained to kill, thanks to bloody Furniss.'

'How's your leg?'

Friday put her foot up on the table, flipped back her skirts and turned her ankle out. An L-shaped scar ran across the back of her calf, vividly purple against her white skin. There was no tissue or muscle missing, but the mark was very obvious.

'Ugly, isn't it?' she said. 'James said it'll fade over time, but I don't know. I wonder if Leo could tattoo over it?'

Sarah rolled her eyes.

'What?'

'You'll be getting your nose tattooed next. Well, Adam and I've decided what we're going to do.'

Friday moved her leg off the table. 'Is it a secret?'

'Yes, I'm not to tell anyone.'

'Well?'

'We're advertising in the papers that "Adam Green Fine Jewellery" are offering free cleaning and valuation of jewellery. Then, when people bring their jewellery in, and they all will because everyone likes something for nothing, especially rich folk, we replace the stones with paste and either sell them on or rework them into new pieces.'

'Can you sell them into a market as small as Sydney's?' Friday asked, peering into the bottom of her empty tumbler. She reached for the bottle.

'Possibly not. Not everything. Adam's talking to Bernard about export opportunities.'

'Back to England?'

'Maybe. I mean, there's enough pinched swag coming the other way.'

'Is there?' Friday was surprised.

'Where do you think Bernard gets half the stock for his shop?'

'Hadn't thought about it. Why would I?'

'Some of the jewellery we'll steal outright,' Sarah said.

'You don't think someone'll notice? Here I am, a rich matron bringing my necklace, earring and brooch set to Adam Green's to get it cleaned, and when I come back to collect it, it's not here any more.'

Sarah rolled her eyes again. 'That particular jewellery we *will* clean, value and give back. But the owner's left a record of where they live, haven't they, so I'll just go to the house and pinch it later. Not all of it, obviously, we don't want the dross. Just a few pieces we think we can best sell intact. And not so much that it looks suspicious, either. We won't need to take much, whether we replace stones or burgle outright.'

'But you don't like doing house burglaries. You told me that ages ago. And what if you get caught, Sarah?'

'What if you get caught whoring?'

'It's not the same,' Friday insisted.

'I won't get caught.'

'You might.'

'I won't.'

'And why are *you* taking all the risk? What's Adam doing?'

'He's risking just as much as I am. The only difference is I'll be going into the houses. I'm good at it, and it won't be very often. Let's be honest, it's not as though women in Sydney Town are so wealthy they own the equivalent of the Crown jewels.'

'That is true. But why, Sarah? You don't have to do this at all.'

'I do. What about Janie and the girls? We have to work twice as hard now to replace the money in the fund. I'll be taking a decent cut from the proceeds. How else can I make that sort of money? I thought I was getting away with robbing Adam but I wasn't, was I? If he'd been any other master I'd be in third class in the Factory by now, doing hard labour. Or on my way to somewhere even worse.'

But it wasn't *just* the Charlotte fund, and Friday knew it. Sarah enjoyed stealing, she relished the challenge and the thrill of it, and living a life that didn't involve challenges bored her absolutely stiff. Also, this was for Adam; despite her insistence that she wasn't interested in him, she was.

'Well, bloody well be careful,' Friday warned. 'If it all turns to shit make sure you're not the only one covered in it.'

Sarah shook her head. 'Adam wouldn't do that to me.'

Would he?

Chapter Ten

Hyde Park had only grown hotter as the afternoon stretched on, the remorseless sun beating down from a boundless sky and drawing up shimmering curtains of heat from the ground. Sunday equestrians trotted briskly around the riding track sweating heavily into their riding habits, their horses' hooves kicking up dust that settled grittily over picnickers and strollers alike. A handful of ladies who'd thought ahead gratefully raised their parasols; those who hadn't resigned themselves to headaches tonight and red noses tomorrow.

Harrie said, 'Thing is, Matthew, we got all this money and it jus' isn't safe. In the safe.' She giggled.

Matthew had moved the second bottle of wine beyond her reach, though she'd already poured herself a glass, now that she'd polished off most of the Moët. It was quite obvious she was drunk and, to be honest, he was more than a little shocked.

Aware he was being very bad-mannered, he nevertheless asked, 'Do you normally drink this much?'

'*Hell* no. *Never* drink. But you know, Matthew, you went to *such* a lot of trouble with this *love*ly picnic, I jus' thought it'd be so *rude* not to have a bit of everything.'

Oh God, it was his fault. She didn't drink and he'd forced the wine on her, and now look what had happened. What on earth would the Barretts think if he delivered her home in this state?

'Nice, though, the wine.' She scowled at her glass. 'Well, the firs' one. This one tastes like —' She burped. 'Ooh, par—' She burped again. 'Pardon. Cat piss.'

He extended his hand. 'I'll have it then, shall I?'

'Nooo! I never said I didn't wannit.' She set her glass aside, where he couldn't get at it. Squinting up at the sky, she remarked dreamily, 'Dunt the sun look like a big fluffy ball of white wool? But, the money! I was talking 'bout the money! Someone tried to steal it so we need a bank 'count. You can open one for us, can't you?' She leant unsteadily forwards and, to Matthew's absolute mortification, ran her hand up his leg until her fingers were only inches from his crotch. 'Please?'

He whipped his leg away and she fell, her palm skidding along the ground. Very slowly she pushed herself upright and examined the dirt stuck to her hand, then wiped it on her skirt. Wincing, he glanced around to see if anyone had noticed.

Perhaps if he sat here and talked to her long enough she'd sober up, especially if she didn't drink anything more. He reached around her and knocked her glass over.

'Oh, I say, how clumsy of me.'

'No, 's all right, there's more, I can see it behind you.'

'Er, no.' He grabbed the wine bottle and made a show of staring intently at it. 'A fly or something appears to have fallen into it.' He felt himself beginning to panic. 'Tell me about this money. How much do you have?'

'Well, 's not all *mine*, not really. Mostly it's Sarah and Friday's. They been saving it. For the Charlotte fund, you know. I think there's 'bout four thousand pounds.'

'*How* much!?'

'Sounds funny, eh? Pooooounds.' She frowned. 'No, that's not right. Four *hundred*. No, there *was* four hundred. Oooh look, is that James?'

Alarmed, Matthew turned to see. Harrie grabbed the bottle off him and, closing one eye, peered down its neck.

'There's no flies in here!'

It *was* James and he was heading straight for them. Christ, Matthew thought, could this possibly get any worse?

'Harrie,' he pleaded, 'would you please give me that?'

'No.' She threw back her head and drank straight from the bottle.

'Good afternoon, Matthew, Harrie.'

Matthew gazed up at James, who appeared to be extremely cross. But James wasn't looking at him, he was glaring at Harrie's shiny red face, her long chestnut hair that had come loose and was all over the place, and the bottle in her hand.

'James —' she began.

'No!' he said, cutting her off. 'Matthew, what is going on here?'

Matthew found himself at a complete loss for words.

'I suggest,' James said to him icily, 'that you get her home as quickly as possible. And I expect to see you for supper at the Australian tonight.'

Giving Harrie a last, extremely disapproving and unmistakably disappointed look, he turned on his boot heel and strode off.

Harrie's face crumpled and she shrieked after him, '*Beard-splitter!*'

Astonished, Matthew gaped at her.

'*Selfish bloody quim-sticker!*'

Matthew waited nervously for James to arrive. He'd had to have a bath when he'd finally reached home, exhausted and sweaty from half carrying Harrie and all the picnic paraphernalia all the way back to Gloucester Street. She'd also been sick, and not very tidily. As predicted, Mrs Barrett had torn a strip off him, and shut the door in his face when he'd tried to help Harrie inside.

He felt utterly deflated, and not just because he was responsible for Harrie's downfall this afternoon. The child-like expression of excitement and expectation on her face when James had appeared in Hyde Park had awoken in him the unpleasant suspicion that she might be taking advantage of him just to get back at James and arouse his jealousy, and the more he thought about it the more he realised he was probably right. He wasn't *completely* stupid. He sighed. Actually, he was, and what's more he was stupid with a half-completed tattoo on his right arm.

He straightened his cutlery and took a sip of his drink — whisky tonight; he'd had enough of wine for one day. But perhaps not all was lost. Harrie was clearly still enamoured with James, but it was possible he might yet embark upon a friendship with her. True, friendship would not involve the level of intimacy that had so impassioned his dreams of late, resulting in embarrassing damp patches on his night attire and bed linen, but it would be better than no contact with her at all. She'd asked him to open a bank account for her and her friends, and he could certainly do that, though perhaps he might not share that little snippet with James.

Also, he really rather liked his lion tattoo, and would return to Leo to have it finished whether Harrie was ever going to see it or not. And she still might. She and James had been playing this silly game for nearly a year; surely soon they must either give in and admit they belonged together, or one or the other would bow out conclusively. If the latter occurred and Harrie was the one requiring consolation, naturally Matthew would step in. He could wait. He'd *been* waiting for ages.

'Good evening, Matthew,' James said. He dropped his hat and gloves onto a spare chair and sat down. Unsmiling, he waved for the waitress and asked for a whisky. 'Have you ordered yet?'

'I thought I'd wait for you.'

James studied the board. 'I'll have the mushroom soup and the beef, thank you,' he told the girl. 'Matthew?'

'I think I might try the hotpot tonight, with the soup to start, please.'

'Sirs,' the girl said and hurried off.

James's gaze settled rather coldly on Matthew. 'Let's get this over and done with, shall we? I take it you were responsible for Harrie's condition this afternoon? Because as far as I'm aware she doesn't drink. And what were the pair of you doing in the park, anyway?'

So, leaving out the bit about his tattoo, Matthew told him, recounting how first Harrie had invited him to tea, followed by, at his instigation, today's outing to Hyde Park, during which he'd failed to take into account her inexperience with alcoholic beverages.

'But it has become obvious to me that I am not the object of her affections,' he said. 'That still seems to be you. I suspect her invitation to me was just a ploy to inflame your passions. Revenge, perhaps, for hiring Miss Harris?' He swapped his soup spoon with his bread knife, then moved them back again, waiting for James's response.

There was a short silence. Then James said, 'Did you think you *could* be the object of her affections?'

Matthew decided there was little point in lying any longer. 'I had hoped so.'

'And how long have you ... harboured this hope?'

'Since, well, since the voyage out, really.'

'I had no idea,' James said quietly.

'No,' Matthew agreed.

James leant back as the waitress delivered his whisky. He waited until she'd gone again. 'And I've sat in this dining room for the past six months wittering on to you about my unrequited love for her. I *am* sorry, old fellow.'

Matthew shrugged, embarrassed. Trust James to be so decent about it.

'What a pickle,' James said.

'Not really.'

'No?'

'How I feel about her doesn't change anything, does it?' Matthew said.

'I'm not sure I understand.'

'Well, Harrie is still refusing to talk to you because of what you did after Rachel Winter died, yes?'

James nodded.

'But today, in the park, you looked at her as though she were despicable, and you wouldn't even allow her to speak. Do you not think a little, well, empathy might be in order? Forgive me for saying this, James, but at times you can be the tiniest bit superior.' There; he'd finally said it.

'Empathy?' James exclaimed, apparently completely ignoring Matthew's last sentence. 'But you saw her. She was *drunk*! She was dishevelled and making a spectacle of herself and her language was atrocious! She was no better than the worst of the trollops out at the Factory!'

Really annoyed by this, Matthew gave the table top a single sharp rap with his soup spoon. 'No, James, that's unkind. She was just Harrie, with too much champagne inside her, and that was my fault. Don't be so judgmental.'

James opened his mouth, then closed it again. Was he judgmental? But she'd looked so awful today, with her hair messy and her face all scarlet; everyone had been looking at her. And the names she'd called him! Emily would never, *ever* have uttered such words, even in her blackest moments. She'd never done anything questionable, or even particularly unexpected. Emily had been composed and dependable, predictable and completely reliable: she'd been the perfect wife for a doctor.

But was that really what he wanted now?

'Different people value different things,' Matthew said. 'You think being drunk in the park is terrible. Harrie thought what you did to Rachel Winter's body was so awful that she can't forgive you.'

'That's very liberal and fair-minded of you,' James said with quite a lot of sarcasm, for him. 'Family trait, is it, that sort of thinking?'

'Hardly. My mother's the most dreadful snob and bigot.'

The conversation ceased as the waitress appeared with their first courses and set the plates before them.

'If you've thrown your hat in the ring,' James said, blowing on a spoonful of soup, 'I can't see how things can remain unchanged.'

'But I haven't. That's my point. She isn't interested in me, so how I feel about her is irrelevant. I'm just suggesting that you might *try* seeing things from Harrie's perspective. Have you, for example, ever apologised for what you did?'

'Apologise? Why?'

'You see? This is exactly what I mean.' Matthew pointed at James with his spoon for emphasis. 'You really can't see why you should, can you? In *your* circles it might be perfectly acceptable to go about hacking up dead people, but in hers it isn't. Where *she* comes from, back home in London, she probably stepped over drunks in the street every day of the week and had friends who quite regularly drank too much. It doesn't mean they were bad people, any more than performing post-mortems makes you a bad person. But you've offended her and now she's offended you.'

'I doubt she'll apologise to me, and you heard what she called me. It was disgusting.'

'For God's sake, James, she was drunk. It's not as if she murdered someone. *You* cut up her best friend. Apologise to her.'

James stared into his soup, then picked something out of it and laid it on his bread plate. 'I'll think about it.'

December 1830, Sydney Town

'Good morning, madam,' Sarah said across the counter. 'How may I help you?'

She was wearing one of several new dresses Adam had paid for with money borrowed from Bernard Cole. Harrie and Nora Barrett had whipped them up in a matter of days and Sarah was very pleased with them, which surprised her as usually she didn't give tuppence about what she wore. Both dresses were of good-quality summer-weight calamanco with bright floral patterns against pale backgrounds. Esther had bought Sarah the dreary sage-coloured item she had, until now, worn every day, which was now too tight as she'd put on a little weight due to her former mistress's cooking. Harrie said that in comparison to that, the warmer colours 'lifted' her complexion, whatever that meant; but Sarah agreed they suited her, and so did the fitted style, which accentuated her bosom.

'Yes,' the woman said, as though Sarah had asked a completely different question. 'I have some items of jewellery — extremely valuable, I might add — and I would like you to clean and value them.' She produced a newspaper cutting from her basket and flapped it at Sarah. 'This is an advertisement from the *Sydney Gazette* stating that this jeweller will perform such services free of charge. Is that correct?'

'Yes, madam.'

The woman wore a bonnet with an enormous brim trimmed with pale pink knife-pleated satin and a posy of artificial blossoms and cherries, the high crown sporting a sprig of apple blossom about a foot long. Sarah was amazed she could hold up her head. Her dress, fastened over a clearly very tightly laced pair of stays, featured pink and burgundy flowers and dark green leaves on a light grey background, and she wore a lace pelerine, white lace gloves, and a burgundy paisley shawl with pink silk tassels. A charming ensemble on a twenty-year-old; unfortunately this woman was easily fifty.

All the pink in her outfit accentuated the broken veins on her face. Heavy bags sagged beneath her eyes and her jowls were heading south, giving her the appearance of a disappointed bloodhound.

Her dentures — Waterloo teeth, Sarah suspected, so she'd paid a lot for them — didn't fit at all well (but then whose did?), and her wig of real but dyed hair peeked from beneath her bonnet, a row of startling persimmon-coloured curls aligned across her forehead and a big one beside each ear. But instead of appearing silly, the woman just looked ... sad, as though she'd been led to believe that something wonderful would happen to her when she grew up, and it never had.

'I expect you to clean everything thoroughly, mind,' the woman said. 'Just because the service is free don't think you can cut corners. And I expect the valuation to be written out in triplicate.'

'Of course, Mrs ...?'

'Tregoweth. Mrs Phillip Tregoweth. Where's the jeweller? I thought I'd be dealing with a proper jeweller.'

'Would you like to speak with Mr Green, Mrs Tregoweth?'

'Yes, I would.'

'One moment please.' This often happened, especially with older women; they didn't think a girl could possibly know the first thing about jewellery, not even how to clean it.

Sarah went through to the workshop and fetched Adam.

'Mrs Tregoweth, is it?' he greeted the woman. 'Good morning, I'm Mr Adam Green, the jeweller. Delighted to meet you.'

'Good morning. Your advertisement says you'll clean and value jewellery at no expense to the customer?'

'That is correct. Do you have your jewels with you?'

Mrs Tregoweth took a large velvet bag from her basket and set it on the counter.

'May I?' Adam asked.

She nodded.

Adam opened the bag and took out several smaller pouches and two flat cases, one of leather, one covered with velvet. The leather case, lined with cream silk, contained an emerald and gold meshwork parure consisting of two bracelets, a ring, earrings, a necklace, and a brooch that could be attached to the necklace as a pendant.

'Have you had the parure valued previously?' Adam asked as he studied the emeralds in the necklace through his loupe.

'No, but my husband obtained a certificate of authenticity from the jeweller from whom he purchased the set. It was very costly.' Mrs Tregoweth simpered slightly. 'He said only the best will do for me.'

'Indeed. And it was purchased here, in Sydney?'

'Oh no, in London, a year or so before we emigrated.'

Adam opened the two smaller bags. The first contained an articulated cannetille bracelet in yellow, red and green gold set with amethyst, jade and topaz.

'This is very nice,' he said.

'My mother's,' Mrs Tregoweth replied. 'A family heirloom.'

The second bag revealed a ring — a spectacularly large, oval, cushion-cut diamond set inside a thin border of midnight blue enamel and surrounded by smaller diamonds.

'Another heirloom?' Adam asked.

'Yes. Very favoured by the royal family in my mother's time, that particular style with the blue enamel.'

The velvet case contained a necklace of perfectly graduated, foil-backed sapphires.

'It's a rivière. That means "river of light", you know,' Mrs Tregoweth explained redundantly. 'Again, it's a rather expensive piece.'

'Charming.' Adam closed the case. 'When would you like to collect your jewels?'

'By the end of the week. We're attending the governor's Christmas Eve reception on Friday evening and I shall need them. In fact, I'd prefer to collect them on Thursday if possible.'

'Of course. My assistant Miss Morgan will need to make a note of your particulars, for the valuation. Thank you for your custom, Mrs Tregoweth. Good day.'

'Good day, Mr Green.'

Mrs Tregoweth gave Sarah her address, one of the very substantial residences at the Bunker's Hill end of Cumberland Street.

'May I ask, do you keep your jewellery at the bank?' Sarah enquired.

'Why?' Mrs Tregoweth said suspiciously.

'You have some very nice pieces, and you'd be surprised by how many of our customers don't. You can't be too careful, in a town like this.'

'Oh, but one can buy such sturdy little iron chests nowadays,' Mrs Tregoweth said. 'And the bank does charge such a lot just for the use of a safety deposit box.'

Thank you, Sarah thought. 'It must be lovely to wear such nice jewellery.'

'It does reflect one's place in society, doesn't it? I do wear mine as often as possible, but, sadly, Sydney is not London.'

'Here you are.' Sarah handed Mrs Tregoweth her receipt.

'Very good. I'll drop by on Thursday at around midday. If you and Mr Green have finished by then, there'll be a shilling in it for you.'

'That's very generous. Thank you.'

When Mrs Tregoweth and her awful pink bonnet had gone, Sarah went through to the workshop. Adam was at his workbench, looking over the woman's jewellery.

'The parure is paste, isn't it?' she said.

Adam nodded. 'Good paste, but someone's taken her husband for a ride. Or perhaps he's taken her for one.'

'Will we tell her?'

'We'll have to. She's expecting a professional valuation. The ring, the sapphires and the cannetille bracelet are genuine, though, and of exceptional quality, especially the ring.' He swivelled on his stool to face her. 'What do you think?'

Sarah sat down. 'She keeps it all at home, on Cumberland Street. The Bunker's Hill end, of course. That bloody awful hat she had on is, according to Harrie, the latest mode, which says to me she likes to keep up with everyone else. The fashion for hiding your jewels when I left London was in a safe in the wall, usually behind a painting, so I'm betting that's where she has hers. She said she often wears her jewellery, so plenty of people will have seen what she owns. If it goes missing after it's been here she won't necessarily assume it's us. Also, she'll be piling it on when she and her husband go to this thing of the governor's on Friday night; if we pinch it, with a bit of luck she'll associate the theft with that outing.'

Adam frowned. 'But why steal it? Why not just take the diamond out of the ring? That's worked so far.'

Sarah draped the bracelet over her wrist and closed the delicate clasp. It was too large, and slid off over her hand. 'Because I want this as well, and the beauty of this is in the whole piece, not just the stones.'

'We can't fence that here, it's too distinctive.'

'It'll just have to go back to England, where I've no doubt it will fetch a very tidy profit. And can Bernard get us a really high-quality paste diamond in the next few days? I doubt it; it would have to be cut to order.' She indicated the ring. 'See here? The stone's not perfectly symmetrical.'

Adam had neither the specific skills nor the equipment to manufacture or cut the leaded glass that formed paste, or 'strass', stones, which were so attractive they were admired and worn even by those who could afford genuine gems. Bernard, however, imported quite a range of both clear and coloured paste, and silver and gold-plated jewellery already set with paste for his own retail business. The loose stones he sold on to various other Sydney jewellers, and several in Van Diemen's Land.

'Yes, I had noticed that,' Adam said. 'But house-breaking? Are you sure?'

'Of course I'm sure.' Sarah slipped on the ring, which again had been sized to fit Mrs Tregoweth's pudgy fingers; it sat crookedly while she admired the huge diamond, its fiery brilliance enhanced by the deep blue enamel surrounding it. 'I wouldn't have suggested it if I wasn't.'

She hadn't liked burgling houses in London, but that was because Tom Ratcliffe had been in charge. He'd dictated everything — which house, what time, what was to be stolen — leaving her no say at all. She'd had to do exactly as she was told, because he'd only ever provided her with enough information to get the job done and to barely keep herself out of trouble. Having her work blind in this fashion had been another of his methods of controlling her. She'd deeply resented it.

But this would be different. This time she would be free to plan the job to the very last little detail and have absolute command over everything. She was good at this, she knew she was, and she wouldn't fail.

'It will have to be this Friday night, after the governor's reception.' Her foot tapped out a rapid little beat as her mind raced. 'I'll be in the house already, hiding, before they arrive home.'

'Christ, Sarah!' Adam exclaimed.

'Oh, stop it,' she scolded. 'She'll be wearing it. What other way is there? Highway robbery on George Street?'

'But if you're caught in the house ...!'

'I won't be. I'll break in while they're out.'

'What about servants?'

'I'll break in *quietly*. For God's sake, Adam, I'm a screwsman and a cracksman, a bloody good one! I know how to do this, all right!?'

Adam closed his eyes, breathed deeply in and out several times, then opened them again. 'If anything happens to you —'

Sarah threw up her hands. 'You'll just say you knew nothing about it. *I'm* the assigned convict, remember?'

'No. That's not what I meant.'

To Sarah, the air in the workshop seemed suddenly very bright and brittle.

Adam rose suddenly, leant across the arm of the workbench separating them, and kissed her, his lips grazing her mouth.

'Oh,' she said.

'I'm sorry,' he said. 'I didn't mean to do that.' But he had meant to do it, and he wasn't sorry at all.

Harrie tucked in Sam, who had fallen asleep the second his little blond head touched the pillow. He'd been galloping around all afternoon whacking his sisters with a wonderfully whippy eucalyptus branch, one of several brought inside to decorate the parlour mantelpiece for Christmas, there being a severe shortage of mistletoe in New South Wales. It was only just past six and normally he refused to get into bed until at least seven o'clock, so his early retirement tonight was a pleasant bonus.

Lewis, however, was as usual bawling his head off. At almost five months he was still a little young for solid food, and didn't actually have any teeth yet, but Harrie's youngest sister, Anna, had been the same — forever grizzling — and Harrie had suggested that Nora try Lewis on a few spoonfuls of stewed apple sprinkled with sugar; Anna had loved that. Nora was downstairs now, waiting for the apple to cool. She didn't want to start Lewis on proper food yet, Harrie knew; he could well be her last baby and though she had to get back to work she also wanted to savour him as an infant for as long as possible. But her nipples were sore and she wasn't making enough milk and he clearly wasn't happy and, well, both Nora and Harrie knew the time had almost come to give up on mother's milk. George wasn't helping either, whinging on about the racket Lewis made and the hours Nora was having to spend with him. What had he expected when he'd made Nora pregnant? Harrie wondered. Lewis to go out and get a job as soon as he could sit up?

George *had* been in a better mood this week, however, out and about getting into the Christmas spirit with various friends even though Christmas Eve was still two nights away, and coming home singing, reeking of booze and noticeably drunk. Fortunately he wasn't nasty in his cups, which was something to be said in his favour. According to Nora, though, he was amorous, and she was having a dreadful time keeping him off her.

Harrie went out into the parlour. 'Hannah, have you had your wash yet?'

'Yes,' Hannah replied.

Walking up and down, joggling Lewis, Abigail said, 'You have not.'

'I have so!'

'Hannah, go to your room and have your wash, please,' Harrie ordered. 'And *don't* wake up Sam.'

'That's not fair! You always —'

'*Hannah!* Will you for once just *do as you're told*!'

Hannah and Abigail both stared at Harrie, startled by her uncharacteristic impatience. Hannah slid off the sofa and headed for the children's bedroom. Lewis started to cry.

'Harrie?' It was Nora, at the top of the stairs, a bowl of stewed apple in her hand. 'Dr Downey is downstairs for you.'

Oh *no*, Harrie thought. She'd not seen him since the terrible afternoon in Hyde Park, and had been dreading what would happen when inevitably their paths did cross. 'Tell him to go away. I don't want to talk to him.'

Stirring the apple briskly, Nora said, 'I did and he refused.' She crossed the room and took Lewis off Abigail. 'Really, Harrie, I'm not your social secretary. Do you not think it's time you put an end to this nonsense, one way or another? Go down and talk to him. Go on.'

Feeling badly flustered and as though her face were on fire, Harrie dragged herself downstairs. James was waiting in the tiny foyer. His top hat was under his arm, he'd removed his gloves, and he looked tired.

She stopped on the third-to-bottom step, the dreadful things she'd called him in the park echoing stridently in her head. Parts of the afternoon had blurred in her memory, but she remembered that all too clearly.

James bowed slightly. 'Good evening, Harrie.'

'Good evening, Dr Downey,' Harrie mumbled.

A short silence.

'How are you?' he asked.

'Well, thank you.'

The back door crashed open and George Barrett staggered in, clearly not expecting to encounter company. 'God's blood! I nearly shat meself then!' He peered at James. 'It's Downey, isn't it?' He stuck out a hand.

James shook it. 'Good evening, Mr Barrett.'

'Sorry to interrupt.' George pointed at the stairs. 'Just on my way up.'

Harrie pressed herself against the wall as George, wafting alcohol fumes, negotiated the narrow staircase.

'Is there somewhere we can speak privately?' James asked.

Harrie's heart pounded even more alarmingly. What was he going to do? Tell her what he really thought of her? Shout at her? Serve her with a summons for lewd behaviour?

'Not really,' she said.

'There must be somewhere, Harrie. Please. This is important.'

He didn't sound as though he wanted to shout at her. In fact, he sounded really quite … unsure of himself. She looked around. They couldn't go outside — the household cesspit reeked to high heaven at the moment — upstairs was too public, and the storeroom was absolutely crammed.

Perhaps Nora wouldn't mind if they used her shop, just for ten minutes. Harrie led the way, carrying the lamp from the foyer. She turned up the wick, illuminating half a dozen pairs of ladies' cotton drawers spread across the counter, left there by Nora this afternoon at the close of business.

'I think we might try Mr Barrett's shop.'

George's premises were just as untidy, but at least there weren't any undergarments on display. Harrie set the lamp on the counter and sat on a stool. James remained standing, which made Harrie wish she'd stayed on her feet as well, but it was too late to rise again now; it would be embarrassing.

James said nothing for almost a minute. Outside several people walked past on Gloucester Street, boots scuffing in the gravel, voices merry and loud. Half a dozen moths fluttered around the lamp. There was a faint smell of whisky. Harrie knew it certainly wasn't coming from her.

At last James said, 'Harrie, I would like to apologise to you.'

Harrie blinked.

'Regarding several matters,' he went on, not quite meeting her eye. 'Firstly, for my rude and pompous behaviour in Hyde Park. It has been brought to my attention that I have been guilty of passing judgment. And I have. I had, of course, no right to do that, and I apologise unreservedly.'

Harrie felt a huge rush of relief and, unexpectedly, a surge of good will towards James. 'And I —' It came out rather squeakily and she cleared her throat. 'And I'm sorry for saying those horrible things. I don't know what came over me. I'd had a little too much of Matthew's wine and —'

James held up his hand. 'Don't. You don't need to explain. It doesn't matter.'

'It *does* matter, James. I'm so ashamed of myself. I behaved no better than a common tart.'

'It does *not* matter. And I haven't finished.' He took a deep breath. 'I also wish to apologise to you for … for my actions after Rachel died. My behaviour then was utterly unforgivable.'

Harrie went very still; this was a matter she'd assumed they would never speak of again, and she certainly hadn't imagined he would apologise for it.

He said, 'I had to know, you see. I had to know *why* she died.

And I didn't stop to think about what effect it would have on anyone else. Not even you. I understand how deeply it upset you and I'm so very sorry.'

Slowly, Harrie shook her head. Suddenly she felt far too warm, dizzy and quite sick. 'But we know why she died. It was Gabriel Keegan, what he did to her on the *Isla*.'

James's face was a picture of empathy. He reached to take her hand but she stood quickly, knocking over the stool, avoiding his touch.

'No, Harrie, I believe she was suffering from hydatidosis, a disease likely caused by tapeworms, and she'd probably had it for years. She died from a cyst on the brain.'

Harrie's eyes rolled up and she passed out; James caught her as she slumped to the ground.

He dashed to the door and bellowed for Mrs Barrett, then knelt beside Harrie, gently tapping her cheeks to revive her. She muttered incoherently, but remained in a deep faint.

He didn't hear Nora Barrett approach, but certainly felt her stinging slap across the back of his head.

'*What* have you done to her? Get your mucky hands off her!'

'No, you don't understand. She's fainted.'

Nora lifted her hand again. 'I'm warning you, mister, get away from her!'

James moved aside a few inches. 'Do you have smelling salts? She's fainted. I didn't touch her. She had a bad shock.'

Harrie stirred. 'James?'

Nora squatted beside her. 'Harrie? Are you all right? Did he hurt you?'

Harrie slowly sat up and rubbed her hands across her face. 'Who?' What had just happened?

'Him.' Nora pointed accusingly at James. 'What did he do?'

'James?' Harrie felt dreadfully confused. 'Nothing. Why am I on the floor?'

'You fainted,' James explained.

Why was James here? And then Harrie remembered; she cried out, and clapped her hands over her mouth.

What had they done? *What* had she and Sarah and Friday done?

'Harrie?' Nora persisted. 'Did he force himself?'

'Yes! Yes, he did!' Harrie wailed, recalling in awful, vivid detail how Rachel had looked after Keegan had finished with her on the *Isla.*

'Harrie!' James exclaimed, horrified.

'Right, I'm getting the police,' Nora declared.

Harrie felt a dizzying surge of panic roar through her. 'The police? Why?' Had she said something when she'd fainted? 'No, please! Please don't.'

'You just said he attacked you!' Nora said, standing.

'I didn't! Not James. He didn't attack me.'

Nora looked from James to Harrie, and back to James again.

'He didn't,' Harrie said again. 'I'm sorry, I was confused.'

Dimly she was aware she had very nearly caused James an enormous amount of trouble, but that insight was swallowed by the horror of realising she'd committed the most hideous crime. She'd helped to murder the man they'd presumed responsible for Rachel's death, and they'd made a terrible mistake. Keegan had raped and badly injured Rachel, but in the end he hadn't killed her.

For the next few minutes, though, she had to pretend everything was fine. She offered her hand to James; he took it and helped her to her feet.

'It's all right, Mrs Barrett, really. James told me something about ... Rachel's death and it ... shocked me. Truly, I'm feeling better now.'

'For God's sake,' Nora said to James. 'You chase her round the streets of Sydney Town for nigh on a year, and the first chance you get to talk to her properly you say something so horrible she faints!'

Looking sheepish, James said, 'Yes, well, I didn't realise she would receive the news in quite this manner.'

'And what are you doing in George's shop?'

'I was hoping for some privacy.'

Nora turned to Harrie. 'Well, you're welcome to bring him upstairs. George has retired and I'm about to join him, providing I can get Lewis to settle.'

'Thank you, but I should be on my way,' James replied.

Nora nodded and left them to it.

James said, 'I'm sorry what I had to say came as such a shock.'

Harrie picked up the lamp and carried it out to the foyer. Her hand was shaking badly and she hoped James wouldn't notice. She felt as though she were stumbling about half asleep; everything seemed slightly blurred, muffled and too slow.

'Yes,' she heard herself say. 'It did.'

'May I call on you again?'

She hesitated. Had the deep rift in their friendship been mended? A lot of things still hadn't been said. What about Rowie Harris? And did any of that matter now anyway, given what she'd just learnt? She didn't deserve James. She didn't deserve anyone.

'If you want to,' she said, hoping her misgiving wasn't too obvious.

'I'd be delighted. Can you manage the stairs?'

'I think so.'

'Good night then, Harrie.'

'Good night, James.'

She closed the door after him and leant her head against it, the painted wood smooth against her clammy forehead.

Murderess.

She'd taken the life of a man who hadn't deserved to die, and she would burn in hell.

After a while she trudged up the stairs to her little room in the attic, lit the lamp with hands that refused to steady and lay on her bed, her head clamouring. It seemed to be crowded with people all talking at the same time: her mother and her siblings; her vindictive past employer Maude Lynch; Walter Cobley; rotten Amos Furniss; old Matilda Bain; James; Matthew; Bella Jackson; Leo Dundas; George and Nora; sanctimonious Reverend Seaton from the *Isla*. On and on they all went, chatter chatter, their voices getting louder and louder, struggling to be heard above one another until she couldn't stand it any longer.

'Stop it, please!' she hissed. 'Just shut up, all of you!'

They did.

She rose and washed her face. She changed into her nightdress, said her prayers, extinguished the lamp and climbed into bed.

And lay there for over an hour in the dark as one by one the voices began again. And this time when she told them to be quiet, they wouldn't.

She got out of bed once more, relit the lamp and draped her shawl around her shoulders. Reaching for her drawing pad and pencils, she settled down to sketch. She was halfway through a stylised rendition of a bat on the wing, the membranes between the delicate arm bones enhanced with a fantastic pattern of curlicues, spirals and tendrils. These she would colour the greens, reds and purples Leo used in his tattoos. The bat's round eyes she would shade a vivid cornflower blue.

The flame in the lamp flickered, dimmed, then flared again. Shivering slightly at the room's drop in temperature, she pulled her shawl tighter.

'I know you're there,' she said after a while, eyes still on her work.

There was no reply, but often there wasn't, just the faintest of creaks from the rocking chair and perhaps a vaporous hint of her own breath condensing in the cooler air.

'James came to visit tonight. He said he was sorry, especially about what he did after you … left us.' She selected the pencil she used for shading, the one with the softer lead. 'Did you know? About what was wrong with you?'

Again, only the gentle squeak of the chair and a thin whistle of night wind under the eaves.

Harrie sighed and finally raised her head. 'I wish so much you were here.'

She'd learnt that if she stared directly into the darkest corner of the room, at the rocking chair under the sloping roof, all she might ever see was the faintest smudge of light. But if she looked instead on an angle, from the corner of her eye, there she would be, her long silver hair falling loose and her skin as pale as the moon.

'I am here,' Rachel said, her voice flat and echoing, sounding as though it came from unimaginable distances.

'No, I mean the way we used to be,' Harrie replied. 'Together again.'

'I'm as here as I can be.'

Harrie nodded. 'I know, and I'm glad. I really am.' She was silent for a second, then said, 'Rachel, we killed him for no reason. We took his life and we shouldn't have.'

The chair gave another creak. A *thoughtful* sort of creak, it seemed to Harrie.

'Shouldn't you?' Rachel said. 'Why not? He deserved it.'

'But did he? I know what he did to you was just awful, but what we did was more than an eye for an eye.'

'No. It wasn't. Think about it.'

Harrie dropped her pencil and her hands crept up to cover her ears. 'I can't *stop* thinking about it.' But she heard what Rachel said next anyway, because the words seemed to come from inside her own head.

'Harrie, I died having Charlotte. Who was Charlotte's father?'

'Gabriel Keegan was.'

'So he did kill me. See? An eye for an eye.'

'But the thing in your brain … You were so sick. Your headaches and those terrible fits.' Surely Rachel, even as she was now, couldn't have forgotten all that?

'It would have been all right if I hadn't had to push Charlotte out. And who made me pregnant, Harrie? *Who was Charlotte's father?*'

Slowly, Harrie's hands came down. 'Oh, Rachel. Do you really think so?'

A knock came at the door and Nora Barrett called from the other side, 'Harrie? Are you all right?'

Harrie got off the bed and opened the door.

'Is everything all right?' Nora asked again, Lewis balanced on her hip. 'I was feeding the baby and I thought I heard you talking.'

'I couldn't sleep,' Harrie said. 'I've been drawing.' Then, to her absolute mortification, it occurred to her that Nora might think James was in her room. 'There's no one in here. You can look.'

'Don't be silly. I was worried you were having a nightmare. But if you're sure you're well?'

'Yes, I am, thank you.'

Nora nodded doubtfully. 'Well, I'll see you in the morning, then.'

'Good night.' Harrie closed the door and turned back to the rocking chair, but Rachel had gone.

Chapter Eleven

Christmas Eve 1830, Sydney Town

Christmas Eve had fallen on a Friday, and many street stalls and shops had advertised they were remaining open for business even later than usual, hoping to cash in on the festive spirit. Everyone seemed to be abroad, the steep and narrow streets of the Rocks crowded with locals determined to enjoy themselves. The pubs were packed and noisy even though the sun had not yet set, windows and doors flung wide to catch the late afternoon breezes off the harbour, and shrieking children with filthy bare feet chased each other up and down alleyways and through dank courtyards.

Matthew had made it to the Bank of New South Wales on George Street just in time. He shot under the elegant archway framing the entrance portico just on closing and hurried up to the clerk, dumping his heavy satchel on the counter.

The clerk looked annoyed.

'Good afternoon,' Matthew said, slightly out of breath. 'I'd like to open an account.'

The clerk made a point of withdrawing his watch from his pocket and examining it, but said, 'Certainly, sir. Have we had the pleasure of your custom previously?'

'You have.'

'And with whom am I conversing?'

Pompous twit, Matthew thought. Surely 'What's your name?' would do. 'Matthew Cutler.'

As the clerk turned his back and flicked through a wooden box containing a series of cards, Matthew glanced over his shoulder at Friday, standing just outside the entrance, looking on.

'Mr Matthew Geoffrey Raymond Cutler? Of Princes Street?'

'Correct.'

'I note you currently hold one bank account with us already.'

'Yes, that's right. And now I'd like another one.' Matthew opened the satchel and drew out the pouch containing the Charlotte fund. 'I think you'll find two hundred and forty-one pounds, seven shillings and thruppence, all in English currency. I'll need a receipt, thank you.'

The clerk looked deeply insulted. 'We *never* receive monies without issuing a corresponding receipt.'

'Good. Look, I don't mean to be rude, but I wonder if you could hurry up? I'm due at the governor's soirée, and you know what he's like when you turn up late.' It wasn't true, but Matthew felt like putting the man in his place.

'Oh! Of course. I do beg your pardon.'

The clerk whizzed through the paperwork and handed Matthew his documents. 'As you have Governor Darling's ear, you might care to comment on what excellent service is to be had at the Bank of New South Wales. Have a wonderful evening, Mr Cutler.'

'Thank you. I most certainly will.'

Outside, Friday said, 'All organised?'

'Yes.' Matthew gave her the papers. 'But I'm still not sure why Harrie couldn't come. Is she avoiding me?'

'No. She's not feeling well.'

Harrie had in fact told Friday she didn't want to see Matthew. She felt deeply ashamed now of taking advantage of him, and was extremely embarrassed about getting drunk and vomiting on him.

In Friday's opinion, the sooner Matthew forgot about Harrie and found himself another girl, the better.

Matthew said, 'I know she and James have ... settled their differences. James told me.' Friday was striding along the street, dodging potholes and piles of horseshit, and he almost had to trot to keep up. 'And, well, I'm happy for them. Really, I am. So you can tell me if she *is* avoiding me.'

'You talk a lot, don't you?' Friday said. 'She's *not* avoiding you. She really isn't well.' She halted suddenly and Matthew only just stopped himself from barrelling into her. 'Maybe you don't know Harrie well enough to realise it, but there's something wrong with her. And I'm only telling you this because obviously you care about her. That business in the park? The swearing and everything?'

'She told you?'

'What she could remember, she did.'

'God, I feel dreadful about that.'

'Not your fault.' Friday gave him a look. 'Well, not *entirely*. Anyway, that's not Harrie at all. She'd never've done that in her right mind. And she never drinks. She's right out of kilter and me and Sarah are very worried.'

'What can I do to help?'

'You already have, opening that bank account. That's one less thing for her to fret about. And you're still happy to do our banking once a week?'

Matthew nodded. 'Though I'm not sure I understand where all the money will be coming from.'

'You don't need to.'

'Well, if there's anything else I can do, please tell me,' Matthew said. 'She might have chosen James, but I can still be her friend.'

Friday said thoughtfully, 'You know, to start with I thought you were pretty useless, but you're not really, are you? You're quite nice.' She pecked him on the cheek, making him blush. 'Well, I'm off to work. Mrs H is closing early tonight. Says cullies should be with their families on Christmas Eve, not out trawling brothels. Ha!'

She waved goodbye and hurried off down the street. Matthew wandered along until he came to a stationer's. He needed to buy some writing paper. He hadn't written to his mother for a fortnight and he must, or she would automatically assume the lack of correspondence was the result of him being struck down by a fatal disease, murdered by ne'er-do-wells, or eaten by natives or dingoes.

What was it, he wondered, that was so distressing Harrie?

'How are you bearing up?' Adam asked.

Sarah glanced at him and, though she made an effort not to, she smirked.

'Will you stop that?' Adam said wearily. It *had* been funny to start with, but now he just felt sick with nerves.

'Sorry, Grandpa.'

It was all right for her. Apparently in London she'd been accustomed to going about in various costumes in the course of executing her scams, but he certainly wasn't. All he'd ever done on the wrong side of the law had been to purchase the odd piece of stolen jewellery. Well, quite a lot of pieces of stolen jewellery, and loose stones, and once even two gold ingots, if truth were told. And some gold and silver plate, and on one memorable occasion a stunningly engraved, solid silver altar suite consisting of a chalice with paten, flagon, ciborium and monstrance stolen from a Catholic church up north, though he'd had that melted down fairly quickly. But he'd not done anything illegal at all in Australia until Esther had run off, and he'd never been involved in anything like *this* before, anywhere.

Sarah had gone out and bought a horsehair wig, the sort old men still favoured, to be accompanied by a fake beard, moustache and muttonchops that looked as though they'd been fashioned from the hair of an elderly white goat. The glue with which she'd stuck the damn things to his face was itching like hell, but he had to admit he barely recognised himself in the looking glass. His rather heavy eyebrows were black, the same as his real hair, but by the time Sarah had rubbed into them the white starch powder she'd purchased for the wig, together with just the lightest dusting over his already pale skin, he looked a good thirty-five years older than his true age, which was thirty.

He'd hired an unliveried gig for the evening, one with a folding hood, which was currently up to hide them from the glances of curious folk on the street, and there were hundreds of those tonight.

'Could we have picked a worse evening?' he grumbled to Sarah as they made their way along narrow and potholed Cumberland Street, the horse stopping endlessly to let folk wander across the road. 'Look at all these people.'

'It's the best time, a busy night,' Sarah said. 'Folk everywhere means we won't be remembered. And it'll be dark soon, with cloudy skies and the moon in the first quarter. A burglar's moon, it's called — just enough light to see by, but dark enough to hide in the shadows. Couldn't ask for better conditions for a night out thieving.'

Earlier he'd been that worried about something going wrong he'd come close to losing his nerve and telling her she wasn't to go ahead with it. But then she'd come prancing down from her room wearing a pair of boy's black trousers stretched taut across her beautiful shapely backside and revealing several inches of bare calf, a dark shirt with the sleeves removed showing off her lovely naked arms, little black lace-up boots, and her sleek hair in a long plait hanging down her back.

Christ almighty, he hadn't known where to look! He'd developed an erection immediately and had to put one of Esther's appliquéd cushions over it. Sarah, though, had wandered casually around the house as though she wore such outlandish costumes every day, apparently not even noticing his discomfort. Fortunately. He'd had to endure it for a whole hour. If she stood with her back to him he was treated to the majestic vision of her rounded buttocks flaring beneath her hips; if she was in profile he got the curve of her bum *and* the lines of her taut thighs; and if she faced him directly he could clearly see where the fabric of the trousers followed the *very* feminine contours of her body at the juncture of her legs. He'd barely been able to contain himself, and felt no less physically frustrated now despite his nerves, the only difference being that his balls ached.

At last they neared the home of Mr and Mrs Phillip Tregoweth, the horse's iron-shod hooves crunching in the sparse gravel littering the unpaved street, which here, at the end of Cumberland, opened out into a wide cul-de-sac. Perched on the pinnacle of Bunker's Hill the house was quite grand, and commanded a view of Sydney Cove, the town and the Domain; in fact, of the entire harbour and the Parramatta River as it snaked inland. It was also, from a burglar's point of view, somewhat exposed, and flanked by slightly smaller though still very elegant homes. A house on the other side of the street featured an ostentatious pond and statue in its garden — and two large brindle dogs staring menacingly through the fence.

'That must be Bella's house,' Sarah remarked.

'Who's Bella?' Adam asked.

Appalled at herself for such an unthinking slip, Sarah darted a look at him. 'Someone Friday's boss knows.' She'd said nothing at all about Bella Jackson to Adam, too afraid he may possibly connect her stealing from him with what he might know of Bella's nasty business practices, and inadvertently half guess the blackmail part of her secret.

The Tregoweths' house was a long, cream-coloured bungalow with a verandah on all sides, its two wings bisected by a looming and somewhat incongruous two-storey pavilion featuring ornamental rectangular columns and a gable. Like several of the neighbouring properties, the Tregoweths' house was surrounded by an iron fence, interrupted by a carriage gate and a hand gate, both at present closed. In the back garden stood an ancient fig, currently boiling with hundreds of bats, chattering, squawking and bitching at one another as they prepared to set out for the night in search of food.

'Off you go,' Sarah said to Adam.

He felt his buttocks clench with nervous anticipation, but handed her the reins and climbed down from the gig; there wasn't time to waste. Feeling his fake moustache to make sure it was on straight, he went through the hand gate, approached the front door and tugged on the bell pull.

Eventually, the door was opened by a girl wearing a grey dress, a white apron and a lace house cap.

'Evening,' she said.

'Good evening,' he replied, doing his best to sound like a sixty-five-year-old man. 'I'd like to speak with Mr Phillip Tregoweth, if you please.'

'Sorry, sir, he's gone to the governor's ball.'

'Oh dear. And must I assume Mrs Tregoweth has accompanied him?'

The girl nodded.

'Nobody home at all?'

'Just me and Mrs Bunyard, but she's going over to her friend's for the night. It's Christmas Eve, you know.'

'Mrs Bunyard?'

'The cook.'

'Ah. But you've not been given the night off?'

The girl's bottom lip came out. 'No, I haven't.'

'Oh. What a shame.' Adam turned away. Then he said, 'You don't know when they expect to return home, do you?'

The girl shrugged. 'Probably not late. No doubt her'll get one of her bad heads and have to come home early.'

'Oh well. At least their driver will be pleased.'

'*He's* got the night off, too. Mr Tregoweth took the curricle. Fancies his driving skills.' She gave a tiny snort of derision.

'Does he? How extraordinary.' Adam raised his hat and had a horrible, bum-clenching moment when he thought his wig might have come off. 'Good evening, then. And Merry Christmas!'

'Merry Christmas to you, too, sir,' the girl said, and shut the door.

Climbing back into the gig, Adam swore.

'What?' Sarah asked.

'There's one servant in the house tonight, a girl. I think she's a bit cross about not getting the night off. When Mrs Tregoweth wakes up tomorrow and finds her jewellery gone, the finger could very well be pointed at her.'

'Bugger,' Sarah said.

Adam wheeled the horse around and they trotted off back towards the southern and less salubrious end of Cumberland Street, then turned. It was fully dark now, and even more folk had ventured out.

'Stop,' Sarah ordered. 'This will do.'

She undid the clasp at the neck of her cloak and let it pool around her on the seat of the gig. She was wearing a boy's jacket and across her body she'd slung her burglary satchel, containing Congreves matches and a candle, her skeleton keys and safe-cracking tools, lemon and menthol lozenges to stave off inconvenient coughing fits, and crystallised fruit for sustenance in case she found herself caught inside the house for any length of time. Some house-breakers carried dried meat but, really, what a stupid thing to have on you when so many people kept dogs! It had been nearly two years since she'd done anything on this scale and while she wasn't exactly nervous, she was fervently hoping she hadn't lost her edge.

'Right,' she said, shoving a cap on her head and tucking her plait under it. 'I'm off. Wish me luck.'

Adam cupped a hand behind her neck, pulled her to him and kissed her, their lips meeting furrily through his drooping moustache.

Sarah giggled. He swore and ripped off the fake facial hair, blinking rapidly at the smarting pain, and pushed her back against the seat, kissing her properly, his tongue gently pressing against her mouth until her lips parted.

It went very well for several seconds more, then Sarah grunted, 'Hmmph!' and whacked him across the ear.

He pulled away. 'Oh God, Sarah, I didn't mean to do that, either.'

'Bloody funny sort of accident.'

Both were profoundly glad for the mantle of darkness hiding skin flushed red with embarrassment and arousal.

'Christ. Look, I'm really sorry.'

Sarah couldn't meet his eye. 'I've got to go.'

'Please, Sarah. Be careful.'

'I will. Stop *fussing*.'

'I'll be waiting.'

Sarah jumped down from the gig. For a second she was there but the next she'd blended into the shadows, invisible.

Adam leant out but couldn't see her anywhere — not on the street, not in the nearby alleyway, not among the crowd.

Would he ever kiss her again?

Sarah trotted down Essex Street then along Gloucester, keeping her head down, just a boy on his way somewhere on Christmas Eve.

He'd kissed her twice now, and she'd behaved outwardly as if nothing had happened, but both times her belly had done slow, lazy flips and she'd felt as though she were spinning and swooping and falling. Into what, though, she didn't know, and that was the danger. She hadn't wanted to get out of the gig; she'd wanted to stay pressed against the seat, feeling the warmth of his skin, the pressure of his urgency, and inhaling his faint sandalwood, lime and fresh-sweat smell. But then the old disgust and fear had roared up from deep inside her like a spew of filth from a cesspit, choking her and filling her with spiky rage, and she'd hit out.

But she couldn't think about that now, and pushed it to the back of her mind. She had a job to do, and couldn't allow anything — not even Adam — to disrupt her concentration.

She followed Gloucester most of the way north, confident she'd become invisible among the crowds, then climbed up to Cumberland Street using the little paths and rocky steps worn into the hill over the past forty years. On Cumberland she ducked across a vacant lot and came out higher up on Princes Street, where three mangy dogs skulked along behind her until she hurled rocks at them and scared them off, then she came down again through the undergrowth, behind the Tregoweths' house.

It looked as though lamps were burning in several downstairs rooms, and at least one upstairs. She removed her cap, jacket and boots and stuffed them under a bush; they wouldn't be necessary in the house and would be a hindrance if she had to wriggle through a small window or negotiate a drainpipe. She scaled the back fence and dropped noiselessly to the ground, fairly confident she wouldn't be set upon by guard dogs. Any dogs on the property would have come rushing around to the front when Adam had knocked on the door earlier, just as Bella's beasts had appeared at her fence. She couldn't believe she'd mentioned Bella to Adam. What was wrong with her?

She made her way through the Tregoweths' rear garden, keeping to the shadows, glancing at the windows every few seconds. And then what always happened when she was about to burgle a house happened: she bloody well had to pee. In the shelter of a bush she undid the buttons on her trousers, pulled them down and squatted, sighing in annoyance as a trickle of warm urine splashed onto the ground, trying not to get any on her feet. But experience had taught her she was far better to do it now than be caught short inside the house for hours on end, her bladder close to bursting.

Finished, she shook herself, yanked up her trousers and closed the buttons. No — still no one at the windows. It was unlikely, with only the servant girl at home, but you could never, ever be too careful.

She crept across the remaining few yards of the garden and up onto the verandah. There were a cane sofa, several chairs and a matching low table, positioned to make the most of the verandah's shady eaves during the summer heat. She tried the back door, which was locked. Both sets of French doors were, too, the rooms behind them dark, though a lamp burnt in the semi-detached kitchen.

Circumnavigating the entire house once, she calculated the height of every window, looked for drainpipes, and judged the various roof angles in case she found herself up there, which had happened before on occasion, then returned to the front of the house and tried the main door, which wasn't locked. Shaking her head in disbelief, she wiped her feet on the mat and opened the door a crack. She listened for a moment, heard nothing and slipped into the tiled entrance hall, shutting the door gently behind her.

The hall was dimly lit by lamplight spilling out from a room farther down on the right; she moved silently towards it, stopping as she reached the doorway. The room, reeking of lemon furniture polish, was a very busily furnished formal parlour containing three large sofas and two plush armchairs arranged around an enormous fireplace. The paintings on the papered walls were of landscapes and miserable-looking people, expensive Turkey carpets covered the floor, and little tables everywhere were crammed with fancy bits and pieces. A lot like Esther's parlour, but bigger, even fussier and clearly paid for with much deeper pockets. The girl who had answered the door to Adam lounged on one of the sofas, her stockinged feet up on a small table, knitting and drinking straight from a crystal decanter.

Sarah smiled to herself; at least the girl was savouring a dash of revenge.

She left her to it and climbed the stairs, looking for the Tregoweths' bedroom. Or perhaps more than one, if they didn't share a bed. Adam should have asked if there were any children, but hadn't. Still, he'd not done too badly, for his first attempt at reconnaissance. And Mrs Tregoweth was very unlikely to have young children at her time of life.

The upstairs light she'd seen from outside came from several lamps on the hall wall, which lit her way admirably. The first room she entered was a small sitting-cum-sewing room, clearly Mrs Tregoweth's refuge if the pale furnishings were anything to go by. There was a vast and beautifully decorated papier-mâché sewing box — for which Harrie would no doubt *die* — sitting open on a table next to a baby's gown Mrs Tregoweth, presumably, was rather skilfully smocking, and a pile of books on a footstool near the window. Not a bedroom, but she checked behind all the paintings just to be sure. Nothing.

The room opposite was made up as a bedroom but didn't look as though anyone slept there. It smelt ... empty. There was no safe there, either.

The next room along was clearly the domain of a male, the bed a massive tallpost with a great slab of a headboard, the mattress covered with a dark quilt, and the yards of mosquito net at present rolled up. The room's other furniture was equally masculine, and bereft of the pots and bottles and brushes you'd expect to see in a woman's chamber. A smaller area off the bedroom turned out to be a dressing room filled with men's clothing, shoes and boots, some of which could do with a good airing. But again, no safe.

Sarah tried the last door, certain it would be Mrs Tregoweth's. It was, and what an overdone room it was. Her bed was as big as her husband's but of white-painted iron, with an elaborately swathed lace net, a pale quilt and perhaps a dozen pillows heaped all over it. Her window dressings were an explosion of lace, a fancy four-branch lamp hung from the centre of the ceiling, and vases jammed with silk flowers perched on every available surface. What an altogether frilly, flowery woman. Silly old trout. The carpet was delicious though; Sarah stood for at least a minute wriggling her bare toes in the luxurious pile.

In here, too, there were at least half a dozen paintings. She headed immediately for the one she knew would be concealing the safe; the only painting hung low enough to be taken on and off the wall with ease, a picture of a King Charles spaniel with bulging eyes and a gormless expression. She lifted it off the wall and there it was; a metal door about twenty inches square set into the wall. Actually, it wasn't what she called a safe at all. Nothing like you got in banks and the bigger shops in London, whose owners paid a premium for the incredibly heavy, iron-clad chests guaranteed to be fire- and theft-proof. Unless someone like her came along.

Putting the dog painting on the floor, she opened her satchel, lit her candle and examined the lock. It was pretty basic but naturally the key wasn't in it. Using one of her tools, she tapped all over the door, listening carefully; a certain pitch would tell her which skeleton key she should use. This was a real luxury: usually she didn't have anywhere near this much time to work out how to crack a safe.

She chose a key, spread a small amount of wax over it, slid it into the keyhole, waggled it slightly, tilted it, and turned. The locking mechanism clicked and the door opened. Inside the box were some papers tied with ribbon, the two jewellery cases and the little velvet bags Mrs Tregoweth had brought into the shop. Both bags were empty, and one of the cases; the only items the woman hadn't worn tonight were those in the emerald paste parure, which Sarah didn't want. She pictured Mrs Tregoweth in the sapphire rivière, the cannetille bracelet and the diamond ring, and was surprised she hadn't crammed on the green glass bracelets, matching ring, earrings, necklace and brooch.

She replaced everything in the safe exactly as she'd found it, relocked it, checked the time on the watch Adam had given her (ten minutes to nine), blew out the candle, and hung the dog painting back on the wall.

Now what? They might not be back for hours, or they could arrive home quite soon. She looked around for somewhere to conceal herself. And then she froze; someone was clomping up the stairs, making enough noise to cause the dead to sit up and complain. She ducked under the bed just as the door opened.

It was the girl, carrying a lamp and humming to herself. Bugger! Would she notice the smell of the just-doused candle?

Apparently not. Sarah observed the girl's booted feet crossing to Mrs Tregoweth's dressing table and heard a drawer slide out. She lifted the edge of the quilt and watched the girl have a good rummage around, then pocket something. She shut the drawer, picked up a bottle of perfume and removed the stopper.

Don't do that, you stupid cow; she'll smell it on you.

The girl evidently thought better of it and put the perfume bottle down. She disappeared into Mrs Tregoweth's dressing room, emerging a minute later wearing one of her mistress's hats and a feather boa, parading about before the full-length looking glass, flinging the feathers this way and that.

'You look charming today, Josie,' she said out loud. 'Thank you, Mr Collier, I think so meself.'

She curtsied to her reflection and the hat slid off, landing on its crown and breaking off one of the artificial magnolias.

'Shit!' She snatched up the bloom and shoved it in her pocket along with whatever she'd pinched.

Hurriedly she returned the hat and boa to the dressing room, collected the lamp and rushed out, closing the door behind her. Sarah waited a few minutes, then rolled out from under the bed, brushed gossamer webs of dust and hair off her shirt and trousers, and looked around for somewhere better to conceal herself.

The dressing room might be a good bet. About ten feet square it had wide shelving on one wall containing shoes, boots and piles of hatboxes, capes hanging from hooks on the opposite wall, more boxes on the floor, and a window framed by voluminous curtains tied back with satin cords. She pushed up the sash and looked outside, noting to her satisfaction a drainpipe only a few feet away. She had considered hiding in the spare room, but that meant she'd have to open Mrs Tregoweth's bedroom door and she'd noticed that it creaked quite loudly.

Drawing down the window again, she left a gap of several inches at the bottom in case she had to leave in a hurry; she didn't want to risk it jamming. Then she sat down on the floor of the dressing room, ate two new moons of crystallised orange peel, and settled in to wait.

Elizabeth Hislop shut her establishment at nine o'clock sharp, even though it meant she had to turn away customers. She always closed early on Christmas Eve; some of her girls had family and they all had friends, and, as Friday had said, she firmly believed Christmas was a time best spent with loved ones, not underneath some cove her girls barely knew. She still paid them their full rate, however; God knew everyone deserved a little bit extra at Christmas.

Friday changed out of her flimsy work costume and into something more suitable for a night out on the jar, and headed straight for the Bird-in-Hand, her favourite pub. She would start there, then pop along the street to the St Patrick's Inn, then maybe duck into the Spread Eagle to see who was out and about. Then she might go down to the Sailors' Grave, and after that perhaps move on to the Crown and Angel. And maybe the Whale Fishery, possibly followed by the Saracen's Head. If she was still in charge of her faculties she'd finish up at the Siren's Arms, as she only had to crawl up the stairs there to get to bed.

The Bird-in-Hand was packed, every seat taken at the long table and dozens standing elbow to elbow or perched on stools, a heavy pall of tobacco smoke hovering above the crowd, the talk and laughter loud. Friday slipped in through the front door and, waving greetings, weaved her way up to the serving counter. Many of the regulars she knew, but there were plenty of strange faces as well, likely folk out for the night on a spree. She ordered her usual gin and leant on the bar, looking out into the crowd.

She quite liked this part of the night, when she was by herself but not alone, but it had taken her a while to get used to it again. After all that time she'd spent with Harrie, Sarah and Rachel, first in Newgate Gaol and then on the *Isla*, she'd had to learn all over again how to be on her own, and it had been hard. She'd had no choice: Rachel was gone now, and Harrie and Sarah both had proper assignments and only a fraction of the freedom she had.

Sydney was a strange little town. She'd been working as a prostitute in Mrs H's brothel for over a year, which as a convict she definitely shouldn't be doing, and not once had there been even a suggestion that the authorities were aware. She wasn't alone, either, as Mrs H certainly wasn't the only madam in town employing assigned convict girls. But not all Sydney's whores were convicts, despite what you read in the papers — far from it. There were hundreds of tarts and perhaps it was just too hard for the authorities to police. Why would they, anyway? Only operating a brothel was against the law: prostitution wasn't.

She certainly worked for her money. And when she wasn't working, she liked to relax and forget about all that and these days, for her, relaxing meant getting drunk.

She would much rather spend her free time with Harrie and Sarah, the way they used to. Sarah, though, was busy with Adam now, and it was obvious where that was heading. Sarah swore she wasn't interested in him, but what a lot of bollocks; she was, and probably she should be. He was a nice-looking man and, it had turned out, a bloody decent one. He knew she'd been robbing him blind and hadn't done a thing about it. But what it all amounted to was Sarah was drifting away, and while it was a nice thing for her, it made Friday sad. If she were the sort of person to get lonely, she'd say that's how she was feeling. But she wasn't that sort of person. Occasionally she did think how nice it would be to have someone special to come home to, but the one time she'd had that — or *thought* she'd had it — the pain of losing it had been so brutal she'd sworn she never wanted to experience it again. But she'd been younger then, so of course it had been hard. She was older now.

As for poor Harrie: what on earth were they going to do to help her? She'd always been the calm, sensible one, whose job it was to soothe and mother them all. But these days she fretted constantly — about Bella Jackson, and James, and what they'd done to Keegan. It was so hard to watch, as though Harrie were slowly unravelling before their eyes.

She'd popped around to the Barretts' yesterday and Harrie had seemed even worse. Mind you, she'd got a hell of a shock herself when Harrie had passed on James Downey's revelation about poor Rachel's head. A brain disease! Jesus Christ. Perhaps they shouldn't have kicked Keegan to death after all. But they had, and there was no changing things now. And whether or not what he'd done to Rachel had actually killed her, he'd still hurt her horribly. He'd had to pay.

And now Harrie was in a right state about *that*. She and James were speaking again, but instead of crossing him off her list of things to fret about, she'd apparently decided she didn't deserve him because of committing such a terrible sin. She, Friday, had had to sit on her hands to stop herself giving Harrie a good clip across the ear. It didn't matter what you said to her these days, she seemed mired in melancholy. Admittedly the business with Keegan *had* been pretty awful — and was even more complicated now — and they were *all* worried sick about the power Bella had over them, but the strain seemed to be ruining Harrie, wearing her down and fraying her from the inside out, until soon there might be no Harrie left, just a little pile of disconnected threads.

She finished her gin and heaved out a long, gusty sigh. She feared Harrie was gradually losing her mind, and knew Sarah did, too.

As she turned to order another drink, someone bumped her newly tattooed arm and she winced. The peacock was finished and it looked fabulous, though it was sore. She thought she might have a little pus developing around the tail feathers, and was finding it very difficult to resist picking her scabs. She was refraining, however, because Leo had explained that if she did, the clarity of the lines would be permanently compromised, so bugger that. There would be no smudged peacock for her.

The barman slid her drink across the bar and she moved into the crowd, looking for somewhere to sit. A hand shot up and a voice called out her name.

Friday made her way across to the long table.

Her voice raised to counter the noise, a pretty dark-haired girl sitting at one end said, 'It is you, isn't it? Friday Woolfe?'

'Sally Minto? From the *Isla*?' Friday hadn't seen Sally since the Factory.

Sally Minto smiled, and shoved along on the bench, making room.

Friday returned the smile and sat. 'God, you look well. What have you been up to?'

Sally really did look good. On the voyage out from England she'd been a skinny girl with pasty, pimply skin and lank hair, and apparently hadn't possessed the gumption to say shoo to a goose. Now she was positively buxom, her spots had vanished leaving only a few small scars, her cheeks were rosy, and her dark brown hair had the sheen of a well-polished saddle.

'I was only in the Factory a week and I got assigned to a baker and his wife on Kent Street, down near Millers Point,' she said. 'I've been there ever since. Can't you tell?' she added wryly, pointing at her small double chin.

'A good assignment, then?' Friday said, fishing her smoking gear out of her reticule.

'I'm happy. Days are long but the work isn't too hard, I've a nice little room to myself, the food's good, the master leaves me alone and I get two half days off a week. I'm living better than I ever did back home. Yourself?'

'I'm a housemaid in a hotel. The Siren's Arms.'

'Are you?' Sally took a sip of her drink. 'That's a fancy dress for an assigned housemaid.'

Friday met her gaze and held it; Sally knew, and Friday didn't care. 'It is, isn't it?' She rolled a sliver of tobacco between her thumb and forefinger and tamped it into her pipe.

'It's nothing like I thought it would be, here,' Sally said. 'I thought we'd be in leg irons, getting whipped and fed gruel and treated like slaves. I do miss my family, though.'

'I think it's different for some of the men,' Friday said.

Sally nodded. 'Mind you, I know a girl, her master's on her every night, poor thing. *And* he's an emancipist himself. You'd think he'd have some sympathy. She's already had a child to him. It's in the orphanage now.'

Friday lit her pipe. Stories like that really annoyed her. Why did the stupid girl put up with it? 'Do you see anyone much from the *Isla*?'

'A few of the girls. I don't know if you'd know them. Lil Foster? The woman who worked in the ship's hospital? She comes into the bakery occasionally.'

'Really? I must tell Harrie. She liked Lil.'

'Harrie was lovely. How is she?'

'Oh, she's well. She's with a nice family and doing quite a lot of sewing.'

'Yes, she was good at that, wasn't she? And what about Sarah? Do you still see her?'

Friday nodded, smoke trickling from her mouth. 'She works for a jeweller.'

Sally laughed. 'That's a good assignment for a convict, isn't it?'

'I'll say. Ha ha.'

'And Rachel? How's she? Did she recover from … well, what happened?'

'No. Actually, she died.'

Sally's hand flew to her mouth. 'From … what that man did?'

'It turned out he made her pregnant and she died having the baby.'

'Oh my *God*.'

'So that's what Janie's doing. She's still at the Factory looking after her girl Rosie and Rachel's baby.'

Sally frowned. 'Janie? Someone told me she'd been assigned up the Hawkesbury River somewhere. At the start of this year.'

'Well, someone told you wrong.'

'Oh. I'd really like to see Janie again.' Sally looked around. 'Good pub this, isn't it? How's your drink?'

'Gone. Fancy another? My treat.'

Sally said yes. When Friday came back, Sally said, 'I'll tell you who else I've seen — that Bella Jackson. She must live nearby because she comes into the bakery now and then and buys our macaroons. Her, or Louisa Coutts or that Becky Haggle.'

'Hoddle.'

'Hoddle. And sometimes Bella has that cove with her, the crewman from the *Isla*? The really nasty one? I nearly died when I saw him.'

'Amos Furniss?'

Sally nodded. 'What's he doing with Bella Jackson?'

'I've heard he works for her now. She lives on Cumberland Street.'

'I don't understand it. She comes in all gussied up in these fancy clothes waving her money around. Isn't she supposed to be a convict like us?'

'She got herself married to a rich old man.'

'Married! But she's *horrible*. Who'd have her?'

Friday gulped her drink. That was three now and she wasn't even feeling muzzy. 'Well, you know what a conniving bloody cow she is. Drink up. I'm going next door to the Pat. Do you want to come?'

'Just for a quick one. And I'll have to tell my friend.'

'Your man?' Friday indicated the sandy-haired lad sitting to Sally's left.

Sally leant in to Friday's ear, though there was no need; the noise in the pub was such now that her companion had no chance of hearing her. 'No, but he'd like to be. I only came out with him to shut him up.'

The lad wasn't very happy about it, but ten minutes later Friday and Sally left the Bird-in-Hand, walked ten yards along Gloucester Street, up the steps and through the double front doors of the St Patrick's Inn. The scene of conviviality inside was identical to the one they'd just left and they stayed half an hour, long enough for Sally to drink a short ale and Friday, relieved to at last be feeling a little drunk, to knock back two more large gins.

Descending the steps on their way out, Friday spied Matthew Cutler walking past and was struck by the most excellent idea.

'Matthew!' she shouted. 'Matthew, wait!'

Matthew turned and spotted her.

Friday leapt down the last three steps and landed beside him in a froth of skirts and a flash of shapely calf, pinching his backside and making him jump. 'Where are you off to?'

'The Australian,' he said, embarrassed and glancing about to see if anyone had observed what she'd done. 'To have supper with James.'

'Oh, what a pity. I'd've come with you but I've been banned from there.'

'Oh dear, that's a shame.' Noticing Sally, Matthew tipped his hat.

'This is Sally Minto,' Friday said. 'She was on the *Isla* with us. Sally, this is Mr Matthew Cutler.'

'Good evening, sir,' Sally said. 'You were a passenger, weren't you? Paying, I mean. Of course.' She blushed.

'Yes, I was. How are you finding life in New South Wales?'

'Very well, thank you.'

Sally smiled prettily at Matthew and fluttered her eyelashes; he smiled somewhat sappily back.

Her work done, Friday said brusquely, 'This is jolly, but we're wasting drinking time. Come on, Sally.'

'Yes, I must be off myself,' Matthew said. 'Don't want to keep James waiting. Very nice to meet you, Miss Minto. It is "Miss", I take it?'

'Yes, it is. Very nice to meet you, too, Mr Cutler.'

Friday dragged Sally off back towards the Bird-in-Hand, but when she glanced over her shoulder Matthew was staring after them. Smirking, she waggled her fingers at him.

Chapter Twelve

Sarah's bum had gone numb. She stood, stretched, moved to the window and checked her watch again: twenty-five minutes past eleven. Christ, she could have emptied the entire house by now.

But at last she thought she heard something. She opened Mrs Tregoweth's bedroom door, checked to make sure the servant girl was nowhere in sight and crept down the hallway to the big window overlooking the front of the house. There was nothing there, but she was sure she'd heard a carriage. She hurried back to Mrs Tregoweth's room and peeked through the window overlooking the back garden.

As she did, light spilt across the rear verandah and a curricle drew up on the carriageway running along one side of the house. A man in a top hat — presumably Mr Tregoweth — climbed out and handed down Mrs Tregoweth. She stumbled and whacked him on the arm. Words were exchanged, though Sarah couldn't clearly hear them. Mr Tregoweth led the horses towards the stable while his wife stepped up onto the verandah and entered the house.

Sarah padded silently into the dressing room, lay on the floor and rolled under the bottom shelf, shuffling her bum and shoulders hard against the wall. All she had to do now was wait for Mrs Tregoweth to go to sleep, then take the jewellery and leave. Of course, it was rarely that straightforward. Wandering around people's houses when they weren't in them was easy; stealing from right beneath their noses was a different matter altogether, and she felt an unpleasant buzz of nervous anticipation ripple through her muscles. But that was all right; only complete idiots didn't feel fear just before a job.

She heard voices, the door to the bedroom creaked open and someone entered. No, two people. A dim, flickering light leached into the dressing room, then grew brighter as the wall lamps were lit.

'Tea, thank you, Josie,' Mrs Tregoweth said. 'And three of those almond biscuits Mrs Bunyard baked this morning.'

'Yes, ma'am.'

Josie, so that really was her name. Josie Light-Fingers.

Mrs Tregoweth's feet appeared in the dressing room. The hem of her velvet mantle dipped then disappeared, hung on a hook. One foot eased a satin slipper off the other, the bunioned, silk-stockinged foot vanished from view, followed by the sound of cracking toe knuckles and groaning. Sarah winced. The other slipper came off and was discarded on the floor with its partner.

Mrs Tregoweth left the dressing room and sat on something that protested squeakily. Her bed? The chair at her dressing table? Not much happened for a few minutes, then Sarah heard her cross the room and take the dog painting off the wall. There was the distinctive sound of a key turning in a lock, some shuffling, then the safe was locked again and the painting replaced.

A knock on the door and Josie called, 'Ma'am? Your tea.'

'Come in.'

A tray rattled as Josie entered.

'Help me with my gown, will you?'

Sarah stifled a sigh; Mrs Tregoweth could be buggering about with her toilet all night.

But with Josie's help it only took twenty minutes and finally she climbed into bed, complaining that now her tea had gone cold. Josie brought her another pot.

As she slurped it in a very unladylike manner and noisily munched her almond biscuits, the door opened again and a man's voice said heartily, 'Ah, all tucked up like a bug in a rug, I see?'

A clink as the teacup was replaced on its saucer.

'What do you want, Phillip?'

Another creaking noise. They could do with a bit of maintenance around here.

'Is there room for me in there?' he wheedled.

Oh *no*!

'After the way you behaved this evening?' Mrs Tregoweth snapped. 'I very much doubt it.'

'Oh, Eunice, be reasonable. I couldn't help that. *She* was flirting with *me*!'

'You could have walked away. But then you never have, have you?'

Sarah very carefully rolled onto her stomach and peeped through the open doorway. Eunice Tregoweth sat propped against her pillows with the bedclothes drawn up to, and tucked tightly under, her armpits. She wore a nightgown fastened at the frilled neck, her hair invisible beneath a lace nightcap. Her vibrant orange wig now resided on a mannequin on her dressing table, looking disturbingly like a decapitated head.

Phillip Tregoweth, tall, sunken-faced and thin, sat hunched on the edge of his wife's bed wearing a floppy nightcap and a calf-length nightshirt; this last revealed white legs bulging with worm-like veins, and flat feet with thick, yellow toenails. He settled a hopeful hand on his wife's knee and she jerked violently away from him.

'Eunice!' he said sharply, 'I wish to exercise my conjugal rights.'

'Then I'm afraid you've come to the wrong place,' his wife shot back. 'You should have considered that when you bought me fake glass trinkets instead of real emeralds. Why don't you go and pester that red-headed whore of yours down on Argyle Street?'

Surely she couldn't mean Friday? Oh God, *surely* not!

'That wouldn't be exercising my *conjugal* rights, would it? That would be exercising my God-given rights as a male. Anyway, they're closed.'

Christ, what an arsehole!

Eunice said, 'Go away, Phillip, and leave me alone.'

'I see that as usual you're going to insist on being selfish,' he replied.

'Yes, I am.'

'It's no wonder I'm forced to look elsewhere for my pleasure.'

'Oh, just get out,' Eunice said wearily. 'Go on.'

Phillip stood, took his candle in its brass chamber stick and left, banging the door truculently behind him. Sarah watched as Eunice opened the drawer in her night table, found a small packet and emptied the contents into her tea. She stirred briskly with a teaspoon, drank it down, grimaced, then tugged the bell pull next to her bed.

When Josie arrived, smothering a yawn, Eunice said, 'You can douse the lamps now, I intend to go to sleep. And lock the door on your way out, will you? I have the other key under my pillow. And Josie? Lock your own door tonight.'

'Yes, ma'am. Thank you, ma'am.'

Sarah made a face. Damn, that meant she would definitely have to leave via a window. Was that a sleeping powder Eunice Tregoweth had tipped into her tea? Fingers crossed it had been. How long would it take to work?

The lamps went out one by one, Eunice removed her false teeth and set them on the night table, and Josie left.

In the dark Sarah couldn't see her watch, so she counted to sixty, ten times.

Eunice Tregoweth's breathing wasn't settling. Mind you, she was probably upset by what her rotten husband had said to her. What a bastard. God, was he really one of Friday's customers? How disgusting. Poor Friday, she really did work hard for her money.

A loud snoring noise came and Sarah jumped. She counted off another five minutes, and another, until Mrs Tregoweth's breathing finally slowed and assumed a reasonably regular pattern.

Sarah turned onto her back, listening with straining ears to the depth and timbre of the breathing, willing the woman with every ounce of her being to be properly asleep. Outside, not far away, a night bird gave a lonely, eerie call.

At last she rolled out from under the shelf and into a crouch. She remained completely still, but after the figure in the bed hadn't stirred for some minutes she uncurled herself and moved across to the tallpost, her bare feet making no sound at all on the thick carpet.

Eunice Tregoweth lay on her side, her mouth open, emitting a series of gentle snores. Her knees were pulled up to her belly and her arms tucked into her chest; with the quilt up around her ears and her nightcap tied at her throat, barely any of her was visible. It was a hot night: she must be sweating like a pig under there.

Sarah padded silently across to the dog painting and carefully lifted it off the wall, resting it on the floor near her feet. She dug in her pocket for the skeleton key and, with both hands to minimise her nervous tremor, guided it into the keyhole and opened the little door.

The interior of the box was in complete darkness, which didn't matter at all as she already knew what she wanted. She gently felt about until her hand closed over one of the small velvet bags; squeezing, she knew she'd found the diamond ring. She tucked it into her satchel, followed by the second velvet bag containing the cannetille bracelet. The two cases containing the paste parure and sapphire rivière she didn't touch; Mrs Tregoweth could keep her lead-glass jewellery, and though the sapphires were pretty and valuable, they weren't spectacular enough to risk stealing and attempting to fence. The ring and the bracelet, however, were a different story. Both would have to be sent back to England, but Bernard could take care of that.

Working more quickly now, but just as carefully, she closed the safe and locked it, listening all the time for a change to Mrs Tregoweth's breathing. She lifted the painting off the floor and, peering into the blackness between the wall and the frame, snagged the cord at the back of the painting over the picture hook and cautiously let go.

The painting fell to the floor, hitting Sarah's bare foot and the polished floorboards with a hollow crack.

Her pulse galloping and sweat popping out all over her face, she whipped her head towards the bed; Eunice Tregoweth had stopped snoring.

'Nnnuunh?'

Sarah held her breath, calculating the distance to the dressing-room door. A fair way, but Mrs Tregoweth was old; she could be across the room and out the window before the old trout even had her feet on the floor.

A snort, a long sigh, nothing for almost half a minute, then the snores started up again.

Feeling faintly sick Sarah silently let out her own breath, and at last allowed herself to rub her throbbing right toes against the back of her left calf. She lifted the painting again, this time holding the cord as she slipped it over the picture hook to make sure it was secure, and kept a firm grip on the frame as she let the cord take the weight. Bloody thing must weigh half a ton; her toes were killing her.

It held.

She limped back to the dressing room. The window sash opened without protest, and she climbed onto the sill and reached across to the drainpipe, testing its strength. It felt secure so she transferred her weight to it, with some difficulty easing the window down again, then descended, wincing as her wounded toes struggled to grip. She climbed down until she was level with a lower-storey roof, crossed to it and scuttled across the tiles until she'd reached the eaves at the far end, then swung herself to the ground using another drainpipe.

She scaled the Tregoweths' fence, retrieved her boots, cap and jacket, and retraced her earlier footsteps until she came out on Gloucester Street, not far from the Argyle Street intersection. Where, as he'd promised, Adam was waiting for her in an alleyway across the road.

She stood in the shadows, silent and hidden, watching him. He'd discarded the wig and fake whiskers and was dressed once more in his normal attire, the black trousers and coat he usually favoured. He was fanning his face with his hat against the night's heat and looked on edge, starting every time a passer-by approached the entrance to the alley. He didn't have to meet her here; they both knew she could easily find her own way home.

She knew he wanted her. There'd been the kisses, and she'd noticed his cockstand earlier. She wasn't blind. Or stupid.

She couldn't deny she was attracted to him — to Friday she could, perhaps, but not to herself — and they worked so well together, but, oh, what she would have to sacrifice! Not just the special bond she had with her precious friends, but also her privacy, her identity, her bed, her time and, most important of all, her independence. And he would always be her master; for the next six years he would hold her assignment papers, he would never forget she'd stolen from him, and he would *forever* be the head of the house. She knew she couldn't tolerate it, and she couldn't have Friday and Harrie believing Adam would take precedence over their friendship.

And what of the secret she carried from her past like a festering sore that wouldn't heal, a corruption that had infected her with shame and soured her view of the world for years? How could she ever make peace with such rottenness within herself, and could she expect it of anyone else?

But Adam's lips were so soft and his eyes burnt with such heat.

She stepped out of the shadows.

Friday arrived at the Black Rat just past midnight. She'd been to all the hotels she'd set out to visit, but when she'd bumped into Molly Bates from Mrs H's at the Saracen's Head she'd decided she didn't feel like going home yet and they'd staggered down to the Black Rat, as mashed as each other.

Like all of Mrs H's girls, Molly was spectacular. She was petite and curvaceous, and used potassium lye to bleach her thick, springy hair a startling yellow blonde. She drank as often and as much as Friday and Mrs H had forbidden them to go out together, but Elizabeth Hislop was the last thing on their minds as they lurched through the door of the Black Rat, giggling and leaning on each other.

Friday, however, was fast reaching the stage of inebriation that, for her, meant she would very soon explode into violence. It was a strange thing but when she hit the mash hard, she inevitably reached a point at which she *knew* she should stop before it was too late. But she never did stop, and after she passed that point there was always a horrible plummeting sensation in her belly and everything that had been fun and exciting only minutes earlier suddenly felt sour and maddening and intolerable.

The pub was still packed despite the hour, its stinking hot, smoky, dark recesses crowded with locals and sailors of many nations harboured up in Sydney Cove while the town's stevedores and provedores plied their trades. Heading for the serving counter Friday and Molly bounced between Chinamen, Arabs, astonishingly tall African men with gleaming skin the colour of coal, Portuguese, ruddy-skinned American Indians, Frenchmen, Maori traders from New Zealand, British tars, Dutchmen and Mauritians.

'Rum?' Friday shouted over the din.

Molly nodded; it was her preferred tipple.

The drinks were served in tankards and were cheap; the barman must be confusing them with the whores working the room, Friday thought, but didn't bother to put him right. She gave Molly hers and they found two stools and an upturned barrel in a corner, out of the way of rough elbows and heavy boots. Friday very deliberately set her tankard on the barrel, backed up to a stool, missed it and crashed to the floor. Stunned, she sat there, her skirts up around her thighs, and burst into hysterical giggles. Shrieking with laughter herself, Molly hauled her up by the arm and, with her foot, edged the stool under Friday's backside.

'There y'are. Have another go.'

Very carefully Friday sat, making sure her arse connected this time. She stared hard into her tankard, checking its contents were still there, and took a long swig.

'Look,' Molly said, waving at one of the whores. 'There's Susannah Moffat from Mrs McShera's house.' She let out an enormous burp. 'Mrs M'll be pleased when she finds out she's been trawling this shithole.'

Friday squinted, seeing two Susannahs. 'How'll she find out?'

'I'll tell her. 'Less Susannah pays back the money she owes me.'

'But that's blackmail.'

Molly shrugged. 'So?'

Friday's view was suddenly blocked by a burly man standing immediately in front of her.

'How much?' he demanded in a heavy French accent.

'What?' Friday was annoyed. She didn't like the French. The men always stank.

The man produced his purse. 'How much? For the fuck?'

'I'm not for sale,' Friday snapped.

'How *much*!?' The man insisted. 'I will double.'

'Are you deaf? Fuck *off*.' Friday aimed a kick at him.

He dodged her boot easily and called her a *chatte*, but he went, melting back into the crowd.

'Arsehole frog,' Friday muttered.

'Christ, here we go,' Molly said.

Friday followed her line of sight: three women were advancing on them, barging their way through the throng, not caring whose ale or rum they spilt. They were whores, the brightly dyed feathers in their hair bobbing angrily and their white breasts wobbling above daringly low necklines.

Excellent, Friday thought; she could do with a bloody good scrap. She knocked back the rest of her gin, gagged slightly and pushed herself unsteadily to her feet.

'Piss off,' the first woman to arrive said. She'd seen quite a number of better days. 'You're queering our pitch. Go on, sling your 'ook, the pair of yis.'

'Might have, if you'd asked nicely,' Friday replied. 'But did you? Nope. So piss off your own self, you dried-up old fus ... fustilugs.'

The tart gaped at her, took a moment to collect herself, grabbed Friday's neck scarf with one hand and threw a punch with the other. Friday ducked and dodged sideways, almost garrotting herself, knocked over the barrel and fell, but recovered and swung wildly back. Beside her Molly stepped in and hit out at one of the woman's companions. Then all five were at it, throwing punches, pulling hair and dislodging wigs, slapping, scratching and kicking. The crowd gathered like flies on fresh horseshit, lustily cheering the combatants on as lace, beads and bits of fabric came loose from dresses, and feathers drifted to the stained wooden floor. But the Black Rat's owner, envisaging at least a temporary dip in his profits if his pet whores were injured so they couldn't work, alerted his cellarman and his doorkeeper and, with some difficulty, pulled the women away from one another.

Friday and Molly were thrown out, but not before Friday had blearily spied Amos Furniss slouched against a wall near the door, tankard in hand, grinning nastily at her.

And the dark-haired girl with him, her face concealed by shadow — had that been Loulou?

Adam brought Sarah a pot of tea and she drank two cups one after the other, she was that thirsty. And hot. She'd left her boots and socks by the back door as they'd come in, and her jacket over the back of a chair. She'd already told him on the walk back everything had gone well, so there wasn't much left to say. The ring and the bracelet were on the dining table, sparkling in the lamplight. Now that she was safely home she felt exhausted and wrung out, but still uncomfortably, expectantly on edge: she knew the night wasn't yet over.

'As far as I could see, the house girl doesn't know where the safe is,' she said. 'Mrs Tregoweth put the jewellery in it herself. So the girl can't reasonably be blamed for the theft.'

'Good.' That had been worrying Adam. He cleared his throat. 'Sarah?'

He was staring at her. He'd discarded his own coat and sat with his shirtsleeves pushed up to his elbows. Unbound, his dark hair fell across his forehead, tendrils sticking damply to his skin. His forearms were pale, and scattered with dark hair. His face was half in shadow, and the eye she could see glittered. A sheen of sweat glistened in the hollow of his throat where his pulse beat. He looked ... saturnine, and a thrill rippled up her spine.

He also looked as though he might be about to say something momentous, and she panicked. She tried to think of some comment to deflect him, but her voice failed her utterly.

He pushed back his chair and moved around the table until he stood before her. 'Sarah,' he said again. His hands gently grazed her bare arms, and he bent to kiss her.

But then he pulled away from her. 'Wait there,' he said, and hurried from the room.

Sarah stared after him, nonplussed. She cupped a hand and breathed into it. No, not her. What was he doing? Brushing his own teeth? Having a pee? She gave way to a nervous, snorted giggle. This was mad. She shouldn't be letting him do this. She shouldn't be letting *herself* do this.

From the shop came the muted sounds of cabinet doors opening and closing, then he was back, in his hands a pool of gleaming gold and sparkling gems.

He scattered the lot on the table, dragged her chair around, and sat down facing her. He fastened a heavy necklace of deep red garnets and pearls around her neck, leaning close enough for her to breathe in his scent, then slid a cobalt-green tourmaline and gold bracelet and a heavy gold bangle up her arms. The hard edges of the pieces were rough against her suddenly very sensitive skin and made her shiver with excitement. On her fingers he placed four of his best rings: diamond; ruby and aquamarine; star sapphire; and chrysolite and diamond. He moved behind her, and she felt him unwind her plait and spread her hair over her shoulders and down her back.

'There,' he said, moving to sit before her again. He ran the lightest of fingers across the scar on her face. 'My girl of shadows. My beautiful girl of shadows.'

Sarah closed her eyes: it was the loveliest thing anyone had ever said to her. She felt a shift of air and his mouth was on hers, gentle at first, polite, then with increasing hunger.

She raised her fists to push him away but Adam's hands closed around her wrists and held them firm.

'Please, Sarah,' he whispered against her face, his stubble scratching her cheek. 'Please let me.'

She opened her eyes, saw the raw desire in his expression, and her belly did another one of those delicious, lazy flips. And though her instinct still warned her she was about to make a terrible mistake, for once she listened to her heart, and she nodded her assent.

He swept her up, knocking over her chair, and carried her down the hall. As he banged her head against the wall on the landing halfway up the stairs, she giggled again, aware that if he'd dropped her on her arse she probably wouldn't have minded. Giggling! For God's sake, she never giggled! But her face was pressed against the damp skin of his throat, and she could smell him again and she felt intoxicated — silly and wild and utterly careless. She grabbed a handful of his hair and pulled his face down to meet hers, kissing him hard. They bounced off the frame of his bedroom door and Adam almost did drop her, and then she was sitting on his lap, on his bed.

She had a second to notice he'd already lit the lamps — when had he done that? — before he was kissing her again, his tongue flickering inside her mouth and his hands roving over her shoulders and back and waist.

And then he was at the buttons of her shirt, opening them one by one until her belly and breasts were bare, except for the garnet necklace, glittering drops of blood against her damp white skin. He slid the shirt off her shoulders and down her arms, and tossed it on the floor. She shivered, but from anticipation, not cold.

He stood and lifted her in one fluid movement, and lay her on the bed. She languidly raised an arm to her forehead, and immediately got an articulated gold bracelet caught in her hair.

'Bugger,' she murmured.

Adam bent over her and very carefully disentangled it, then removed it from her arm altogether.

'It looks superb on you,' he said, 'but perhaps isn't very practical for love-making.'

He took off his own shirt then, revealing a pale, elegantly muscled chest and a flat belly with a line of black hair disappearing under the waistband of his trousers.

Sarah stared. He was beautiful.

'You're beautiful,' he said, and for a confused moment Sarah thought he'd somehow voiced her own thoughts.

He opened the buttons on her trousers and slid them down and over her feet. Fighting an urge to place her hands over her groin, she closed her eyes again — she knew he was gazing at her.

'*So* beautiful,' he whispered.

The bed creaked as he lay beside her, and she started as his hands slid over her warm flesh. She opened her eyes and touched him back, tentatively at first, then with increasing confidence. Beneath her palm his skin felt like the finest silk velvet, the contours of his body a gift just for her. When his hand moved down her belly to the place between her legs, she thought she might cry out, the feelings were so extraordinary, so unexpected. So rude, too. Her face flaming, she couldn't look at him.

'Sarah,' he groaned, his voice rough. 'I don't think I can wait. Not this time.'

What was he saying? She'd never had a lover before. She gave the tiniest nod, hoping it was the right thing to do, and *very* much hoping she wasn't going to miss out on anything because of it.

He rolled onto his back, shoved down his trousers and kicked them off, then positioned himself between her legs.

His erection jutted out like … well, she didn't know what it was like. She'd only seen one before and that had been vile. But this time, though she was nervous, she wasn't frightened, and she certainly wasn't angry. She did, however, feel as though she was about to lose control of herself, she wanted Adam so desperately.

He propped himself on his elbows, cupped his hands behind her neck, and kissed her passionately. Then he pushed himself into her, letting out a long, guttural groan.

It hurt, and she didn't care. She raised her legs, wrapped them around Adam's waist, drew him in and held on while he drove into her. The pain subsided to a sting that very quickly became something else building inside her. His back became slippery with sweat and then it dripped off his chin as he arched his spine above her, every muscle in his body taut as seconds later he emptied himself into her.

'Oh good Christ,' he moaned. His arms shaking, he lowered himself onto her, his hair falling across her face. 'Bloody hell.'

He lay inert for a moment. She could feel the wild pounding of his heart against her own chest, as though their bodies for a few moments had joined. He rolled off her and stared at the ceiling, panting.

'I'm really sorry, Sarah. That was ungentlemanly.'

Sarah felt ... odd.

Adam said, 'I need a few minutes, but in the meantime ...'

He rolled her onto her side and snuggled behind her, pulling her against his chest and belly, his left arm holding her. His leg snaked between hers to separate them while his other hand crept over her hip and down to the slippery mess he'd left between her legs. Slowly, with his fingers, he began to circle the swollen flesh there. Immediately, the feeling that had been building when he'd been inside her was back, a tingling and a sort of itching that made her toes want to curl. She made a noise and bit her lip, embarrassed, and realised she was wriggling and tried to stop and couldn't. He increased the pressure of his fingers and the sensation intensified, and she was pushing against his hand and he was pushing against her, erect again, and suddenly there was an incredible, wild burst of sensation down there and she cried out and arched backwards, almost nutting him in the face with the back of her head, and getting the beginnings of terrible cramp in her toes.

And then he was on her again, and it wasn't until afterwards that he noticed the faint tinge of blood on the bed cover.

He stared at her, his expression shocked and a little bemused. 'Oh God, Sarah, I'm sorry. I just assumed.'

She put her hand over his mouth. 'Don't. Don't spoil it.'

He moved her hand away. 'I'm *so* sorry, Sarah. If I'd known —'

'You'd have what?'

After a moment he touched her face. 'I still would have asked if I could.'

She laid her head on his shoulder. 'I'm glad.'

She would tell him one day, but not now. Or maybe she wouldn't.

Friday awoke with the usual monstrous headache, bilious stomach and feeling of deep, persistent dread.

But at least she was in her own bed.

She rolled onto her back an inch at a time so her brains could keep up and not protest too painfully. A vicious shaft of sunlight stabbed into her room through the gap in her curtains, turning the inside of her closed eyelids a searing orange. The day already felt hot.

Warily opening her eyes she glanced at the clock; it was a quarter to ten. She sat up, holding her pounding head. A towel covered her pillow and a bucket sat on newspaper spread on the floor. How had they got there?

Groaning piteously, she pushed off the bedclothes and eased her legs — covered with fresh bruises — over the side of the bed. She was wearing her shift from last night and her arms were also bruised; her lovely peacock in particular had a big purple and red blotch across its head and some of the scabs had bled. Shit. Her jaw was sore, too. She felt around with her tongue and discovered she'd lost another tooth. Fortunately it was a back one; if it had been from the front Mrs H would've had her guts for garters.

Her mouth suddenly awash with spit and her stomach clenching violently, she lunged for the bucket and vomited horribly and loudly, her skull feeling as though it might burst. With trembling hands she used the towel to dab at her mouth and streaming eyes and thought, For fuck's sake, I must stop doing this. Her bowel gave an ominous grumble and she knew she only had a minute to get down to the privy near the stables.

She struggled into a robe, shoved her feet into her comfortable black boots, picked up her bucket of sick and unlocked her bedroom door.

'Dear oh dear, don't you look a sight.'

Elizabeth Hislop stood in the hall bearing a tray on which sat a pot of tea, a plate of bread, butter and jam, and a small brown bottle.

'Can't stop, got the shits,' Friday said quickly, noting the opium bottle gratefully. That would fix her head, though she'd leave it until she'd finished whipping the cat, or it wouldn't stay down.

Elizabeth stood aside. 'I'm not surprised, the state you were in last night.'

Friday rushed past, heading for the stairs. Halfway down, on the landing, she had to stop to be sick again, clenching her buttocks tightly. Outside she dashed across the yard into one of the two privies, slammed the door, yanked up her shift and threw herself onto the seat just in time.

'God almighty,' she muttered, her head in her hands as her bowels emptied explosively into the pit below.

The smell was atrocious and she vomited into the bucket a third time, doing her best to breathe through her mouth, which wasn't easy while being sick. Her head throbbed mercilessly and her stomach muscles protested, but when it was over she felt thoroughly emptied, and somewhat better. She used the squares of newspaper on the nail in the privy wall to clean herself, then tipped the bucket down the hole. Exiting on wobbly legs, she warned an approaching Jimmy Johnson to use the other privy; looking alarmed, he smartly changed direction towards the neighbouring door.

While Friday was dashing downstairs, Elizabeth knocked on Molly's bedroom door. When no response was forthcoming, she knocked more loudly, waited another minute, then let herself in with the master key.

Molly lay in bed, the bedclothes pulled up to her ears, her tangled and knotted hair spread across her pillow like a ransacked bird's nest.

'Wake up, Molly.'

'I am awake.'

'I want to talk to you.'

Molly rolled over and peered at Elizabeth through bloodshot eyes.

Elizabeth said, 'What have I said to you about leading Friday astray?'

'Oh, for Christ's sake.' Molly propped herself on one elbow, gave a liquid burp, and pressed her hand over her mouth. She swallowed and grimaced. '*I'm* not leading her astray, she's leading herself astray.'

'It's you who takes her out drinking.'

'Oh, it bloody is not. She hardly ever goes out with me. And if it wasn't me, she'd find someone else. Or she'd drink by herself. She *does* drink by herself.' Molly rolled onto her back and stared at the ceiling. 'Face it, Mrs H, she's an inebriate. And there's nothing you can do about it.'

Moving closer to the bed, Elizabeth glared down at Molly. 'Yes there is. I can fire you. Then she can't go out drinking with you.'

Molly sat up, wincing at the pain in her head. 'No, you can't.'

'Who says? You?'

'That's right.' Molly hoicked and spat into an empty tumbler on her night table.

Folding her arms over her ample bosom and raising her chin, Elizabeth said, 'I think you'll find I can.'

Molly's own chin came up. 'You think so? You just try it. Because if you do, I'll tell the authorities you're paying assigned convict girls to work in your whorehouse.'

Elizabeth stared at her in icy silence for a moment, then crossed to the door. But before she opened it she turned and said, 'You're a nasty piece of work, aren't you?'

Outside in the yard Friday washed her hands and rinsed the bucket using water from the rainwater overflow barrel, then went back inside. Mrs H was closing the door to Molly's room, rather forcefully.

'She's no more fit than you are,' she said angrily. 'What did the pair of you get up to last night? And why are you covered in bruises?'

'I'm not,' Friday said, pulling her robe closed.

'You are. There's one on your chest, and your wrist, and is that one on your cheek? You *know* what I think about my girls fighting! What if one of your customers saw? I run a superior establishment — I can't be seen to employ girls who roll around in the gutter belting the living daylights out of folk!'

'They weren't folk.' Friday trudged into her room and slumped onto the bed. 'They were sixpenny jack-whores. And they started it. Reckoned we were trespassing.'

Elizabeth knew damned well where such women worked. 'You were in the Black Rat again, weren't you?'

'Sorry, Mrs H,' Friday mumbled. She didn't like it when Elizabeth told her off. It made her feel like she was five years old.

'I should think so! For God's sake, Friday, have some respect for yourself.' Elizabeth passed her the opium. 'I think it's high time you did something about your drinking, don't you?'

Forgetting she'd told herself something very similar less than half an hour earlier, Friday said, 'Why? What's wrong with it?' She sat up, removed the glass stopper from the opium bottle and took two sips.

'What's wrong with it? Look at yourself!' Elizabeth laid her hand on the back of Friday's head and made her look towards the looking glass on her dressing table. 'Go on!'

Friday did, and got quite a fright. Her hair was knotted and wild and something had stuck big clumps of it together, her face was deathly pale and her lips dry and cracked, her eyes were bloodshot, she had a blossoming bruise on her right cheek, and the black kohl she'd applied the previous afternoon was smudged halfway down her face. No wonder Jimmy Johnson had looked frightened.

'*And* you smell like an unwashed bar rag!' Elizabeth said. 'I've lost count of the number of times you've come home like this. It worries me, Friday, it really does.'

Friday said nothing.

'Apart from the fact you're ruining your looks and your health, not to mention bringing the name of my house into disrepute, have you not thought about what might happen if the police pick you up?' Elizabeth caught sight of the clothes strewn all over the floor. 'Did you wear that out last night? Where are your nice dresses? Why are you wearing that flash tat again?'

Friday still said nothing. The opium had begun to ease into her blood, washing through her like a velvet wave, smoothing away her headache, comforting her bruised flesh, wrapping her in soft cotton gauze.

'Are you listening to me?'

'Yes.'

'Never forget you're a bonded convict, my girl. If you're picked up you'll be back in the Factory so fast your feet won't touch the ground. And not in first class, either.'

'I know that.'

Elizabeth rolled her eyes. 'Well, why carry on like this, then?'

The door opened and Molly stuck her head in. 'How you doing?'

'Bit rough,' Friday replied. 'You?'

'Same. I swear, never again,' Molly said, darting a sly glance at Elizabeth. 'I'm going back to sleep for a few hours.'

'Well, open your window before you do,' Elizabeth ordered sharply. 'Your room smells like a sailor's socks marinated in rum.'

A moment later Molly's bedroom door clicked shut.

'You haven't answered my question,' Elizabeth said.

'What question?' Friday caught sight of her boss's reflection in the looking glass and prepared to duck; Mrs H looked like she could happily slap her across the head.

Elizabeth let out a long, loud breath. 'You know very well what it was. Why do you keep doing it?'

Several plausible excuses flashed through Friday's mind but she couldn't share them with Mrs H, and she knew they weren't the real reason anyway, and she didn't want to lie. She owed Elizabeth Hislop more than that.

'I don't know,' she said eventually. She lay back on her bed and rested her arm across her eyes. For a second she almost fell asleep. 'I go out to get as mashed as I can. It's the only time I get any peace and quiet. From this.' She tapped gently on her skull. 'And I just can't stop. And I don't want to. I like it. Except for the horrors.'

'Well, it's ruining you. You do know that, don't you?'

Friday shrugged. 'I don't know if I care.'

'You should care.'

'Why?'

'Because people depend on you. Your friends Sarah and Harrie certainly do. And what about whoever it is you're supporting in the Factory? And you've a lot of friends here. That's enough "shoulds", isn't it?'

'I'm fed up with "shoulds",' Friday muttered. 'I'm always doing what folk tell me I should do.'

Elizabeth gave an incredulous snort. 'What a lot of bloody rubbish! I've *never* known you to do anything anyone has said you *should* do!'

Friday had the grace to giggle. 'No, I don't suppose I do, do I?'

Sitting on the end of the bed, Elizabeth said, 'You're just like my man. He was a drinker.'

Friday recalled that Mrs H's husband was at sea, captain of a trading ship, though to her knowledge he hadn't been back to Sydney for some time.

'Did he give it up?' she asked.

'Give what up?'

'The drink. You said he *was* a drinker.'

'Oh. No, not as far as I know,' Elizabeth said. 'He pushed me to the absolute limit. Coming home blind drunk whenever he was in port, swearing and shouting, hitting me, breaking the furniture, upsetting my girls. When he actually *did* come home, that was. Sometimes I wouldn't see him for days, and then his ship would be gone and I wouldn't know until I read it in the paper. Then I'd have to go to the bank to see how much of my money he'd taken to pay for the damage he'd caused around the town and settle his debts.'

Friday lifted her arm and peeked at Elizabeth through one bleary eye. 'Why didn't you throw him out?'

'Oh, because I love him and I'm stupid,' she said crossly.

'So why haven't we met him?'

'One day he broke my jaw and it was the last straw. I'd had enough. I told him I didn't want to see his face again until he'd decided he'd rather have me than the booze. When he did that, then he could come home.'

'When was that?'

'Five years ago. I'm still waiting.'

Shocked, Friday stared at her.

Elizabeth moved to the door. 'I'm going to have to say the same thing to you, Friday. And I will say it, if you don't start taking better care of yourself. I'm not happy about those new tattoos of yours, either. They look cheap and I'm worried they'll deter your customers. I'd rather you didn't get any more. Now, I'm going to send Jack up with some hot water. You badly need a wash.'

She went out, shutting the door behind her.

Friday closed her eyes and heaved out a big, rancid sigh. She'd forgotten to ask Mrs H if she'd put the bucket in her room. She was right, though: she did have to stop drinking like this. But she'd told the truth — she did like it, and she truly couldn't imagine how she could ever get through her nights, or her mornings for that matter, without her gin.

Just the thought of it alarmed her and she staggered off her bed to the dressing table and dug around in a drawer for the bottle stashed there. There was another on top of her clothes press, out of sight at the back, but that required too much effort to reach today. She took several eye-watering gulps and got back into bed, slipping the bottle beneath the pillow.

Chapter Thirteen

January 1831, Sydney Town

Friday helped herself to one of the shortbread biscuits Sarah had arranged on a plate and set on the table. She was getting quite domesticated these days. Also, recently — very recently, in fact — something about Sarah had changed, and Friday had a pretty good idea about what might have happened. Yes, there'd certainly been some big changes in the Green household since Esther had buggered off. For a start, it was nice to sit inside at the table like normal folk, something they'd only once been permitted to do when Esther had been in residence. Friday didn't know about the others but she'd been getting fed up with balancing her arse on a bucket in the backyard, with lizards and the like skittering across her boots. Truth be told, she didn't mind the little slinky ones — they were quite sweet. It was the bigger ones with the blue tongues that gave her the shits.

Peering down her cleavage for errant shortbread crumbs, she said, 'Well, we know there'll be another demand, don't we? We just don't know when.' Spotting a crumb, she dug it out and flicked it on the floor, then looked at Sarah and Harrie and added truthfully, 'I've thought about this until my head hurts, I truly have. But I just can't see how we can get the upper hand.'

What was really vexing Friday was how to begin the conversation. She eyed Sarah and raised her brows, hoping Sarah would take the lead. She'd lured Harrie to Adam's house on the pretext of discussing their next move regarding Bella, but what she and Sarah most wanted to talk to Harrie about was her state of mind. They were extremely concerned about her, and the time had come to get to the bottom of whatever was so distressing her. Adam was out visiting Bernard Cole, and they knew they'd have at least an hour to themselves.

'Is that what's been upsetting you so?' Sarah asked Harrie. 'All this worry about Bella?'

Nodding thoughtfully, Harrie turned her teacup round and round in its saucer. 'It feels like a huge weight, crushing me into the ground. Like rocks on my chest. Sometimes I feel as though I can't breathe.'

She certainly looked like she'd been having trouble breathing lately, Friday thought. Her face — normally quite rosy across the cheeks — was the colour of fine flour, encouraging the freckles on her nose to stand out, and even her lips were barely tinged with pink, making her appear like a portrait that had so far only been sketched and not yet coloured. Making her look like a ... ghost.

Friday said, 'I feel that way, too, love, now and then. I really do. You know, deep in my heart I don't regret what we did, but sometimes I do wish we hadn't done it.'

'I don't,' Sarah said. 'He deserved it.'

There was a silence, then Harrie said, 'No, we were right to kill Keegan. An eye for an eye. That's what Rachel says.'

In the parlour, Esther's mantel clock struck the hour, the muted, mellow gong ringing hollowly through the house.

'*Rachel* says?' Sarah repeated.

'Yes.'

Sarah and Friday exchanged uneasy glances.

'When you dream about her, you mean?' Friday asked.

Harrie shook her head. 'Not in my dreams. When I talk to her.' She raised her eyes and stared directly at Friday. 'She's back, you see. Rachel's come back.'

The hairs on Friday's arms rippled. She risked a glance at Sarah, who stared back at her, her dismay evident.

'What do you mean, she's come back?' Now the tiny hairs on the back of Friday's neck were standing up.

'She's *here*,' Harrie said crossly, as though Friday were being stupid. 'She's returned from … wherever she's been.'

'Oh, Harrie, love, there's no such thing as ghosts,' Sarah said. 'That was just a game, with Esther. To scare her.'

Harrie's face flushed a dull, angry red. 'There *is*! Ghosts are real! Aren't they, Friday? Everyone knows that! And Rachel *has* come back. She talks to me, at night, in my room. And I talk to her. Tell her, Friday! You saw the *Flying Dutchman* on the *Isla*!'

But Friday couldn't, because she wasn't completely sure herself. She reckoned, though, if anyone was likely to come back from the dead it would be angry little Rachel, who had so abruptly been ripped away from all those things she'd wanted in her life. And from her baby daughter. Friday shivered.

'Don't you dare, Friday,' Sarah warned. 'Harrie, we know you've been very worried lately. Might you have imagined Rachel?'

Harrie banged her open palm on the table, making Sarah and Friday jump. 'No, I haven't! I knew you wouldn't believe me. She's real! I can see her and hear her. She *talks* to me! She told me we were right to kill Keegan, and she tells me all the time that I'm not …' Harrie paused to swallow, and added in a voice not much louder than a whisper, 'I'm not unhinged.'

'Nobody said you were,' Sarah said.

'You haven't said it, but you think it, don't you?' Harrie stood and collected her shawl and bonnet. 'You don't have to believe me, but perhaps that's what you need to do, to see her. Just believe. Have you ever thought of that?' At the door she said accusingly, 'I would have thought you'd *want* to see Rachel again.'

And she left.

Sarah and Friday sat in rueful silence. At last, Friday said, 'That didn't go very well.'

'Christ, what if she *is* going mad?'

Friday said, 'But sensible folk like Harrie don't go mad.'

'They don't talk to dead people, either.'

'Sarah?'

'What?'

'Do you really, truly, honestly not think there's any such things as ghosts?'

'No I bloody don't!'

'Lots of folk do, you know.'

'Well, I'm not one of them.'

'But what if there are?'

Sarah sighed and sloshed the teapot to see if there was any tea left. There was and she poured it into her cup. 'Then I'll be wrong, won't I? But I doubt it. Have you ever seen one?'

'I saw the *Flying Dutchman*.'

'You saw some strange waves and a lot of low cloud and spume, the same as I did.'

'Everyone else on the *Isla* saw a ghost ship.'

'No, not everyone. The captain didn't.'

'Christ, you're stubborn.' Friday shook her head despairingly. 'Well, I suppose what matters now is either Rachel has come back, which you reckon is impossible, or Harrie's gone barmy.'

They both knew that a female convict too sick to work would be returned to the Factory, and that one suffering from hysteria or mania could find herself confined to the hospital there or, even worse, the lunatic asylum at Liverpool — an awful prospect. But Harrie still seemed capable of carrying out her duties at the Barretts'. For now.

'Should we go and have a talk to Nora?' Friday suggested. 'If anything's amiss she'll have noticed. Can you get away tomorrow morning?'

'Good idea. I'll check with Adam when he gets in.'

'Speaking of Adam, have you got some news?'

'News? No.' Sarah blushed to the roots of her hair.

Friday laughed. 'You liar. Come on, out with it.'

Sarah saw she wasn't going to be able to hide much from Friday, and suddenly felt very self-conscious. 'Oh, all right. We ... well, we slept together.'

'About bloody time! How was it? Good? He looks like you'd get your money's worth.'

Sarah smiled to herself. 'Yes, it was good.'

'Best you've had?'

'I've nothing to compare it with.'

'What?' Friday was aghast. 'Really? Harrie I can understand, she's such a saint, but I just assumed with you. I thought you and that flash man of yours — what was his name? Ratface?'

'Ratcliffe. No. He tried often enough, but I couldn't stand him. So yes, Adam was my first.' Then Sarah put her hands behind her head, gazed up at the ceiling, and said, 'Shit.'

'What?'

'I've just lied to you.'

Friday asked, 'Is there any tea left in that pot?'

'It's nearly cold.'

'Then it'll have to be gin, won't it?' Friday took a flask from her reticule, fetched two glasses, poured a measure of gin into each, and pushed one across the table towards Sarah. 'Do you want to tell me?'

Sarah brought down her arms and studied her fingers, picking at one with a thumbnail. 'Only if you promise me you won't ... well, that you won't think badly of ...' She trailed off. 'Christ. That you won't think less of me.'

And Friday knew then that Sarah was about to tell her something momentous; until now, she'd never once indicated that she cared what anyone else thought of her — not even Harrie, Rachel or herself.

'Sarah, have a bloody good look at who you're talking to. Have you ever looked down on *me* for who I am or what I've done? For what the hell I *do*?'

Sarah had to think about that. 'No,' she answered honestly. 'I haven't.'

'No. And I won't do it to you.'

Seconds ticked by until Friday began to think that Sarah might have changed her mind. Finally, she began.

'I don't have any brothers or sisters and my mother and father were quite old when I was born. They were both high church and fanatically religious. My father was a tyrant and a violent bully, and my mother was too frightened of him to leave him.' Sarah's jaw tightened. 'Well, that's what I told myself. Better to think that than to believe she condoned what he did. And now she's dead so I can't ask her.'

'What about your father?'

'He's still alive, last I heard. Unfortunately.'

'And that's what he did? He beat you?' Friday asked. But she knew it had been much worse than that. Sarah was a strong girl in both mind and body. She would have endured beatings as stoically as she'd tolerated everything else that had happened to her over the last few years, and then left the memory where it belonged — in the past.

Her eyes on the table top, Sarah shook her head. She was swallowing and swallowing, as though trying to dislodge something hard and sharp, like a fishbone, from her throat.

Gently, Friday said, 'He fucked you, didn't he?'

Sarah sat very still, the rapid tapping of her foot beneath the table the only indication that she'd heard. At last, she nodded. 'In the end, yes.'

'How old were you?'

'Just a child. I can't remember. Eight?'

'And how long did it go on?'

271

'Until I was fourteen and left Leeds for London.'

Friday rubbed her hands across her face. She'd heard this story far too many times, but it still made the bile rise up in her throat.

'And you never told your mother?'

'I tried, and she told me not to lie. She said my father would never do anything that wasn't prescribed by the Bible. And then when she finally caught him, she told me it was my fault. They both did. They told me I was wicked and damned to hell.' Baring her teeth, Sarah scooped up her glass and hurled it at the wall, where it smashed into a thousand pieces.

Friday eyed the wet patch on the wallpaper and the shards of glass all over the floorboards. 'Where do you keep the brush and pan?'

While she swept, Sarah went on.

'I *hated* him, Friday, and her.'

'You don't think she really might have been scared of him?'

'No, I don't, and I don't want to hear you say that.'

Friday shut her mouth.

'And I hated their rotten church and endless praying and his stinking breath and disgusting flabby old body and his filthy prick,' Sarah spat, 'but most of all I hated *myself*.' She leant forwards, elbows on the table, head in her hands.

Friday finished cleaning up, took the broken glass outside and dumped it in the cesspit. When she returned, Sarah had poured herself another gin.

'So now you know,' she said. 'And I don't want to say anything more about it, if you don't mind. And *don't* tell Harrie. It'll only upset her.'

'Fair enough. Can I ask, though, does Adam know?'

'No. He thinks I was a virgin.'

I bet he doesn't, Friday thought. With his looks I bet he's put himself about enough to tell the difference between a maiden and a girl who's had a few sausage suppers. 'So will this be regular with you and him, do you think? Are you "walking out"?'

Sarah went red again. 'I don't know about walking out, but I haven't slept in my own bed since the first time we did it, and that was two weeks ago.' She licked her finger and rubbed at an invisible mark on her sleeve. 'Actually, I was going to ask you, I think I might have hurt myself slightly. Every time I pee I feel like it's on fire.'

'What's on fire?'

'Down there.'

'Your minge?'

Sarah nodded, but Friday was already laughing. And relieved; Sarah was embarrassed, but at least that awful look of haunted bitterness had gone from her face and she'd calmed down.

'It's not funny,' Sarah complained. 'It's bloody sore.'

'I know. It's from too much rutting. You've irritated the bit you pee out of.' Friday made a circle with her thumb and forefinger. 'Say this crease here is your pee-hole, and my finger here is him going in and out all night.'

'Not *all* night.'

'All right, most of the night, then. They rub together and this bit gets irritated, and sometimes you can get an infection as well.'

'Oh, that'll be nice. What can I do to ease it?'

'Bathe it with warm water and about half an ounce of borax three or four times a day, rub on a bit of laudanum before you pee, and drink a lot to flush everything out. Small beer, obviously, nothing stronger. And lay off the sex for a while. Or at least until it improves.'

'When will that be?'

'Couple of days? You don't have to stop doing everything, though, do you? Just sticking his cock in.'

'You have such a way with words.'

'I know. Er, Sarah, have you been using anything?'

'To avoid falling? Well, my courses are always regular, so for the days in the middle he pulled out, but lately he hasn't, because you can't get caught close to when you're due.'

Friday gaped at her in astonishment. 'Who the hell told you that?'

'The girl who lived next door to us. Her mother told her.'

'And how many brothers and sisters did this girl have?'

Sarah counted on her fingers. 'Eleven.'

'For God's sake, you can fall any time, whether the cove pulls out or not.'

Sarah paled visibly. 'Oh *no*! What if I'm ...?'

'Christ, Sarah, for a smart girl you can be a proper idiot. But don't worry.' Friday patted her arm reassuringly. 'There's plenty of things we can do if we have to. But you're not to let him near you until we've been to the chemist. We need to get you sorted.' She hesitated. 'Unless you *want* a baby?'

'No, I do not want a baby,' Sarah shot back. 'What a stupid thing to suggest. And you've got the cheek to call *me* an idiot!'

'Would Adam not marry you?'

'I've never thought about it. And now that I just have, if he asked me I'd say no.'

'Why?' Friday said, though she was very relieved to hear Sarah say so.

'Because he's already married, you fool.'

'Oh. That's right. I'd forgotten about her.'

'And he'd have to know where she is, to divorce her. So that isn't going to happen, is it?'

'Would you want it to happen?' Friday asked.

'No. I like things the way they are.'

Good, Friday thought. Bloody good.

Friday paused impatiently on the footway while a horse and cart loaded with barrels and wooden pallets exited from an alleyway, then hurried on down George Street. She wasn't happy. She should be, but she wasn't. A dog trotted past, a small one, its mangy head low and its prominent eyes darting in all directions like rolling brown marbles, and she felt like giving it a good kick.

Sarah had *said* she liked things the way they were with her and Adam, but Friday didn't believe her. If Adam could actually marry her, and he asked her, Friday had a bloody good idea Sarah would say yes. It was written all over her face every time she looked at him. And if that happened, that would be the end of the closeness between her and Sarah. And Harrie. Adam would come between them all, whether he meant to or not, so even though Friday thought he was a decent cove, he made her just about septic with jealousy and she hated it.

But Sarah and Adam getting together meant the end of the three of them anyway. Friday could feel it in her bones. Everything they'd been through, all they'd done to try and keep Rachel safe and then care for her and Charlotte — that bond would surely be fractured now. And it wasn't really Sarah's fault because she deserved a bit of happiness, but Friday was angry all the same. It might have been different if Harrie had taken up with James, because James in a way had been with them almost from the beginning, and he'd done what he could to help them in his own stuffy manner, but so far Harrie hadn't taken up with James, so it didn't matter.

She felt as though everything was slipping beyond her grasp. She didn't know what to do about Bella and her blackmail demands, she was frightened by what might be happening to Harrie's mind, she hated the thought of losing Sarah to Adam, and every day she worked for Elizabeth Hislop she grew more tired of servicing stupid, piggish men. *And* she thought she might have a dose of the clap, which meant a visit to that do-gooder, Chandler. It seemed the only release she got these days was when she was drunk or on the end of Leo Dundas's needles. And she still had a twelve-and-a-half-year prison term to serve in this uncivilised, flyblown, lonely bloody colony at the end of the bloody earth.

She picked up her skirts and crossed the street, running the last few yards to avoid some arrogant swell trotting past on a big, black horse. She raised her fist at him but was ignored. A second later she spotted Adam, dithering in front of a stall selling cut flowers, quite likely deciding which bunch to buy for Sarah. She bit her lip to stop herself from calling out, Freesias! She likes freesias! But he probably knew that already.

She watched him for a minute. There was no doubt he was a handsome man with his dark hair and eyes and those good lines to his face. Nice arse and legs, too. If he was her cup of tea she might even make a play for him herself. She didn't blame Sarah, actually. They really were a good match — a pair of dark little rats sneaking around town robbing things.

But she was going to do it anyway.

'Hello, Adam,' she said.

'Friday. Good morning. I'm just buying Sarah some flowers.'

'I can see that. Dahlias are her favourite.'

'Are they? Yes, those are a pretty colour, but I think I prefer the scent of the freesias. Don't you?'

Their eyes met for quite a long moment; Friday annoyed herself by looking away first. Adam pointed to the bunch of freesias he wanted and paid the flowerseller.

Friday decided to come straight out with it. 'I've just been to see Sarah. You and her seem to be getting along very well.'

'Yes, we are,' Adam replied, setting off back up George Street in the direction from which Friday had just come, the freesias dripping water down his trousers.

Friday hadn't intended to go back that way, but she would have to if she wanted to talk to him.

'I've known her for quite some time, Adam, and, well, I probably know her a lot better than you do.'

'Go on,' he said, pinching a slightly bruised petal off a bone-white bloom and discarding it.

'Well, what I'm going to say is for Sarah's sake as well as yours.'

Adam's brows went up slightly but he remained silent and kept walking.

'She has quite a murky past, Adam. She ran with a pretty rough crew in London and got used to pleasing herself. And because of that, I know for a fact she isn't prepared to settle down, and especially not with just one man. Ever, probably.' Behind her back, Friday crossed her fingers to nullify her lies.

Adam stopped and turned to face her. 'Isn't she?'

'Nope. Sorry. At best you're wasting your time and at worst you could really regret it.'

'Are you sure?'

Friday sighed. ''Fraid so.'

'Yet she's willing to share my bed?'

'For now. But, I'm sorry to say, you can't assume it's just your bed she's sharing,' Friday added, feeling like the biggest shite that ever lived.

Adam was silent for some time. Then he said, 'You're very fond of Sarah, aren't you?'

The question startled Friday. She didn't know what to say, so she resorted to her usual uncouth and bellicose tactic. 'Yes, I am. And if you tell her what I've just told you — even a single word — I'll know and I'll bash the daylights out of you, all right?' Though she wasn't sure she could. He wasn't a big man but he was fairly handy-looking.

Adam nodded thoughtfully. 'You know, I do understand, Friday.'

She didn't know how to respond to this, either. So she turned on her heel and marched away without looking back.

If she had, she might have seen the flicker of uneasiness cross Adam's face before he, too, walked off up the street.

Sarah was not pregnant, though somewhat alarmingly her courses arrived over a week late. By then Friday had taken her to the chemist and advised her on the best sea sponges to buy, and later shown her how to boil them with a pinch of borax powder, then soak them in lemon juice and quinine before use. She'd also recommended Sarah purchase a small stock of dried tansy, plus some oil of kill-bastard — though the chemist would probably refer to it as juniper — to have on hand in case the sponges failed.

Sarah felt content despite everything that was going on around her — there was now more than enough money for Adam to pay the rent on the shop and house, and for her to contribute to the Charlotte fund again as he was paying her a very fair wage. And so he should — she was doing half the work. She'd told him about Charlotte, and Janie and Rosie. It had come out one night when she'd at last explained why she had systematically stolen from him for so long. She certainly, however, had not said a word about Gabriel Keegan or Bella Jackson's extortion.

And having a man in her life was new and, she had to admit, *very* exciting. Intoxicating, in fact. It was lovely to be with Adam at night as well as during the day. He made her feel safe after she'd spent so much of her life knowing she wasn't, and having to tolerate the consequences. But Harrie, Friday and Rachel had made her feel safe, too. Friday and Harrie still did.

But it was a fragile sort of contentment. She didn't trust it and knew it could be shattered by any number of things: her and Adam getting caught thieving; Bella Jackson's next strike; Harrie's precarious state of mind. In the pit of her belly was an endlessly stirring worm of unease reminding her that nothing nice lasted forever — that sometimes it didn't last very long at all.

She was putting some things away in the top drawer of the dressing table in Esther's old bedroom — now hers and Adam's as it was the largest and nicest in the house — when she noticed the open door of the clothes press. Adam had jammed something into one of the drawers and now it wouldn't close properly, and therefore neither would the cupboard door, and that sort of thing always irritated her.

She slid the drawer all the way out, removed socks, gloves and a couple of rumpled cravats she'd never seen Adam wear, and that's when she found it, right at the back hidden under a hideous emerald-checked woollen scarf Esther *must* have bought for him: a sheet of paper folded in half.

Because it was tucked away she knew it was private, but that had never stopped her before. The date on it was two weeks earlier and it had been signed by the secretary of His Excellency the Governor. Her jaw dropped as she read that the marriage application of Adam Eli Nathaniel Green, holder of a conditional pardon, and Sarah Carys Morgan, bonded convict late of the ship *Isla*, had been approved, and that permission had been given to publish the banns.

What marriage application?

Blood pounded in her head and she felt horribly dizzy. She sat on the bed, read the document again and felt her breath catch painfully in her chest as she realised that Adam would have had to forge her signature to lodge a marriage application. He'd just gone ahead and done it, without even asking!

She was out of the bedroom and halfway down the stairs before she was even aware of it. The shop was closed for the day but Adam was still in the workshop. She stormed in, marched across to the bench and flung the paper at him.

'*What* is the meaning of this?'

He tried to catch it and missed, but Sarah could see from the distinctly uncomfortable look on his face that he knew what it was.

He removed his spectacles. 'You found it, then,' he said, polishing the lenses on a cloth, not meeting her eye. The paper lay on the floor.

'Yes, I bloody did.'

'Hidden at the back of my drawer.'

'You forged my signature,' Sarah accused. 'You scrivening bloody *bigamist*!'

'Just a minute, Sar—'

'What do you think I am, Adam? A chattel?' Sarah knew her face was bright red and she didn't care. 'It's not on the papers from the Factory, you know! You don't get to marry me as of right! You didn't even bloody well ask!'

'Sarah, let me explain.' He half stood but gave up and sat again as she loomed over him.

'No! There's nothing *to* explain. You're the same as ... all the rest of them! You're just a selfish little shite!' She inadvertently spat on him, and didn't care about that, either. 'What on earth made you think I'd be happy with this?' She snatched up the paper and threw it at him a second time. 'The next Mrs Green while there's still a first Mrs Green? Fuck off!'

'Sarah, please!'

'*No!* I'm going back to the Factory. I'll tell them you're an unfit master.' She was very close to tears now, but refused to let Adam see her cry. She marched across the room, the heels of her boots ringing on the floorboards. 'I'll tell them you wouldn't leave me alone! I'll tell them you're a lech! I've got rights, you know!' And she went out, slamming the door behind her.

Adam sat on his stool, staring despondently between his knees at the floor. He sighed, then slowly spun around and plonked his elbows on the bench, his forehead resting on the heels of his palms. Bernard had told him it would be a mistake to forge Sarah's signature on the marriage application, but he hadn't been able to think of any other way around it.

As a bonded convict, she was under the authority of the state, and because of that they were both required to apply to the governor for consent to marry, which was demeaning and humiliating, but those were the rules, unless they were happy to cohabit without a marriage certificate, and he wasn't. He wanted Sarah as his wife. Providing permission was granted the banns would be read in church on three consecutive Sundays, then he and Sarah could marry. The wedding, however, would have to take place in the registry office, as he couldn't see Sarah converting to Judaism just to suit him. He wasn't an overt practitioner of his religion, and had never attended the divine worship he knew was held in the privacy of a number of the seventy-odd Jewish homes in Sydney Town, but neither could he bring himself to completely abandon his own faith. Perhaps he would, though, if that was the only way to marry Sarah.

He'd lodged the application only three days after Esther had gone, he'd made up his mind that quickly. Bernard had been delighted with the idea, but had been sworn to secrecy until he, Adam, had had a chance to talk to Sarah about it. He'd mulled the matter over and over in his mind, and had *almost* asked her to be his wife, but his nerve had failed. What if she turned him down? She was so independent. Worse, what if she turned him down and laughed at him? He didn't think he could bear that. Then Friday had bailed him up in the street with her speech about Sarah's dark past and what have you and, though he hadn't entirely believed her, it had unsettled him.

So he'd decided to wait until he'd received the memorandum of approval from the governor's office. Surely that would encourage her to say yes? Then when it had arrived he still couldn't summon the nerve to ask her, and now she'd discovered it. He really should get a decent lock for his drawers, though he doubted there was one made that could keep Sarah out. It was her own fault for being so, well, inquisitive, and it would be amusing if he didn't feel so wretched and she wasn't so upset. And anyway, apart from the marriage application, he had no secrets from Sarah. A misunderstanding or two and a story not yet told, perhaps, but certainly no secrets.

He retrieved the paper from where it had landed beneath the bench, and went to find her.

Friday and Harrie stood before Rachel's grave at St John's Cemetery in Parramatta. They'd just come from the Factory after visiting Janie and the girls, and Harrie had some flowers she wanted to lay. It was hot and still in the cemetery and Friday used her shawl to blot the sweat from her face and neck. A couple stood in silence before a grave some distance away, and a pair of crows argued noisily in a tree by the O'Connell Street lych gate, but otherwise they were alone.

Making sure she didn't step on Rachel's actual grave, Harrie reverently placed the bunch of yellow roses at the base of the headstone. It was a nice piece of sandstone about three feet high with a plain curved top, though it had tilted slightly as the soil over the grave had settled. They should have waited the full year before having it erected. On the headstone was engraved:

SACRED

to the memory of

RACHEL FLORA WINTER

Who departed this Life

3rd March 1830 in the 17th Year of her age

REVIRESCO

'What does that actually mean?' Friday asked. 'That word, "Reviresco"? Did we choose it?'

'I did,' Harrie said. She was on her knees now, pulling weeds from around the headstone. 'The stonemason suggested it. It means "I will rise up".'

'Sarah? Let me in.' Adam knocked on the bedroom door again. 'Sarah?'

'Go away!' she shouted.

The knob turned, but she'd shot the bolt.

'Sarah! Open this door!'

She could tell he was losing his temper. Bugger him. A rattling thump resounded as he rammed his shoulder against the door.

'*Sarah!*'

She ignored him. If she waited long enough, hopefully he'd go away.

There was a moment's hiatus, then an almighty crash and the door flew open as the bolt splintered away from the frame. Adam charged in, just managing to stay upright.

Sarah leapt off the bed and ran to the window. 'Don't you dare come near me!' she warned, shoving up the sash. 'I'll scream. Everyone will hear.'

'Sarah, please, just shut up and listen. I never married Esther. We weren't married.'

She stared at him. 'You were so.'

'We weren't.' Adam brushed a shard of wood from his hair. 'She already had a husband when she was transported. We couldn't marry.'

'But she was Mrs Green.' Sarah felt as though the plug had been pulled on her innards and they were all falling out.

'I know. She called herself Esther Green, but she was really only ever Esther Kopelmann. I'm not a bigamist, Sarah, and I couldn't marry one.'

She let go of the window sash; the cord was loose and it came down with a bang. 'Is that why she hated you?'

'Not really. Though it didn't improve matters.'

'Why, then?' Sarah moved away from the window. Adam stood on the other side of the bed and she was glad: for now she felt it was important to keep a distance between them.

He parked his hands on his hips and stared at his boots for several moments. Then he raised his head and held her gaze. 'I had an affair. A short one. Lust, not love. She found out.'

Sarah wasn't surprised. Esther Green would surely drive any man into the arms of another woman. 'How do I know you wouldn't do that to me?'

'You'll have to trust me. But you're not very good at that, are you?'

That was true.

Adam took a step closer. 'So now you've heard my confessions, will you tell me yours?'

'I don't have anything to confess.'

'I think you do. That first night we had together when I noticed, well, the blood, you said to me, "Don't spoil it." You wouldn't let me speak. Why not?'

'I was embarrassed.' And she had been.

'Because it was your first time?'

'Yes.'

'But it wasn't really, was it?'

'It was!'

Adam shook his head and leant against the bed's footboard. Softly, he said, 'I don't think it was, Sarah. And I thought that even before our first night together. Because of how you see the world. Because you're so ... aloof. And so stubbornly wilful.'

Sarah felt resentment and anger flood through her again. She didn't want to be forced to tell him her miserable story. Not now. She wasn't ready. 'All right then, I lifted my leg for the entire crew of the *Isla* on the way here from England. Does that make you feel better?'

'No, because I don't believe that, either. That isn't who you are.'

'Well, I don't give a shit what you believe, Adam Green!'

'I think it's something between the two, something that happened a long time ago,' he went on, poking and prodding at her like a doctor looking for a rotten tooth. 'Something that was pretty bloody awful for you.'

Her eyes narrowed. 'Who have you been talking to?'

'What? No one.'

'Well, you're wrong. Nothing happened.' But her voice was shaking badly — she could hear it and she could feel it.

He moved around to her side of the bed. 'What happened, Sarah?'

She sat on the mattress and covered her mouth with her hand, then took a deep, ragged breath.

'My father. It was my father.'

She felt the gentle weight of Adam's hand settle on her shoulder.

'Ah, Sarah. Christ.'

Nothing was said for the longest time. She was too afraid to look at him.

'Do you despise me?' she whispered at last.

'Oh God, Sarah, I could never despise you. I love you.'

'Sometimes … sometimes I despise myself.'

'Don't say that, please. It's wrong.' Adam tilted her chin so she had to look at him. 'Will you marry me?'

'No, Adam. I won't.'

The visitors' room at the Factory was occupied, so Sarah, Janie and the children were outside in the yard, sheltering in a sliver of shade thrown by a wall. Pearl sat on the ground not far away, knitting. Fat, lazy flies buzzed everywhere and Janie repeatedly swatted them away from the babies, who sat in the dust in their clouts, with a cabbage-tree-leaf fan.

She asked, 'What do Harrie and Friday think?'

'I haven't talked to them yet. Not about him proposing.'

Janie's eyebrows went up.

'Well, I can't talk to Friday about it, she's jealous enough as it is.' Sarah recounted what Friday had said to Adam, which Adam had told Sarah the following day. 'And I don't want to worry Harrie with my woes. She's got enough of her own.'

'She were a bit odd when they come out last Sunday.' Janie took an almighty swipe at a glistening bluebottle crawling along Rosie's leg. Rosie started to cry. 'Got ya, ya bastard. Sorry, Rosie, love.'

'We're worried she's losing her mind.'

'Yeah, Friday were saying. I doubt it, though.' Janie flicked the splattered fly off the fan and wiped her finger on her skirt. 'She's just havin' a bad patch. She worries too much. It'll pass.'

'Do you think so?'

''Spect so. But I think *you're* mad if you don't marry your Mr Green.'

'I've just *told* you why I can't.'

'You've told me why you won't,' Janie said.

'Well, would you, if some cove forged your signature on a marriage application and didn't even ask you?'

'If he owned a jeweller's shop and were as nice as Friday and Harrie reckon your Mr Green is, I would, yeah. And as for all this bollocks about giving up your independence!' Janie snorted. 'Wake up, girl! You're a bonded convict. What've you got to give up? You're just being a stubborn bloody baggage, that's all.'

'I am not.'

Charlotte tipped over backwards, hit her head on the hard ground and started to cry. To cover her annoyance at Janie, Sarah picked her up and cuddled her, patting her bare back. 'Her nappy's wet.'

'Pearl!' Janie called. 'Clouts!'

Pearl produced a fresh nappy from her knitting bag. Janie took Charlotte from Sarah and, working quickly and efficiently, laid her down and changed her.

'Bum,' Rosie said, pointing at Charlotte's little white bottom. 'Lotta's bum.'

'That's right, sweetie, it is, too.' Janie lifted Charlotte and swung her high. Charlotte giggled and made a grab for the brim of Janie's bonnet. Janie handed her back to Sarah.

'You're the most stubborn bloody person I know,' she said.

'They should have their smocks on,' Sarah observed. 'They'll be getting burnt from the sun.'

'Don't change the subject. If you won't marry him 'cos you don't love him — though you do; it's all over your sour bloody mug — then marry him for other reasons. Use your smarts.'

'Meaning?'

'Marry him so he won't send you back here. Marry him so he'll never dob you in for all the swag you've robbed off him. Marry him for his money.'

'God, you're a mercenary cow, Janie Braine.'

'That's good, coming from you.' Janie nodded at Charlotte. 'Marry him for her. You vowed you'd do everything you could to take care of her, didn't you?'

And Sarah nodded.

Because she had.

February 1831, Sydney Town

Sarah and Adam were married at the Sydney Town registry office on the morning of the 24th of February. It was a Thursday but Nora and George Barrett had given Harrie the whole day off, and Friday was still stood down from her duties at the brothel — much to Elizabeth Hislop's ire — while recovering from her bout of gonorrhoea.

Sarah wore a royal blue silk dress, paid for by Adam and made by Harrie, who'd nearly exhausted herself staying up several nights in a row to finish it in time. It was neither ostentatious nor adorned with fripperies, but was beautifully cut and sewn and suited Sarah perfectly. It was, she told Harrie, the loveliest dress she had ever owned. In her hair she wore freesias to complement those in her bouquet, and Adam presented her with a pair of drop earrings containing perfectly matched sapphires. Adam himself wore a new black cutaway coat and white breeches. Bernard Cole gave Sarah away, and afterwards everyone gathered for a small wedding breakfast at Adam's house, after Adam had carried Sarah, embarrassed and giggling, across the threshold of the front door.

Matthew Cutler came by, and was delighted when Sally Minto also appeared for an hour; the Barretts arrived with their children; Elizabeth dropped in with a gorgeous batiste nightgown for Sarah and a bottle of best whisky for Adam; James turned up with a dozen very fine lead-glass wine goblets; and the neighbours drifted in and out with gifts of food. Jared Gellar also sidled in bearing a present — a beautifully carved piece of greenstone from New Zealand — declared hearty congratulations and spent much of his visit eyeing up Friday; and from the Factory Janie sent a pair of pillowcases she'd embroidered, and a misspelt note wishing Sarah and Adam all the luck in the world and featuring Charlotte's and Rosie's hand prints. During the breakfast Sarah threw her bouquet and hit Harrie in the face with it.

It was a lovely day, Sarah thought at the end of it. She only hoped she'd done the right thing.

The following Sunday, Harrie, Sarah and Friday took a whole day off to spend together, travelling out to the Factory to take Janie and the girls a piece of Sarah's wedding cake. Elizabeth had offered Friday her landau, and Jack to drive it, after extracting a firm promise from both that they would not stop off at every public house on the way. Initially Harrie had worried she might not be able to go, as George Barrett had insisted Nora couldn't spare her, especially as she had just had Thursday off. But after Nora pointed out that Harrie had worked through many of her Sunday afternoons off helping her fill dress orders and was owed far more than two days' leave, George reluctantly agreed.

So now they sat in the landau with the hoods raised against the sun, fanning themselves and watching the countryside shimmer in the summer heat through the windows, the gauze shades up to let in the warm breeze. Friday had her boots and stockings off and her skirts hoisted past her knees. Poor Jack, sitting outside in his shirtsleeves, was cooking. The seats, which had seemed luxurious hours earlier when they'd set out, now felt like unforgiving planks against backsides stuck to shifts damp with sweat.

'This is the first time we've all been back to the Factory together,' Harrie observed unnecessarily.

'Well, I couldn't get away, could I?' Sarah said. 'Not while Esther was being such a cow.'

'That's the worst thing about being assigned,' Friday said, 'not being able to please yourself when you do things. We've got hardly any freedom at all.'

Sarah laughed. 'We're not supposed to. We're convicts.'

'I think we're a lot freer than some girls,' Harrie said. 'And you *can* please yourself now, Sarah. You've just married your master.'

'Not really. I still have to work. Not that I'm complaining.'

Harrie gazed out the window. After a minute she said, 'Do you know what else you could do?' She turned to look at Sarah. 'Not now, but perhaps in a year or so? Now that you're married?'

'What?'

'You could raise a child.'

Sarah slapped at a fly. 'I don't want a child.'

'I don't mean your child.'

Friday frowned. 'What *are* you talking about?'

'Charlotte,' Harrie said. 'Sarah could adopt Charlotte.'

Sarah and Friday stared at her, their heads gently wobbling in time with the motion of the carriage.

Eventually Sarah said, 'But I'm an assigned convict. I wouldn't be allowed.'

'But Adam isn't. He has a conditional pardon. He could adopt her.'

'But what about Janie?' Friday asked. 'We can't just take Charlotte off her.'

'She'll be taken away when she turns four and put in the orphanage, anyway,' Harrie said. 'And so will Rosie.'

'Oh, well, I might as well adopt Rosie, too, then,' Sarah said.

'No. Rosie has a mother,' Harrie replied with unexpected vehemence.

Friday and Sarah exchanged worried glances: that didn't sound like Harrie at all.

Sarah leant back against the seat and blew out a long breath. 'And what if Adam doesn't want to adopt someone else's child? Why would he? He didn't even know Rachel.'

The knuckles of Harrie's clasped hands were white. 'Would you at least talk to him about it? And you wouldn't have to raise her by yourself. Friday and I would help as much as we could, wouldn't we?'

'Well, of course I would,' Friday said. 'I've got to work, though, remember. I don't know how much time I could … put into it,' she added weakly, feeling unpleasantly as though she were trying to wriggle out of committing herself. She loved Charlotte, but she *did* have to work.

'But that's the thing,' Harrie said. 'If Sarah adopts Charlotte, you won't have to put money into the fund any more. We won't need it. You can stop working for Mrs H. I know you don't like it.'

Sarah sat up straighter, picked a piece of fluff off her skirt, then fixed Harrie with a very level stare. 'You know, Harrie, I never thought I'd hear myself say this, but that was really bitchy of you.'

Harrie's mouth trembled and her eyes glittered with tears. 'I didn't mean it to be.'

'It bloody was, though. You're blackmailing me into saying I'll adopt Charlotte! What's wrong with you?'

'I am not!'

'You are. You *know* I know Friday hates working in the brothel.'

'Then why shouldn't she be allowed to stop working there?' Harrie shot back, her voice rising and her cheeks flushing a dull red.

'Hey …' Friday began, but was ignored.

'She *can* stop,' Sarah said, raising her own voice. '*I* can pay for Charlotte's care if need be, by myself. I can afford it now.'

Friday said, 'No you can't.'

Sarah flapped a shushing hand at her. 'Shut up. But if Friday wants to chuck in her job that's up to her, not me! Why do *I* have to be the one to give her a reason not to work for Mrs H?'

'Because you can!' Harrie was shouting now. 'You can give Charlotte a home and you can set Friday free.'

'Why are we stopping?' Friday asked, looking out the window.

Sarah slid to the edge of her seat and jabbed a finger right in Harrie's face. 'Why don't *you* give Charlotte a home and fucking well set Friday free? Why don't you marry James Downey and adopt Charlotte yourself?'

Jack appeared at the window, his hat pulled low over his forehead. 'Oi! What's going on in here?'

Harrie burst into noisy tears. 'I *can't*, all right? I can't marry James! And if I'm not married I can't adopt her, so *you* have to, Sarah.'

'Women's business, Jack,' Friday said quietly. 'Go away, eh?'

Jack touched the brim of his hat and disappeared from view. The landau bounced on its springs as he climbed back into the driver's seat and a second later they were off again, the horses straining into their harnesses.

Friday lay a soothing hand on Harrie's forearm. 'Calm down, love.'

Harrie swatted the hand away. 'No, I *won't* calm down. You don't understand! If we don't adopt her she'll go to the orphanage and she'll *die* there and we'll have lost *both* of them!'

'I didn't say we couldn't have her,' Sarah said, her voice conciliatory now she'd realised how upset Harrie was.

'You don't want her, though, do you?' Harrie accused.

'I did *not* say that, Harrie. I just meant it would be a lot to ask of Adam.'

'It would, too,' Friday agreed.

'And a lot to ask of me,' Sarah added. 'And poor little Charlotte. You know I'm not very good with children.'

'Yes, I know,' Harrie said so bluntly that Friday laughed. 'But she'd be so much better off with you than in the orphanage.' And she put her face in her hands and started weeping again.

Sarah suddenly knew what this was about. '*You* really want her, don't you?' she asked gently.

Harrie nodded, tears squeezing out between her fingers and running down her hands. 'More than *anything*.'

Sarah glanced at Friday in dismay: they both knew Harrie was asking for something she just couldn't have. She was an unmarried, assigned convict girl at the long end of a seven-year sentence, and she was mentally unstable and didn't seem to mind who knew it. No one in authority would give her custody of a small child.

Harrie lowered her hands, wiped her nose on her sleeve and peered at them through bleary eyes. 'I love her. I love her as much as I love Rachel. To me she *is* Rachel. And every time I hold Lewis I see Charlotte. Every time he cries I hear *her* when she was a tiny baby. And Rachel ... Rachel's telling me *I'm* the one Charlotte needs, *I'm* the one who should have her after she leaves Janie. And I *can't* have her.'

Friday and Sarah exchanged a 'bloody hell' look.

'Is there really no way you'd marry James?' Friday asked.

'I can't,' Harrie said flatly.

'You keep saying that, but why not?'

'He hasn't asked me.'

'Only because you won't talk to him. He would if you gave him the chance.'

'The last time I talked to James he told me we'd murdered an innocent man!' Harrie burst out.

'Harrie, for God's sake!' Sarah said, wincing and pointing through the hood of the carriage towards the driver's seat. 'Keep your voice down!'

'But hang on, didn't Rachel tell you we'd done the right thing?' Friday said. 'An eye for an eye? I thought you were square with that?'

The most awful look of confusion and guilt crossed Harrie's face. 'I thought I was but now I don't know. I've asked her and asked her to explain it again but she just won't talk to me about that any more.'

'Is that why you won't have anything to do with James?' Sarah asked shrewdly. 'Because you think you're such a terrible person?'

'No. He's found someone else. He's got Rowie now.'

'My fat arse he has,' Friday said. 'She cooks his meals and he eats them, and that's the end of it.'

'Harrie?' Sarah probed. 'I'm right, aren't I?'

Harrie, who'd been staring at her hands in her lap, slowly raised her head. 'I *am* a terrible person. I'm rotten and evil and I'm a murderess.'

After a short silence Friday said, 'You can sew really well, though.'

Sarah laughed, and then they all did, though Harrie's laughter had a discordant, hysterical edge to it.

Friday patted her knee. 'Don't worry, love, when the time comes we'll work something out. One of us will have Charlotte, and Rosie too, if Janie can't keep her when she's assigned. You don't really want to see Rosie in the orphanage, do you?'

Harrie shook her head.

'You'll see. Things have a way of sorting themselves out. And anyway, it isn't for ages yet. Charlotte's only just turning one. We've got years.'

Part Three

Phantoms on their Errands Glide

Chapter Fourteen

March 1831, Sydney Town

The afternoon was so hot that even the rosellas in the tree outside the workshop window had ceased their usual bickering, and slumped now among the wilting leaves like tattered, dusty trimmings on an unloved hat.

'God, I can't stand this,' Sarah said as sweat trickled down her face and pasted strands of hair to her cheeks. She pushed away the oil lamp and wiped her face and hands with a cloth. 'I'm going to leave this soldering until tonight.'

'Might not be any cooler,' Adam murmured. 'Could even be worse if the breeze dies. Damn.' Blinking rapidly, he put down the brooch on which he was working.

'What's the matter?'

'Sweat in my eyes.'

'You'll end up with blight if you're not careful.'

'No I won't.' Adam removed his spectacles and carefully blotted his eyelids.

'That's looking nice,' Sarah said, referring to the brooch.

'It had better be. It's driving me to distraction. I hope the bloody things go out of fashion soon.'

Adam had spent the past three hours using white horse hair to sew more than a hundred tiny pierced seed pearls onto a mother-of-pearl frame backed with a gold clasp, a task guaranteed to make anyone's eyes burn, regardless of the temperature. The finished product would be charming, however: a pearl-encrusted fleur-de-lis only an inch and a half high.

The bell over the shop door rang.

'I'll get it.' Sarah rose, her shift sticking unpleasantly to her bum and legs, and hurried through to the shop.

Two police constables stood before the counter, while another hovered near the door. They all stared at her impassively.

Sarah's stomach plummeted; she felt instantly disoriented and gripped the counter with one hand. 'Can I help you?' she heard herself say.

'Senior Constable Durrant,' the eldest of the constables said. 'Is Mr Adam Green the owner of this shop?'

Sarah nodded slowly, her heart pounding thunderously.

'Is he here?'

No! No he isn't!

'Sarah?' Adam appeared in the doorway.

The senior constable faced him. 'Adam Green?'

'Er, yes.'

'Adam Green, I'm arresting you on suspicion of receiving stolen goods.'

Adam's mouth fell open. 'What?' He shot a shocked glance at Sarah. 'What stolen goods?'

The senior constable flipped up the hatch in the counter: it tipped over with a resounding crash and he stepped through, pushed past Sarah, grabbed Adam's arm and pulled him around.

'Get off me!' Adam exclaimed. 'What the hell do you think you're doing?'

'I'm warning you,' Senior Constable Durrant told him, 'if you don't come quietly, it'll be both of you I'm taking up the street.' He produced a pair of manacles and clamped them around Adam's wrists. 'Right, have a look,' he ordered his colleagues.

'Have a look for what?!' Sarah demanded, panic sweeping over her in great, crashing waves.

She was ignored. One of the younger constables went to the drawers behind the counter, and methodically rummaged through them one after another. From the last he extracted a black velvet bag.

He emptied the contents into his hand and, clearly thrilled with himself, exclaimed, 'It's here, boss.'

'You just planted that, you *bastard*!' Sarah spat.

'I did not!' the boy said, his face going as red as the contrasting collar on his blue uniform jacket.

He must have; Sarah had never seen the brooch of gold and carved red coral in her life. She glanced at Adam. He shook his head, looking equally baffled.

He said, 'I don't know anything about that.'

'I'm sure you don't,' Durrant agreed.

'Someone's set me up.'

'Let's leave that for the magistrate to decide.' The senior constable gripped Adam's sleeve and pulled him through the gap in the counter.

'No! You can't take him!' Sarah grabbed Adam's other arm and jerked him back.

'Let go, girl,' Durrant warned.

'It's Mrs Green to you, arsehole,' Sarah snarled, yanking even harder on Adam's arm.

Adam's eyes flared in panic. 'Sarah, don't.'

'I'll ignore that,' Durrant said.

Sarah could see that, unlike his underling, Durrant wasn't particularly happy to be arresting Adam — he was simply doing his job. It didn't make any difference, though: Adam had been framed and she would not allow them to take him away. She let go of him and ducked through the gap in the counter, her intention to block the door so they couldn't move him into the street. But the other constable, a tall, red-headed boy — a currency lad, by the look of his wide shoulders and long legs — pushed her violently to one side and opened the door. She tripped over her skirts and fell. Durrant swore but didn't stop, concentrating on manoeuvring a struggling Adam through the doorway.

Sarah scrambled to her feet, spat on the red-headed constable's jacket, and launched herself outside after Adam and Durrant. Someone shoved her again and she went down once more on her hands and knees in the filth of the street, a passing horse and gig swerving to miss her. Then she was hauled to her feet, but not by either of the younger constables — they were already marching up George Street with Adam and Senior Constable Durrant.

'Adam!' Sarah shrieked over the noise of the busy street. '*Adam!*'

Stumbling, he looked back at her, but was jerked forwards again.

Mr Jellicoe, the cutler from next door, who had picked Sarah up off the ground, demanded, 'What's going on? Where are they taking him?'

'He's been arrested.'

'Oh my Lord!'

Sarah set off up the street, wiping her bleeding palms on her skirt.

'Mrs Green!' Mr Jellicoe called. 'Sarah!'

She stopped.

'Your shop. Should you close up?'

Christ. She dashed back, rushed around inside shutting all the windows, and locked both doors. Outside again she pelted off up George Street, arriving at the police office located between the market sheds and the old burial ground, moments after Adam and his escort entered the narrow gate in the high stone wall surrounding the compound.

The policeman on guard slammed the gate in her face.

She gripped the iron railings hard enough to turn her knuckles the colour of bone, watching as Adam was led inside the building. '*Adam!*' she shrieked, so violently she tasted blood.

But she was too late; they'd taken him to the watch house.

'On your way, missus,' the guard told her. 'Go and weep at home.'

Sarah glared at him, her top lip curling on one side to reveal a rather sharp little eyetooth. 'Weep? Fuck you! I'll not be wasting good tears when he'll be out by tonight.'

The guard leant into his side of the gate. 'Any more of that and I'll arrest you for indecent language.'

Sarah leant into her side. 'Fuck. Off.'

'Fuck off yourself,' the guard growled.

Sarah did. Actually she would have liked nothing better than to lie down in the road, curl up with her arms over her head and cry, but there were things she had to do.

She headed off back down George Street. Not to fetch Bernard Cole, or James Downey or anyone else with authority, but to find Friday and Harrie, the two people she knew could comfort her best, the souls she trusted most, and who she knew would never let her down.

Friday's cully left feeling a bit short-changed, but from the window Friday had seen Sarah hurrying up Argyle Street, and she knew she wouldn't be bothering her at work if it wasn't extremely important.

In the privacy of Elizabeth's office, Sarah explained what had happened. She was definitely crying now, since no one but Friday would be witness to her loss of control.

'And you're sure the brooch wasn't Adam's doing?'

'Of course I'm sure!' Sarah snapped, and blew her nose on a dainty lace handkerchief Friday had found in a drawer in Elizabeth's desk. 'We've been fencing stuff, but we've not been receiving. Everything we've bought's been on the up or it's come through Bernard, and yes he does send swag back to England on the sly, but everything he imports always has the correct paperwork. And if it doesn't it certainly *looks* like the correct paperwork. You'd never tell the difference. And the tax is always paid. But none of that's the point here. The point is I've never seen that brooch before in my life.'

'And Adam wouldn't have accepted something without you knowing?'

'These days Adam doesn't even breathe out without me knowing, he's been trying so hard to make everything right.'

Friday scowled and helped herself to two measures of Elizabeth's brandy. She passed one to Sarah, who took a huge, shuddering sip.

'Who would want to frame him?' Friday asked.

'I can't think of anyone. Only Esther, but she's long gone.'

'What about Bernard?'

'Bernard?' Sarah looked shocked. 'I don't think so. Why would Bernard want to do that?'

'I don't know. Just a thought.'

Sarah knocked back the rest of her drink, gagging slightly. 'If Adam goes to gaol, I'll have to go back to the Factory and he'll lose everything.'

'Bloody hell. Really? As his wife, don't you have any rights?'

'Yes, but I'm still a bonded convict. I'm still serving a sentence so I'm not allowed to run a business by myself.'

'Bloody Bella Jackson does,' Friday muttered. She stared into her empty glass, as though wondering where the contents had gone, and poured herself another drink.

'But the authorities don't know about that, do they?' Sarah snapped, anger drying her tears. 'They think ... Well, I *assume* they think her husband is running those businesses. If Adam goes to court, the magistrate will know it's just me and him in the shop, and that I'm an assigned convict. So if he's gaoled, that'll be that. I can't afford to go back to the Factory, Friday. What about the Charlotte fund? And Bella's bound to make another demand. And apart from all that, I just bloody well *refuse* to do nothing while everything Adam has is taken away from him because some *bastard* has set him up.'

Friday emptied her glass a second time. 'But what can you do? He'll get a bloody stiff sentence, an ex-convict committing a crime here.'

'He *didn't* commit a crime. I don't even know who to ask for advice. You'll be mashed in a minute,' Sarah said, watching Friday pour a third brandy. 'Stop that.'

'James might know.' Friday slumped forwards, elbows on her bare thighs, her face in her hands.

'Is Harrie talking to him at the moment? Should we get —' Sarah stopped. Friday was crying. 'What's the matter?'

'Oh shite, Sarah. I've been a right bitch. I did the most terrible thing.'

For an awful, dreamlike moment Sarah thought Friday was about to say *she* had framed Adam.

'I told Adam he shouldn't even think about taking up with you.' Friday's expression was wretched. 'I said you'd never settle down with any man, and sort of suggested you'd make his life a misery. In fact I more or less implied you're a tart. I couldn't *help* it, Sarah. I'm sorry. I was jealous. And I've felt that rotten and it's been eating a bloody great hole in me ever since.'

'I know,' Sarah replied mildly. 'He told me.'

'What?' Friday was outraged. 'I swore I'd beat the living shite out of him if he said a single word!'

'Well, he did.'

They burst out laughing, and then they were hugging fiercely, and then crying again.

'It doesn't matter that I married him, Friday,' Sarah said. 'I love him, but ... well, I love you, too.' She brushed at a tear-dampened patch on the shoulder of Friday's robe. 'Adam's ... extra. It will always be you and me and Harrie, no matter what else happens. Always.'

'You're not roaring 'cos I tried to scupper everything?'

'Of course I'm not. You did it from here.' Sarah touched the place just below Friday's left breast. 'And he didn't listen to you anyway. He has a lot more backbone than you obviously thought.'

'Obviously,' Friday said, her face sour. 'D'you know, that's the first time I've heard you say you love him?'

'Is it? God. I suppose it is, isn't it?'

'You do love him, don't you? You really do.'

Nodding, Sarah's face crumpled again, and Friday's heart ached for her.

'Well, come on, then,' she said. 'We haven't got time to sit around bawling. Let's go and get Harrie and make a plan.'

Harrie was stunned — aghast and immediately brimming with concern for Sarah. While Sarah recounted to her what had happened, Friday took Nora Barrett downstairs for a quiet word.

'We've been worried sick about Harrie,' she said without preamble. 'She told us a little while ago — actually *admitted* to us as plain as you please — that she's been having conversations with the ghost of our friend Rachel. The girl who died at the Factory?'

'Yes, I know who Rachel was.' Nora shifted Lewis from one hip to the other. He grabbed at her hair and she put him down on the ground and watched him crawl jerkily off to annoy Angus the cat, who had been contentedly lolling in the sun at the bottom of the back steps.

'Have you noticed anything odd about the way she's been carrying on?'

Nora said, 'I quite often hear her talking in her room at night. Lewis! Be careful, he'll scratch you!' She wrinkled her nose disapprovingly. 'Friday, have you been drinking?'

'I might have had a small one, for medicinal purposes. Well, don't you think that's a bit, um, barmy? Talking to a dead person? Or even to yourself?'

Nora shrugged. 'I don't know. It's harmless, isn't it? She has been a bit highly strung lately, I'll grant you that, but she never lets it get in the way of her work. She's marvellous with the little ones, and good around the house, and the best needle-worker I've ever encountered. And *is* she barmy? Quite a few folk have the second sight, Friday. It's just something they have to live with.' She fixed Friday with rather a stern look. 'I suggest you and Sarah learn to live with it, too, instead of hounding her. She came home very upset after that talk you had with her, you know.'

Friday felt guilt and embarrassment prickle her face. 'Did she?'

'Yes, she did. So leave her be.'

'But what if it isn't that?' Friday said. 'What if she is, well, unhinged?'

The inevitable happened and Angus scratched Lewis, who shrieked like a teakettle. Nora picked him up and joggled him. 'Then we'll deal with that if we have to. I'm going upstairs. I want to hear what's happened to Sarah's man.'

And she turned and went inside, leaving Friday standing on the steps feeling stupid and as though in some really mean way she'd let Harrie down.

Instead of crumbling further beneath the weight of more awful news, Harrie felt galvanised by a sense of injustice she'd not experienced in many months — not, in fact, since she'd realised Gabriel Keegan was going to get away with what he'd done to Rachel. Adam Green was a decent man, and Sarah's husband now, and if Sarah said he'd been falsely accused of a crime, then Harrie believed her. If Adam went to gaol Sarah would suffer, too, and Harrie had had enough of her friends suffering. She could not stand aside, mired in her own misery and mental confusion, and simply watch something terrible happen. Last time, with Rachel, she'd not been vigilant enough: perhaps this time she could do better.

She desperately wanted to talk to Rachel about it — Rachel would know what to do — but that night she didn't appear. Harrie sat up until five o'clock in the morning, her head nodding and her eyelids leaden, but the rocking chair in the corner remained resolutely empty and still.

Angus, back from a successful night's hunting, pushed open Harrie's bedroom door, padded in on silent paws and hopped up onto the bed, where he collapsed, stretching himself out.

Harrie eyed him distastefully and murmured, 'You're a mucky cat, you are.'

She fetched a cloth, quietly pushing the door closed on the way, and wiped the bright blood off Angus's whiskers. He tossed his furry black and white head from side to side like a recalcitrant infant, his top lip caught on a yellowing fang, but eventually succumbed.

'I don't think she's coming, Angus.'

He blinked at her.

'Perhaps she wants me to make up my own mind.' Harrie folded the cloth so the blood smears were hidden. 'And I can, you know. I'm not as silly and as mad as everyone thinks.'

Angus sat up and proceeded to clean his backside.

Harrie sighed. 'I'm so tired of this, Angus. I'm so tired of being frightened and worried and angry.' She gently tugged Angus's tail. 'But I'm glad in a way this has happened to Sarah. I know it's a terrible thing to say, but at least we're all together again. She's going to need Friday and me.'

The lamp flickered and Harrie glanced hopefully at the rocking chair. Nothing. Disappointment sour in her belly, she climbed under the bed covers, doused the lamp and lay in the darkness. But still she couldn't sleep, though Angus did, emitting a whistling snore, his legs twitching as he chased rats, bandicoots and other tasty treats through his dreams. After a while the sky outside her window lightened almost imperceptibly, and she got up again to watch the sun rise.

Bats streamed overhead, just a few outriders at first, then a long, tapering cloud. A lone bat broke away from the column and swooped down towards Harrie's small window, its translucent wings slicing through the heavy dawn air, so close she leant out to touch it.

'Hello, you,' Harrie whispered.

With Nora's blessing, Harrie went around to Sarah's house as often as possible to keep her company. Adam, now in Sydney Gaol, had been denied bail, and Sarah had not been permitted to see him and was consequently in a complete state, oscillating between fury and despair. Bernard Cole took time off from running his own business to come in and help Sarah with the shop, but she was terrified the Principal Superintendent of Convicts would be notified of what had happened and send her back to the Factory.

Harrie and Bernard were both in attendance the day Jared Gellar arrived. He swept in, setting the bell over the door jangling madly, greeted Bernard jovially and barged past him into the workshop.

'Sarah, my *dear*! Such a dreadful state of affairs!'

Instantly irritated, Sarah barely glanced up from the ring she was polishing. 'Mr Gellar.'

'Jared, what are you doing here?' Bernard asked, trotting in after him.

Jared ignored him. 'You must call me Jared, Sarah. We are, after all, to be business partners from now on.'

Sarah turned to Bernard and then Harrie, as though they might know what he was wittering on about. Obviously, they didn't. 'Are we?'

'Yes, indeed,' Jared declared. 'I've just come from the gaol. Adam has asked me to step into the breach while he's, well, indisposed, and naturally I've agreed. It's the least I can do to help out a friend.'

Sarah's heart plummeted. 'But ...' She turned to Bernard. 'Did you know about this?'

He shook his head, clearly as surprised as she was.

'Why are you allowed to see Adam and I'm not?' she said to Jared. 'I'm his wife.'

'I gather there may be concern in some quarters that you yourself may have been involved in the matter of the received goods.'

'There *were* no received goods!' Sarah exclaimed. 'That brooch was planted. Do you think he did it? Because if you do, you can just bugger off!'

'Sarah, sweetie, settle down,' Harrie soothed. 'He's only saying what he's heard. Aren't you, Mr Gellar?' she added sharply.

'Well, he can bloody well say it somewhere else.'

'Of course I don't believe he did it,' Jared insisted. 'And yes, I *am* only passing on what I've heard. But I do believe that's the reason you've not been permitted to speak with him — so you can't connive regarding the matter of his defence.'

'Then why can't *I* get in to see him?' Bernard asked. 'I've tried and I'm not allowed, either.'

Jared shrugged. 'You'd have to speak to the chief constable about that.'

'I have.'

'Anyway,' Jared said, 'Adam has asked me to take over for him here, to keep the business going. If worse comes to worst and he's sent to gaol for any length of time —'

'He won't be,' Sarah said quickly.

'But if he is, I've agreed to take you on as an assignee so you can stay here, in your home.'

'But wouldn't that mean *you'd* have to live here, too? In this house?' Sarah asked. What a hideous thought.

'Yes, actually, it would.'

'I don't believe you,' she said flatly. 'Adam would never have agreed to that.' He knew Jared Gellar gave her the shits.

'I can assure you he has agreed,' Jared said smoothly. 'I realise this is not an ideal state of affairs, Sarah, and of course you're distressed by what has happened. I do understand that. So are we all. But this really is the best solution.'

'Did he give you a letter for me?' Sarah demanded.

'No.'

'Well, in that case, I'll only believe it if I hear it from Adam myself.'

Jared looked to Bernard for help, but Bernard, his arms tightly crossed, was staring intently at the floor.

'But you're not permitted to see Adam,' Jared said. He sounded exasperated now, and Sarah was glad.

'I haven't seen him *yet*,' she replied. 'But I'll make bloody sure I do.'

Jared said, 'I've a few things to attend to, and a trunk to pack, but I'll be back this evening. I trust there will be a room prepared for me?'

'I'll do that,' Harrie volunteered.

Jared nodded. 'Thank you. Good day, ladies, Bernard.'

After he'd departed Bernard, Harrie and Sarah stared at one another.

'Tosser,' Sarah muttered.

'That was a shock,' Bernard said.

Sarah asked, 'Bernard, can you hold the fort? I'm going down to the gaol. Harrie, I think we're going to need Friday.'

Sydney Gaol was small, given the town's population, and severely overcrowded. Sanitation was appalling, security lax, and trade on the black market thrived. Bordered by George, Harrington and Essex streets and Essex Lane, the gaol covered a full block and consisted of an exercise yard and various sandstone buildings, the whole surrounded by a high stone wall. It wasn't high enough, however, to conceal the gallows that loomed permanently in the yard and attracted huge crowds on Gallows Hill above the gaol on hanging days. Then, Essex and Harrington streets thronged with onlookers keen to watch the spectacle of those convicted in the colony of serious crimes drop to their deaths, their necks snapped or, on a particularly entertaining day, strangle as the result of a badly positioned noose. Hawkers did a brisk trade in oysters and baked potatoes, the police turned a blind eye as tankards of ale were passed through pub windows, and small children rode on their fathers' shoulders for a better view.

Within the gaol walls were two prison dormitories in the style of army barracks, one for men and the other for women and their children, most of whom slept on wooden barracks beds on the ground, plus separate apartments for debtors and six secure cells for the condemned. The remaining buildings in the compound accommodated the soldiers who staffed the gaol and a handful of administrators. Sarah knew — *everyone* in Sydney Town knew — living conditions inside the gaol were atrocious, but she tried not to think about this as she furiously rattled the bars of the entrance gate on George Street.

'Hey! You! Open up!' she shouted at the lone redcoat leaning against a sandstone wall.

He looked around as though she were perhaps addressing someone else.

'No, you! Let me in!'

The soldier swallowed the last of the bread roll he was eating, hitched his musket higher on his shoulder and sauntered across to the gate. Friday and Sarah saw he was barely a man, the sprinkle of mild spots on his cheeks testimony to his youth.

'What?'

'Open the gate, please,' Sarah said, doing her best now to control her temper. 'I'd like to visit my husband.'

'Who's that, then?' the soldier asked, eyeing Friday.

'Mr Adam Green.'

The boy consulted a creased piece of paper he dug out of his pocket. 'No. Permission denied.'

'Why?' Sarah demanded. 'I know for a fact he's been allowed other visitors.'

'Because it says on this piece of paper. No visitors.' The soldier poked at a lump of bread stuck between his front teeth. His eyes slid once again towards Friday, who was ostentatiously adjusting her low-cut bodice.

'Will you take a bribe?' Sarah said.

'What's on offer?'

Friday stepped up to the gate, reached through the bars and ran her hand down the front of the boy's breeches. 'Anything you fancy.'

He swallowed audibly. 'Fifteen minutes,' he said to Sarah, producing a key and letting them in, then relocking the gate behind them.

He led them swiftly across the compound to a barracks building, said, 'Wait here,' and disappeared inside.

He was back a minute later. To Sarah he said, 'Go inside, turn left, there's a little chamber. He's in there. Like I said, fifteen minutes, that's all.'

Another soldier passed, giving them a hard look, and the boy saluted smartly.

They weren't the only civilians in the gaol compound, Sarah noticed; two men in good black coats — solicitors, perhaps, or even barristers? — were leaving the barracks building, a pair of coves were unloading bulging sacks from a dray in the yard and a workman was hammering noisily away at something on the gallows. She could also hear plenty of noise from the cells and the larger barracks — shouts of men and women, screams, and, incongruously, laughter.

'Well?' the young soldier said to Friday.

'Well, yourself,' she said back, winking at Sarah. 'Come on then, find us a corner. I'm not getting my dress dirty, but.'

The boy reddened, unsure of himself now, and clumsily took her elbow.

Sarah didn't wait to see where they went. She ducked into the barracks building, reeling at the indescribable stink — easily as foul as Newgate Gaol had been — and slipped into the small, plain room on the left. A high barred window let in a miserable spill of light, illuminating initials and words scratched into the sandstone walls. The place stank of urine.

Adam sat at a rickety table. He looked exhausted and unshaven, and she could smell his body odour from the doorway. To her horror, his ankles were encased in irons linked by a heavy chain. At the sight of her he lurched up, tipping his chair over, and embraced her.

'Sarah, oh God, Sarah!'

'They wouldn't let me in to see you!' she said, her face squashed against his bristly neck. 'We had to bribe our way in.'

He stood back, holding her at arm's length. 'Christ, you look tired. Are you all right? Who's we?'

'Me and Friday. She's, er, entertaining one of the guards.'

Adam snorted. Sarah laughed a little, too, but it was a brittle sound. She was tense and frightened, and so, obviously, was he.

'We haven't got long. Jared Gellar turned up. He said you've asked him to take over the business while you're in here. And take over me! As my master!'

Adam cupped her cheek with a grubby hand. 'You can't stay there by yourself. You won't be allowed. And I need you to do something for me, Sarah.'

They sat down, holding hands across the table.

'Could Bernard not have stepped in?' Sarah asked.

'I couldn't get hold of him. I did send messages, through my barrister.'

'He never got them. And he isn't allowed past the gate, either. He's tried.'

They stared at each other, eyes full of fear.

Adam said, 'Christ, do the police know what we've been up to? Are they watching Bernard, do you think?'

'But wouldn't *I* have been arrested, too, if that were the case? And Bernard, by now?'

'I would have thought so. Perhaps it's just me. God, I hope so.' Adam released Sarah's hands and rubbed his face.

'But why Gellar?' she asked. 'You know I can't stand him.'

Adam gazed down at the scarred table top, then let out a huge sigh full of regret. 'I didn't *ask* him to take over the business, Sarah. He came here this morning to tell me he *will* be taking over.'

Sarah sat very still, watching his face. For a few long seconds all the background noise coming from the prisoners' barracks seemed to fade away.

'I haven't told you this, and maybe I should have. When I opened the shop I borrowed money from him. Quite a lot of money. But with the way Esther was, to date I haven't been able to pay him back. This morning he informed me that if I didn't install him as manager, he'd call in the loan. We're doing quite well now, you and me, but we can't afford that. It would mean the end.'

'The bloody liar. He told me you'd asked him!'

'I expect he thought you wouldn't get in to see me.'

Sarah felt sick. 'Oh God, Adam, if you do go to gaol, he'll take it all. That's what he does. You said so yourself.'

'Yes, I know. So I'll have to make bloody sure I don't.'

'But how? You don't —' Sarah broke off, realisation draining the blood from her face. 'Was it him? Did *he* set you up?'

Wearily, Adam nodded. 'I think so, to get me out of the way. But I can't prove it. With me gone no doubt he thinks he can just buy up the business when it mysteriously starts to fail.'

'But why bother framing you? Why not just call in the loan?' Sarah said. 'If you owe him that much money, wouldn't that ruin us just as surely without him having to muck about making sure you go to gaol?'

'Because he knows Bernard would lend me the money. Bernard's a very wealthy — and generous — man.'

'Well, why haven't you asked Bernard?'

'Sarah, Bernard is a very good friend and you don't borrow money from close friends. Would you?'

'No,' Sarah said. And she wouldn't.

'If you have to, you borrow it from professional moneylenders, like Jared Gellar.'

Sarah thought for a moment. 'Is that all of it, then?'

'All of what?'

'All your secrets. You weren't really married to Esther, you had an affair, and you made a stupid decision to borrow money off Gellar. Anything else?'

Adam's mouth twitched in a smile. 'No, that's everything now.'

'Well, I'm not having that two-faced, speeling bloody magsman in my shop. Your shop,' she amended. 'Or my home.'

'You have to, if you don't want to go back to the Factory. You only have to put up with him until I can prove he framed me. But for God's sake, be careful. Lock your door at night. If you have to, just leave. Just walk out. But I think you'll be safe. It's in his interests to keep you happy. You're the jeweller — you're the one who'll keep the business afloat. He won't want to destroy things completely, just run the books down. I've told him to give you a weekly wage so you can continue paying for Charlotte's care and he's agreed. But I want you to watch him, Sarah. Watch everything he does. Go through his things. There must be something I can use.'

'How can you prove you've been set up while you're stuck in here? You can't.'

Adam said nothing: they both knew Sarah was right.

She asked, 'When will you go before the magistrate?'

'My solicitor, Arthur Hocking, says possibly within the month. The barrister I've hired is a fellow named Augustus Evans. Bloody expensive but they're thin on the ground.'

'Will it be Rossi?'

'Don't know yet. I hope not.'

Captain Francis Rossi, police magistrate and superintendent of police, was known to be hard on recidivist convicts.

Sarah glanced over her shoulder, worried about their time running out. 'What does your solicitor say?'

Adam's face was grim. 'That if I can't prove I was set up I'll be convicted. Tell Bernard to find out what he can. I've asked Arthur Hocking to put his ear to the ground as well, but I think Bernard's far better placed to dig out that sort of information.' He paused. 'And so are you.'

Sarah nodded. 'I'll do everything I can. And so will Friday and Harrie.'

'But be careful.' Adam took her hand again. 'Please.'

'Are you all right in here?'

'Hardly. There are a hundred of us jammed in the men's barracks and it's so crowded we can't all lie down at night, we have one bucket to shit in, as you can tell it stinks to high heaven, *I* stink, and I'm starving.'

Sarah remembered she had something for Adam. From the pockets of her dress she took several links of smoked sausage, two bread rolls and half a small cheese.

'And this,' she said, passing him two one-pound notes and two half-sovereigns she'd taken from the money drawer. 'Keep it in your boots or the hem of your trousers.'

Adam wolfed down a sausage in four bites, and hid the rest of the food in his jacket.

The door was thrust open and the young soldier from the gate stuck in his head. 'Time's up. Out.'

Sarah stood. Adam rose, too, and embraced her tightly.

'Hurry up,' the boy urged.

'Take care,' Adam murmured.

'You too,' Sarah whispered back. 'I'll find out what I can.'

And then she was outside again, blinking in the harsh sunlight.

'All right?' Friday asked, leaning against the barracks wall.

Sarah nodded.

'You don't look all right,' Friday said as they walked towards the gate.

'He thinks Gellar did it.'

'What? Framed him?' Friday was shocked.

'And so do I. But we can't prove it. Well, not yet. How I'm going to tolerate him in my house I don't know.'

'Shite, Sarah. Does Gellar know you know?'

'No. I don't know. I don't think so.'

'Well, I'd keep it that way, if I were you.'

Sarah kicked angrily at the gravel underfoot. 'God, Adam looked awful. And he stank.'

'He's in gaol. We ponged, too, in Newgate. Remember?'

'It hurts, Friday.'

Friday touched Sarah's arm. 'We'll get him out, don't worry.'

'Will we? Really?'

'We'll bloody well die trying.'

'Thanks for taking care of the guard.'

Friday shrugged. 'Another lonely boy. No skin off my neb.'

Sarah smiled faintly. 'Have you got rid of your dose of clap?'

'Not quite, and I have to say I'm sick to bloody death of flax-seed tea and squirting zinc up my minge. But who cares? The 57th are shipping out any day. By the time he notices he'll be halfway to India.'

Sarah laughed properly for the first time in days, and as they exited the gaol gate Friday blew the young guard a kiss.

Jared Gellar settled into the bedroom Adam had occupied when Esther had been the lady of the house. Sarah remained in the chamber she shared with Adam, the lock now repaired after he'd broken it the day they'd argued about getting married. She made sure she shot the bolt every night.

Jared had not made any physical approaches towards her, but he watched her all the time, and it disturbed her deeply. He'd only been in the house three days, and already she could quite happily do away with him and tip his body into the cesspit in the backyard. While she confined herself to the workshop, he generally stayed in the shop to deal with customers, where he was admittedly very charming and competent, or attended to the paperwork. He complimented her cooking, which she was aware was decidedly average, told her she was a very able housekeeper and a highly skilled jeweller, both of which were true, and said she looked 'fetching' in the mornings, which was rubbish as she barely slept and knew she looked rough.

And often, the hairs on the back of her neck would prickle as she bent over her work and she would turn and there he'd be, leaning against the frame of the workshop door, a smarmy little smile on his handsome face, silently observing her. At first she'd asked him what he wanted and he'd only shaken his head, his girlish curls flopping over his forehead in a way that made her want to get up and slap him, so now she just gritted her teeth and ignored him. God help her if Adam didn't come home soon.

If Jared was aware she strongly suspected he was responsible for framing Adam, or even that she knew he'd blackmailed his way into Adam's business and home, he gave no indication, and she certainly wasn't going to mention either. The more oblivious he thought she was, the better.

On the fifth day after he moved in Jared was absent from the shop the entire morning. When he returned he locked the shop door and sat Sarah down in the dining room.

'I have something to tell you, Sarah.'

His expression was grim and she braced herself for bad news. 'I've been to the magistrate's court. Adam went up this morning.'

For a moment Sarah couldn't comprehend what he was saying. '*Court?!* He's been in front of the *magistrate*?'

Jared nodded solemnly.

'Why didn't you *tell* me?!' she almost shrieked.

'I didn't know myself until yesterday afternoon. I didn't want you to worry.'

He'd been to watch Adam in court, and Adam wasn't here now, and that could only mean one thing.

'What happened?' she demanded hoarsely, her heart pounding so furiously she could barely breathe.

'He was convicted, Sarah. Five years' confinement at Port Macquarie.'

Five years! Sarah thought she would faint. She gripped the edge of the table and held on as a wave of dizziness consumed her and pinpoints of light sparkled across her vision. And it was *all* this ... this *maggot's* fault. 'Rossi?' she whispered.

Jared nodded.

'You ... *bastard*!'

'I thought it was for the best. You couldn't have changed anything, Sarah.'

Dimly, she realised he thought she was cursing at him for not telling her about Adam's trial. And maybe if she had gone, she might have done something to sway the magistrate. 'I could have! I could have given a character reference!'

Jared looked genuinely uncomfortable. 'A character reference, from his own wife, a prisoner of the Crown?'

'Oh, fuck you, Jared Gellar! And why was the trial brought forwards? Tell me that?'

He appeared wounded. 'It wasn't, really. Not by much.'

Sarah lurched up out of her chair. She couldn't stop her tears, and brushed them angrily from her cheeks. 'I'm going to see him. They can't stop me from saying goodbye.'

'They can, I'm afraid. He's already gone. On a ship about an hour ago.'

* * *

That night, as Sarah lay in bed unable to sleep, she heard stealthy footsteps approaching along the short hallway from Jared's room. She held her breath as a weak flicker of lamplight appeared beneath her bedroom door.

A gentle knock. 'Sarah?'

Oh God.

'Sarah, I would be delighted if you'd let me in.'

You dirty, treacherous pig.

'He need never know, you know. And I'd make it worth your while.'

The door rattled, but as usual she'd locked it.

'Sarah?'

She stared at the ceiling, a single tear trickling into her hair, her heart feeling flayed by grief.

After a while she heard Jared go away.

Chapter Fifteen

Late March 1831, Sydney Town

'Where is he now?' Friday asked.

They were having a council of war — her, Sarah and Harrie, around Sarah's dining table. Sarah had just told them about Jared's attempt to get into her bedroom the previous night.

'I don't know and I don't care,' she said.

'Well, you should care,' Harrie declared. 'He's sneaky. You should keep an eye on him all the time.'

Friday raised a brow. 'That's not like you. What's happened to "all folk have their good points"?'

Harrie was a picture of bitter resignation. 'I think I've finally learnt my lesson. And he *is* sneaky. And ... menacing.'

'Menacing!' Sarah's lip curled. 'He's rotten to the core.'

'You could go back to the Factory, you know,' Harrie said. 'You'd be safe from him there.'

Friday leant away from the inevitable explosion.

'*No!*' Sarah whacked her hand on the table. 'I won't! If I'm not here there'll be absolutely nothing to stop Gellar stealing Adam's business.'

'I know this isn't much comfort,' Friday said hesitantly, 'but at least Adam was only sent to Port Macquarie. It could have been worse. He could have ended up at Moreton Bay. Or Norfolk Island.

He probably won't be worked to death where he is. I mean, he's good with letters and numbers. He might get a clerk's job.'

'No, it isn't much comfort,' Sarah shot back. 'Five *years*, Friday. He could still die of some disgusting disease. And he's *innocent*!'

Friday busied herself tamping tobacco into her pipe. Port Macquarie had recently been opened to free settlement, and the convict population in the gaol there no longer consisted of the hardened recidivists of earlier years, but five years was a very long time if Adam for some reason remained confined to the gaol, or was assigned to a labourer's job, or did fall ill.

'Are you sure Gellar wants to take over the shop?' she asked.

'Of course he bloody does! That's how he makes his money! And how can I pay my share of the Charlotte fund if I'm stuck in the Factory or scrubbing someone else's dirty floors? I can't, can I? And what about Bella's next demand?'

'I would've thought Bella Jackson'd be the least of your worries right now.'

'Well, that's bloody short-sighted of you. We *have* to pay up next time, and we might not have the money if I'm not earning any.' Sarah's body was stiff with tension. 'If we don't pay she'll dob us in. How's that going to look for Adam, already in gaol? I was assigned to him when we killed Keegan, remember. What if the police get it into their heads he was involved? They'll hang him, right next to us.'

'We do have the money,' Friday countered. 'Not that I want to sodding well give it to her, of course.'

'For the next demand we do,' Harrie said, 'but what about after that? You said yourself she won't stop until we're ruined.'

Friday nodded reluctantly, because she had.

'So I *have* to stay here,' Sarah declared. 'And I'm going to. Bugger Gellar.'

They fell silent while they absorbed this.

Eventually Friday asked, 'Has he tried anything else on, apart from last night?'

Sarah frowned, remembering. 'There was one little incident, when Esther was still here.'

'You didn't tell us that,' Friday said accusingly.

Sarah waved a dismissive hand, because it hadn't really mattered then. 'He was here one night for supper and he and Esther were swapping ghost stories and he put his hand up the back of my skirt. I thought it was a spider.'

'Christ, he fancies himself, doesn't he?' Friday remarked. 'Mind you, he isn't a bad-looking cove.'

'*You* have him, then,' Sarah said.

'No, thanks. Not my cup of tea.'

Harrie said crossly, 'This isn't a joke, you know, Friday.'

'I know it isn't.'

'So what are we going to do to keep him away from Sarah?' Harrie demanded.

Sarah slumped visibly. 'God almighty. The day I lift my leg for Jared Gellar will be the day I ... God, the thought just absolutely makes me sick. If he made me, I'd —' She retched and put her hands over her mouth. 'Sorry. Every time I think about it I think of poor Rachel.'

They fell silent again, lost in their own sad memories.

Suddenly Friday asked, 'What sort of ghost stories was he swapping?'

Sarah said, 'What?'

'You said he was swapping ghost stories. With Esther. What sort of stories?'

'Oh, she was going on about being haunted by Rachel.' Sarah frowned again, trying to remember. 'Actually, no, I think it was Adam who raised the subject, and Gellar said he'd once had to sell a house because it was haunted. And no one local would buy it because they all knew.'

'So he believes in ghosts?' Friday asked.

'Well, he said he did.'

Friday sat back in her chair, a grin spreading across her face. 'Then let's haunt *him*. I had a great time scaring the shit out of Esther. It was a real hoot. What d'you reckon?'

Sarah stared at her, then started to smirk. 'It might work, though Gellar isn't unhinged like Esther was. But if we did it right, if we're really clever, we could use his fear against him.'

'Well, we *are* clever, aren't we? Well, you are.' To Harrie, Friday said, 'How does that sound? Are you in? Shall we bring Rachel out of retirement?' Then immediately regretted it.

'I'll ask her,' Harrie replied.

'Sarah, I need to go along to the bank,' Jared said. 'Will you be all right here by yourself?'

Well, I have been every other time you've ponced off, she thought. 'Yes. How long will you be?'

'I don't know. Possibly an hour or so?'

She nodded and turned back to her work. She was resetting a pendant containing a rare and costly pink topaz. The piece was around forty years old and the claws had worn down to the point that the gem was loose, and the owner was quite rightly concerned that it may fall out and be lost. It was a lovely stone and she was tempted to replace it with paste, but even just the thought of all that would entail — consulting with Bernard regarding a perfect strass replica, lying to the customer, falsifying the valuation documents — exhausted her. Adam had always played an essential role in the scams they'd operated and while he was away she didn't have the energy or heart — or frankly, at the moment, the nerve — to carry on by herself. Also, Gellar wasn't aware she and Adam had been on the flash, and she had no desire to provide him with anything else he could use against them.

She waited a good ten minutes after Gellar had gone to ensure he didn't return unexpectedly, then locked the shop door and belted up the stairs to his bedroom. The door, as she'd half expected, wouldn't open, so she fetched the spare key, unlocked it, and started searching. She found some interesting items — several bottles of tincture of opium on the night table; a purse containing nearly two hundred English pounds wedged under the chest of drawers; and stuffed beneath the mattress a book of rather well executed drawings depicting naked men and women doing extremely rude things to one another (dirty bugger) — but not what she was looking for. Unless he'd hidden it elsewhere in the house, which she doubted, it could only be in one other place. She climbed on the bed and jumped — and saw it, shoved out of sight on top of the tall clothes press.

She moved a chair over and stood on her tip-toes, just managing to grab the trunk's handle and almost knocking herself out swinging it down. She dragged it over to the window where the light was better. Two thick straps enclosed the trunk, and a solid-looking lock fastened the lid. Undoing the straps she pulled on the lid but it remained firmly shut. Locked, of course.

Undiscouraged, she fetched her burglary satchel from her room and got to work. A few minutes later the trunk was open and its contents — a thick bundle of papers tucked into the silk lining of the lid — spread across the bed. There was a lot of stuff she wasn't interested in; documents pertaining to a printery business Gellar owned in York Street, a butchery in King Street, and a tea warehouse, a boot and shoe warehouse, and an ironmongery in George Street. No wonder he had plenty of dosh. But there were also papers relating to the importation of wine, spirits and tobacco, and these were far more interesting because the more she read, the clearer it became that Jared Gellar had not paid customs duties on a fair proportion of those goods, thereby making a significantly more handsome profit when he sold them on.

So he wasn't just immoral — he was bent.

She shuffled through the papers — invoices, receipts, letters, several ships' manifests relating to voyages across the Tasman to

New Zealand — until one document in particular caught her eye, a short letter ending with the signature *Augustus A. Evans, Esq.*

The same Augustus Evans who had stood for Adam in court? Surely there couldn't be two barristers of the same name, not in a town this small. She skimmed through the note, which thanked Gellar for his *much appreciated contribution*, and assured him that the usual arrangements had been made to facilitate the seamless progression of Gellar's latest delivery of goods from England via the usual channels. On one hand it said nothing, but on the other it told Sarah everything she needed to know: Gellar was bribing Customs officers to look the other way when ships carrying his goods arrived in Sydney, and that this Evans cove was involved in the racket.

Which meant Augustus Evans was also crooked.

April 1831, Sydney Town

'What's this?' Leo Dundas jammed the cork back into a bottle of raw alcohol. 'A delegation of pretty girls? Well, I've no complaints about that.' He raised his voice. 'Put the kettle on, Walter!'

'We're here on business, Leo,' Friday said as she turned the sign outside the shop to read *CLOSED*, then shut the door. 'Don't forget my appointment's at three, but.'

This afternoon Leo was starting on the outline of the new tattoo to cover the ugly, smudged anchor and initials on her upper right arm: a Chinese dragon to begin on her shoulder and extend all the way down, the tail wrapping around her forearm and ending on the inside aspect of her wrist. They'd debated the design for hours, discussing colours and patterns specific to the shape and lines of Friday's arm, and Harrie had completed the flash last week. Friday couldn't wait.

'I could hardly forget, could I?' Leo said wryly. 'Business, you reckon? That sounds serious.' He wiped the last of the needles he was cleaning and carefully slotted them back into their mother-of-pearl case. 'Come through.'

Walter was in the other room, getting cups down from the shelf and lining them up on the old table. A loaf of fresh bread sat on a chopping board, its hot, crusty smell filling the room. Walter's dog was sprawled across the end of the cot, and immediately began to growl, though it didn't bother to get up.

'Yous're just in time,' Walter said. 'I been to the bakery.'

'You look well, Walter,' Harrie said.

He did. He'd had a proper haircut and was wearing a new blue shirt tucked into his trousers, which had been neatly patched, and a decent pair of boots.

Walter ducked his head, blushing. 'Thank you.'

Sarah picked up a cup and peered into it, frowning at the brown rings staining the china.

'Ignore it. It won't kill you,' Friday said.

Leo gestured at the chairs. Friday and Sarah took them, while Harrie perched on the little cot, as far from the dog as she could manage. Humming, Leo sliced the loaf, then sat in the remaining chair at the table.

As Walter filled the teapot with boiling water from the kettle, Leo asked through a mouthful of buttered bread, 'Can the boy stay?'

Sarah nodded, and Walter grabbed a bit of bread and shyly settled himself next to Harrie. The dog immediately snuggled next to him.

'So, what's this about, then?' Leo asked.

Friday helped herself to a slice of the loaf. 'Sarah's in the shit,' she began, and explained what had happened to Adam.

Leo, who had only met Sarah twice and barely knew her, listened in silence, wading his way through the bread and drinking several cups of tea.

'We were hoping,' Harrie said when Friday had finished, 'that with all the people you know, you might be able to help us.'

'How?' Leo asked.

Friday said, 'We thought you might be able to ferret out some dirt on Gellar. We know he's crooked.'

'You said that.' Leo wiped buttery fingers on his trousers. 'But *how* do you know?'

Friday hadn't gone into detail regarding this. She glanced at Sarah, who nodded. 'Sarah broke into his trunk and went through his papers. He's been dodging the customs duty on imports.'

Leo's craggy gaze fixed on Sarah. 'Interesting.'

'That Gellar's bent?' Friday said.

'No, this one being a female cracksman. You don't get many of those.'

Sarah rolled her eyes. 'Can you help us or not?'

'Can I help *you*, you mean,' Leo said mildly.

'No. If Sarah goes back to the Factory she can't earn money,' Harrie said. 'Which means we'll be short for the Charlotte fund, which means B—'

'Harrie! Shut up!' Friday glared at her.

Harrie clapped her hands over her mouth, horrified by what she'd almost let slip.

'Is there possibly something you lasses aren't telling me?' Leo asked. Silence. He buttered another piece of bread. 'Well, another day, perhaps. But I'm not lifting a finger unless I get the answer to this question.' He pointed at Sarah. 'From you, this time. Is your husband guilty as accused?'

'No, he bloody is not! He was framed by Jared bloody Gellar!' Sarah stood, the legs of her chair scraping the floor. 'I'm going. I don't have to listen to this.' To Harrie she exclaimed, 'I told you expecting anything useful from a decrepit bloody old sea dog was a stupid idea!'

Leo sighed and gestured with the butter knife. 'Sit down, lass. If you want my help, I'm entitled to an honest answer.' In a very loud whisper he said to Friday, 'You're right, she isn't a very trusting soul, is she?'

Sarah glowered at Friday, but sat down again, arms folded across her chest. She breathed slowly in and out, visibly calming and gathering herself.

'I know Gellar's been bribing someone in the Customs office to dodge paying duties, and that a barrister called Augustus Evans is also in on it. The *same* cove who represented Adam when he went up before Rossi. Yes, a coincidence, isn't it? But I want more. I want to know everything about Gellar's crooked dealings, and the name of every shady cove he's gammied up with since he arrived in this town.' She hesitated, then added, 'Please.'

'And how long ago was that?'

'About eight years.'

Leo's hairy brows went up. 'Tall order.'

'If you're as sharp as Harrie says you are, you can do it.'

'Are we, boy?' Leo asked Walter, who shrugged and went red again.

'We can fight back if we know what we're dealing with,' Friday said. 'The more dirt we have on him the better. But we've got something in mind anyway.' She told Leo about their plan to 'haunt' Gellar, based on the manner in which Sarah had persecuted Esther.

Leo started to laugh. 'That's a new one,' he said. 'I've not heard of that before.'

'And if that doesn't work, we'll blackmail him with whatever you find out.'

'I want to know everything about him, anyway,' Sarah said, 'whether we blackmail him or not.'

'Yeah, what's that Bible quote?' Friday said. '"Know thy enemy"?'

'That's not from the Bible,' Harrie said.

Friday frowned at her. 'Yes it is.'

'It's from Sun Tzu's *The Art of War*,' Leo corrected.

'Who the hell's Sun Soo?' Friday said.

'An ancient Chinese military strategist. Very clever cove. But you're quite right — it pays to find out everything you can about your enemies. I'll see what I can do. Might take me a while, though. Does anyone want this last crust?'

Walter launched himself across the room, grabbed it and fed it to his dog.

Eyeing him sourly, Leo asked, 'Any other business? While you're here?'

'I've finished my latest lot of flash.' Harrie took a roll of papers from her basket on the floor and passed them across the table. 'Don't get butter on them.'

Leo moved the chopping board and butter dish out of the way, wiped his hands on his trousers again and carefully opened the roll. He studied them one by one, then said, 'Harrie, lass, these are stunning.'

Friday and Sarah both leant over for a look. Harrie had drawn a series of five stylised ships on wild seas, each one progressively more spectral than the last. With the skilful use of shading she'd managed to convey a truly evocative sense of abandonment and hopelessness. Within the white spaces that were the tattered remains of the ships' sails, she'd added the intricate Celtic spirals and knots she'd learnt from Leo's *Book of Kells*. And in every image, hovering just above the ship's bowsprit, was her signature bat.

'The *Flying Dutchman*?' Leo asked.

Harrie nodded.

'Is this what you actually saw?' Leo had heard all about the sighting from Walter.

'Sort of.'

Leo slowly shook his grizzled head. 'These are easily as good as your bat series. I don't know what to say, lass. I'm impressed.'

Harrie went pink with pleasure.

'They're gorgeous, Harrie,' Friday said, 'but what sailor'd want the *Flying Dutchman* tattooed all over him? Wouldn't that be, I dunno, bad luck?'

'Plenty do.' Leo was sharp. 'I'm surprised you haven't come across any, in your line of business.'

Friday gave a bark of laughter. 'Fire away. You can't insult me.'

'Probably not.' Leo grinned, his gold tooth glinting. 'A lot of tars view seeing the *Dutchman* as a badge of honour.' He tapped the roll of drawings. 'Anyway, these are art. Pure art. Which reminds me, Harrie lass, how's that tattoo I did for your young man?'

Harrie returned his look blankly. 'Pardon?'

'The Chinese lion and the peony. Yin and yang?'

Harrie switched her gaze to Sarah and Friday. What was he talking about? James had never been tattooed. Had he? Not that she'd seen much of him — in any sense of the phrase — since he'd apologised to her just before Christmas. He'd been very busy with his duties apparently, and so had she, much to her relief. Why was Friday giggling?

She said to her, 'What are you tittering at?' then asked Leo, 'Are you talking about James Downey?'

'No. This was a lad called Matthew.'

Friday burst out laughing.

'*What* is so funny?' Harrie wasn't at all amused.

'Matthew got a tattoo!' Friday hooted. 'For you!'

'Oh, he did not!' Harrie exclaimed.

'Aye, he did,' Leo confirmed. 'I thought he was your young man.'

Harrie felt her face reddening. She'd never actually discussed her private affairs with Leo — she didn't know him *that* intimately. 'Well, he isn't. I went to tea with him once, that's all.'

'And got blind drunk on a picnic and whipped the cat all the way home,' Friday added, laughing so hard now her eyes were leaking.

'Shut up, Friday,' Sarah said, her hand over her mouth covering her own smile. 'Don't be such a cow.'

'He was desperate to impress you, you know,' Leo said.

'Ah, poor Matthew,' Friday said, cackling her head off.

'How did you know about it?' Sarah asked her.

'I turned up when he was getting it. But I didn't tell you, Harrie, in case he wanted it to be a surprise.'

'It's a surprise, all right.' Harrie felt terrible.

Sarah couldn't help it: at the miserable, guilt-ridden expression on Harrie's face she started to laugh, too.

'Now don't you be a cow,' Friday said.

Sarah belted her on the arm.

'So this Matthew *isn't* your young man?' Leo asked.

'No, he isn't.' Harrie scowled at Sarah and Friday.

'Well, then, who is? That Downey cove?'

'No! No one is. I don't have a young man. And I don't bloody well want one!'

'You do,' Sarah said.

'I *don't*!'

Friday said, 'Matthew's taken now, anyway. Sally Minto's got her claws into him and I don't think he minds at all.'

'Well, I hope *she* appreciates his tattoo,' Sarah said.

'She'd better. I bet he suffered for it,' Friday said, knowing full well that not everyone received the sort of pleasure and release from the needle that she did. 'Did he, Leo?'

'Aye, he did actually. Poor bugger.'

Friday and Sarah caught each other's eyes and were off again, and even Harrie giggled this time.

Leo and Walter shook their heads.

Sarah felt a little more cheerful. Even though she wasn't sure if she trusted the salty old bugger, Leo was going to help them by digging up some dirt on Gellar, and she'd had a good laugh at his shop the other day. Before she'd gone all odd Harrie had always said laughing helped a person to feel better, and she was right. It really did. She hoped Adam was finding something to laugh — or at least smile — about in Port Macquarie.

She set Jared's plate of breakfast down on the table in front of him.

'Thank you, Sarah. This looks very nice.'

She'd burnt the black pudding on the edges and made sure the egg yolks were still runny — not the way he liked them. He was doing his best to flatter and court her favour, but she didn't know why he was bothering. She certainly wasn't encouraging him.

She sat down and started on her own meal. After a while she said, 'Did you hear that noise last night?'

'What noise?'

'Creaking, on the stairs. And a sort of dragging. Was that you?'

Jared swallowed. There was a piggy little blob of egg stuck in the corner of his mouth. 'What time?'

Sarah shrugged. 'I didn't look at the clock. Two? Half past?'

'No, it wasn't me.'

'And you didn't hear it?'

He shook his head, staring at her.

'It was quite loud,' Sarah said. 'Certainly woke me.' She cut up a piece of black pudding, popped it in her mouth, chewed and swallowed. 'Friday's dropping around this morning. Is that all right with you?'

Jared waved his fork. 'Yes, that's fine.'

Sarah knew it would be — he couldn't keep his eyes off Friday. She finished her breakfast, waited for Jared to wipe his plate clean with his bread, cleared the table and carried everything out to the kitchen. As she filled the washing-up basin with hot water from the kettle, Jared went past on the way to the privy, yesterday's *Sydney Gazette* under his arm. He'd be in there for at least half an hour, but at least he used the crapper and not the pot.

Friday arrived just before ten, flouncing through the door and laying it on with a trowel.

'Mr *Gellar*, it's so nice to *see* you!' She flitted across the shop, set her elbows on the counter and leant forwards, giving Jared an excellent view of her cleavage. 'Is Sarah in?'

'It's lovely to see you, too, Miss Woolfe. May I say that's a very charming gown you're wearing today?'

'You don't think it's a little snug?' Friday grabbed the bodice under the arms and yanked it so her breasts heaved. 'It's such a divine colour, though, I can't resist wearing it.'

'No, no, it's perfect.'

She raised her arms and removed her hat, allowing her hair — strategically left unpinned — to tumble down over her shoulders. Jared watched every tiny movement she made.

'Well, is she?'

'I beg your pardon?'

'Sarah? Is she in? She *is* expecting me.'

'Oh! Of course. I'll fetch her.'

Friday smirked as he trotted off to alert Sarah, who appeared a moment later.

'Morning, Friday. Come through. You'll have to talk to me while I work — I'm right in the middle of something.'

Jared gallantly lifted the hatch in the counter to let Friday through.

Her hand 'accidentally' brushed his thigh as she swished past, and she smiled invitingly. 'Thank you, Mr Gellar.'

'My pleasure entirely.'

In the workshop Friday sat on Adam's stool. 'Talk about leading him around by his cock,' she said under her breath. 'This is going to be so easy.'

'I wouldn't be too sure of that.' Sarah picked up her pliers. 'He's not stupid. And if you don't eventually give him what you're flaunting, he'll be roaring.'

'Should I tone it down a bit?'

'Just pace yourself, that's all. Don't overdo it.'

Friday was affronted. 'When do I ever overdo things?'

Sarah looked at her sideways.

'Oh, all right. But he's not going to jump on me today, is he?' Friday dropped half a dozen pea-sized pearls into the palm of her hand and rolled them around, admiring their sheen. 'He's so sure he's got three silly, downtrodden convict girls at his fingertips and all the time in the world to do whatever he likes with us. What a tosser. I'm just … stoking the fire.'

'Well, I'm just saying, don't stoke it too obviously.'

'You know me, I'm never obvious.'

Sarah snorted. 'Have you heard from Harrie?'

'She dropped by yesterday, but only to say Leo's not got anything yet. I expect it'll take a while. Digging up shite on people can be a delicate business, you know.'

'I'm sure. There'll be plenty to find, though, I'll bet my life on it.'

'Have you heard from Adam?'

Sarah shook her head, her mouth set in a grim line.

'Well, don't worry, you'll get a letter soon. The place is full of specials so he's bound to be able to get writing paper.'

'Just because lags are educated doesn't make them generous or decent,' Sarah snapped.

'No, I know, but they might not *all* be scum.'

'*And* they're sending lunatics there now.'

Friday nodded. 'I heard that, too. And cripples.'

Sarah rubbed her hands over her face. 'Christ, Friday, five bloody years.'

'I know, love.' Friday squeezed Sarah's arm. 'I know.'

'All right, ladies?' Jared called from the doorway.

'Oh, fuck off,' Sarah whispered.

'Has he tried anything else?'

'Keep your voice down and your back turned,' Sarah warned. 'He pinched my arse a few days ago, and yesterday he had me up against the wall on the stairs and tried to feel my tits. And he's *always* watching me.'

'Bastard. Did you give him a good boot in the bollocks?'

'I tried to but my skirt got in the way. I'm getting so sick of it, Friday. I'm looking over my shoulder the whole time and I'm barely sleeping at night.'

'Ask Bernard to put an extra lock on your door.'

'I will.'

'When are we going to start haunting him? I'm looking forward to that.'

Without looking, Sarah asked, 'Is he still in the doorway?'

'No, he's back in the shop. I think there's a customer.'

'I made a bit of a start this morning. Are you ready to leave?'

Friday nodded. 'I've an appointment to see the doctor shortly. Why?'

'On the way out, just say, "Are you sure you'll be all right?"'

'What for?'

'Just do it.' Sarah stood and moved through to the shop, where Jared was returning a tray of cufflinks to a display cabinet.

'Friday's on her way,' she said.

Jared locked the cabinet door. 'So soon? Well, do come by whenever you like, Miss Woolfe. You know you're welcome here any time. I wouldn't like to feel Sarah was being deprived of the company of her friends.'

'Very kind of you, Mr Gellar.' Friday smiled prettily, pecked Sarah on the cheek and made for the door, where she turned and said, 'Are you sure you'll be all right, Sarah?'

Sarah waved a dismissive hand. 'It was just a noise. Probably the house settling. I'm not sure she really is back.' She paused, then added darkly, 'At least, I hope not.'

Friday caught on. 'You don't want me to stay with you?'

'I'm fine. Go on, you'll be late.'

Friday waggled her fingers in farewell and left, closing the door behind her.

Returning to the workshop, Sarah resumed work. It wasn't long before she sensed Jared's presence in the room. As predicted.

'Sarah, what did you mean when you said to Friday you're not sure she really is back? Who?'

Sarah gave a reluctant sigh and swivelled on her stool. 'I wasn't going to say anything, but do you recall when you came to supper — last October, was it? — and Adam told you Esther thought this house was haunted? Well, it was, by the ghost of a girl named Rachel Winter. It was the reason Esther left. The poor woman was frightened witless. She couldn't bear it.'

'Poor woman, my arse,' Jared said coarsely. 'The pair of you clearly couldn't stand each other.'

Sarah's heart gave a little jolt of alarm, a reminder that she must be very careful. Just because he behaved like a boor didn't mean he was obtuse. 'That's true, we didn't get on. She thought I was to blame for Rachel's spirit being here.'

Jared moved across to the workbench and leant against it. 'Who exactly was this Rachel?'

Sarah turned again so she could see his face. 'A girl who was transported with me and Harrie and Friday. We were very close. She died giving birth in the Factory.'

'Who was the father?'

Sarah frowned. What the hell did that matter? Also, she most definitely didn't want Jared connecting them to Keegan in any way. 'We never knew.'

'Like that, was she?'

'We all are, Jared. We're convict whores, remember?'

He didn't even have the grace to look embarrassed. 'And this ghost went away when Esther left?'

'Seemed to.' Sarah manufactured a vaguely regretful expression. 'I suppose in a way it *might* have been my fault Rachel haunted this house, but only because this is where I was assigned. Esther was just as much to blame. If she hadn't been so unpleasant to me, and if she'd granted me leave to go to the cemetery when Rachel was buried, perhaps Rachel would have stayed in her grave.'

'What do you mean?' Jared seemed uneasy.

'It was extremely unpleasant here when all the haunting business was going on. There was a very nasty sense of ... resentment in the air. I can't help thinking Rachel may have been angry with Esther.'

'Because she stopped you from —'

'Attending the burial. Yes. I was very upset.' What an understatement.

'And you think the ghost was persecuting Esther for that?'

'And for being such a constant bitch to me.' Sarah shrugged. 'But then Rachel always was very protective of us.'

'And when Esther went, so did the ghost?' Jared asked again, as though to reassure himself.

Sarah turned back to the workbench, gave the silver bangle she'd been engraving a quick polish with a cloth and squinted at it. 'All the strange activity stopped, if that's what you mean. The bad smells and the furniture and everything moving around and the food going off and the creaks and rattles and bangs in the night.'

'Good God! That's certainly a relief to hear.' Jared pulled nervously at his cravat. 'Sounds like an absolute nightmare!'

Sarah raised her head and looked him squarely in the eye. 'Well, I *thought* it had stopped, until last night.'

George Street's new market sheds had not long been completed, replacing the bark and slab huts, rough stalls and open ground that had previously constituted Sydney's central market. After numerous and ongoing complaints from nearby residents and shopkeepers, the livestock market had been moved south to Campbell Street in the valley below Brickfield Hill, taking its flies and noisome stinks with it, and there was talk of the hay and grain farmers following in due course. It was also quietly hoped that with them would go the less salubrious stallholders — those who sold second-hand goods, ready-made hot foods, and medical preparations of questionable quality — leaving the George Street market to good, honest Sydney citizens shopping to simply feed families and stock store shelves.

Smirking to herself, Friday hurried towards one of the market's many entrances, looking for something to grab to eat before her doctor's appointment. That had been clever of Sarah. Whatever hints she'd dropped to Gellar about Rachel's ghost reappearing must have been good ones, judging by the way his gob had been flapping open.

She spied a familiar figure about to enter one of the long sheds. 'Harrie! Oi, *Harrie*!'

Harrie stopped and waved. She had one of the junior Barretts with her, the naughty, annoying one named Hannah.

Friday hurried over. 'I've just been at Sarah's. It's started,' she said, rubbing her hands with glee.

'What has?'

'You know.' She inclined her head at the child, indicating she needed to watch what she said. 'The return of our friend.'

'Oh. Right. How is Sarah?'

'Pretty fed up. He's been pawing her again.'

Harrie made a face. 'I've been meaning to visit but Lewis and Sam have been sick for the last two days. I'll go in the morning if I can get away.' She put out a hand. No Hannah. 'Oh God, where's she gone?'

Friday spotted her disappearing into the fruit and vegetable shed. They trotted after her but lost sight of her again once they entered the noisy, dimly lit building. The shed was two hundred feet long, about thirty wide and divided into multiple stalls piled high with fresh produce, and crowded with shoppers.

'Oh Lord, what if someone steals her?' Harrie fretted.

'Wouldn't be the end of the world, would it?'

'Don't be horrible.'

They eventually found her in the grip of an irate-looking costermonger, her mouth and hands stained dark red with plum juice.

'Is this your kiddie?' the man demanded.

'She's … yes, she is,' Harrie said for simplicity's sake.

'Well, you owe me one shilling and tuppence. She's pinched and eaten eight of me prime plums.'

Friday laughed down at Hannah. 'You'll be shitting through the eye of a needle tomorrow, won't you?'

'Did you help yourself?' Harrie asked.

Hannah nodded. 'I were *hungry*.'

'Why didn't you stop her?' Harrie asked the costermonger.

'I didn't see her, did I? She were down there in front of me stand. She's only a dot.'

Harrie opened her purse and counted out the money. 'Thank you for not fetching the watch.'

The costermonger humphed. 'What do you think I am, with her just a kiddie?'

'I appreciate your generosity.'

The man tipped his hat as Harrie dragged Hannah away by the hand. As soon as they were out of the shed, she removed a length of sturdy twine from her basket.

'Nooo, I *hate* the twine!' Hannah whined.

'I'm sorry, Hannah, but I did tell you what would happen if you misbehaved.' Harrie tied one end of the twine to the back straps of Hannah's pinafore and looped the other around her wrist. 'Where are you off to now?' she asked Friday.

'Appointment with the doctor.'

'James?'

Friday shrugged. 'I usually see old Chandler. I need a note for Mrs H to say I'm fit for work.' She was fairly sure her recent bout of gonorrhoea had now passed. 'Though it was James who sewed up the dog bite. I'll get Chandler to check and make sure I don't have rabies after all, though obviously I don't. It's been months and months and I haven't bitten a single person. Shall I say hello to James for you if I see him?'

'No, it's all right, thank you,' Harrie said hastily.

'Why not? Christ, don't tell me you aren't talking again!'

'No, it's not that.' Harrie wouldn't meet Friday's eyes. 'I just don't feel … up to seeing him at the moment.'

'Oh, for God's sake, Harrie. He's said sorry, hasn't he? Look, why don't you just get off your bum and go and visit him at home?'

Harrie was shocked. 'I couldn't do that.' She gave the twine a good jerk as Hannah bounded off after a woman carrying a litter of kittens in a basket.

'Why? Because of Rowie?'

'Have you had a proper look around?' Harrie said, wrenching the conversation in another direction. 'It's a lot nicer with the new sheds, don't you think?'

'It's a market,' Friday said dismissively. She found shopping boring and never did it if she could avoid it. The girls Elizabeth employed at the Siren's Arms hotel did all the shopping, and the cooking, and Friday ate whatever was put in front of her, as long as it wasn't oysters. 'Don't change the subject.' It was too late now anyway. She waved. 'Speak of the devil.'

'James?'

'No, Rowie.'

Harrie whipped her head around. Approaching was a very pretty girl wearing a pale pink dress and a cream bonnet trimmed with pink ribbons. She was petite and slender yet shapely, had lovely, gleaming black hair falling in loops over her ears, and looked far better than a convict girl had a right to. Then, with a squirt of annoyance, Harrie remembered that Rowie Harris wasn't a convict — she had a ticket of leave.

Friday pecked Rowie on the cheek. 'Nice to see you, Rowie. How's things with you?'

'Can't complain. Good to see you, too, Friday. How's the leg?'

'Mended. Rowie, this is my friend, Harrie Clarke.'

'Oh, so *you're* Harrie.' Rowie offered her hand.

Reluctantly, Harrie took it, catching a pleasant whiff of perfume. Rowie's palm was warm and dry, unlike her own, which was now sweating.

'James is always talking about you,' Rowie said. '"Harrie says this, Harrie did that." It's very nice to finally meet you.'

James? Bloody *James*? 'Thank you,' Harrie said stiffly.

'How's the ...' Friday gestured vaguely at Rowie's middle.

'A little better. Comes and goes. You must come and visit again, Friday.'

Rowie regularly dropped by at the Siren to catch up on the gossip, but Friday had been rather remiss at returning the courtesy.

'You're right, I should,' she said.

'You, too, Harrie. Come in the evening. I really think James would like that. In fact, I know he would.'

Harrie thought furiously, who the hell are you to know what James would like? 'I'm really very busy. I have two jobs, you know,' she said. Then realised how rude that sounded. 'But, yes, perhaps one evening we could drop by.' She wouldn't, though.

'That would be lovely,' Rowie said. 'And who's this dear little girl?'

Hannah was picking her nose.

'This is Hannah Barrett. She belongs to the family I'm assigned to,' Harrie explained.

Rowie bent down. 'Good morning, Hannah.'

Hannah ignored her, fascinated by the lump of snot on the end of her finger.

'Hannah, say good morning, please,' Harrie prompted, though silently she applauded the little girl's disgusting manners.

'Mornin'.'

'What a sweet thing,' Rowie said. 'Well, I should get on with my errands. Nice to see you both. And please come and visit. James would love it.' She gave a little wave and headed off towards the meat, poultry and dairy shed.

'See? She's perfectly nice,' Friday said.

Harrie scowled.

'Shall we visit?'

'No.'

'Why not?'

'I just don't want to talk about it, Friday! Not now, anyway.' Harrie slapped Hannah's hand away from her nose. '*Hannah*, will you stop doing that?'

Friday said, 'Well, I've got ears when you're ready.'

'Thanks. I know. I know you have.'

'Good. Now, I've really got to go or I'll be late.'

When she'd disappeared into the crowd, Hannah said, 'Harrie, has Friday got a baby?'

Startled, Harrie looked down at her. 'No. Why?'

'Then why's she got her bubbies out?'

'Oh, Hannah, don't ask so many questions.'

Chapter Sixteen

Nibbling a hot potato, Friday strode down George Street, turned right onto King then followed Pitt north towards Dr Chandler's surgery. Hearing the rattle of a vehicle approaching from behind, she moved to the edge of the road, but suddenly had to leap for her life as, in a flash of midnight-blue paintwork and a jingle of harnesses, the gig swerved directly at her, barely missing her. A hoot of harsh laughter issued from beneath the gig's raised hood before it sped off down the street, wheels hurling up gravel. Friday launched her potato in an almighty lob, cursing the air blue as it exploded harmlessly against the oiled black canvas.

Her anger hadn't subsided by the time she arrived at the doctors' surgery to discover at least a dozen other patients sitting outside, waiting to be seen.

'Hoi, wait your turn!' someone demanded as she stamped up to the door of the little cottage Lawrence Chandler had converted to medical rooms.

'You can wait *your* bloody turn,' Friday snapped. '*I've* got an appointment.'

'You get back here!' the woman spluttered. 'Who do you think you are?'

'Queen Adelaide,' Friday shot back.

The woman, a bony specimen wearing a shawl tucked into her waistband and a lumpy brown bonnet, lurched up off the ground and marched over.

'You. Wait. Your. Turn,' she repeated, emphasising each word by jabbing Friday's freshly tattooed arm with a sharp finger. 'I've got two very ill kiddies, one with a shocking case of blight and the other with galloping consumption. *You* don't look poorly at all.'

'Oh but I am.'

'Prove it!'

Friday whipped up her skirt, revealing the ragged purple scar on her calf. 'Dog bite. *Rabies*!' And she bared her teeth and barked like a deranged dog.

The woman's eyes bulged and she backed away, then turned and fled, slowing only to scoop up her two startled children.

A window creaked open and James's head appeared. 'What on earth is going on out here?'

'Is old Lawrence about? I'm here for my appointment.'

'He's running at least an hour and a half late. We had an emergency this morning.'

Friday pouted. 'Well, Christ, I can't wait that long!'

'Was that you making dog noises?' James asked.

'Might have been.'

James heaved a sigh and pulled out his watch. 'I can see you now, just briefly, otherwise you'll have to wait for Dr Chandler.'

A moment later Friday was sitting in the chair beside James's desk. 'I actually do have an appointment, you know.'

'I'm sure you do,' James said. 'A man arrived earlier today having almost severed his foot with an axe. Dr Chandler had to tend to him, because of course the poor fellow couldn't afford to go to the infirmary. It's set us very much behind, but I can spare you about fifteen minutes. Providing you promise not to bark. I assume that isn't why you're here? It is rather late for the onset of hydrophobia. Obviously you were very lucky there.'

'I've had the clap. I've been seeing Chandler for that. I need a note for my boss to say it's gone so I can go back to work.'

'*Has* it gone?'

'Hard to say. I think so. I don't stink any more and the burning's stopped.'

'Well, I heartily approve of Mrs Hislop not allowing you to work while indisposed,' James said. 'Not all, er, madams are as conscientious.'

Friday snorted. 'Easy for you to say, you aren't losing her any money. She's been right shitty at me. I didn't *ask* for the clap.'

James fiddled with the implements on his desk, aligning a scissors perfectly between his stethoscope and a tongue depressor. 'I will have to carry out an examination. I cannot issue a statement of fitness without doing so.'

Unexpectedly, Friday felt embarrassed, which made her angry all over again. 'Mrs H wouldn't expect anything less,' she snapped.

'Then please recline on the examination couch.'

Friday removed her hat and lay down on the worn leather bench, her booted feet hanging over the end. 'Skirts lifted?' she said, determined to make James feel as uncomfortable as she did.

He set a lamp on the small table strategically placed at the end of the bench, and turned up the wick. 'If you please.'

'Knees up round my ears?'

'Slightly bent will be sufficient, thank you.'

Friday did as asked. James had a thorough look, and a good sniff, but didn't touch her. 'Thank you, you may lower your skirts. I see no evidence remaining of any venereal affliction, and will issue a note to your employer accordingly.'

An unguarded expression flitted across Friday's face that looked very much to James like disappointment.

'You don't want to return to work?'

'No, it's time I went back.'

But James knew what he'd seen. 'I might as well look at the site of the dog bite while you're here. Would you please turn over onto your stomach.'

He palpated the purple L-shaped scar on Friday's right calf. It had healed remarkably well, testament, in all likelihood, to her general good health and sound eating habits, and to his skill with a needle and catgut, if he did say so himself. It was somewhat lumpy, but that was to be expected, and the lurid colour marred her attractive pale skin, but there was no avoiding that.

'Ugly, isn't it?' Friday remarked.

'Is there any pulling with activity? Stretching? Running?'

'I can feel it when I stretch. I hardly ever run, though. I was thinking of getting it tattooed.'

'The scar?'

'Yes. I don't want a bloody great purple mark down the back of my leg.'

'It will fade with time, you know. Scars always do.'

Friday rolled over and sat up. 'Well, I don't want to wait that long.'

'I wouldn't recommend it. The skin is new and still very delicate. If you must do it, I suggest you wait a while.'

'Maybe,' Friday said, hopping off the couch. 'Been to see Harrie lately?'

'I'm afraid not. We've been extremely busy with all the dysentery going about since Christmas. And I'm not sure it's any business of yours anyway.'

'Maybe not, but this is. She thinks she's seeing Rachel's ghost. And she talks to her, at night. Regularly. Me and Sarah are worried sick.'

James sat at his desk. 'How long has this been going on?'

'Ages. Months and months.' Friday tapped her head. 'Sarah reckons she's losing her mind, but I don't know about that. Nora Barrett says she's managing her duties perfectly well. Perhaps Rachel really has come back.'

James felt his pulse quicken as he thought back to his last encounter with Harrie. Her behaviour *had* been rather out of character. 'Is she demonstrating any other symptoms of lunacy?'

'I don't know, you're the doctor. You've seen her. What do you think?'

'Friday, as I've just said, I've seen far too little of her of late. I'm asking you for *your* opinion.'

'Well, there's no need to be snippy about it.' However, Friday recounted to him the precarious state of Harrie's nerves, and her endless worrying and evident fatigue, but also how lately she seemed to have rallied somewhat, rising to the challenge of supporting Sarah in her time of crisis.

James said, 'That is her forté, though, isn't it, giving comfort to others?'

'Christ, you make her sound like a bloody saint.'

'In some ways she is quite a paragon of virtue.'

If you only knew, Friday thought. 'You didn't think that when she was drunk in Hyde Park.'

'I had no idea she was suffering such ... mental distress.'

'No, you're too busy tending to everyone else. Folk you don't even know. What about plying your trade a bit closer to home, doing some good for someone you actually care about?'

'I'd be delighted to, if only she'd —' James stopped, reluctant to discuss his personal affairs any further. Especially with Friday. 'This note: do I mark it attention of Mrs Elizabeth Hislop?'

Friday nodded.

'And when would you like to be declared fit for work?'

'Oh, now, I suppose.'

James dipped his pen into a bottle of ink, wrote the note, then rolled his blotter across the lines. 'May I suggest the use of sheaths to prevent future afflictions of the type you've just suffered?'

'You can suggest it but it isn't going to happen. You try and get the buggers to wear them. Apparently it feels like shagging with a Wellington boot on your tool.'

This didn't surprise, or shock, James; he'd heard such complaints before. 'Well, please consider the possibility. I'm sure Mrs Hislop would prefer healthy employees.'

'No, she'd prefer a popular and busy brothel. And we always make the cullies wash beforehand. It's why our house is so clean and Mrs H can charge such outrageous prices.'

James gave up. Friday wouldn't, he was sure, comprehend the finer points of a lecture on how venereal diseases could be transmitted. The reason Elizabeth Hislop's establishment had a reputation for being relatively disease-free was that she didn't allow her girls to work when they were infected.

'And you said Harrie is still with the Barretts?'

'Yes. Why?'

James handed her the note. 'Good day, Friday.'

He'd make a point of visiting Harrie as soon as he could, busy be damned.

Starving now and regretting chucking her potato at Bella the Bitch, Friday stopped at a street vendor on the way home and bought some hot roast pork and pickles on a bap. It was a warm day, the kind that made you sticky and itchy under your clothes, but thunder clouds were piling ominously in the sky to the west, which likely meant heavy rain before nightfall, and then the streets would stream with filthy water and everything would be slick with mud.

She didn't want to go back to work. It had been nice having a rest from having to lie under stupid, sweating, grunting pigs. But she had no choice; she had to make money, now more than ever. Well, at least Mrs H would be happy with her return.

She wandered down the carriageway at the side of the Siren's Arms, licking pickle juice off her fingers, and unlocked the gate into the narrow alleyway leading to the brothel. The cobblestones in the alley were covered with a thin film of moss, and Friday reminded herself to ask Jack to give them another scrape. At night, especially during winter, they could be treacherous. The August before, Hazel had taken a tumble and landed on her arse — she hadn't been able to sit down for days.

Entering the brothel's backyard, she stopped short, astonished, then shouted, 'Oi, get out of there, you mangy bloody goat!'

The privy door banged open and Loulou emerged, rearranging her robe. 'Who the hell are you calling a goat?'

Friday pointed.

The beast in question — a shaggy, mean-looking billy goat with wickedly curved horns — turned from its dinner of freshly laundered antimacassars hanging on the washing line and stared balefully through evil yellow eyes.

Lou shot back into the privy.

'Get out!' Friday whipped off her boot and hurled it. 'Go on, bugger off!'

The boot bounced off the goat's rump. It barely flinched.

The back door opened and Elizabeth Hislop appeared. 'What's all ... oh!' The door shut again.

Friday sidled around the animal, intending to herd it out of the yard, but Elizabeth reappeared with a pistol and fired it, aiming at the sky. The goat leapt into the air and scrambled for the gate, its hooves skidding on the yard's cobbles. It left a trail of little dark turds in its wake. A moment later Friday and Elizabeth glimpsed it on top of the wall on the far side of the alleyway, and then it was gone.

Elizabeth broke open the pistol. 'How the hell did that get in here?'

'Same way as it got out, I suppose.'

'Just look at my good linen. Ruined!'

Friday called, 'You can come out now, you gutless article.'

Lou emerged from the privy, red patches high on her cheeks. 'Don't you dare call me gutless! I can't *stand* goats!' Glaring at Friday, she stomped up the steps into the house.

Friday hooted with laughter. 'You should have shot the ruddy thing,' she said to Elizabeth. 'You could have served it in the pub. Goat stew.'

'I don't hold with shooting things,' Elizabeth replied. 'Gives me nightmares.'

Friday followed Elizabeth inside. 'Serves Lou right. She's *always* in the bog.'

'She is not,' Elizabeth said as she unlocked the door to her office. 'She wouldn't have time to work if she was. Why does it bother you?'

'*Everything* she does bothers me.'

Elizabeth put the pistol in a drawer and sat at her desk. 'But why?'

'I don't know.' Friday flopped into a chair. 'She just gets on my tits.'

She couldn't tell Mrs H the real reason — that she was *sure* she'd seen Lou with Amos Furniss at the Black Rat — because she'd kept from Mrs H the fact that she, Sarah and Harrie were being blackmailed by Bella, and Lou's appearance with Furniss could only mean she was also involved. The mystery of who had tried to break into Mrs H's safe hadn't been solved, either. But who else could that have been but Lou? Molly had said she'd seen her coming down the stairs as they'd gone into the office that day: perhaps Lou had spied Sarah with the bag containing the Charlotte fund. It was obvious when you thought about it.

'Well, don't *let* her get on your tits,' Elizabeth said shortly. 'Try and act your age. Now, how did you get on with Dr Chandler?'

Friday dug around in her reticule for James's note and passed it to her. 'I'm fit for work as of now.'

Elizabeth read it. 'That's a relief. I'm sick of telling your regulars you're indisposed with a stomach complaint. They've been asking for you constantly.' She opened her mouth, and shut it again. Then she said, 'No, bugger it, I will say it. You've also had at least half a dozen new gentlemen asking for you. Well, most of them were gentlemen. A couple were tars.'

'Have I?' Friday tried to sound enthusiastic.

'Yes, you have. They were asking for the redhead with the tattoos.'

'The tattoos you said were cheap and would put the cullies off?'

'Well, obviously I was wrong. It seems word has spread of your ...' Elizabeth flapped a hand in Friday's direction, 'bodily decorations, and it appears they have a certain erotic appeal.'

'That's not why I get them, you know,' Friday said. 'They're for ... well, they're for me. And I'm not stopping, either. When this dragon on my arm's finished I'm getting one on my leg, and after that I'm thinking about a great big one on my back. Except I might have to wait for that because I want Harrie to do it, and she isn't ready.'

'She doesn't do any actual work with the needles, though, does she?'

'Not yet, but I've got a feeling Leo's going to start her. He reckons she's born to it.'

'Well, Leo Dundas always did have an eye for a business opportunity.'

Friday was suddenly alert. 'D'you think he'd take advantage?'

'Leo? Not at all, not of someone like your Harrie. He's far too decent. And soft-hearted. But if she's as talented as he seems to think she is, they'll be run off their feet with custom, the sailors that come through this port, and I hear he's already busy.'

'Actually, so is Harrie.' Friday considered how much she wanted to tell her. 'You know Sarah, whose man's just been sent up to Port Macquarie?'

Elizabeth nodded.

'Well, it turns out the cove managing the shop and supervising Sarah is as crooked as a dog's hind leg. Jared Gellar?'

'Never heard of him. What does he do?'

'When he's not being a lech he buys up ailing businesses and does a bit of importing, *without* bothering to pay the customs duties.'

'And Sarah's husband put him in charge of her?' Elizabeth was horrified.

Friday decided to tell her everything. 'Keep this under your hat, but Sarah thinks he's the one who framed Adam. Adam owes him money and he threatened to call in the loan if he wasn't put in to manage the business when Adam was arrested. Sarah hates him. He's slobbering all over her, the dirty bastard, and she and Adam are convinced he's going to skim the profits off the shop until it goes bankrupt, then buy it up cheaply. Or something. I don't really understand it myself.'

'I do,' Elizabeth said.

'But she won't leave. She could go back to the Factory, but she won't.'

'Good on her. She's a strong girl, that Sarah. But what's this got to do with Harrie?'

'We've both decided, me and Harrie, that we have to help her.'

'Of course you do. You're her friends.'

'So we're going to scare the shit out of Gellar by pretending the ghost of our mate Rachel's come back from the dead to haunt him. That'll keep the bugger in line.'

Elizabeth looked sceptical. 'And how do you propose to do that?'

'There're ways. You'd be surprised. A lot of work, though, so I'll be pretty busy as well.'

'I hope you know what you're doing, Friday. This Gellar sounds like quite an unpleasant character.'

'He is. That's why we're doing it.'

'Well, as long as it doesn't interfere with your duties here.'

'It won't.'

'Good. Will you start back today?'

Friday nodded. 'I'll go and get dressed.'

She went to her room in the hotel to change into her work costume, wash and make up her face, then returned to the brothel to wait in the salon. Lou appeared and folded herself elegantly into an armchair, her tiny satin-slippered feet tucked under her backside.

'Back from your holidays, then?' she asked.

'Don't be a bitch, Lou,' Hazel said. 'She had the clap. She couldn't work.'

'That's what *she* says.'

'No, I definitely had it,' Friday said. 'And I'm sure I caught it off one of your cullies. Still, that's what happens when you hang around the Black Rat. Isn't it, Lou?'

'I wouldn't know. I've never been to the Black Rat in my life.'

'Are you sure? Didn't I see you there on Christmas Eve?'

'Certainly not. But perhaps that's where *you* caught it?'

Friday said, 'Oh, shut up, Lou. You're getting on my goat.'

Hazel, Molly and Esmerelda roared, because they'd all observed the little drama in the yard through the house's rear windows.

Too busy glaring at each other, however, Lou and Friday barely noticed.

Sarah had just scrambled down from the attic when Jared arrived back from one of his frequent visits to the bank. She'd been up there drilling tiny holes alongside the beams in the ceiling of his bedroom with an auger she'd purchased from Mr Skelton, and hoped there weren't tell-tale cobwebs in her hair or clinging to her clothes.

He stuck his head into the workshop. 'I'm back. You can prepare my dinner now, thank you.'

She went out to the kitchen and arranged on a plate a cold collation of meat loaf, hard-boiled eggs, shop-bought pork pie, bread and cheese, and took it in to the dining room, together with a tankard of ale.

'It's on the table,' she told Jared in the shop.

'Thank you, Sarah. I'll lock up for thirty minutes.' He regarded her reflectively. 'I've the most raging appetite today.'

Sarah ignored him, opened the cupboard beneath the stairs, found the feather duster and headed for the parlour, which hadn't been dusted since Adam had been taken away.

'Aren't you eating?' Jared asked from the doorway.

'Not hungry,' Sarah replied.

She leant across the sofa to flick dust off a vase on a table behind it, when suddenly she was shoved face down onto the couch and her skirts hauled up over her back. Jared's hands were all over her bare bottom and she felt the pressure of his knee as he attempted to separate her legs. Twisting like a cat, she curled up, turned over and struck out at him with the duster, jabbing him in the eye with the wooden handle.

He clapped a hand to his face, stared down at her for a second, then lurched out of the room.

Slowly Sarah sat up, shaking wildly. She thought she might vomit, and where his hands had been on her bum felt … *filthy*.

She hiccupped, swallowed hard, and held her hand over her mouth for the longest time until she was sure nothing was going to come out. No spew, no sobs, no crying out for Adam.

When her heart had slowed and she knew she could walk without her legs failing, she made her way out to the dining room. Jared was at the table, eating his pork pie. His eye was watering furiously.

He paused, a forkful of pie halfway to his mouth, and looked at her.

Sarah pointed the duster at him. 'If you ever touch me again, I swear to *God* I'll kill you.'

The following day both Sarah and Jared were attending to customers in the shop when Walter arrived. He waited quietly just inside the door, his scruffy little dog at his feet, until Sarah was free, then wordlessly handed her a note across the counter and left.

It said simply, *News. L.*

'Not bad tidings, I hope?' Jared asked, trying to look over her shoulder. All morning he'd behaved as though yesterday's horrible incident had never occurred.

Sarah refolded the note and slid it down her bodice. 'Not at all. But I do need to go out, just for an hour. Harrie needs my help. May I?' It stuck in her craw to have to ask permission, but in practice Gellar was her master, so ask she did.

Jared withdrew his watch from his pocket. 'Well, it's almost midday. I suppose I can find myself something to eat. Yes, go on.'

Sarah shot off to grab her bonnet and reticule, and was out the door before he could change his mind. She hurried down George Street, arriving at Leo's shop at the same time as Walter. As he politely stepped back to let her through the door first, his dog nipped at her heels as though she were a tardy sheep, however one sharp look from Walter sent it scampering into the back room.

Leo was finishing with a customer. 'Won't be a minute. Go through, put the kettle on.'

Sarah didn't want a cup of tea so she stood in front of the hearth, making menacing faces at Walter's horrible, growling little animal.

'You'll only aggravate her, doing that,' he remarked as he put the kettle over the fire.

'Doing what?'

'Making them ugly faces. If you want her to settle, you have to make a nothing face.'

'Who says?'

Walter shrugged. 'Dunno. Just works.'

Sarah settled her features into what she thought was a perfectly neutral expression. The dog exploded into a fusillade of barks.

From the other room Leo shouted, 'Shut that bloody dog up!'

Walter giggled. 'No, like this.' His young face went smooth and blank.

The animal immediately stopped barking and rolled over on the floor.

'Walter the dog boy,' Sarah said sarcastically. 'Has it got a name?'

Walter nodded. 'Clifford.'

'*Clifford?* But isn't it a bitch?'

'She is.'

'Clifford's a man's name.'

'I know.'

'Well?'

'I like it. And it suits her.'

Sarah shook her head.

Leo appeared. 'Right, I've another customer shortly, but I heard something last night you could well be interested in, Sarah.' He lifted the teapot, only to find it empty. 'Walter, where's my cup of char?'

Bugger the tea, Sarah thought. 'What was it? What did you hear?'

'I was in the Crown and Angel yarning to a cove, and he was telling me he'd had a very interesting chat with someone in the Welch Harp concerning your mate Gellar. So I trotted along there and found said cove, bought him a tankard or five and God knows how many Jamaica rums, and got the story out of him. This cove, who could barely stand up by the time I left him, reckons he's paid now and then by that barrister fellow Augustus Evans to do the odd bit of dirty work, rent collection and evictions and the like, and the scuttlebutt coming from that quarter is Gellar did frame your man.'

Sarah wasn't at all surprised: it confirmed her and Adam's suspicions and did fit with what she already knew about Gellar. Still, she was puzzled.

'I'm still not sure when he could've done it.'

Leo raised an ink-stained hand. 'Hold on. This cove could have been talking through his arse. Thank you, boy,' he said as Walter set a steaming cup of tea in front of him.

'Well, was he, do you think?' Sarah's mind was racing.

Leo shook his head. 'No, to be honest, I suspect he was telling the truth. The poor bugger couldn't keep his trap shut in his cups if his life depended on it. Likely he'll be discovered floating face down in the harbour before too long.'

'Ah!' Sarah almost shouted. 'I know when it was!'

'Gellar?'

'Yes! At our wedding — he must have hidden the brooch in the back of the drawer then.'

'There's more, though,' Leo said. 'The cove in the Crown and Angel also dropped a few hints about some import deals Gellar was heavily involved in, to do with these upoko tuhi from across the Tasman.'

'These what?'

'Upoko tuhi. Preserved, tattooed Maori heads. The Maori are the native people of New Zealand. It's their heads being traded and stolen.'

Sarah made a disgusted face.

'Do you not the read papers? Listen to this.' Leo reached for the *Sydney Herald* lying on the table and ran his finger down the front page. 'Here we are.' He cleared his throat. '*Whereas it has been represented to His Excellency the Governor, that the masters and crews of vessels trading between this colony and New Zealand, are in the practice of purchasing and bringing from thence human heads, which are preserved in a manner peculiar to that country: And whereas there is strong reason to believe, that such disgusting traffic tends greatly to increase the sacrifice of human life among savages, whose disregard of it is notorious, His Excellency is desirous of evincing his entire —* Christ, what's this word?' He shoved the paper under Sarah's nose.

'Disapprobation.'

'— *disapprobation of the practice abovementioned, as well as his determination to check it by all the means in his power; and with this view, His Excellency has been pleased to order, that the Officers of the Customs do strictly watch and report every instance which they may discover of an attempt to import into this colony any dried or preserved human heads in future, with the names of all parties concerned in every such attempt.*' He heaved a sigh at the effort of reading such a formal passage of text. 'And it goes on to say there'll be *certain and dreadful consequences* if the practice continues. Aye, and this bit: *His Excellency further trusts, that all persons who have in their possession human heads, recently brought from New Zealand, and particularly by the schooner* Prince of Denmark, *will immediately deliver them up for the purpose of being restored to the relations of the deceased parties to whom those heads belonged*, etcetera, etcetera.' Leo smiled at Sarah. 'So that's Gellar buggered, unless he plans to smuggle the things in now.'

'God, that's … revolting.'

'Apparently Gellar's just shipping them — someone else is arranging for them to be stolen to order. It's to do with the tattoos, or moko. The higher the rank of the owner of the head, the more valuable it is to collectors.' Leo tapped the newspaper. 'You might be able to use this to your advantage. I'm not sure how, though.' He lowered his voice. 'I *have* heard it said Bella Jackson's masterminding the racket.'

'Really?' Sarah sat quietly, thinking. Then she said, 'Well, I can't say I'm particularly shocked about any of it. Gellar's such a shite.'

'It's only hearsay,' Leo said, 'and from a tosspot at that.'

'No, he did it,' Sarah said. In her heart, she knew it. 'And he'll be right in the middle of this head-smuggling business. Well, thank you very much for your help. I really do appreciate it.' She reached for her reticule. 'How much do I owe you?'

'Don't insult me, lass. I don't want paying.'

'I insist.'

'And I insist you don't. Any friend of Harrie's is a friend of mine.' Leo put his elbows on the table and leant forwards conspiratorially. 'Mind you, if one of these days I'm ever in need of a master crackswoman, I'll know who to come to, won't I?' He grinned and gave her a wink.

And Sarah grinned back, treating him to one of her wide and rarely seen Sarah specials.

Sarah carried the tureen of roasted and boiled vegetables through to the dining room, set it on the table and removed the lid.

'Don't bother serving, dear,' Ruthie Cole said. 'We can all help ourselves, can't we? No need to stand on ceremony.'

She was as short and as round as her husband, with a matching twinkle in her eye, and as they were the senior couple at tonight's supper party Sarah had seated them one at each end of the table. Harrie and Friday sat along one side, while she and Jared were opposite. Esther's precious cutlery hadn't been polished since she'd run off so Harrie had given it a bit of a clean that afternoon, and in the lamplight it gleamed softly, arrayed around the table like a muted silver necklace.

'I'll carve, shall I?' Bernard offered.

'Allow me,' Jared said.

He stood quickly, grabbed the carving knife and, with notable skill and speed, shaved off slice after slice of moist, pink-grey beef; such speed in fact that droplets of fat flew out and spattered his trousers.

'Oh dear,' Ruthie said. 'White kerseymere. That'll stain.'

'It won't. Sarah works absolute wonders in the laundry,' Jared insisted ingratiatingly.

'Good for you, Sarah!' Friday said.

Sarah made a rude gesture behind Jared's back. The supper party had been her idea, a carefully orchestrated occasion at which Bernard was primed to reminisce about Esther's 'haunting' in an effort to make Jared feel as uneasy as possible. She'd gone to see Bernard the day before yesterday and informed him of what she'd discovered via Leo, then explained what she intended to do about it. He'd been truly scandalised and aggrieved on Adam's behalf, then amused, though quite disappointed, to realise that Esther's haunting had been manufactured. He'd believed it had been genuine, and had thoroughly enjoyed it, which inspired Sarah to hope she might get away with it a second time. Ruthie Cole had also been recruited, and both had agreed to do anything they could to help Sarah clear Adam's name, and put the boot into Jared if at all possible.

Unable to relinquish her role as a housemaid even for an evening, and disregarding Ruthie's suggestion that they all help themselves, Harrie forked slices of meat onto the plates and served the vegetables. Jared poured the wine and raised a toast.

'To health, happiness and good fortune,' he said brightly.

'Except for Adam's,' Sarah said. 'He won't be getting anything of the sort locked up in some shithole in Port Macquarie.' She jumped slightly as Friday tapped her ankle under the table, and scowled.

But Friday was right — she needed to keep her mouth shut. It was so hard, though. What she yearned to do so badly it made her physically shake was beat the living daylights out of Gellar — smash her fists into his face and drive her boots into his belly and groin until he screamed for mercy, and then keep going until he never made another noise again, just as they'd done to Gabriel Keegan — but if this were to work, if they hoped to manipulate him in the manner in which she planned, she *had* to control her feelings. She couldn't even let on she was aware of his business rackets. She did have a perfectly valid excuse to feel some antipathy towards him, however, and behave accordingly — his lewd gropings would have offended most women, and surely even a man as arrogant and coarse as he was must know that.

Bernard said, 'Perhaps a minute's silence in recognition of absent friends?'

'Indeed.' Jared immediately lowered his glass and his head, gazing at his plate, face grave.

You lying, turncoat bastard, Sarah thought.

Friday signalled the minute's passing by tucking into her supper. Speaking with her mouth full, she said, 'I know we're here to talk about how to get Adam out of gaol, but are we really going to be able to do that?' She wiped a dribble of gravy off her chin with the back of her hand. 'I mean, we all know he was set up, but we couldn't find anything to prove that before he went to trial. How are we going to do it now?'

'We can't. It's too late,' Sarah said hopelessly. But she didn't mean it. All this had been carefully rehearsed the day before while Jared had been out.

'What about his colleagues, other people in the jewellery business?' Harrie suggested. 'They might have heard something.'

Bernard said, 'What do you think, Jared? You must be at your wits' end wondering how to help.'

Ploughing through his supper, Jared choked and coughed.

'Bean go down the wrong way?' Sarah asked.

Red-faced, Jared nodded, reached for his wine and took a hearty gulp. 'I do beg your pardon. Yes, I've been thinking long and hard racking my brains about what to do.'

'Why don't *you* talk to Adam's friends and colleagues?' Bernard said, knowing Jared was aware that would be a waste of time. 'The girls here wouldn't know where to start and, well, they're not really in a position to make those sorts of enquiries, are they?'

'Why don't *you* talk to them?' Jared replied. 'You're in the trade.'

'Yes, I could, of course. But first I think I'll pay a visit to Arthur Hocking. Adam's solicitor? I know the man. Decent sort. And that barrister fellow, what was his name?'

'Evans. Augustus Evans,' Jared said.

'Yes, that's him.' Bernard poured more gravy onto his meat. 'Well, that's a start, at least. It's probably all we can do for now. Have you heard from him yet, Sarah?'

'No, nothing.' Sarah's voice was as flat as the Yorkshire puddings she'd made to accompany the beef.

'It's a dreadful business,' Ruthie Cole remarked. 'Such a lovely boy, Adam. To think of him all alone in a filthy cell hundreds of miles up the coast.'

Sarah regarded her at the end of the table. In her lace house cap and with her round face and rosy cheeks, bright, teary eyes, and her grey/brown hair she looked like a little upset squirrel. And she knew Ruthie wasn't acting: she really was very upset about Adam.

'I don't think he will be alone, dear,' Bernard said. 'He'll be in a barracks, probably.'

'Still,' Ruthie said, 'it's a bad business.' She cleared her throat nervously. 'And Bernard tells me on top of everything else your ghost is back!'

Sarah nodded. 'It does seem so.' From the corner of her eye she noted Jared staring at her intently.

Bernard dabbed at his mouth with a napkin. 'But why, I wonder? Last time you thought it might have been trying to stop Esther from mistreating you. What could have brought it back this time?'

Sarah gazed deliberately at Jared. 'I really don't know.'

'Not "it". *Her*,' Harrie corrected. 'Her name is Rachel. And you're very distressed, Sarah. Perhaps she's come to give you support. She's like that.'

Oh no, Sarah thought, her heart missing a beat. Keep to the script, Harrie!

Bernard explained to Jared, 'I was here for a few weeks during the last manifestation, looking after the business while Adam was away, and I can assure you it was *not* a pleasant experience, what with the noises and the smells and the *very* strange activity. Extremely disturbing! Poor Esther was beside herself.'

'We had a ghost once,' Ruthie said. 'Did Bernard tell you, Sarah?'

'The little girl in the cesspit?'

'Yes, Pansy. Very sweet, but so sad.'

'Rachel wasn't sweet, was she?' Friday said, topping up her glass again with claret.

'She was so!' Harrie protested. 'She was a darling.'

Friday laughed. '*Sometimes* she was a darling. Bloody good with the broads, too. You should have seen her play, Bernard. But sometimes she was the most bad-tempered little thing ever.' She sighed and was quiet for a second. 'I'd give my left arm, even with my new tattoo, to have her back, though. Anyway, I didn't mean when she was alive. I meant the last time we saw her, in this house.'

'You saw her as well? The ghost?' Jared asked, startled.

One of the wall lamps flickered and went out. Looking alarmed, he half rose from his chair, then sat down again when no one else appeared bothered.

Sarah thought: sod, too early. She'd made sure the oil in the lamp was low, but had hoped it might have lasted a little longer.

'Only once or twice,' Friday said, 'And she wasn't being very darling then, I can assure you. Sarah and Harrie saw her more than I did. They both have the sight, especially Harrie.'

'Can you ... sense when there's a presence here?' Jared asked Harrie.

'Oh yes. So can Sarah.'

Jared shifted his gaze to Sarah, a vein in his neck visibly pulsing.

She waited a moment or two to heighten the tension, then said, 'What do you think, Harrie? Is she here now? Can you feel anything? I can.'

Harrie laid her knife and fork neatly across her plate, clasped her hands in her lap and closed her eyes. Everyone forgot supper. Nothing happened for the longest time, though almost no one at the table was expecting that anything actually would. A late cicada buzzed shrilly from some unseen hiding place, and in the tree outside a pair of night birds bickered.

Another lamp flickered to a mere pinpoint of light.

The door from the back porch into the dining room creaked open, bringing with it a sulphurous whiff of cesspit from the yard.

Bugger, Sarah thought, and got up and closed it. By the time she'd returned to her chair, Harrie had opened her eyes again.

She smiled delightedly. 'Yes, she's here.'

Jared's gaze darted wildly around the room, his eyes huge.

Harrie was looking at a point halfway up the wall behind Bernard, but of course there was nothing there to see. God she's good at this, Sarah thought.

Harrie appeared to listen for a moment, then she said conversationally, 'We're talking about what to do about Adam, to get him out of gaol.' She cocked her head to one side, said, 'Well, ask her yourself,' and glanced across the table at Sarah.

Sarah panicked — they hadn't practised this bit! She pretended to listen, then ad-libbed, 'I do, Rachel. I miss him horribly.' She shot a pleading look back at Harrie. 'I can't see her any more. Is she still there?'

Ruthie suddenly shivered at the other end of the table, and pulled her shawl more tightly across her shoulders.

Harrie shook her head. 'No. She's gone now.'

'Out of —' Jared's voice came out as a high-pitched squeak. He cleared his throat noisily and tried again. 'Out of the house?'

'Oh no,' Harrie said cheerfully, and pointed to the closed door behind Ruthie. 'She went out there, into the hallway.'

That wasn't in the script, either. Disconcerted, Sarah caught Friday's eye.

Harrie gave a little start, turned to Friday and said rather testily, 'What?' Then, 'Oh! And she said she's really, *really* angry.'

'But what's she angry *about*? That's what *I* want to know,' Friday boomed with theatrical inflection worthy of Drury Lane's Theatre Royal.

'She said she will not have Sarah treated badly,' Harrie replied.

'Oh dear,' Bernard said. 'It does rather sound like a repeat of last time, doesn't it? But Sarah, you're not being mistreated, are you?'

'Not at all,' Sarah said woodenly. 'I really don't understand why she's here again.'

Beside her she felt Jared go very, very still.

So he'd received the message, but would he heed it? And even if he did, keeping his dirty hands to himself was not going to be enough, for she'd decided she would not stop persecuting him until he'd confessed to framing Adam.

Jared came down to breakfast the following morning looking as though he'd spent a week on the jar. Puffy mauve bags marred the skin beneath his bleary eyes, his skin was pasty white and his hands shook badly as he poured himself a cup of tea. He looked like Sarah felt.

'Eggs do you?' she asked.

'Thank you.'

Though she knew very well he hadn't, she asked, 'Did you sleep well?'

'No, I didn't.'

'Upset guts?'

'Nightmares. I hope.'

'Really?' Sarah plopped two fried eggs onto his plate and a couple of rounds of black pudding, then served herself.

Jared poked his knife into his egg yolk and watched as it oozed out onto the plate. 'After what transpired at the supper table last night I had a couple of fingers of brandy to settle my nerves and managed to get to sleep, but then had the most hideous dreams. I dreamt I heard rapping and knocking noises half the night, and that my bed chamber was filled with a horrible, other-worldly light. It went on and on, the noises and the lights, until an hour or so before dawn.'

Sarah knew exactly what time the noises had stopped, because she'd been up in the attic making them, and crawling around with a lamp covered with a glass mantle coloured a sickly greenish-yellow, shining it through the holes she'd drilled the other day.

'I don't think you were dreaming,' she said. 'I heard all that, too.'

Jared appeared dismayed. 'And a scratching at my window, just prior to sunrise. My *upper*-storey window.'

Sarah wondered what that had been; certainly not her doing. A possum? There were dozens in the town's trees and they often scampered across rooftops on noisy little feet. But it gave her an idea. 'Harrie believes Rachel sometimes appears as a bat. Perhaps it was her, trying to get in.'

Jared blanched.

'Anyway,' she went on, delighted with his reaction, 'I thought you said you'd had experience with this sort of thing? Didn't you say you once owned a house that was haunted?'

'We did, yes. In England. That was nothing like this, however. I never actually saw that ghost.' He shuddered. 'I couldn't abide actually *seeing* one.'

'Who's we?'

The barest flicker of discomfort crossed his pale face. 'My wife and I.'

Sarah might have guessed he was married. She decided to rub it in. 'I didn't realise you're a widower.'

'I'm not.' He went back to his eggs. 'My wife remains in England.'

It was time to test his mettle. And his intentions. 'Well, it could very well get worse here. It was pretty grim last time. If you don't like it you could always go back to your own lodgings.'

Jared put down his fork. 'Look, Sarah, I'm not completely stupid. I gather that this spirit of your dead friend has become offended by my treatment of you. Which, I admit, has been somewhat cavalier.

But I'm not entirely to blame for that. You're an attractive young woman and a man has certain needs and entitlements, and in the eyes of the law I am currently your master. I had hoped we might come to an arrangement — for which, I should add, I would have been more than happy to reimburse you — but it seems I am to have the shit scared out of me should I pursue that course of action. So I won't. You may go about your business unmolested, by me at any rate. I assume, consequently, that this ... Rachel will now go away and leave us alone, therefore I may continue to reside here in peace. Am I right?'

Sarah held his gaze, not daring to look away. If any of the ghost carry-on were real, he would be correct. She thought quickly. 'What if she suspects you mean me harm in some other way?'

Again that flicker of unease on his face. 'Then she'd be a very intuitive ghost, wouldn't she? I don't mean you harm, Sarah. I am managing Adam's business during his absence, and there is nothing else to it. Why, what did he say to you when you spoke to him in the gaol?'

Sarah had been waiting for this question, and knew it would be a mistake to lie altogether. 'He told me you have a stake in the business, by way of money you lent him when he opened the shop. I thought he'd ask Bernard Cole to step in, but he didn't. He said that wasn't my concern, as long as the business keeps running.' If Jared believed Adam thought she wasn't clever enough to understand how the business worked, or was not entitled to know, so much the better.

'Well, I intend to make sure it does. I'm not leaving.' He picked up his fork. 'Anyway, if I left you'd have to go back to the Factory. Have you thought of that? You'd lose everything you have.'

'Not *everything*. As a married woman, even as a convict, I do have recourse to some rights.'

'But no claim to Adam's business, or his money, or the lease on this building. All you have is his name and possibly a few things he might have given you. It's not much, is it?'

'I certainly have the right to complain to the police about what a filthy-minded lech *you've* been.'

'Well, do your best. You've no proof, and I doubt they'd believe you, you being what you are.'

It was a deliberate little jab of unpleasantness, now he'd apparently accepted he wasn't going to get her into bed. Sarah felt her temper rising dangerously because of it, and because he was right.

'If Rachel doesn't leave, I'll know you're up to no good.' Shite, now she'd said too much.

He didn't respond this time, but neither did he look at all happy.

That night Jared lay in bed, waiting for sleep to overtake him. He'd had several fingers of whisky and a good sip of opium to help him on his way, but was still very much on edge. Last night the awful pus-yellow light and the rapping had been deeply disturbing. He'd felt as though the noises and the thin, sickly shafts of illumination had been heralding the imminent arrival of that wretched dead girl. Her spirit was already here in the house causing mischief, and that was bad enough, but his worst fear was that she herself would appear to him and he would have to look upon her cold, dead face. It was true, what he'd told Sarah about the ghost in his home in England; he hadn't seen it with his own eyes. To see the walking dead, he believed, would be to experience the greatest terror of all.

He was facing a dilemma. He could simply pack up his things and walk out of this damned awful house, away from this horrid ghost business and Sarah bloody Green, who was turning out to be a lot harder to manipulate than he'd expected. She was clever, sharp-tongued, bad-tempered, and unexpectedly loyal to Adam, all of which were adding up to quite an obstacle. Adam clearly underestimated her — fortunately. If Adam had told her that he, Jared, had blackmailed his way into managing the shop, she could well have suspected him of framing Adam. But women — as

Adam had obviously realised — couldn't be trusted with matters of commerce, and were far better relegated to the cooking hearth or between the sheets. Though he had to admit Sarah was a damn fine jeweller.

He still wanted her, however, despite his promise to keep his hands off her, and he most certainly still wanted Adam's business. In a matter of months Adam and his new wife had somehow managed to turn a moderately successful jewellery enterprise into one of the most profitable in the town. Normally he, Jared, only bought up ailing companies at bargain prices, but Adam's was so attractive he knew he'd sincerely regret not acquiring it. Adam himself, of course, had been the major impediment to that scenario, but thanks to the carefully planted coral brooch — happy wedding day! — Adam was rotting in Port Macquarie penitentiary and would be for the next five years. With any luck he might even die there. All Jared had to do now was run the business down by siphoning off the profits and declaring bankruptcy, after which he'd purchase it cheaply, then rebuild it.

Sarah's skills as a jeweller clearly contributed greatly to the success of the business, so it was vital she be kept on side and remain in the house and working. He'd done his best to court her favour, although several times, he knew, his behaviour had upset her. She seemed to have no idea of the natural order of things: he was her master and she was a convict assignee, and as such he had certain privileges. She'd wake up to the truth of her situation one day. He was confident she wouldn't pack her own bags; she was far too stubborn, and that suited him just fine. And when she did wake up, when she realised her husband wouldn't be back for years — if, in fact, he *ever* came back — she'd change her mind and choose him. After all, within the year he would outright own the jewellery business for which she seemed to hold such a passion.

He scratched his belly under his linen nightshirt and rolled onto his side, wondering why the whisky and the opium weren't working. Perhaps his head was too full of thoughts. Maybe he should have another drink. Or toss himself off? Yes, that was far more appealing.

His hand closed around his cock and, thinking about when he'd had Sarah face down on the sofa with her skirt up, he rubbed and squeezed until he was erect. He'd just got a good rhythm going when a loud, flat banging came at the bedroom door. He stopped pulling, his cock shrivelling immediately.

The banging came again and he sat up, almost too frightened to look across the room. With suddenly shaking hands he struck a Congreves match and lit the lamp on his night table, his eyes darting towards the door, noting with enormous relief that it was closed and the key was still in the lock.

Then, with a surge of horror, he watched as the key began to move, bit by bit sliding out of the escutcheon plate until it parted company completely and fell with a clatter to the floor.

'Jaared,' a hollow, sighing voice came from the hallway. 'Jaaaared.'

Very slowly, the door opened.

That hideous yellow light again, filling his room. And in the doorway, a ghastly apparition of a girl, her face as white as bleached cotton, bloodless lips, black shadows beneath sunken eyes, and long tangled hair as pale as her dead, dead skin.

Jared let out a fear-strangled squawk.

The figure glided into the room, feet concealed by the soiled hem of her ragged grave clothes, and came to a halt at the foot of his bed. He caught a whiff of fresh dirt and a dark hint of something far more rank.

It said nothing, but stretched out an imploring hand, as if to say, Come with me. Come with me down to where the soil is cold and the worms writhe and feed. Keep me company, Jared, for I am so *lonely*.

He screamed again, loudly this time, and tried to move, but found his limbs were immobilised by terror.

Sarah appeared in the doorway, clad only in her nightdress and with her hair awry, and ran across the room to his side.

She touched his shoulder. 'Stay still. I know what to do. She's done this before.'

Jared heard himself rasp, 'Get it out! Just get it out!'

'Go away, Rachel!' Sarah commanded. 'You're not wanted here. Go on, go back to where you came from.'

The figure retreated, gliding backwards. But in the doorway it halted and raised a small white hand, a black-nailed finger pointing directly at Jared.

In a wispy, child-like voice it intoned, 'You shouldn't ... have made me ... angry.'

Jared whimpered and a fear-propelled fart blatted out of him. At his side he heard Sarah gasp.

But at last the thing turned and was gone; the sickly light faded and he could hear the creak of the risers as it slowly descended the stairs.

'Oh God. Oh fuck,' he said, his head sinking into his hands.

A loud thump came from somewhere near the ceiling. Sarah hurried to the door and closed it.

Jared pushed back the covers, his heart thumping wildly, and perched on the side of the mattress, shaking violently. 'Will she come back?' he asked.

'Tonight? I've never known her to appear twice in one night. But who can tell?'

God. She'd said that on purpose to scare him, he was sure of it. 'Weren't you frightened?'

'Of course I was. I *am* frightened. Who wouldn't be? But Rachel was my friend. I'm fairly sure she doesn't mean *me* harm. And, as you just saw, she'll do my bidding. You're the one who should be shitting yourself, not me.'

I bloody am, Jared thought, don't you worry about that.

But still not enough to leave.

'I'm going back to bed,' Sarah said. 'I suggest you lock your door.'

'It *was* locked,' Jared replied.

He eyed the bottle of opium on his night table. A few really good swigs of that, plus half a tumbler of whisky, would see him off to sleep without doubt. He'd be lying awake in terror the rest of the night, otherwise.

'Good night,' Sarah said, closing his door behind her.

She crossed the landing, opened her own door and shut it again without going in. Then she crept downstairs, avoiding the ones that creaked, through the house and out to the back porch where young Jimmy Johnson from the Siren's Arms waited in the shadows.

'Was that you making all that noise?' she whispered tersely.

'I fell down them bloody attic stairs,' he complained, holding up the lamp with the yellow mantle. 'Just about busted this, too. Think it'll still work, but.'

'Come on,' Sarah said, taking his elbow.

With the moonlight guiding their way, they crossed the yard to the gate in the high back fence and slipped through. Jared Gellar's bedroom window looked out over George Street so they had no fear of being seen.

Friday and her friend Molly from the brothel loitered behind the fence, smoking their pipes. Molly looked a right picture. She'd wiped some of the rice flour off her face but it was still thickly caked around her eyes and jaw line, and all over her neck and hands, and was positively plastered through her normally yellow-blonde hair. In fact she looked worse than she had in Gellar's bedroom, as though she were now rapidly decaying. Her white, mud-smeared nightgown still ponged, of course, as it would after rubbing gone-over meat all over it.

'You did a great job in there, Molly,' Sarah said. 'Thanks ever so much'

'My pleasure. Thought I was going to ruin everything when he farted, though. I had a *hell* of a job keeping a straight face.'

'Christ, so did I. You did well, too, Jimmy,' Sarah added, patting the boy's arm. 'Thanks.'

Jimmy beamed with pleasure.

'Here's your key,' Molly said, handing back the spare to Gellar's room that she'd used to dislodge the key already in the lock.

'Has it done the trick, though?' Friday asked.

Sarah shrugged. 'We'll have to wait and see, won't we?'

Chapter Seventeen

May 1831, Sydney Town

Harrie had at first been perplexed then disappointed by the failure of the others to see Rachel when she'd manifested at Sarah's supper party. Very quickly, however, she'd realised that Rachel hadn't wanted to be seen, not even by Sarah and Friday, and though she didn't understand why, she knew there'd be a reason.

Nevertheless, for an entire day she'd worried that Rachel might have moved permanently to Sarah's house, perhaps to help Sarah, or — far worse — to punish Harrie for something she didn't even know she'd done. But no, she hadn't been abandoned, as last night Rachel had appeared in her usual spot in the rocking chair under the eaves, and Harrie had experienced such a sense of relief she'd almost wept.

She could hear Hannah calling for her, and went to the top of the stairs.

'What is it, Hannah? I'm up here!'

'There's a man at the door!' Hannah shouted. 'That Mr Downer! Will you talk to him?'

Harrie froze. Oh God, what was he doing here? She'd have to go down — she couldn't expect Hannah to tell him to go away. She handed Lewis to Abigail. 'Would you tell your mother I've just gone downstairs? Tell her Dr Downey's called?'

Abigail wiped dribble off Lewis's chin and nodded. Her mother and father were in their bedroom, arguing loudly.

Harrie reluctantly trudged downstairs. James was at the back door, hat in hand, listening patiently to Hannah explain how it was her job to go around the yard every morning and pick up Angus's turds and chuck them over the fence, as it always seemed to be her who trod them into the house on the bottom of her boots.

'Thank you, sweetie. You can go up now,' Harrie said.

'I don't want to. I want to stay,' Hannah said.

'Well, you can't. Up you go.'

Hannah didn't move.

James dug in his coat pocket and produced a shilling. Hannah took it and danced up the steps and inside.

'You shouldn't bribe children,' Harrie said.

'It was expedient,' James said. 'I'd like to talk to you, Harrie. Preferably not out here in full view of the neighbours.'

'There's nowhere else to go,' Harrie said unhelpfully. She didn't want a repeat of last time, when Nora had jumped to the wrong conclusion.

James sighed. 'Then out here it will have to be.' He sat on the step, his back to the door.

Hesitantly, Harrie drew her skirts around her legs and joined him.

'I saw Friday a week or so ago,' he began, 'at the surgery.'

'Yes, I saw her at the markets, on her way to an appointment with Dr Chandler.' Harrie suspected she knew what might be coming next, and resisted the urge to put her hands over her ears.

'Well, she saw me instead.' James turned to her. 'And she told me she and Sarah have been concerned about you.'

Harrie studied her fingernails. They were ragged and could do with a good tidy. 'Yes, I know.'

'Do you know why?'

Well, she wasn't going to lie. Why should she? It wasn't her who couldn't see what was glaringly obvious. 'They think I'm losing my mind because I've been talking to Rachel.'

James was silent for a moment. He reached down and wiped a film of dust off the toe of his boot. Then he said, 'And by Rachel, do you mean your memories of her before she passed away, or do you mean Rachel as in her ghost or spirit returned to the here and now?'

'Her ghost here now, obviously,' Harrie said. 'What would be the point of talking to memories?'

'And does her ghost talk back to you?'

Harrie gave him a hard look. His tone was gentle and compassionate but something in his eyes made her suspicious. 'Don't make fun of me, James!'

'I'm not, Harrie! I assure you I'm not.'

Warily, she said, 'Yes, she does talk back, actually.'

'In what way?'

'What do you mean, "In what way?" She opens her mouth and words come out.' Harrie frowned. Was that what actually happened, though? Or did she hear Rachel's words in her head?

'No, that's not what I mean.'

Harrie could see he was struggling to put his thoughts into words.

James tried again. 'I mean do you, well, do you just chat to each other? Or do you ask her questions, or perhaps ask her for advice?'

'Sometimes I ask her for advice,' Harrie said, not meeting his eye now. 'When I'm unsure about something. And it always helps. It really does. There's nothing wrong with that, is there?'

James took the longest time to answer, and now *he* wouldn't look at *her*. 'Harrie, the concern I have isn't the fact that you think you can see Rachel's ghost. Plenty of people believe they see ghosts.'

'I don't *believe* I can see her, I *can* see her!'

He ignored the interruption. 'My concern is *why* you feel the need to converse with an imaginary Rachel. And, perhaps even more importantly, the subject of those conversations.'

'For God's sake, I am *not* imagining her!'

James met her gaze. 'All right, let's say you're not. Let's say for argument's sake that she has manifested as an apparition. Why, Harrie, would you rather seek counsel from the ghost of a dead girl than from a living person? Why not from Sarah, or Friday? Or even me? Can you not see how delusional and morbid your behaviour is? Can you not see why Sarah and Friday are so concerned for you? Why *I'm* so concerned?'

'You don't understand,' Harrie said flatly. And he didn't, but then he couldn't because he knew nothing about what they'd done to Gabriel Keegan or Bella's blackmail or anything else, and she could never tell him.

'No, you're right, I *don't* understand.'

They sat in silence, feeling as though a wall of insurmountable proportions had been erected between them.

Finally, James said stiffly, 'Are you sleeping well? You look tired.'

'I'm managing.'

'How is your appetite? You seem to have lost some weight.'

'I'm all right.'

'Have you had heart palpitations? A racing pulse? Feelings of dread or approaching doom?'

'No!'

Harrie had in fact been experiencing all those things, though she wasn't going to tell James that. She hadn't told anyone.

James let out a heavy sigh. 'Harrie, please hear me out. You need a rest. I think you're exhausted and possibly experiencing some form of hysterical or maniacal episode. The hallucinations and hearing of voices you're describing are a serious concern. I'd like to arrange for you to go somewhere to recuperate for a month or so.'

Waves of panic and utter dismay surged through Harrie, leaving her skin clammy and her heart pounding. 'No! I won't!'

He wanted to send her to the Factory hospital. Or perhaps even worse, Liverpool Asylum. The madhouse.

'Will you not even consider it?'

'*I'm not mad, James!*' Harrie almost shrieked.

'I didn't say you were. I said you *may* be suffering from hysteria. Or something similar. I really do think you need a rest.'

Harrie did her very best to calm down, which was extremely difficult as her entire body was vibrating with fear, anger and a monumental sense of betrayal. After everything he'd said to her — his silver-tongued apologies and admissions of disapproval and fault-finding — and here he was judging her yet again!

'I don't need a rest, and I especially don't want to listen to you. So please go away, James, and don't ever come back. I *never* want to see you again!'

Yet another dreadful, brittle silence stretched out between them.

Then James asked, 'Do you really mean that?'

'I do.' Harrie rose, tears searing her eyes. 'Now *please* leave.'

James stood as well, gazed at her with immeasurable sadness for a moment, put his hat on his head and walked away.

Essex Street was its usual steep, potholed, rutted self, but the advantage of it being so difficult to traverse was that only pedestrians ever tried, resulting in a notable lack of the horse and bullock shit that normally fouled Sydney's streets. Harrie, Friday and Sarah appreciated this as they laboured their way up, skirts lifted to avoid treading on hems, though they were not enjoying the eye-watering stink emanating from the nearby soap- and candleworks, even though it was well past seven in the evening.

'What if she tells us something terrible?' Harrie asked. 'Or something we're really better off not knowing?'

'Oh, how the hell can she?' Sarah scoffed. 'She'll be making the whole bloody lot up.'

'I dunno about that,' Friday said. 'I used to get my cards read at home, and they can be pretty on the nail, these old didikai mots.'

'*Is* she a gyppo?' Harrie asked.

'Must be, if she can read the cards.'

It had been Leo's idea to visit the tarot-card reader. Harrie had arrived at his shop several days earlier feeling very despondent and withdrawn, and when he'd said to her, 'Cat got your tongue?' she'd burst into tears.

He must have felt bad about it because he'd sent Walter out for cakes, and over a cup of tea she'd told him what had transpired with James, and that she'd decided it was for the best. She and James weren't meant to be together, and it was silly pretending it was ever going to happen — especially with a man of James's calibre, even if he was judgmental and narrow-minded. And Leo had reminded her that not long ago she'd said she didn't even want a man, so why the unhappy face?

When she couldn't answer him, he'd startled her by confiding that whenever he felt at odds about a matter, he visited a woman named Serafina Fortune, who was a dab hand at reading the cards. Harrie had nearly smiled at the thought of Leo hunched over a table spread with a lace cloth and brightly coloured tarot cards, bursting to know what the future held for him. Then she'd recalled he'd been a sailor most of his life, and that sailors were incredibly superstitious, and the idea hadn't seemed so strange after that.

'Is that her real name?' she'd asked. 'Serafina Fortune?'

'You'd have to ask her that,' he'd replied. 'But I wouldn't, if I were you.'

'Well, I won't have the chance. I don't want my cards read. I've nothing to be undecided about. I've made up my mind.'

And Leo had regarded her thoughtfully and said, 'Are you sure, lass? You don't think you might regret your decision?' which had been extremely irritating of him, especially as she suspected he'd taken against James, even though he didn't know him.

She'd told Friday and Sarah, and predictably Friday thought it was an excellent idea to have their cards read, while Sarah said it would be nothing but a scam. But here they were anyway, traipsing up Essex Street looking for Serafina Fortune's house.

'Is this it, do you think?' Friday said.

They were halfway up the hill between Cambridge and Cumberland streets, outside a cottage with a moon and stars painted on the front door.

Sarah made a production out of squinting at it.

'What are you doing?' Friday asked.

'Looking for a sign saying *Fools and their money welcome here*.'

'You know, you shouldn't be so suspicious of everything. It makes you ugly and gives you wrinkles.' Friday knocked loudly.

A young woman opened the door.

Friday said, 'Er, we're looking for Serafina Fortune. Is she home?'

'Yes,' the woman replied.

'Well, can we see her?'

'You are.'

Harrie was slightly taken aback. She wasn't what they'd been expecting. This woman was perhaps in her late twenties and looked quite well off. Her features were sharp but not at all unattractive, though her expression was a little guarded. She wore her treacle-coloured hair in fashionable braided loops over her ears, and a dress of costly, bronze-coloured calamanco patterned with tiny white flowers, beautifully cut and fitted to her trim, shapely figure. There wasn't a single flowing scarf, oversized ear hoop (though she was wearing small gold earrings), decorative coin or inch of colourful embroidery to be seen, and neither was she a withered, stoop-backed crone, which surely you had to be to have mastered the mysteries of the tarot?

'And you're the one who does the cards?' Friday asked, looking her up and down.

Serafina Fortune nodded. 'How many readings were you wanting?'

'Three,' Friday replied, as Sarah said, 'Two.'

Serafina Fortune shrugged. 'Well, it's Tuesday anyway.'

Sarah said, 'And that means …?'

'Tuesday's two-for-three day. Come in.' Serafina stepped aside.

Friday had to stoop to enter, though Harrie and Sarah were short enough to avoid bumping their heads on the low lintel.

The interior of the cottage appeared to consist of just two rooms, the parlour they'd entered directly and possibly a bed chamber, and was cosily furnished if somewhat dimly lit, as the curtains were drawn across the windows and only two lamps were burning.

'Please take a seat.' Serafina indicated six chairs around an oval table that took up a lot of space. She pulled out a chair for herself, sat and opened a large box whose lid and sides were ornately inlaid with marquetry. From it she lifted a battered tin, set it to one side and said, 'I'd prefer you to pay in advance, if you don't mind.'

'What if we aren't satisfied?' Harrie said, having completely forgotten she'd told Leo she wasn't going to have a reading.

'Oh, I expect you will be.'

'Really? How much do you charge?' Friday asked. She spoke directly to Serafina across the table, holding her gaze for longer than was necessary, her mouth curving in a small, private smile.

A short, uncomfortable silence fell.

Meeting Friday's smile with a faintly amused lift of her eyebrows, Serafina replied, 'Four shillings per person.'

Sarah snorted.

'And your friend for free,' Serafina reminded them.

'Hold on a minute,' Sarah interrupted. 'How do we know this isn't all just a racket?' She pointed rudely at Serafina. 'We don't know the first thing about you. I mean, you could be the world's worst magswoman.'

'Sarah!' Harrie was mortified.

Serafina coolly returned Sarah's gaze. 'What would you like to know?'

'Well, for a start, what brought you to New South Wales?'

'I was transported.'

'Ha! See!' Sarah was triumphant. 'She's as crooked as we are!'

'Speak for yourself!' Harrie said.

Serafina added, 'As were the three of you.'

'Lucky guess, especially in this town,' Sarah said. 'Transported for what?'

'Fraud.'

'What did I tell you?!' Sarah crowed. 'You might as well chuck your money down the crapper.'

Frowning, Friday asked, 'Fraud with the cards?'

Serafina said, 'Not directly, no.'

'But you can really read them?' Friday persisted.

Serafina didn't seem at all perturbed by the question, or Sarah's derision. 'Yes. Among other things.'

Friday barely hesitated. 'Bugger it, I'm getting mine done. It's only four bob.' She slid her money across the table.

Sarah shook her head despairingly.

Harrie thought four shillings was a bit steep, but opened her purse and handed over the money.

Serafina unlocked her tin, dropped in the coins with satisfying clinks, closed it and returned it to the larger box.

'Who would like to go first?'

'I will.' Friday hitched her chair closer to the table.

'Right, then.' Serafina was businesslike now. 'Do you prefer a particular deck? French? Italian? The Visconti, perhaps?'

'Just the usual,' Friday replied, clearly having no idea.

Serafina took a red cloth bundle from the box, unwrapped it and extracted a pack of large cards. She shuffled them expertly in spite of their size, tossing them from hand to hand so dextrously the images on them blurred. Harrie, Friday and Sarah glanced at one another, expressions bleak, mouths pressed shut against raw memories. Rachel had shuffled the cards like that. Harrie brushed the heel of her palm against her eye and swallowed hard.

Serafina set the cards before Friday and, with a sly sideways glance at Sarah, said, 'I'll do a general reading first, to assure you I do have the necessary skills. Touch the cards, please.'

Friday did, Serafina took them back and shuffled again, then asked Friday to cut the deck. From the bottom half she laid out five cards in the shape of a cross. The cards were beautifully but quite bizarrely illustrated. Serafina tapped her teeth while she studied them.

'You live by your wits and your personal charms, and at times this causes you sorrow, anger and pain. You've never known the passion of real love. You once *thought* you did, but all you'd done then was confuse love with the bonds born of dependence and desperation. And now you fear you never will know true, deep love, because of what you —' She abruptly stopped and glanced up at Friday. 'Well, you don't need the cards to tell you that, do you?'

Friday stared at her, her mouth unbecomingly open and a faint tinge of red blooming on her cheeks.

Serafina returned to the cards. 'Your mother left you — died or disappeared? — some years ago and your father was nothing more than a shadow. Your closest family are not connected to you by blood, but they mean more to you than blood ever has. You have suffered much loss. You have borne a child and lost her.' She looked up again and said bluntly, 'You should stop grieving, girl. She would have died anyway, whether you'd been with her or not. The poor little thing was defective.'

Friday and Harrie gasped. Even Sarah felt her heart jolt; how could this woman have known that Friday had left her baby alone?

'There is a core of darkness within you and you must be wary of it,' Serafina went on. 'If you're not vigilant it will literally be the death of you. You should strive to choose a path that is not so self-destructive. There is also a darkness without, in the form of ...' Frowning, she picked up a card. 'This is the Magus, but manifesting as he has in this spread between *these* cards —' she tapped two others '— signifies almost a complete inversion, with the Magus exhibiting attributes remarkably similar to those of the Empress. Very unusual, I have to say. Anyway, this external darkness represents a very significant threat to you. And this card here?' She pointed to one depicting a tier of goblets. 'You drink far too much.' She gathered the cards and shuffled the deck again. 'Do you have a specific question you'd like to ask?'

Friday swallowed, then nodded.

'Keep it to yourself.' Serafina set the deck before her a second time. 'Hand, if you will.'

Friday placed her palm on the cards, Serafina cut and spread seven.

'This is interesting. The answer is yes, and before too much time has passed.'

Friday's face lit up and she almost clapped.

'But be warned,' Serafina said quickly, 'the path won't be easy, and there will be considerable resistance from external forces. However, if you persist, you will be rewarded beyond anything you might ever have dreamt. As to the specifics — tall and strong and, yes, definitely dark. There is this, however.' From the spread she slid two cards across the table.

Friday eyed them uncomprehendingly. 'What do they mean?'

'Justice, and the Eight of Swords? Quite possibly more gaol time, which could be connected to your first reading, but more likely to this one.'

'Well, that stinks.'

Serafina shrugged. 'Everything has a price. Who's next?'

384

'Did you get a good answer to your secret question?' Harrie asked Friday. She felt decidedly nervous now. The woman's comment about Friday's baby had been uncanny.

'Bloody good, actually,' Friday said. 'Except for the gaol bit.'

'If the cards say something's going to happen,' Harrie said, 'does it always *have* to happen?'

'I can't really tell you that,' Serafina replied. 'I read the cards for a lot of people, but I don't always hear how things turn out for them. In fact, hardly ever.'

'All right, do mine, please,' Harrie said in a rush, before she could change her mind.

Sarah felt uneasy, and more than a little angry; Harrie, as usual, was being far too trusting with someone she didn't know. It was probably all right for this Serafina woman to tell Friday things — Friday was tough, but Harrie wasn't, especially not at the moment. And Serafina appeared to have been disturbingly accurate so far, which frankly was a real shock.

Sarah *had* seen this kind of thing before — she *didn't* altogether disbelieve in it — and it gave her the willies. Maisie, a girl in Tom Ratcliffe's crew in London, had been able to read the cards, and scry, but she'd been so raddled by opium she'd never had the wits to harness her talent. Serafina Fortune clearly did, however. What if she actually did tell Harrie something really awful, as Harrie herself had suggested on the way here? Sarah had done everything she could to deter her and Friday, and it hadn't worked, and the worst thing about it was she suspected Serafina could see right through her attempts.

The first spread of five cards told Harrie she was surrounded by children — hardly a revelation — that her mother was very unwell and hovering between this world and the next, and that someone in her family would soon be in trouble with the law.

As soon as Harrie heard this, her bottom lip quivered, then she burst into tears. 'Robbie!' she sobbed. 'That'll be Robbie!'

'That's enough!' Sarah moved to collect up the cards, but Serafina blocked her.

'Leave them. I haven't finished.'

'You bloody have.'

'This isn't your reading,' Serafina said, indicating Harrie, now noisily blowing her nose. 'Ask her what she wants.'

'I think you've heard enough,' Sarah said.

'No, I want to know the rest. I do,' Harrie replied through her handkerchief.

Sarah shot a glance at Serafina, expecting to see at least a small smirk, but her face was impassive.

'Are you sure?' Friday asked, her arm around Harrie.

Harrie nodded, hiccupped and tucked her handkerchief into her sleeve. 'Sorry, it gave me a fright, that's all. Really, it isn't unexpected. He's been heading that way for a while. And so's the prediction about Ma. She was sick before I left. Really.'

Serafina went on to tell Harrie she had considerable artistic ability, and that soon she would 'grant her illustrations life and breath'.

Harrie frowned. 'I'm not sure what that means. Do you know?'

'No. I expect you will, when it happens.' Serafina slid a card from the spread. 'This card, the Moon, is a concern. It can be associated with tension, confusion, fear and worry, imagination and illusion. And pregnancy, so beware of that.'

Sarah and Friday exchanged a startled glance.

Harrie flushed. 'Well, there's not much chance of that, is there?'

'The Moon is mistress of the oceans within the mind. When the tides are out of kilter, we become ill. You've been unwell, haven't you? A time of darkness and despair?'

Harrie shook her head.

'There isn't a lot to be gained from lying to the tarot, you know,' Serafina said matter-of-factly. She indicated a third card, a naked girl pouring water from a jug into a pool. 'This is the Star and, in this spread, for you, she brings enlightenment. Do you believe you have visitations? From a spirit who gives you peace of mind, perhaps?'

Her eyes shining with delight, Harrie exclaimed, 'I do! Yes, I do.'

Sarah mouthed 'Jesus Christ!' at Friday, who nodded wearily back.

'Take comfort where you can. Sometimes there is precious little to be had.'

Serafina gathered up the cards. 'Any specific questions?'

Harrie nodded. 'Two. Can I have two?'

Serafina shuffled, cut and lay out the cards again. She studied them for a full minute, then said, 'The answer to the first question is yes, but you will have to suffer more loss to achieve it.'

The look on Harrie's face was an odd combination of hope and dismay; it was obvious to Sarah and Friday what the question had been.

'And like her —' Serafina indicated Friday, 'you've suffered plenty already. The love of a child will be involved, and commitment to a promise you've made. The answer to the second question is also yes, though again, initially you'll have your share of heartbreak around that.' She looked Harrie directly in the eye. 'Most women do, you know, one way or another. But there's also a warning here, involving water and tides, which connects back to the Moon and Star cards.'

'What sort of warning?' Sarah demanded.

'Who can say?' Serafina opened her hands, palms up. 'I'm only the oracle. I only pass on the message.'

Sarah didn't believe her. As Serafina gathered the cards, she said, 'You can do my reading now.'

'I thought you weren't having one?' Friday said. 'Didn't you say this was a load of old shite?'

'So? I'm allowed to change my mind, aren't I?'

'God, you're contrary sometimes,' Friday grumbled.

Ignoring the bickering, Serafina prepared the cards and set the cut deck before Sarah, who gave the topmost card the lightest of touches.

Serafina lay out the five-card spread and studied it. 'You're a very complicated person,' she said eventually.

Friday let out a bark of laughter, which turned into a grunt as Harrie elbowed her in the ribs.

'Do you want the short or the long version?' Serafina asked.

Sarah shrugged.

'Short, then. I'm getting tired. You're fierce and cunning and you don't trust easily. Your blood family has been largely responsible for that. Your mother was weak. Dead now, is she?'

Sarah nodded.

'And your father is a selfish, childish and possessive bully. Who hides behind … what?'

God, Sarah thought. He hides behind God.

'Sadly, not dead,' Serafina went on. 'But when you do finally allow yourself to trust, you are eternally loyal. In the past you've been a loner, though that's changed over the last couple of years.' She moved a card out of the spread. 'Three characters moved into your orbit who have become extremely important to you, and now there is a fourth.'

'Adam?' Harrie suggested.

'I see he is in trouble,' Serafina remarked.

Sarah said tersely, 'Well, obviously, I know all this.'

'I'm sure you do,' Serafina said, sweeping the cards into a neat pile.

'So tell me something I *don't* know.' Sarah snatched up the pack.

'Sarah! Give them back!' Harrie protested.

'She doesn't need them,' Sarah said. 'Do you?'

For a long moment Sarah and Serafina stared at each other, neither willing to be the first to look away.

At last Serafina said, 'Actually, no. Not really.'

Friday was confused. 'Why not?'

'She has the sight.' Sarah raised the cards. 'These are just a front, something she hides behind.'

Friday and Harrie gaped at Serafina as though she'd just grown a second head.

Serafina gave a small, one-shouldered shrug, as if it were really neither here nor there that her secret was out, and settled more comfortably in her chair, her pale, long-fingered hands in her lap. 'You have a specific question?'

'I do.'

Serafina remained still for a moment, her eyes half closed. The left side of her top lip twitched once, then she spoke. 'Yes, you will. *He* will.'

Her shoulders slumping visibly with relief, Sarah used her sleeve to wipe away the sheen of nervous sweat that had suddenly appeared on her forehead.

'Furthermore, there's a very strong connection between how that comes about, and these two.' Serafina indicated Harrie and Friday. 'In other words, they'll help you. But of course you know that.'

Sarah nodded.

'Also, and using the imagery of the tarot, there's a powerful link with the Magus. The same Magus, perhaps, who appeared in her reading?' Serafina nodded at Friday. 'Hers as well,' she added, indicating Harrie, 'though I didn't mention that, not after the other bad news. I'm seeing a very unpleasant and dangerous force. Do any of you know who this man is?'

Sarah raised her eyebrows at Friday. 'Gellar?'

'Could be.'

'Someone known to the three of you for some time?' Serafina suggested.

'But we haven't known Jared Gellar that long,' Harrie pointed out.

'Not bloody Amos Furniss?' Friday said, disgusted.

Sarah said, 'But this is about me. Why is bloody Furniss in *my* future?'

'Whoever he is,' Serafina said, 'and despite the darkness around him, he contributes to your salvation in a totally unexpected way.'

'Really? So not Furniss, then,' Friday remarked. 'He'd be the last bugger to help *us*.'

'And if I *were* reading the tarot for you,' Serafina said to Sarah, 'I would have turned over the Death card.'

There was a sudden and dread-laden silence.

Sarah felt sick. Not Adam, surely? 'Who's going to die?'

'The Death card doesn't necessarily mean death.' Serafina paused. 'I can't always tell. But sometimes it does.'

'It isn't one of us, is it?' Friday asked in a small voice.

Sitting forwards, Serafina leant her elbows on the table. 'That isn't my feeling, no.'

Harrie looked ready to weep again. 'But do we know this person? Please, can you tell us that at least?'

Serafina sighed. 'You do, but I doubt you'll mourn their passing.'

'Well, that's all right, then,' Sarah said.

'However, I've already told you, there will be other losses,' Serafina warned. 'But the bond between you four girls is extremely strong, and together, one way or another, you'll weather those storms.'

'Three,' Sarah said.

'Pardon?'

'There's only three of us.'

Serafina blinked. 'Yes. Three.' She regarded them across the table. 'You've been through a few fairly wild storms already, haven't you?'

Sarah, Harrie and Friday returned her gaze in uncomfortable silence. It suddenly occurred to Sarah that, given Serafina Fortune's apparently genuine gift, they could well have made a serious mistake coming to see her. What else had she seen in the murky depths of their pasts?

Serafina caught her eye. 'My readings are strictly confidential, and I'm known for my discretion. I hear and see all manner of things, matters my customers most definitely would not want made public. As for my predictions, take heed of them, but keep in mind I may see only one possible pathway. There could be others. Also, of course, I'm not always right.' She stood, pushing back her chair, and said to Harrie, 'You work for Leo Dundas, don't you?'

Harrie sucked in a quick breath. 'That's extraordinary. Did you sense that from me?'

'No. I know Leo quite well, *very* well in fact,' Serafina said, darting a vaguely apologetic look at Friday, 'and he's told me he has a convict girl called Harrie working for him. Your friend here called you Harrie. How many convict girls called Harrie can there be in Sydney?'

'So that business about Harrie's illustrations wasn't a prediction at all,' Sarah said. 'You already knew she's an artist.'

'She only draws flash, though,' Friday said. 'On paper. They don't live and breathe.'

'What exactly did you mean by that?' Harrie asked.

'Actually, I don't know,' Serafina replied with unexpected frankness. 'I really do only pass on what I see. I often have no idea what it means.'

'Make an educated guess,' Sarah suggested.

'Perhaps Leo is going to teach Harrie to tattoo.'

Alarmed, Harrie said, 'Oh, I don't think I could do *that*.'

Delighted, thinking of the tattoo she was planning for her back, Friday said, 'Oh, I was hoping he would! That would be *lovely*. You could do mine.'

Serafina held the door open. Clearly their session was over and it was time for them to leave.

As Sarah brushed past her, she asked, 'How much of us could you see? Of our pasts, I mean?'

Serafina said, 'Enough. But it's not my place to judge. Or tell tales. Besides, I don't care. It's none of my business.'

Sarah studied Serafina Fortune's face and saw nothing that suggested the woman felt otherwise, but as the door closed she sincerely hoped they wouldn't come to regret their visit.

'I think I'll try the fish for a change,' James said. 'Rowie's been spoiling me with mutton and beef at least four times a week.'

'You do look like you've filled out a little,' Matthew remarked.

'A little? I can barely close the buttons on my trousers. I shall be forced to go on a reducing regime if I put on any more weight. I'll have to have a word with her.'

'Why?' Matthew asked. 'Is she forcing you to eat two helpings of everything she cooks?'

'Well, no,' James said, disgruntled. 'I must say, Matthew, that being in love for some reason seems to have brought the more impertinent aspects of your character to the fore.'

Matthew buttered a bread roll. 'On the other hand, you were a bit on the thin side, especially after, you know, your bereavement. For a while there you were looking very close to gaunt. Anyway, I'm not in love.'

James grunted. 'And how is Miss Minto?'

'Very well, thank you.'

'Everything on course?'

'What do you mean?'

'The last time we dined together you mentioned you intended to ask for her hand.'

'I still do,' Matthew said, dabbing with his napkin at a tiny smear of butter on his mouth.

'When?'

'When the time is right.'

James waved to attract the attention of the waitress. 'Are you sure you're making the right decision?'

'Why wouldn't I be?'

'I'll have the celery soup to start, followed by the fish, thank you,' James told the girl. 'Matthew, what will you have?'

'Soup, and the mutton in caper sauce, please.' When the girl had departed with their orders, he added, 'Sally's kind-hearted, industrious and really rather pretty, and I'd be lying if I said I wasn't physically attracted to her.'

'She's not Harrie Clarke, though, is she?'

'Well, I can't have Harrie, can I?' Matthew said flatly.

James took a sip of his sherry. 'Neither, it seems, can I. She told me the other day in no uncertain terms she never wants to see me again.'

'Yes, but she's said that before, hasn't she?'

'She meant it this time, Matthew. I know she did.'

Matthew was briefly silent. 'What brought this about?'

'I told her I believe she's suffering from hysteria or something similar and that she might benefit from some form of therapeutic rest.'

'You told her she's mad? *Honestly*, James!'

'I didn't, not in so many words.'

'I'm not surprised she never wants to see you again. She probably thinks you want to commit her to the asylum.' Matthew paused. 'She isn't, though, is she? Mad?'

'Have you spoken with her lately? This business about conversing with Rachel's ghost and what have you? Things are clearly not right with her.'

Matthew froze with his glass halfway to his mouth. 'What business?'

James recounted his conversation with Harrie.

'I had no idea!' Matthew said, appalled. Though he did recall Friday telling him Harrie was 'out of kilter'.

'Too busy squiring your new paramour?'

'Too busy clearing the decks for you, actually.'

The waitress arrived and set steaming bowls of soup before them.

James blew on a spoonful. 'Well, actually, I do appreciate that, Matthew. I know how you felt about her.'

'How I *still* feel about her. But I know when I'm beaten and I've no intention of spending the rest of my life as a bitter, lonely bachelor starved of physical company.' Matthew pointed at James. 'And neither should you. So don't give up.'

'Yes, well.'

'What do Friday and Sarah think about Harrie?'

'Friday's worried. It was she who mentioned it to me, during a visit to the surgery. I understand Sarah is, too.'

'Well, why don't you go and have a proper talk to them? They know her better than anyone else.'

'Why don't *you*?' James dragged a piece of celery string out of his soup. 'And then you can tell me. You seem to have enjoyed better relations with them than I ever have.'

Matthew regarded him for a second, then laughed. 'You're scared of them, aren't you?'

'Yes, to a certain extent I am.'

'Actually, so am I. Especially Sarah. Friday's not so bad, once you get used to her ways.' Matthew decided, however, that now was not the time to disclose to James that he and Friday went regularly to the Bank of New South Wales together to do the girls' banking. 'Though I certainly wouldn't want to find myself on the wrong side of her.'

'Definitely not.'

'I think it would be better if you talk to them, James.'

James sighed. 'Yes, I expect you're right.'

'But tread gently. I gather Sarah has her own troubles at the moment.'

'Yes, I'd heard. Someone was gossiping about it. Her husband's been sent to Port Macquarie?'

'Five years, for receiving.'

'That's unfortunate,' James said.

'Well it is, actually. Apparently he was framed.'

'Who told you that?'

'A friend.' Leo Dundas wasn't strictly a friend, but after the hours Matthew had spent in Leo's tattoo shop they knew each other well enough now to stop in the street and exchange news pertaining to shared acquaintances. 'And while Adam Green's away, his business is being run by a fellow Sarah loathes. He's living in the house, too, overseeing Sarah. You can imagine the atmosphere.'

'Indeed.'

The waitress removed the empty soup bowls and delivered their main courses with a flourish.

James regarded his baked fish smothered with béchamel sauce. 'What sort is it?'

The girl said, 'Don't know what it's called here, sir, but cook says it tastes a bit like John Dory.'

'I'll have another glass of sherry to go with mine, if you please. Matthew? Hock? Claret?'

'Claret, thank you.'

The waitress scuttled off.

'*Would* you commit her to the asylum?' Matthew asked, liberating a slice of mutton from its lake of caper sauce.

'Harrie? Of course not! It's a ghastly place. I wouldn't send my dog there. Lawrence is acquainted with a very Christian couple who own what is evidently a charming property at Elizabeth Bay. They open their home to young women requiring somewhere peaceful to recuperate. I mentioned Harrie to Lawrence, and he thinks he could arrange a place for her.'

'Who would pay?'

'There are no fees. These people are apparently rather well off. I would, however, make a considerable donation to their charitable organisation.'

'That would be very generous of you,' Matthew said.

'It would be, if Harrie conceded to go. But clearly she won't.'

'Not even to a private home?'

'I didn't even get that far. When we discussed the matter she was exceedingly grumpy with me and told me I didn't understand.'

'About?'

'This spirit manifestation business.'

'Rachel returning as a ghost?'

James popped a forkful of boiled carrot into his mouth and nodded while he chewed.

'Well, *do* you understand?' Matthew asked.

Swallowing, James replied, 'Well, obviously she's having some sort of extended delusional episode.'

'But what if it's true? What if Rachel really has come back?'

'Oh, for God's sake, not you as well!' James snapped.

'I'm just saying. "There are more things in heaven and earth", or whatever it was Shakespeare said.'

'I didn't know you read Shakespeare.'

'I don't, really. But just because you don't believe it doesn't mean it isn't true. Or real.'

James drew in a deep breath and let it out very slowly. 'To be honest, Matthew, what I care about is Harrie's welfare and happiness, and at this point in time she seems neither well nor content. I am not a physician who specialises in disorders of the mind, but I am capable of recognising the characteristics of a patient in considerable mental distress. She must have help of some sort.'

'Well, get it for her, then.'

'I'll do my best,' James said tersely.

'If there's anything I can do.'

'Yes, I know.'

They ate in silence for a while. At last Matthew asked, 'How *is* it working out with Rowie Harris? Apart from you overeating, I mean? You've never been tempted?'

James glanced up from his meal. 'I can't say it hasn't crossed my mind. She's certainly an attractive girl. And an excellent homemaker.'

'So ...?'

'Well, that's all she is — a comely girl who makes a good pork pie. And I want more than that.'

'Yes,' Matthew muttered. 'I know what you mean.'

'Anyway, I have my doubts about her moral underpinnings. She's often visiting Friday at Elizabeth Hislop's establishment. She seems to hold very fond memories of her time there. Apparently they were close, herself and Friday, though I understand Friday has only called on her at my house once or twice.'

'She must miss Friday, though,' Matthew said. 'And the other girls at the brothel. I know you don't approve of brothels, but I expect the ambience there must be quite jolly at times.'

'Jolly!'

'Well, you know, all those young girls together.'

'I think the sooner you marry, the better, Matthew.'

'The company, James. She must be quite lonely, stuck in the house with no one to talk to but you.'

'Well, thank you very much.' James folded his napkin and lay it on the table. 'She does get visitors, you know. There's a woman who comes to see her after hours fairly regularly. I've glimpsed her passing the front window but Rowie's never introduced her. And she has other friends.'

'No male suitors?'

'If she has any I don't see them.'

Matthew stifled a burp behind his hand, then set his knife and fork neatly across his plate. 'So, what are you going to do about Harrie?'

'I don't know. Yet.'

Chapter Eighteen

Sarah had thought deeply about Serafina Fortune's answers to her secret questions, and though they'd been positive, the woman had also said her predictions didn't always come true and that they were only one potential future outcome. There was also the possibility she'd been making the whole lot up, though Sarah — despite her inherent mistrust of people who told fortunes for a living — didn't think this was likely, given the accuracy of her readings of their pasts.

But she'd also talked of losses still to come, and Sarah was convinced she'd been concealing bad news from them. It made commercial sense, really. If Sarah could see into the future, *she* wouldn't go about telling people their friends and loved ones were about to drop dead, which would certainly guarantee an end to any repeat business.

Still, Serafina's answers had given her hope, something to hold on to during the darkest hours of the night, when she couldn't sleep and everything seemed at its most bleak.

Gellar was well and truly frightened now, but was showing no signs of leaving. He must want Adam's business very badly. Her hate for him was such that the mere sight of him made her gorge rise, but she was able to summon the strength to behave in a moderately civil manner towards him, and remained determined to continue the charade of the house being haunted for as long as necessary. What she had to do now was extract from him a confession to the effect that he'd framed Adam, one she could present to Police Magistrate Captain Rossi in the hope of having Adam's conviction for receiving quashed.

A lot easier said than done, of course. Why the hell would Gellar admit to it? She certainly wouldn't if she were him.

Jared thumped down the stairs and strode through the dining room to the back door.

'No time for breakfast. God, what's that smell?' he said as he thrust his stockinged feet into his long black boots. 'I've an early meeting this morning.' The harried expression on his face changed abruptly and he withdrew one foot from a boot. 'Is this ...?'

Sarah turned away, terrified she would laugh.

'Christ, it is! It's *dog* shit!'

There was a clatter as the other boot flew off.

Sarah looked; Jared was staring down, appalled, at the shite squashed all over his feet and trouser hems.

'How did *that* get in my boots!?' he demanded.

'Rachel?' Sarah suggested. 'She did that before, to Esther.'

'For *fuck's* sake!'

Jared tore at the buttons on his trousers, yanked them down over his hips and stepped out of them, revealing a pair of fine linen knee-length drawers that hugged the considerable mound of his genitals, and kicked viciously so the trousers sailed off to a corner of the dining room. Sarah tried to avert her eyes, but, mesmerised by the spectacle of Jared's tantrum, found she couldn't. His hairy but shapely lower legs were encased in short, white silk stockings, held up by gay red garters. He ripped them off, hurled them after the trousers, and stomped off back through the hall and upstairs, his bare feet leaving shitty prints behind him.

Sarah remained at the table, hands over her mouth, stifling her giggles.

When Jared reappeared — in clean trousers and another pair of boots and reeking of lavender soap — he said in a tight voice, 'The water in the bowl in my room is filthy. And will you please launder my clothes. Thank you.'

When he'd gone, Sarah fetched a stick and flicked his dog-shite-laden clothing and boots out the back door, congratulating herself on a job well done, even if she did have to clean up the mess herself. It hadn't brought her any nearer to getting him to confess, though, had it? What she needed was some form of threat that would put the wind up him even more than being haunted did, and that would render him thoroughly malleable. He was already very much on edge — what could she produce that would tip him over?

And then, in a blinding flash of enlightenment, it came to her. She recalled several snippets of information Leo had given her, something she'd seen among Gellar's papers, and a scene from her wedding day, and it all fell into place, leaving her wondering why she hadn't thought of it before.

She had to talk to Friday.

'Bloody dangerous,' Friday said, whipping up her skirt to reveal the purple scar on her calf, as yet untattooed. 'Look what happened to me.'

'That was just bad luck,' Sarah replied.

'No, that was Furniss's sodding rabid dogs.'

'They weren't rabid. You'd be in your grave now if they were. Anyway, and no offence meant, I'm a lot better at sneaking round houses than you are.'

They were in Elizabeth Hislop's office, which she'd kindly offered them yet again so they could speak privately.

'But why? What are you looking for?'

Sarah said, 'Something that will connect both Gellar and Bella Jackson to this business of trafficking native heads from New Zealand. He's been there recently, that's obvious. He has ships' manifests from trips across the Tasman, and he gave Adam and me a piece of greenstone on our wedding day — two-faced bastard — and Leo said he heard that Bella's masterminding stealing the heads to order. If I can prove a connection, we can blackmail him into admitting he framed Adam.'

'Can't we just blackmail him now, without you having to break into Bella's house?'

'There's nothing specific in his papers, nothing that says, *Pinched and smuggled to Botany Bay, one dozen Maori heads, by order of Bella Jackson*. He's not that stupid,' Sarah said. 'Unfortunately he's not stupid at all.'

'Bella isn't either, you know.'

'Yes, I *do* know that, thank you.'

'What if you don't find anything?'

A little burst of panic spurted behind Sarah's ribs: she didn't want to consider that. 'Stop asking me all these questions.'

'Don't snap.'

'I'm not.'

'You are. But what if you *don't*?'

'I don't know.' Even the very prospect of not finding anything flooded Sarah with desperation and despair. 'I really don't. I think this might be my last chance.'

Friday made a worried face. 'You'll have to get into the bloody house first. And, more to the point, out again.'

'I know. Obviously, it'll be far easier if the place is empty, but even if Bella and Clarence and Furniss aren't there, those dogs will be, won't they?'

'Well, that's their job, terrorising trespassers. I should know,' Friday said sourly. 'Actually, they mightn't be home this Saturday night. Apparently there's some sort of reception in town for toffs.' She laughed. 'Not the dogs, I don't mean. Dogs don't go to receptions. But Clarence is a snob, he's bound to go, and he'll take Bella. That's why he married her.'

'Furniss, though?'

'Dunno. Doubt he'll be driving them; Bella's already got a driver. With any luck Furniss'll be in the Black Rat frittering his money on pox-raddled whores.'

Sarah thought about it. 'The servants. They'll still be there.'

'Probably. You can creep around them, though, can't you?'

'Of course I can. So that just leaves the dogs.'

'Rather you than me.' Friday shuddered. 'What we need is one of those coves from the travelling menagerie who tames lions and bears and other mad animals.'

Sarah started to smile. 'We've got one.'

When Sarah arrived home the mail had been delivered and there among the business-related bits and pieces was, to her utter delight, a letter from Adam. She left the *CLOSED* sign on the door — to hell with customers — and hurried through to the dining room.

She yanked off her bonnet, dropped it on the table, sat down, cracked the seal on the letter and … froze.

What if he was horribly sick? What if he'd been assigned to a really back-breaking job and it was killing him? What if he was starving to death? Could she bear to know any of those things?

But she had to. She had to know.

Slowly — warily — she unfolded the letter and began to read the cramped writing:

10th of May 1831
My Beloved Sarah
   I am surviving here. The worst aspect of my
Incarceration is that I cannot be with you. I miss you
desperately and think of you every minute of every day. My
Heart feels as though it has been torn out. I had no idea I
was to go before Rossi the day I did, and I tried so hard to
get a message to you. I am so sorry, Sarah.

When I arrived I was confined to Barracks for a month. They refer to it here as 'Acclimatisation' but the inmates call it 'breaking your spirit'. This practice is just for Specials — those educated Recidivists, of which, apparently, I am one, the authorities fear are too clever and too fond of stirring the political pot to remain in Sydney.

Food rations in Barracks are meagre and leave a fair bit to be desired, but there is a vegetable garden attached to the Barracks in which many of the lunatic and crippled prisoners work, so at least we won't die of scurvy. The Barracks, as expected, are foul, crowded, and infested with the usual assortment of fleas, cockroaches and rats. Fortunately, most of the truly nasty inmates were shipped off to Moreton Bay and Norfolk Island when the Town was opened up for settlement last year, so I suppose I should be grateful. There is also a newly built Female Factory here, where the poor women apparently bash away making nails all day.

I have recently been assigned to the Deputy Assistant Commissariat as a Clerk, hence this letter. I now have access to as much paper, ink and nibs as I can safely steal, though I had to pay a Premium to have this posted by the Convict who works in the position above me.

I have also written to Arthur Hocking asking him to begin preparations for an appeal against my Conviction. I greatly fear, though, that an appeal will not be successful. But I must try. I know how busy you must be in the workshop by yourself, Sarah, but have you discovered anything that might be of assistance to me? If you have, tell Bernard and he can inform Hocking.

I will write again as soon as I am able. If you have written to me I won't have received your letter — Specials are not permitted to either receive or send correspondence

*in case their literary plottings bring about the Downfall of
the British Empire.*

*I love you and miss you desperately, and I would give
anything to be at home with you. However, I am slowly
coming to terms with the likelihood that I will be here at
Port Macquarie for the full five years. Five years is a long
time. I am not an unreasonable man and although I feel as
if I am stabbing myself in the heart as I write this, I don't
expect you to wait for me, Sarah. Should you receive an
offer from someone with better prospects than mine, you
should take it. I will understand, but I hope with all my
selfish heart and soul that such an offer never arises.*

   Yours Now and Always,
   Adam

In a fit of pain and rage Sarah flung the letter as far away as
possible. No! She would *not* go off with some other cove! What a
bloody stupid idea. She *would* wait for him. For five years — or for
ten, or for twenty, if she had to.

She struggled to swallow the enormous, burning lump in her
throat. He was giving up, letting the prison suck the life out of him,
and the thought of it made her want to shriek at the top of her
voice. And he hadn't received her letters. Where were they? Stuffed
in some officious bloody commandant's drawer?

She stood up and kicked the table leg as hard as she could,
then sat down again, took off her boot and cradled her toes, tears
streaming down her face.

No matter what it took, she was bringing him home.

Friday rose from the bed, but her customer, a regular named Ralph
Kidd, grabbed her wrist and pulled her back.

   'Where are you going?'

   'Just to the window, to close the curtains.'

'Leave them. I like being able to see the night sky.'

Friday sank down beside him again, and let him draw her head onto his chest. She didn't mind Ralph Kidd. He was perhaps in his early thirties, and had been coming to see her every week for ages despite being married and the father of four young children. He was tall and thin, though his shoulders were wide, and if she had to describe him in one word it would be 'blond'. His hair, cut close, was so pale it was almost white, and his skin was fair. When his face was composed he looked grim, but a rare smile revealed good, white teeth, which Friday appreciated as healthy teeth meant pleasant breath.

He always booked an hour with her, though he only used half of that for sex. During the remaining time he talked and so, to her enduring surprise, did Friday. While he discussed his ship-building and refitting business, his children, whom he loved, and his wife, whom he also loved — though she wouldn't do the things in bed he wanted, which is why he came to see Friday — she told him about what she'd been doing, though never anything too personal or private. He knew she had a friend whose husband had been sent to Port Macquarie, and another assigned to a family on the Rocks, and that she was committed to supporting the child of yet another who had died. He told her he thought she was amusing, honest and generous in the way she gave herself to him sexually, but they both knew she had to — it was her job.

'How's the one going with the husband in the penitentiary?' he asked, stroking her hair. Friday had never told him Sarah's and Harrie's names, and she never would.

'Not very well. Desperate to have him back.'

'I can imagine. And there's no way she can prove his innocence?'

Friday shook her head, her hair sliding against his skin.

'Why doesn't she approach his solicitor or barrister and seek an appeal?'

'That'll be the day. The barrister he had in court, some cove called Evans, was bent and working with the bastard who framed him.'

'Augustus Evans?'

'That's him.'

'I know him. I see him socially sometimes. Who did frame your friend's husband? Or aren't you in a position to tell me?'

It suddenly occurred to Friday that Ralph Kidd could be more than just a cully with fresh breath. 'Jared Gellar. Oily bugger fancies himself rotten? Has businesses all over town and does a bit of importing.'

Her heart sank as she felt Ralph shake his head.

'I don't know him personally. I have heard his business dealings are somewhat shady, however.'

'But you know Evans?'

'Yes. But I did hear Gellar's name mentioned recently.'

Friday sat up and faced Ralph, her heavy breasts bouncing. He raised a lazy hand to stroke a nipple.

'To do with what?'

'I was at a private soirée the other night and I wasn't actually part of the conversation, but I did happen to overhear something to the effect that he may have played a little fast and loose concerning some import deal involving Bella Shand. Or was it her husband?'

Friday's pulse quickened. 'Who was saying this?'

'Eli Chattoway. You won't know him. Oh, actually, you might.'

'Don't think so. And how did everyone react?'

'There wasn't an "everyone", there were only two people having the conversation, Eli and someone else. But they both laughed. At Gellar's expense, I gathered, not Mrs Shand's.'

'Do you think this Eli cove would talk to me?'

Ralph ran his fingers down Friday's belly to her pubic hair. 'Possibly, but you might have to pay a price. He's a bit of a roué, old Eli. Have you got another customer after me?'

'No one booked.'

'Do you want another five pounds?'

'That'd be nice,' Friday said, trying at that moment, but failing completely, to see a difference between Ralph Kidd and dirty old Eli Chattoway.

When she finally went downstairs, she went straight to Elizabeth's office.

'Do you know someone called Eli Chattoway?'

'Why?'

'I need to talk to him.'

Elizabeth gave her a suspicious look. 'What about?'

'It's … I just do. Do you know him or not?'

'I hope you're not in some sort of trouble, Friday.'

'Do you *know* him?'

'Unfortunately, yes.'

'Where would I find him?'

'Either drunk somewhere, or stuffing his face, or terrorising some poor girl. A deeply unpleasant man, Eli Chattoway. I banned him from here years ago. I don't think you do want to talk to him, Friday.'

'I do. Where does he live?'

Elizabeth sighed, and told her. 'I'm not happy about this, Friday. And don't go into his house. The man's a pig.'

Friday didn't waste time. The following day she wasn't due to start work until one in the afternoon, so at ten she set out to walk over the hill above the Rocks to Fort Street on the other side, overlooking Darling Harbour, where Chattoway lived. It had been raining all morning and the road had turned to shite, but she was wearing her sturdy boots and took care to avoid the worst of the mud and puddles, though once she almost ended up on her arse.

She was also wearing one of Mrs H's elaborately styled, bright auburn-coloured wigs.

'To hide your identity,' Elizabeth had said when she'd knocked on Friday's bedroom door earlier that morning and presented it with a flourish. 'Just in case something goes wrong. You don't want him knowing what you really look like. Not with that hair of yours.'

Bemused, Friday had accepted it but now she was regretting the decision because the bloody thing was making her head sweaty and itchy and she felt like throwing it away. God knew how Mrs H wore one all the time. But she kept it on: if Elizabeth Hislop, who actually knew this Eli Chattoway, thought she should make the effort to disguise herself, then perhaps she should.

She came to the house Mrs H had described to her. It was new, quite a flash one constructed from sandstone, near a row of terrace houses, also newly built. Chattoway's home was two-storey, with double chimneys and tall windows on both levels. Obviously he had plenty of chink. She lifted the ring on the door knocker and banged it.

Eventually, the door was opened by a long-faced, sallow-skinned girl in a housemaid's costume.

'Mr Chattoway, please,' Friday said brightly.

'Have you got an appointment?'

Given Eli Chattoway's reputation, Friday took a punt. 'Yes.'

The girl stepped back to let Friday in. 'He's still in his chamber. I expect he's waiting.'

God, Friday thought. She wiped her boots on the coir mat, then followed the girl inside and up a smart staircase.

'Where's Mrs Chattoway?' she asked.

'In her grave,' the girl said over shoulder.

When they reached the upper floor the girl hared off down the hall until she came to a closed door. She turned, said, 'Rather you than me,' then knocked loudly.

Friday felt an unpleasant chill ripple across her buttocks. She'd said exactly the same thing to Sarah, but in reference to Furniss's mad dogs.

A cracked voice from within croaked, 'What?!'

The girl pushed open the door and fled.

Friday stepped in. The room was gloomy, the curtains still drawn, and it stank — of unwashed body and whisky, the latter smell no doubt emanating from the unstoppered decanter on the night table. A mound lay in the bed, the nets and drapes looped untidily over the canopy rails. The mound grunted and lifted its head.

'Who the hell are you?'

'Mr Chattoway?' Friday asked hesitantly. It *really* ponged in here: this could be a lot nastier than she'd thought.

He wore a stupid nightcap with a long tail on it, and a voluminous linen gown with a stain of some sort down the front. He was very fat and had ruddy cheeks, intelligent piggy eyes, wet red lips and enormously bushy grey muttonchops.

'Speak up!' he barked. 'I didn't order a girl!' He reached for his pocket watch on the night table and peered at it. 'Did I? What day is it?'

'Thursday, sir. I've come to ask you for some information.'

'Turn around,' Eli Chattoway said, pushing himself into a sitting position.

'What?'

'I said turn around.'

Friday did, feeling the old man's gaze all over her.

'Are you sure you're not a whore?'

Friday thought she'd keep that to herself for the moment. She moved closer to the bed, trying not to breathe through her nose. 'I've been told you know something about a man named Jared Gellar.'

Chattoway snorted. 'That spigot-sucker.' Grunting, he leant over and poured himself a tumbler of whisky. 'I know a lot of things.'

'Something to do with a business deal concerning Clarence Shand? Or his wife Bella?' Friday prompted. Mentally she crossed her fingers. 'Maybe something about Gellar playing the crooked cross?'

'You labouring types and your charming vernacular.' Chattoway sipped his whisky thoughtfully, his eyes never leaving Friday.

It gave her the shits.

'If I tell you what you want to know, it'll cost you.'

She sighed inwardly. 'What's your price?'

'You.'

Now there was a surprise. But she'd already made up her mind she would pay it; Chattoway's information could be the key to forcing a confession from Gellar. Also, she owed Sarah, for being so jealous of Adam and trying to ruin their blossoming love affair.

She nodded. 'But you have to tell me first, or no deal.'

'Fair enough,' he said with the arrogance of someone accustomed to having things go his way. 'Open the curtains. I feel like a bloody mole in here.'

Friday did, noting he was even more repulsive with sunlight spilling across his puffy face. She perched expectantly on the end of the bed.

'Jared Gellar is your basic crook dressed up in fine clothing. Always was, always will be,' Chattoway said. 'For the last twelve months or so, until very recently, he's been sailing between Botany Bay and New Zealand with a cargo of, among other things, preserved and tattooed Maori heads hidden in the hold of that schooner of his. Some purchased, and some stolen. And not just any old heads — the very best. Heads that once sat on the shoulders of exceedingly royal New Zealanders.'

A terrible itch sprouted beneath Friday's wig, but she dared not scratch it in case the sodding thing shifted. Or even worse, fell off. 'And Bella Jackson? Shand, I mean? What about her?'

'Mrs Shand, Clarence's *delightful* new wife, takes orders from collectors of such items, ethnologists and what have you, and arranges for their acquisition. Forwards the payments, has the graves dug up, liaises with whomever does the killings if necessary, that sort of thing. Her and that henchman of hers, Amos Furniss.'

Friday knew her mouth had sagged open; she snapped it shut and almost bit her tongue.

'Gellar, however, apparently wasn't happy with his cut of the proceedings so he stole four of the heads and sold them himself to collectors in England. Bella Shand is aware, of course, that they're missing, but not who took them.' Chattoway smirked. 'It'll be *his* head separated from his shoulders when she finds out. And she will, eventually.'

'How do you know all this?' Friday was delighted. This was *exactly* the leverage they needed.

'I have my methods. This whole grubby little town operates on deceit, favours owed and backroom deals. I doubt it will ever change. Look at its genesis. Now, I think we'll start with a bit of fellatio. Come here.' He threw back the bed covers and pulled his nightgown up to his middle. The smell in the room suddenly got worse.

His belly bulged over his lap but Friday could still see his cock, lying limply on sparse grey pubic hair. God, it would be one of those ones she'd have to work on forever, she could tell, with her jaw getting cramp and her lips chafing and dribble going everywhere. His legs were fat as well, the skin mottled like that pink and white marble you got in the houses of the very rich, and a brown-stained bandage covered his right leg from his toes to his knee. Gout, obviously.

'Come here, my love,' he crooned. 'Come closer.'

She moved around the bed to stand beside him, noting the cheesy excrescence oozing out from under his foreskin, and dry yellow flakes littering the surrounding hair and skin. Her stomach roiled and she stifled an acidic burp. No wonder he stank.

'Ah, I ...'

'Hurry up,' he said, his voice as sharp and ragged as oyster shells now.

411

He grabbed her arm and jerked her down towards his groin, but she twisted out of his grasp, relieved he hadn't taken hold of her hair, which would have come off in his hand.

'Let me just prepare first,' she said. 'If I'm to lie with you, there's something I need to do.'

'Do it here, in front of me,' Chattoway countered, idly stroking himself, without any discernible effect. 'I like watching that sort of thing.'

Blocking her nose from the inside, Friday bent down and tickled him beneath his chin. 'No, let's keep a sense of mystery, shall we? Do you have a room for ablutions?'

'There's probably water in the kitchen, if that's what you want,' Chattoway grumbled. 'Ask Ivy.'

'I won't be long.' Friday blew him a kiss and flitted out the door, closing it behind her.

Outside, in the hall, she retched repeatedly. Wiping her watering eyes on her sleeve, she rushed to the stairs and trotted down, heading for the front door.

But it was locked; that stupid girl must have the key.

She hurried through to the back of the house, past the indoor kitchen — clearly Chattoway was *very* well off — and into what appeared to be the back porch. She tried the door there, and that was locked, too. *Bugger.* Ducking into a small room off to one side containing several trunks, a heavy coat on a hook and two pairs of Wellington boots, she dragged a trunk over to the single tiny casement window, climbed up and looked out. Ivy, the servant girl, was in a narrow yard behind the house, hanging laundry.

Friday unlatched the window, set her palms on the sill, thrust her head and shoulders through the opening — and discovered the rest of her was too big to fit through.

Fuck.

She scrabbled her boots against the inside wall and felt herself wriggle through the gap a few more inches, but that was it: she was well and truly jammed.

'Oi!' she called to the girl at the washing line. 'Oi, I'm stuck!'

Ivy looked to her left, then her right, then shrugged and bent to pick up another huge pair of white drawers.

'Behind you!' Friday yelped. 'The window!'

Finally, Ivy turned — and dropped the drawers on the muddy ground. 'What are you doing up there?!'

'Pomading the hair on my minge. What does it look like? Come and give me a hand.'

Ivy crept closer. 'Where's Mr Chattoway?'

'Upstairs lying in bed like a big fat toad playing with himself and expecting me back any minute. Here, grab my hands and pull.'

Ivy wiped her hands on her apron, took hold of Friday's and pulled.

Friday grunted in pain and tossed her head. Ivy shrieked as the wig fell off.

'Shut up, he'll hear us!'

'It's all right — he can't move fast with his bad leg.' Ivy started to giggle, revealing several missing bottom teeth, and clamped her hand over her mouth. 'Can you go backwards?'

Friday tried. 'Not now, I can't.'

'Is it your skirts? Are you wearing a dress or an ensemble?'

'Bodice and skirt. Undo the buttons, will you?'

While Friday supported her weight on her hands against the wall — she felt like she was being cut in half now — Ivy struggled with the buttons on her skirt.

'Hurry up, I'm passing out here.'

Ivy tore open the last two buttons, grabbed Friday's hands again and gave an almighty yank. Friday shot out, leaving her skirts behind, and landed on the ground, naked from the waist down except for her boots and a pair of pretty, pale blue stockings.

Blushing fiercely, Ivy ran to the back door, unlocked it and disappeared inside. She reappeared a moment later with Friday's skirt.

'Hurry, he's coming down the stairs! I can hear him! I'll tell him I haven't seen you.'

Quickly she relocked the door, darted over to the washing line and resumed hanging laundry.

Friday stepped into her skirt, did up the top button, snatched up Mrs H's wig and asked, 'What's over the back fence?'

'A bit of a drop then the military hospital and the fort. If you go hard right along the fence you'll get to Windmill Street. It'll take you up to —'

'Princes Street, I know. Thanks, love,' Friday said. 'You want to get yourself someone decent to work for.'

'Can't. I'm assigned.'

'Tell them he's raped you.'

'He bloody has.' Ivy's face was scarlet again.

Christ almighty. Friday scrambled onto the high fence. 'Go to the Siren's Arms on Harrington Street. Ask for Elizabeth Hislop. She might be able to help. I'll tell her to expect you.'

Ivy gave a little wave, then Friday was over the other side, tumbling down a long greasy slope until her progress was halted by a soggy clump of bushes. She stood up, wiped herself off, and headed towards Windmill Street, wondering what Mrs H was going to say about the state of her wig.

Saturday, 28 May 1831

Sarah and Friday were walking north along Cumberland Street, their skirts held high to avoid the muck; it had been raining heavily for several days and the deluge hadn't improved the condition of the streets any. But the sun had shone for several hours this afternoon, and now that evening was approaching the air felt a little drier and the autumn wind a tad less fractious.

Sarah half turned and called, 'Come on, keep up!'

'It's not me, it's her,' Walter replied, gesturing at Clifford, who was stopping every ten feet to lift her leg.

'God, how can such a small dog be so full of piss?' Friday said.

Walter caught up. 'I don't think she's weeing, I think she's marking her territory.'

'Well, she must own all of Argyle and half of Cumberland Street by now,' Sarah grumbled. Then she said, 'Harrie wanted to come today, but I said she couldn't.'

'While you break into Bella's? She'd fret herself to death.'

'She's worried about Walter.'

'Oh, you'll be all right,' Friday said to him. 'You're a tough little bugger, aren't you?'

Walter shrugged, his ears turning red.

'I told her that,' Sarah said.

Friday pointed. 'We'd better stop here. That's Bella's house over there.'

'Yes, I do know where she lives.' Suddenly Sarah almost tore off Friday's sleeve, dragging her behind a hedge. 'Keep your head down, Furniss is opening the gates.'

Crouching behind someone's manicured shrubbery, they watched as Amos Furniss dragged wide first one and then the other of the carriage gates at the side of the Shand residence. Nothing happened for a minute or two, then a vehicle appeared, presumably from the stables behind the house — not Bella's smart curricle, but a roomier landau lacquered a deep forest green with a coat of arms on the door — and parked in the carriageway.

A minute later Bella and Clarence, both attired extremely elegantly, appeared on the verandah at the rear of the house (actually the front), and climbed aboard. Or at least Friday assumed it was Clarence Shand; she'd never encountered him until now. Shorter than Bella, and older by a good twenty years or more, he had a bit of a belly above thin, bandy legs. His face she couldn't see clearly from their vantage point in the bushes. He held himself well, though, and managed to exude an air of authority bordering on arrogance as he handed Bella into the landau.

Furniss shut the gates again after the carriage had departed, then vanished from view himself. A moment later the two dogs appeared, racing wildly up and down the carriageway, clearly delighted at being let out of wherever they'd been confined.

'Shit,' Sarah said.

'Can they smell us?' Friday asked nervously.

'Maybe,' Walter said. 'I could smell that filthy bastard Furniss,' he added, the cords in his neck stretched tight and his fists clenched.

Friday eyed him with alarm, startled by the anger rolling off him. She knew Walter disliked Furniss — Harrie had told her — but she'd never said why.

Clifford's bristly hackles were up and her short little legs splayed as she eye-balled the dogs still bounding around across the street. A dreadful, low growl emanated from her throat. Walter lay a hand on her head, and the growling subsided to a barely audible rumble.

'You'll never get past Furniss *and* the dogs,' Friday said.

Sarah's hand tapped up and down on her knee. 'Just wait a while.'

They did.

Half an hour later, as the late afternoon light began to decay, tinting the rain-rinsed sky a vivid pink and orange, Furniss appeared once more, let himself out through the hand gate, and strode off down Cumberland Street.

From the bushes, his face pinched with loathing, Walter watched Furniss walk past.

'Now?' he asked when Furniss was out of sight.

'Not yet.' Sarah raised her eyebrows at Friday. 'I'll give it fifteen minutes. What about you?'

'Ten, I'd say.'

Betraying his nerves, Walter snapped, '*Now* what?'

'Servants,' Friday said.

They were both wrong. Barely five minutes passed before two more figures appeared, sidling along the carriageway, backs to the wall of the house, doing their best to keep their distance from the dogs.

'Bugger me, look who it is,' Friday said. 'I didn't know they were working for Bella. She must have got Clarence to have them assigned.' But hadn't Sally Minto said something about the pair of them coming into her bakery? Friday hadn't realised she'd meant they'd come in *with* Bella.

Louisa Coutts and Becky Hoddle were evidently as frightened of Furniss's animals as were Friday and Sarah. Clearly dying to sprint the last few yards to the hand gate, they restricted themselves to a brisk walk, the dogs stalking them closely, then let themselves out. Once through and with the gate safely closed again, Becky gave the dogs the finger with both hands before she and Louisa hurried off.

'Still at her beck and call, washing her filthy smalls and doing her dirty work. Haven't they gone up in the world,' Sarah remarked.

'Better than Liz Parker,' Friday said, referring to Louisa and Becky's previous boss.

'Barely.'

'Do you think there's anyone else in there?'

'If there is, it'll only be some poor little house girl,' Sarah said. 'I'll be all right. Walter? Are you ready?' She slipped out of her jacket and skirt to reveal her burglary outfit of trousers and sleeveless shirt, and settled her satchel over her shoulder.

He nodded. 'Someone'll have to hold Clifford. She can't come with me.'

'Christ,' Friday grumbled, 'that'll be me, obviously. Give her here.'

As Walter picked up Clifford, her legs paddled furiously and she wriggled and squirmed, but he managed to thrust her into Friday's arms.

'There we are,' Friday said. 'What a good little girl you are! Now, you be good and stay with Auntie Friday.'

Clifford snapped at Friday's face with sharp white teeth, missing her nose by less than an inch.

'Fucking hell!' Friday exclaimed, holding Clifford out at arm's length. 'You'd better hurry up, Sarah, before I'm torn to shreds.'

'Better be quick, anyway,' Walter said. 'I dunno how long I can do this for. I've never tried it before.'

Sarah unlaced her boots and toed them off. 'Come on then, let's get started.'

'You got a pocket?' Walter asked Friday.

'What for?'

He produced a bulging paper twist. 'Aniseed balls. She loves them. If she plays up, feed them to her one by one.'

'*If?*' Friday tucked a struggling Clifford under her arm. 'God almighty.' As Sarah and Walter moved off into the deepening shadows, she called after them, 'Good luck!'

'What sort of dogs are they?' Sarah asked.

The animals stood in Bella's carriageway, ears pricked, watching their every move as they crossed the street. One let out a barrage of barks.

'Dunno, really. Mastiffs? They're beautiful.'

'They are not. I still say we should poison them.'

Walter shook his head vehemently. 'No! It's not their fault. That bastard's *ruined* them. Just give me five minutes.'

'Quick as you can, then.'

And in case Walter's amazing dog-wrangling turn didn't work, she'd brought along two small pieces of raw mutton treated with cyanide, tightly wrapped in oilcloth in her satchel. That would *certainly* do the trick, though, of course, then Bella would know her property had been broken into when she came home to find two dead dogs in her yard.

Walter stepped off the roadway, walked up to the wrought-iron fence and peered through; the dogs immediately raced over to him, barking and slavering. Staring calmly at them, he didn't flinch, his hands wrapped casually around the bars within easy reach of the beasts' teeth.

They stopped barking. One sat down, followed by the other. They both tilted their huge heads to one side, whining slightly.

Seconds ticked past. Sarah couldn't see, but she was sure Walter was doing his 'nothing' face. One of the dogs took a moment to nip at something near its nether regions.

The whining stopped.

Walter opened the gate and went inside, hands extended, palms down, fingers curled out of harm's way. The dogs ambled over and had a good sniff.

'You can come in now,' he said over his shoulder.

Her heart pounding thunderously, Sarah crept in and closed the gate, and waited until Walter moved off down the carriageway, the dogs flanking him, rubbing against his legs like a pair of overgrown house cats. Christ, she hoped he knew what he was doing. She followed, and when he'd settled himself on the verandah, the dogs sitting expectantly before him, she set to work unlocking the nearest door.

It took her less than a minute. Once inside she stood very still, listening, but heard nothing, no sign that anyone remained in the house. She started with the large desk near the far wall — Bella's, judging by the elegantly feminine desk accessories — picking the locks on each drawer and, lighting the lamp on the desk, going through the papers contained within, but finding nothing that made any mention of a business relationship with Jared Gellar. In fact, she could see nothing that could be used against Bella in any way at all; everything seemed to relate to perfectly legal commercial transactions concerning Clarence's import company. Which made sense, as Bella was a convict and forbidden from setting up her own business. Sod it. Perhaps she kept her dodgy paperwork somewhere else. Upstairs, or even at different premises entirely?

She put everything back exactly as she'd found it, relocked the drawers, picked up the lamp, glanced out at Walter to make sure he was still in one piece, and began a tour of the house. Clarence's desk was in a small library, but also held no documents of use, though letters from his bank indicated his businesses and investments were doing extremely well. She found no other repositories of papers downstairs, and no safe, so in silence she climbed the stairs, hesitating once again on the topmost landing to listen for the presence of anyone else. The upper floor was unlit and as the building was constructed from sandstone there was nothing to hear, not even the creaks and groans of a house settling for the evening.

She went through each room. Clarence's bedroom was what you'd expect of a man, albeit expensively and very stylishly furnished, though his wall safe contained bundles of crude and explicit letters signed by several different males. She wondered if Bella knew. Or cared. Bella's chamber was also extremely tasteful, which was a surprise. Her clothes press overflowed with lovely gowns and gorgeous accessories. She had an entire chest filled with exquisitely soft linen and sateen corsets and demi-corsets, beautifully embroidered lawn shifts and petticoats, and the finest linen drawers; the latter a garment, everyone knew, worn only by wealthy women or those with serious pretensions. Sarah really had to suppress her desire to squat and piss all over the lot.

Bella's safe contained some good jewellery, a silver-framed miniature portrait of a fat middle-aged woman, and some letters on yellowing paper that began, *To My Dearest Son*, on which the signature had been deliberately obscured with blobs of ink. Letters to a brother of Bella's from their mother? Even Bella must have had a mother. From Bella to her son? Surely not, but if he existed, God have mercy on the poor boy. Sarah was very tempted to read the letters, but the thought of Walter holding off the dogs downstairs stopped her. Again, however, there was nothing in the safe she could use.

A bubble of panic rose in her chest, and she forced herself to swallow it.

She crossed to the dressing table, littered with beauty tools and preparations; two extravagant wigs on stands, pomades, creams and salves, skin-bleaching solutions, tweezers, brushes, a mortar with pestle, perfumes, powders, rouge and kohl and tinted balms, plus a range of lotions. Opening a bottle of the latter, she sniffed and winced, recognising beneath the sweet scent of roses the bite of chalk and almonds that indicated quicklime and arsenic, which she knew was used to remove body hair. A bit strong, though, this particular concoction. She'd prefer to have hairy armpits — which, in fact, Adam said he found rather alluring — than scorch herself ragged with this. She smiled slightly as it occurred to her what might have happened to Bella that day on the *Isla* when she'd burnt her face. Wrong bottle of lotion?

But, dismayingly, there was nothing here for her. Reluctantly she trotted back downstairs, extinguished the lamp and returned it to Bella's desk.

Out on the verandah, Walter was still sitting with the dogs.

'Have you finished?' he asked, his voice wavering. He didn't turn away from the animals. 'I'm getting bloody tired.'

'I'm done. Let's go.'

Walter rose and followed Sarah to the gate, the dogs closely flanking him as before. As he and Sarah stepped through, Walter turned and gave the dogs a last hard stare and they lay down with their big heads on their paws, as exhausted as he looked.

'That's not easy to do, you know,' he said, wiping his brow as they crossed the street to Friday's hiding place in the shrubbery. Sarah hoped Clifford hadn't torn her to pieces.

'I'm absolutely sure it isn't. I'm very impressed. And grateful.' She smiled and gave his hand a squeeze.

Startled, he smiled back.

Friday wasn't in pieces but Clifford nearly was, lying on her side, looking very sorry for herself, next to a pool of dog vomit reeking of aniseed.

'What did you do to her?' Walter exclaimed.

'She was mean to me,' Friday said, 'so I gave her the whole lot in one go. Did you get what you wanted?'

'Nothing,' Sarah said. 'Not a single bloody thing.'

Friday's face fell. 'Shite. What do we do now?'

Chapter Nineteen

June 1831, Sydney Town

It was Sunday afternoon and Friday, Harrie and Sarah were sitting on a rug in Hyde Park watching well-off people kitted out in expensive riding habits trot round and round the perimeter on smartly groomed horses. It had rained again that morning, though it was fine now, and the sun was drawing a light veil of mist out of the ground, spreading a shimmering mantle over the low, bare hillocks of the park.

'So, what have we got?' Friday asked, leaning to one side and scratching her bum. 'The damp's coming through this rug.'

Sarah glanced over her shoulder to make sure no one else was close enough to overhear, raised a fist and flicked up a finger. 'One scared-shitless crook.' Another finger. 'Nothing to prove he stole those heads from Bella, or even that he was directly involved in bringing them across the Tasman for her. My money's on her keeping all her really important papers somewhere they'll never be found.' She paused. 'Or maybe she doesn't document that side of the business at all. I wouldn't.' And finally her ring finger. 'One husband — mine — we have to get out of Port Macquarie as soon as possible.'

'You know, I really was worried he'd leave after Molly,' Harrie said. 'I was so sure he would.'

Sarah shook her head. 'Lucky for us he's such a greedy bastard. Anyone else would have run a mile.'

'She was good, wasn't she?' Friday smiled at the memory of Molly's grotesque, rice-flour-caked face.

'I know we only have hearsay about him cheating Bella,' Sarah said, 'but it's *accurate* hearsay, and he'll know it when we confront him with it because he's guilty.'

Friday nodded. 'It'll rattle him.'

'It has to more than bloody rattle him. It has to make him *confess*.'

'What if it doesn't work?' Harrie said.

Sarah turned on her. 'Then Adam'll rot in gaol for the next five years, won't he? Why do you always have to be such a doom-monger?'

'Stop it, Sarah,' Friday said. 'That's not going to help.'

Sarah's shoulders slumped and she touched Harrie's knee. 'Sorry, love. It's just that I'm —'

'I know,' Harrie soothed. 'It's all right.'

'You're right, though. What if it doesn't work? It *has* to work.'

'Well, hang on,' Friday said slowly. 'You just said he's scared shitless of Rachel, so he must think she's real. What if we tell him *she's* told us he pinched Bella's heads, and that we'll tell Bella if he doesn't sign the confession. Rachel'd know that sort of thing, being dead herself.'

Sarah stared at Friday for a full minute, then her pale face broke into an enormous smile, as though the sun had come out. 'Friday?'

'What?'

'That might just be the best idea you've ever had.'

'Really?' Friday was delighted.

Nibbling a fingernail, Harrie looked worried. 'I'm not sure if it works like that, if spirits can know those sorts of things. I don't know if Rachel —'

With as much patience as she could muster, Sarah took Harrie's hand and said very gently, 'I don't know if it works like that either, but will you please, just for now, pretend that it does? For me? So Adam can come home?'

Reluctantly, Harrie nodded.

Friday let out a breath she hadn't realised she'd been holding. 'Good. Shall we go with that, then?'

'Yes, and I want to confront him tonight,' Sarah said. 'There's no point putting it off. And I'd like you both with me. Can you get away?'

Harrie and Friday nodded. Harrie added, 'But not until about half past six. I told Nora I'd help her get a gown cut out later today, even though it's my day off. It's an urgent order. Is that all right? I'm sorry, I didn't know. But I promise I'll come.'

'Of course it's all right.' Sarah squeezed Harrie's hand. 'As long as you're there.' She reached for Friday's hand, too. 'As long as you're both there. I really don't think I can do this by myself.'

Sarah had just finished washing the supper dishes when Friday stuck her head round the kitchen door. As usual, she'd come in through the backyard gate. Sarah could smell alcohol on her breath, but she wasn't mashed, just a little bright-eyed. She was probably nervous. So was Sarah.

'All set? He's not gone out, has he?'

'He's at the table, reading the paper.'

'Harrie here yet?'

Sarah shook her head. 'I hope she doesn't change her mind.'

'She won't. She won't let you down, Sarah. You know that.'

'I know. I know she won't.'

Friday glanced over her shoulder. 'Speak of the devil.'

Harrie appeared in the doorway, puffing slightly, her hair escaping from beneath her bonnet. 'Sorry I'm late. I had to run all the way.'

'You're not late, love,' Sarah replied. Suddenly her eyes filled with tears. She dabbed them away with the hem of her apron.

'All right?' Friday asked.

Sarah nodded.

'Good girl. So, are we doing this?' Friday went on. ''Cos if we are, we should just get in there, no mucking about.'

The nervous tension buzzing through them was as discomfiting as it had been the night they'd followed Gabriel Keegan along Phillip Street, but this evening, although there would be no killing, the stakes were higher. Then, their motivation had been revenge — now, they were desperate to secure Adam's freedom, perhaps even his life.

Friday pulled them into an embrace and for a moment they relaxed against one another.

Then Sarah broke away, took off her apron, and led them inside to the dining room.

'Jared?' she said. 'We'd like to talk to you.'

'Yes?' He closed his paper.

His recent encounters with the supernatural entity that had taken up residence in the house were taking a visible toll. He'd lost weight, the lines of his face now sharp and angular, and his previously energetic curls lay limp against his skull. Instead of the handsome, confident man he'd been when he'd arrived, he was now beginning to resemble a hungry fox; but one that would *not* let go of the little bird clamped in its jaws. He was wary, too — of every noise, creak and sigh the house made, as though something might lie in wait for him around each corner and in the depths of every murky shadow.

The girls took seats around the table.

Sarah said, 'I have something to tell you, Jared, about Rachel. Well, *from* Rachel, actually.'

'Yes?' Jared said again, but much more cautiously this time.

Something made a scratching sound at the window and he started badly. The sun had set but a ribbon of ruby light remained on the horizon; he rose and drew the curtains against it, turning up all the lamps in the room as he returned to his chair.

'When we were transported here,' Sarah said, 'there was a convict on our ship named Bella Jackson. She's known here as Bella Shand.'

A tiny flicker of recognition in Jared's eyes, quickly pinched out.

'Do you know her?' Friday asked.

'I've heard the name.'

Sarah continued. 'Well, we certainly know who she is, and so did Rachel.'

Jared made a circling, 'get on with it' motion with a limp hand. 'And?'

'Rachel sees a lot of things, Jared. Doesn't she, Harrie?'

'She exists in two different dimensions, you see,' Harrie explained. 'And when she isn't here, she's with the others. She's with the dead.'

An uneasy look from Jared. 'What's this got to do with Bella Shand?'

Friday ignored the question. 'And sometimes some of those dead folk are upset because they've been disturbed. Someone might have, let's say, stolen their bodies, or even just parts of their bodies? And they might want them back.'

Jared went very still.

Sarah let the silence spin out like a long line of silk from a busy spider. Finally, she leant forwards. 'Rachel knows, Jared. She knows you stole those heads off Bella.'

Jared's lips went white and a tic started in his left eye. 'You're mad. I did no such thing. I don't know what you're talking about.'

'You brought a shipment of tattooed heads back from New Zealand for Bella and kept four of them to sell yourself.'

'I did not.' The flesh on Jared's face seemed to have shrunk even tighter over his bones, just like one of the heads he'd stolen.

'Rachel says you did.'

'Prove it.'

'We don't have to. I'm sure Bella will. When we tell her.'

Friday shook her head ruefully. 'She'll be *roaring* when she finds out you played the crooked cross on her. Dearie me, I'm glad I'm not walking in your boots.'

'Oh.' Jared sat back in his seat, eyes narrowing. 'Oh, I understand now, you trio of conniving bloody bitches.'

'Sticks and stones, Jared,' Friday remarked.

'This is extortion, isn't it?'

'Well done.' Sarah did a couple of slow hand claps.

'In exchange for you not informing Bella Shand about this *alleged* theft, you want me to ... what? What *do* you want?' Jared glared at Sarah.

'I want a confession from you in writing,' Sarah said, returning the glare just as forcefully, 'stating clearly that you framed Adam. Because you did, didn't you? You set him up.'

Another scraping noise came at the window, but this time Jared didn't seem to hear it. Though Harrie did.

Jared shrugged, as though fabricating an associate's complicity in a crime was all in a day's work. 'And if I do, you'll keep your counsel? All of you? About everything?'

Sarah nodded.

He rubbed his forehead with his fingertips, stared unseeingly ahead for several moments, then muttered, 'Get me paper and a pen.'

Sarah fetched from the chiffonier a sheet of paper and a nib in a holder, lay them before Jared, and stood at his side.

'And it will all end with this?' he asked.

'You have our word.'

He scribbled quite a lengthy sentence. Over his shoulder Sarah read: *I confess that I, Jared Gellar, planted a coral brooch at the premises of Adam Green, George Street, then anonymously informed the Sydney Constabulary that Adam Green had received said brooch as stolen property.*

Her heart almost in her mouth, Sarah shot a glance at Friday and Harrie, then demanded, 'Now sign it.'

Jared put down the pen. 'No. Fuck you, I won't. I don't trust you.'

An almighty rattling and scratching came at the window: Sarah, Friday and Jared all cried out in alarm and turned towards the racket.

Only Harrie remained calm. She crossed to the window and drew back the curtains. Outside, its wings beating wildly against the glass, hovered a bat. Its belly was covered with pale fur and in its sharp-eared head glittered round, intelligent eyes.

Harrie grasped the bottom of the sash and thrust it up.

'*No!*' Jared shouted, and dashed for the door into the hallway.

But Friday gave him a shove, knocking him into the chiffonier. Emitting a furious, high-pitched chittering, the bat launched itself up off the windowsill and flapped clumsily into the dining room, its wings — two feet from tip to tip — brushing the wall and the ceiling. It tumbled, tried to gain height, hit the wall again and flapped over Jared, who shrieked and struck out at it. The thing retaliated, tearing at his scalp with the sharply curved claws on its feet. He ducked and flailed wildly but it dropped again, raking his face this time, then landed on the table where it came to rest on its belly, wings half folded and pointed elbows raised, staring beadily at him.

Then, to Sarah's appalled fascination, it began to drag itself towards him, bony, membrane-covered arms working, mouth agape to reveal sharp little teeth, that ear-piercing chittering filling the room again.

As blood poured down his face and soaked into his collar, Jared snatched up the pen, scribbled his signature on his confession, made a break for the back door and wrenched it open. They heard him tear down the yard to the gate, the rattle of the bolt as he wrestled with it, an echoing slam as the gate flew open and bounced off the fence, and then ... nothing.

'Well,' Harrie said, looking around the dishevelled room.

A picture had fallen off the wall, a pair of candlesticks and a vase lay on the floor, the vase in a dozen pieces, and blood had spattered across the wallpaper above the chiffonier and onto the dining table, a few garnet-red drops on the confession letter.

The bat gave a single chirrup.

Harrie gathered it carefully in her hands and carried it to the window. 'Time to go,' she said, and launched it into the air. 'Take care!'

The creature flapped its wings, found the evening breeze and rode upwards in ever-increasing spirals until it disappeared from view.

'Was that ...? Oh my Christ,' Friday said in an extremely shaky voice.

'Perhaps I shouldn't have opened the window,' Harrie said with a tiny smile. 'Bats will get into everything if you're not careful.'

Sarah sat down at the table and burst into tears.

The next morning Sarah rose with the sun, filled the copper, lit the fire beneath it, and cleared out Jared's room. She hauled his trunk down from the top of the clothes press, helped herself to one or two of his papers, and filled it with everything else of his she could find. She dragged the trunk downstairs, bumping heavily on every step, and outside to the back porch. That way, if he came back for his things, he'd have no reason to enter the house.

Then she stripped his bed, threw everything into the copper, and scoured the room from floorboards to ceiling. The more she scrubbed, the better she felt. At nine o'clock, she put a sign on the door saying the shop would be closed for the day. She had more to do today than just wash away the grubby vestiges of Jared Gellar's presence.

At a little after ten she changed into one of her better dresses, brushed her hair, chose a decent bonnet, locked the house and set off up George Street for the police office. On the spur of the moment, she reversed direction completely and headed for Harrington Street to ask Friday to come with her. She'd been determined to do this by herself, but now that the time had come she wasn't sure she could. She needed her friends with her.

Friday, of course, agreed.

In the yard behind the Siren's Arms, she remarked as she fiddled with the ribbon on her hat, 'But I hope we don't have to stand in a bloody queue all day. I have to start work at one. If it takes ages, shall I see if Harrie can get away? One of us should be with you, eh?' She gave Sarah's hand a squeeze.

The gate leading to the brothel opened, and Elizabeth emerged. 'Good morning, girls. Going shopping?'

Sarah and Friday exchanged a glance.

'Oh dear,' Elizabeth said. 'Do I want to know?'

'Can I tell her?' Friday asked Sarah.

'Might as well. It's no secret.'

Grinning hugely, Friday said, 'We got Jared the Bastard Gellar to sign a confession last night, admitting he framed Adam.'

'Oh, well done! Should I ask how you managed that?'

'Probably not,' Sarah replied. The less said about the previous night's odd climax the better.

Friday said, 'So we're off to petition Captain Rossi.'

Elizabeth looked both thoughtful and amused. 'Fancy that. As it happens, I know Francis Rossi rather well. Not in a biblical sense, of course — I'm far too old for that these days — but I have had business dealings with him.'

'What sort of business dealings?' Friday waggled her eyebrows.

'Confidential, and staying that way. But can I suggest it could be to your advantage, Sarah, and certainly to your man's, if I came with you? Would that be acceptable to you?'

It most definitely would be — Sarah shared a grin with Friday.

Half an hour later they arrived in the gloomy waiting room outside Captain Rossi's office, crammed, as predicted, with folk hoping to petition the police magistrate for clemency — or at least leniency — on behalf of husbands, wives, offspring and lovers currently snagged in the cogs of the colony's judicial system. Someone had brought with them a crate of chickens, whose incessant squawking was doing nothing to lessen the din.

'Christ, we'll be here for bloody ever,' Friday grumbled.

'We will not.' Elizabeth patted the auburn curls peeking from beneath her smart hat and approached a window in the wall, behind which stood a young clerk, his head down as he perused some documents.

'Excuse me, good morning,' Elizabeth announced.

'One moment, I'm busy,' the clerk responded through the grille, not bothering to look up.

Sarah glanced at Elizabeth, whose lips were now clamped in a straight line paralleling her narrowed eyes. That had been a mistake.

Elizabeth said, 'Do you not value your job, young man?'

Finally, the clerk raised his head. 'Pardon?'

'Captain Rossi is a personal friend of mine. I don't imagine he'll be overly pleased to discover what a rude pup he has out here embodying his public face. Do you?'

The boy rolled his eyes at the waiting crowd: it hardly mattered what a roomful of criminals' relatives thought.

Elizabeth nailed him with a terrible glare. Gone was the attractive, cuddly, mother figure Sarah knew; here instead was the hard-faced, iron-willed businesswoman who'd built up a chain of brothels in London, survived transportation, then clawed out a very comfortable life for herself in Sydney. The full transformation was perhaps somewhat wasted on this smart-arsed boy, but still a treat to see.

He swallowed audibly. 'How may I be of service?'

'That's better. We need to see the captain immediately. Please arrange it.'

He consulted his list. 'May I have your name, please?'

'Mrs Elizabeth Hislop, on behalf of Mr Adam and Mrs Sarah Green.'

'He's with someone at the moment, but you can go in next.'

Friday elbowed Sarah and smirked.

'Thank you, young man. I appreciate your assistance.' Elizabeth produced a card from her reticule and slipped it through the gap beneath the grille. 'This is the address of my establishment. Please feel welcome to visit, with my compliments. Just the once, of course.'

The clerk's face reddened as he realised what he was being offered, but he tucked the card carefully into a pocket all the same.

They didn't have to wait long. Francis Rossi's office was reasonably spacious and comfortably furnished. He himself was in late middle-age with a crest of silver-white hair brushed back from his forehead and matching muttonchops, and was quite a striking-looking man.

'Elizabeth! How delightful to see you!' he said, coming out from behind his desk to take her hand. 'Not in trouble with the law, I hope?' he added, smiling at his little joke. She operated a brothel, a fact of which he was clearly aware, an activity just as illegal in New South Wales as it was in England.

He was a Frenchman born in Corsica, and Sarah had to listen to his odd accent carefully. She looked at Friday, who shrugged. Apparently, however, Elizabeth understood him perfectly.

'Please, do take a seat,' Captain Rossi said as he returned to his own.

They all sat, on uncomfortable, ladder-backed wooden chairs clearly designed to encourage people to get off them and leave Rossi's office as quickly as possible.

'What can I do for you? I take it you are here on business?'

'We are,' Elizabeth replied. 'Sarah? Would you care to explain to Captain Rossi what has happened?'

Sarah's mouth was suddenly bone dry and her belly felt oddly hollowed out. So much depended on the next few minutes. If Rossi accepted Gellar's confession, Adam could be on his way home in as little as a week. If he rejected it, she had no idea what to do next. She just couldn't *bear* to think of Adam languishing in gaol hundreds of miles away for the next five years. She fought back tears and cleared her throat. To her horror a big lump of phlegm came up. Desperate to spit it out but knowing she couldn't, she swallowed instead, suppressing a shudder as she felt it slide down.

Devoid of all her usual confidence, she hesitantly recounted the background to Adam's arrest. Halfway through Rossi waved his hand, saying he recalled the court case. It hadn't been that long ago, after all. So she focused on her suspicion that Jared Gellar had framed her husband and operated in tandem with Augustus Evans to see him convicted. She told Rossi she'd simply put it to Gellar that he'd planted the brooch for the purposes of taking over Adam's business, leaving out everything to do with Rachel, and Bella, and certainly last night's episode with the bat, and that he'd confessed. She produced Gellar's scrawled confession and passed it to the captain.

He read it carefully. 'What are these brown marks? Surely they are not blood? Where is this Gellar person now?'

'It is blood, but it's mine,' Sarah replied quickly. 'I nicked my finger slicing a loaf. I haven't seen Jared Gellar since last night, after he wrote that.'

'How do I know this is Gellar's own hand and not a forgery?'

Sarah whipped a document from her reticule and placed it on the captain's desk. 'These are papers certifying he paid customs duty on an inbound cargo at the end of last year.' It had been the *only* evidence she'd been able to find among his papers demonstrating he'd paid import tax of any kind. 'See the stamp and the Customs officer's signature at the bottom? They're genuine. And that's Gellar's signature there. It matches the signature on the confession, and the rest of the writing in general.'

Rossi studied the papers, then gave her a long, measured look. Finally he asked Elizabeth, 'Is this all true?'

'I wasn't present last night when Gellar wrote his confession, but I can attest that, as a master, his conduct was extremely unbecoming towards Mrs Green, and that word on the street suggests he did indeed frame her husband, Adam,' she replied, carefully not answering Rossi's question.

'Why did you not make a complaint against him and request to return to the Factory?' Rossi asked Sarah. 'You would have been safe from him there.'

'Why the hell should I?' Sarah replied, her spirit flaring. 'That's my husband's business he was trying to steal. That's my *husband* he framed. I wasn't going to give up!'

Then she recalled to whom she was speaking, and shut her mouth.

The captain gave her another pointed look, but all he said was, 'You do realise you will have to return to the Factory now, anyway? As a convict without a ticket of leave, you may not remain at liberty if this Gellar has absented himself, and while your husband is in gaol.'

'But what about her business?' Elizabeth asked.

'Her *husband's* business. She will have to close it.'

Sarah and Friday exchanged a dismayed glance.

'But I can't do that,' Sarah said. 'What about our customers? The good will? Our income?'

Rossi shrugged as though he was not particularly bothered, and she realised he probably wasn't. His concern was managing the constabulary and the judicial business of the town, not the commercial affairs of individual citizens. And Sarah wasn't even a citizen. She was a convict.

'The confession, Francis,' Elizabeth prompted.

He read it again. 'Yes, I will consider it.'

Elizabeth persisted. 'And you'll consider it in a favourable light? Oh, but of course you will. I am, after all, aware of how very generous you can be when the mood takes you.'

His head remained bowed, unmoving. For a moment he was very still.

Then he met her eye. 'You understand, Elizabeth, that this would mean all favours have been called in and all debts repaid?'

'I accept that.'

Sarah realised she was holding her breath.

He nodded, satisfied. 'Then I will authorise the release of Adam Green from Port Macquarie penitentiary as soon as possible. And the arrest of this Jared Gellar.'

Sarah slumped forwards on her chair, put her head in her hands and closed her eyes.

Dimly, she heard the captain add, 'But you, Mrs Green, must go back to the Factory until your husband's return.'

Friday and Sarah stood on the street outside Bella's house. As always, the dogs were watching, snouts pushed against the railings of the carriage gates, strings of spit dangling from slack jaws. But they weren't going in that way — today they intended knocking on the small side door at the other end of the building.

'Ready?' Friday asked.

'As I'll ever be.'

'I hope Gellar's found himself somewhere clever to hide.'

'Do you?'

'Not really.'

Friday tugged at the hem of her jacket and straightened her hat, and they crossed Clarence Shand's manicured lawn, rounded the end of the house and knocked on the low door recessed into a tiny porch. Clearly it was a tradesman's entrance — the knocker was nothing fancy and the door itself was on the street side of the wrought-iron fence, so that anyone using it wouldn't be torn to shreds by the dogs.

Nothing happened. Sarah knocked again, harder this time.

Eventually they heard footsteps, the squeak of bolts shifting, and Becky Hoddle opened the door. She remarked, 'You've got a cheek, coming here.'

Friday said, 'Nice to see you, too, Becky. We want to speak to Bella.'

'Have you got an appointment?'

'No, we haven't got a bloody appointment.'

'Then no, you can't. She's busy.'

'It's business, Becky,' Sarah said. 'Can you go and get her?'

Becky dithered, clearly debating whether to do as they'd asked or slam the door in their faces and risk Bella's wrath if what they had to say was in fact important. 'Hold on.' She pushed the door onto the latch and disappeared.

Back a minute later she said, 'She says you're to come in.'

Friday and Sarah followed her through the house and into the parlour both girls had already seen. Bella was at her desk, writing in a ledger. Christ, Friday thought, doesn't she do anything *but* work? And blackmail people and drive around town in that gig of hers scaring the shit out of folk? All her bitter rancour for the woman rose up as a hard, sour lump in her throat and she felt her face grow warm as she struggled to contain her temper.

Bella put down her pen. 'You can go, Becky.'

Becky left.

'What do you want?'

Same rude bloody cow. Friday bit back a smart reply. And still wearing too much make-up, and *still* as skinny as a rake, if not skinnier. God, how did she stay alive with so little meat on her bones? The veins on her hands stuck out like blue worms against her white skin and her weasel eyes were huge black pits ringed with kohl. Her clothes, though, were gorgeous, the bitch.

'To make a deal,' Friday said bluntly.

Bella snorted a laugh. 'Then I won't offer you a seat. You won't be here long enough.'

'We don't want to pay you any more extortion money,' Sarah said. 'We have information we think you might find useful. We're willing to exchange it for an end to you blackmailing us.'

'Give me the information and I'll think about it.'

Friday snorted this time. 'Fuck off. How barmy do you think we are?'

Bella sat back and raised her eyebrows.

Ignoring the implied insult, Sarah said, 'It doesn't work like that. You give us your word there'll be no more blackmail demands, and we'll give you the information.'

'All right. I give you my word,' Bella said.

Friday said, 'I don't believe you.'

'No.' Bella smiled unpleasantly, revealing long, yellowing teeth. 'And so you shouldn't.'

'Suit yourself, then.' Friday shrugged. 'Don't hear what we've got to say. But that's no way to get ahead, is it? Or *four* heads, to be precise.'

The smile disappeared from Bella's face. She sat forwards again. 'Are you referring to my upoko tuhi?'

'Yours?' Friday said. 'They're not yours if you stole them in the first place. *And* it's illegal to traffic in them now. As I'm sure you know.'

'What information do you have?' Bella asked, addressing Sarah.

Sarah studied her for a moment. 'Do we have a deal?'

Bella reached for a sheet of paper, dipped her pen into a silver and cut-crystal inkwell, wrote a sentence, and handed it over.

Sarah and Friday both read, *I, Bella Shand, do state that I will no longer require Friday Wolfe, Harrie Clark or Sarah Morgan to compensate me in relation to the matter that occurred in 1830.* She'd also signed and dated it.

Very clever, Friday thought. They could never take that to the police as evidence of blackmail — it didn't mean anything. As if they ever would, though: they'd have to admit to why they were being blackmailed.

'Good enough for you?' Bella asked.

It was as good as they were going to get, and Friday and Sarah both knew it. Sarah nodded.

'I'll ask again, then. What information do you have?'

Sarah gave Friday the satisfaction of answering.

'Jared Gellar stole your heads, and sold them to collectors in England. Go and talk to Eli Chattoway. He might be able to give you a few more details.'

If it was at all possible, Bella's skin turned even paler. The white rice powder on her face actually seemed faintly yellow now, and above and below her silk scarf the cords on her neck were sticking out like the roots of a Moreton Bay fig. Her nostrils flared and her fists in her lap were clenched; she looked as though she was about to explode.

Sarah raised Bella's note. 'How do we know you'll honour this?'

'You have my word. Becky!'

Becky Hoddle appeared immediately.

'These two are leaving. See them out.'

Just before Becky closed the door on them, Friday and Sarah heard Bella roar, '*Furniss!!*'

'I'm not going back to the Factory,' Sarah said, 'and that's the end of it.'

Harrie was worried. She'd ducked up to Sarah's after she'd finished helping Nora with the midday meal, to see how she was getting on. 'But what if Captain Rossi tells the Principal Superintendent? What if they actually come and arrest you? Won't that make it even worse?'

'Grab the end of this, will you?' Sarah passed Harrie the corner of a sheet, and together they draped it over the washing line and pegged it.

'Sarah? What will you do?'

Sarah grinned. 'Wait and see what happens. It doesn't matter. Everything's good now and Adam'll be home any day.'

'But will he? It could take weeks to get him out. Perhaps even months.'

'God, Harrie, you're such a worrywart!'

'I know. But that doesn't change the fact you're supposed to be assigned, and at the moment you're not. You'll get into terrible trouble.' Harrie sighed in exasperation: Sarah was in such a jubilant mood and wasn't listening to anything. 'And where do *you* think Gellar is? What do you think will happen to him?'

'Who the hell cares? Good riddance to the bastard.'

Harrie had noted the trunk on the back porch and wondered why he hadn't come back for his things. But he was probably on the run, hoping to avoid arrest — and now, of course, Bella Jackson. Friday said no doubt he was on a ship halfway back to England by now.

When they'd talked about doing a deal with Bella involving what they knew about Gellar, Harrie had initially felt uneasy. They'd given him their word after all, and they'd double-crossed him almost immediately. But if he had left the colony, their arrangement with Bella couldn't result in any nasty repercussions for him. He would never return to New South Wales, either, because he'd always be wanted by the police, so as far as she, Harrie, had been concerned, giving his name to Bella to end the blackmail had turned out to be relatively painless. It hadn't been Gellar she'd been concerned for, because she'd loathed him — it was herself. She never liked to go back on her word, no matter to whom she gave it, but above all she didn't want the blood from another death staining her conscience. She couldn't bear that happening all over again. She was feeling better now, quite a bit better, and she desperately wanted to stay feeling that way.

Sarah was looking at her. She was frowning slightly and had

two clothes pegs sticking out of her mouth, which reminded Harrie of a picture she'd seen once of a walrus.

'What?' Harrie asked.

'The other night, when the bat came, did you know that was going to happen?'

'Not until I heard the scratching noises at the window,' Harrie said truthfully. 'Then I did wonder.'

'Wonder what?'

'I ... just wondered.'

Sarah bent to pick up a pillowslip. 'Was it a wild bat?'

'Well, I don't know any tame ones. Do you?'

'No, I mean, was it ...' Sarah pegged the linen, then shook her head as though trying to dislodge an unwelcome thought. 'Never mind. It all worked out in the end, didn't it?'

Harrie agreed it definitely had. 'Have you asked Bernard Cole if you can be temporarily assigned to him?'

'No, but that wouldn't work anyway.'

'Why not? He might come and stay here.'

'He's away on business for the next few weeks.'

'You're just saying that.'

'I'm not.'

Harrie didn't believe her. Matthew, perhaps? she wondered. Would he agree to live at Sarah's house for a short while? 'There must be something we can arrange.'

'There's no need. He'll be home in no time, just you wait and see.'

The following day Sarah received a letter from Police Magistrate Captain Francis Rossi informing her that the formal process that would culminate in the quashing of Adam's conviction for receiving stolen goods had begun. He would be released from the convict penitentiary at Port Macquarie as soon as this process had been completed, in approximately a month's time, and passage would be secured for him aboard a ship bound for Sydney. The whereabouts of Jared Gellar was currently being sought.

Sarah screwed the letter into a tight ball and threw it across the shop. It bounced off the wall then rolled under the cabinet displaying watches and snuff boxes.

A month! A month was a bloody *eternity* away!

Harrie chose a pear, squeezed it, frowned when her thumb sank immediately into the overripe flesh, then selected another. This one was better — firmer, and its fragrance was delicious. How you could get hard, and perfectly ripe, and near-rotten pears in the same bin, and be asked to pay the same (overinflated) price for them all, she didn't know.

'You buying, or just mauling 'em to death?' the costermonger demanded.

'I wouldn't have to "maul" them, as you so colourfully put it,' Harrie shot back, 'if I could trust that they were all of the same high quality. But they so obviously are not.'

'Don't blame me, blame them bloody farmers out at Parramatta. Not enough rain, too much rain, too many possums, birds, worms, aphids, you name it.'

'Possums aren't responsible for pears picked too early.'

The man heaved a sigh. 'You want any or not?'

'Yes, I'll have this half dozen, thank you.'

Harrie paid and moved through the shed to the vegetable stalls, where she selected a cabbage, a bunch each of spinach and silverbeet, a bright orange pumpkin (though not a really big one as she had to cart it all the way down to Gloucester Street), carrots and a swede, much of which would go into a soup for tomorrow. She'd stop in at her favourite butcher for beef bones on her way home.

She left the markets via the George Street exit and headed off, her loaded basket hooked over her arm. Glancing across the street, she glimpsed James and quickly looked away, hoping he hadn't seen her.

But he had: she heard him calling out to her. Damn. She kept walking.

And then he was beside her, a hand under her elbow.

'Harrie, stop, please.'

She looked at the ground, saying nothing.

'I wanted to see you. I need to know how you are,' he said.

'Am I still mad in the head, do you mean?' she said, and wasn't sure why. She wasn't even angry with him any more. He'd only been trying to help. Of course he wasn't going to understand about Rachel — he was a man of science, not supernaturalism.

'I never said that, Harrie. And I never would. I care about you very much. Surely you must know that by now.'

This was an uncharacteristically revealing and personal thing for James to say, and it made Harrie distinctly uncomfortable. She felt herself blushing. 'Shouldn't you be at your surgery?' she asked, trying to change the subject.

'I have to see my tailor. New shirts.'

'Oh.' Say something else! she thought. Anything. 'Sarah's husband is coming home. His conviction's being quashed.'

James's fair eyebrows went up. 'Well, that's good news, isn't it?'

And Harrie had an idea.

'James, would you do something for me? A favour? It's quite a big one.'

'For you?'

She nodded. Then, without even asking what the favour was or what it might cost him — which was utterly contrary to the cautious and measured James she knew — he said yes.

And something in her shifted.

On the pretext of helping him pack, Harrie went with James to his little house on York Street, delighted at last to have a legitimate excuse to see where he lived. His new shirts, he said, would have to wait another day. She wondered if Rowie Harris would be there, and felt exceedingly prickly at the prospect of seeing her again. But of course she'd be there. That was her job.

James's house, or rather cottage, turned out to be rather sweet. Someone had spent a good few hours in the garden — probably not James; according to him his wife had been the one with green thumbs — which contained tidily pruned camellias, daphnes and lavender, and fuchsias peeping from shaded corners like rubies and amethysts on holly-green velvet.

When they arrived Rowie Harris was standing at the table in the main room up to her elbows in flour, a smudge on the end of her adorable little nose.

'Dr Downey!' she exclaimed. 'What are you doing home?'

What a cheeky question, Harrie thought. This is James's house, not yours.

'Rowie,' James said. 'Have you met my friend Harriet Clarke? Harrie, this is Rowie Harris, my maid of all work, I suppose you'd call her.'

'Yes, we have met, at George Street market. Lovely to see you again, Rowie,' Harrie lied.

Rowie extended a floury hand, then changed her mind. 'You, too, Harrie.'

'Well, I'd better hurry up,' James said. 'I need to get back to work shortly. Rowie, where's my small trunk, do you know?'

'Why? Where are you going?' Rowie sounded alarmed.

'To stay at the home of Harrie's friend Sarah Green while her husband is away. She's assigned to him and doesn't want to go back to the Factory, so I'll be supervising her until he returns.'

'Oh.' Rowie tugged at the ties on her apron. 'Well, wait for me. It'll only take me a minute to get my things together.'

Harrie said, 'What for? You don't need to come.'

Rowie stared at her, her floury fingers touching her throat. 'But who'll look after Dr Downey?'

'Sarah will,' Harrie replied. 'She's very capable.'

'But I do everything for him.'

I bet you do, Harrie thought, a wave of jealousy crashing through her. 'You won't be needed, thank you, Rowie.'

'James?' Rowie said, gazing at him pleadingly.

James, James, bloody *James*! Harrie felt her jaw clench.

'I could cook all your favourite meals,' Rowie wittered on. 'And do your laundry just the way you like it.'

James was embarrassed now. 'Really, Rowie, I know Sarah Green quite well, and I'm sure she runs a perfectly comfortable house. And it will only be for a month or so. Why don't you make the most of my absence and have some time to yourself? Visit with friends, perhaps? Now, I really must pack.' And he hurried into his bedroom and shut the door before she could protest any further.

Rowie turned back to her baking, picking up a mound of dough and slamming it onto the table so violently an explosion of flour puffed into the air.

Harrie wondered what on earth was wrong with her. What an extreme reaction. It wasn't as though they were married and James had just announced he was sailing around the world for the next ten years. Was she jealous? But she didn't even know Sarah. Did she?

And what was Sarah going to say when she discovered James was to be her new master?

Harrie met James on the street outside Sarah's house at six o'clock that evening. Nora Barrett had kindly given her an hour off, and he'd arrived straight from the surgery on Pitt Street, having paid a boy to transport his trunk on a barrow.

'Are you ready?' she asked him.

'Yes, though I do wish you'd discussed this with her beforehand.'

'I couldn't. I only thought of it when I saw you today, and I didn't have time this afternoon.'

Harrie opened the shop door and went in. Sarah was at the till, cashing up.

'Hello, Harrie.' Sarah's eyes widened slightly as she noticed Harrie's companion. 'Good evening, Dr Downey.'

'Good evening, Mrs Green,' James said, removing his hat.

'Look, it's still just Sarah. I've only got married, not ascended to the throne.'

Ignoring her sarcasm, James said politely, 'I'm pleased to hear your husband will soon be home.'

'Yes. Thank you. I'm very pleased myself.'

'Have you found yourself a temporary master yet?' Harrie asked eagerly.

'No. Why?'

'Good, because I've found one for you!'

Sarah eyed her suspiciously. 'Who?'

'James! Isn't that kind of him? So now you won't have to go back to the Factory.'

Her mouth open, Sarah stared at him. 'You?'

James nodded.

'You do understand I can't stay here by myself? You'd have to live here?'

Another nod.

'But we hardly know each other.'

'Sarah, I expect we know each other rather better than do many bonded convicts and their masters at first meeting.'

This was true and Sarah couldn't deny it. 'I'm very busy in the workshop *and* with the customers. There's only me to do both jobs. So I won't have time to cook fancy meals or muck about starching shirts.'

'I'm sure your everyday cooking is more than adequate,' James replied.

'You could send your laundry home to Rowie. It would give her something to remember you by,' Harrie suggested.

'I work long hours myself,' James said. 'You're therefore unlikely to find me under your feet.'

'And I certainly won't be under yours.'

'Would it be a suitable arrangement, then, do you think?' James asked. 'Just until your husband returns?'

Slowly, Sarah nodded. 'Yes, actually, I think it might.'

James smiled, but not at her — at Harrie.

Chapter Twenty

During the third week of June, a boy arrived at Mrs Hislop's house with a note for Friday. She wasn't at work, instead spending a morning sleeping off a hard night of going around the pubs, but Elizabeth slid the note beneath her bedroom door.

When Friday finally dragged herself out of bed at midday, with the usual dreadful case of the horrors, she spied the note on the floor and her heart plummeted; she knew exactly what it was.

Slowly, with shaking hands, she broke the seal and read it.

> To Friday Wolfe, Sarah Morgan, Harrie Clark
> This time the payment is £200.
> I _know_ you can afford it.
> Go to the old burial ground on George Street at midnight on the second Sunday in July. My man will be waiting for you.
> Give the £200 to him.
> B

Friday screwed her eyes shut and roared, '_You fucking slag!!!_'

Clutching her throbbing head, she sat on the bed, the note in her lap. Bloody Bella bloody Jackson — the dog-faced, coney-catching, mutton-hawking bloody hedgewhore had double-crossed them. She'd kill her — she'd bloody *kill* her.

She read the note again, carefully this time. *Shite*. The second Sunday in July was only a few weeks away.

Someone knocked on the door.

Oh, go away.

The door knob rattled furiously. 'Friday!' Elizabeth called. 'Unlock this door.'

She trudged across the floor and turned the key. The door opened to reveal Mrs H, and Ivy from Eli Fat Toad Chattoway's house. Ivy waggled her fingers in a little wave.

'Was that you bellowing your head off?' Elizabeth snapped.

'Might have been.'

'Well, don't. It lowers the tone. Ivy's starting in the laundry today. She's replacing the girl I fired last week for pinching the soap. She wanted to come and say hello.'

And suddenly Friday grinned. 'Nice to see you, Ivy.'

Ivy returned the smile with a gap-toothed one of her own. 'Mrs Hislop's taken me on. It's all official and everything.'

'You're a sweetie, Mrs H,' Friday said, giving Elizabeth a peck on the cheek. 'Thanks.'

Elizabeth flapped a theatrical hand in front of her face. 'Honestly, Friday, you could turn milk with that breath. Run along now, Ivy. Annie will show you what to do, all right?'

Ivy dropped a quick curtsy, mouthed 'Thank you' at Friday, and trotted off towards the stairs.

Elizabeth stepped into Friday's room and closed the door. 'What were you screaming about? I could hear you down in the kitchen.'

'Nothing.'

'It was a bloody loud nothing.' Elizabeth spotted the note on Friday's bed and made a move towards it, but Friday got there first and tucked it inside her robe under her arm.

'Show me.'

'No, it's private.'

'Look, are you going to tell me what's going on?' Elizabeth demanded. 'Because I know something is. And it has been for a while, hasn't it?'

For a second Friday felt like confessing everything, but what good would it do? Nothing would change.

'I can't tell you. Really, I'm sorry, I just can't.'

'You're being blackmailed, aren't you?'

Friday felt her cheeks redden, and turned her face away.

'If it's money you need, I can help, you know,' Elizabeth said.

'I've got money. But thanks, I appreciate your offer.' Friday hesitated, then asked, 'Why are you being so kind?'

'You remind me of someone,' Elizabeth said. She examined her perfectly manicured fingernails for a long moment. 'Someone who was very dear to me.'

Friday opened her mouth to ask who, then decided Mrs H was entitled to her secrets, too. If she wanted to tell her, then one day she would.

Elizabeth lay a plump hand on Friday's arm. 'Well, I'm always here if you want to talk to me about it. Believe me, there's nothing worse than carrying the weight of a secret all by yourself.'

But Friday didn't have to suffer the burden of this secret alone, and for that she thanked God.

'What time will James be home?' Friday asked.

'I don't know,' Sarah said. 'I'm not his wife.'

'Well, where is he?'

'Still at the surgery, I expect.'

Friday had called an emergency meeting at Sarah's. She'd grabbed Harrie on the way, telling Nora it was *essential* she come out for an hour, and now here they were once again sitting around Sarah's dining table, where they seemed to have done so much of their planning, plotting and worrying. She fished Bella's latest note out of her pocket and passed it to Sarah.

She read it quickly. 'Double-crossing bitch,' she said for about the fifth time since Friday had told her. 'I knew we shouldn't have trusted her.'

'I didn't trust her,' Friday said. 'Not really. Did you?'

'What do you think? There's no honour among thieves. I should know.' Sarah gave the note to Harrie. 'Do we have the money?' she asked Friday.

'We do. And I got Matthew the other day to withdraw Janie's payment for the next few months, so that's all right. But there'll be hardly anything left.'

'How much? By my reckoning there should be about fifty pounds, after this. Is that right?'

Friday nodded. They all knew fifty pounds would be a small fortune to many, but not to three girls regularly being blackmailed, who also had three dependants in the Parramatta Female Factory.

'How does she know we can afford it?' Harrie asked.

'What?'

'She's underlined the word "know" as though she's sure of how much money we have in the bank.'

'She can't know,' Sarah said. 'Apart from us, Matthew's the only other person who knows that.'

'The bank clerks must,' Friday pointed out.

'She can't be bunging them,' Sarah said. 'Can she?'

Harrie frowned. 'How would she even know we have a bank account?'

Sarah turned to Friday. 'You haven't told anyone, have you?'

'Why the hell would I?'

'More to the point, would you remember?'

'No need to be snarky. Of course I haven't bloody well told anyone. Oh shite.'

Sarah pounced. 'What?'

'Well, it was Mrs H who gave me the idea of us having a bank account. We were talking about it in her office. But I can't remember if I said anything about how much money we have.' And she really couldn't.

'And?' Sarah prompted.

'She might have been listening at the door.'

'Who?'

'Lou. I *told* you she's been spying on me. I'm bloody *sure* she's working for Bella.'

'More likely Bella's made a shrewd guess,' Sarah said. 'She runs a brothel, she'll have a good idea of how much money you make. Christ, she's probably managed to find out how much Adam and *I* earn. Though I bloody hope not. She'll be blackmailing us for that next.'

They lapsed into silence until Harrie laid the note on the table, gave it a little push so it skated away from her and said in a deflated-sounding voice, 'I thought this was all behind us.'

Friday gave her a genuinely sympathetic look. 'Did you?'

'No, I suppose not. Not really.'

'It was worth trying,' Sarah said. 'It did all seem a bit easy, didn't it? The lying cow.'

'We're back where we started, aren't we?' Harrie said.

'Well, no.' Friday folded the note and stuck it in her pocket. 'We got rid of Gellar and Adam's coming home. Have you heard anything, Sarah?'

Sarah scowled. 'No, I bloody haven't. Rossi said it would be a month and the month's not quite up yet. If I could I'd be down at the wharf every day to meet the ships but I can't leave the shop.'

'When's Bernard back?'

'In a few days, I think.'

'How are you getting on with James?' Harrie asked.

Sarah's face relaxed. 'Actually, quite well. Better than I expected. He's a lot less fussy than I thought he would be. I thought he'd have to have his sausages all lined up on the plate half an inch apart facing in the same direction and his handkerchiefs folded into perfectly symmetrical squares and all the rest of it, but he's not like that at all. And he does a lot of things for himself. Comes from being in the navy, I suppose. Thoughtful, too. He seems to know when I don't feel like talking.' She blushed and started to smirk.

In anticipation Friday giggled, too.

'The other night he was having a bath in front of the fire in the parlour. I forgot and barged in to get my mending and there he was standing in a foot of water in all his glory. I nearly died and so did he.'

Friday shrieked with laughter.

'You,' Sarah said, pointing at Harrie, 'don't know what you're missing.'

'Don't be coarse,' Harrie said.

'And you stop being so stubborn and stupid. The man's really quite spectacular. Mind you, I didn't see him for two days after that. Went out early and came home late he was that embarrassed.'

Friday was still tittering as she walked home along Harrington Street. Things *were* looking up, in spite of the fact Bella had made another blackmail demand. Harrie and James were talking again, Sarah was tolerating James living in her house surprisingly well and so far her sarcastic tongue hadn't driven him back to his own cottage, and surely it couldn't be much longer before Adam himself arrived home.

There had been no sign of Jared Gellar. His trunk still sat on Sarah's porch, the ends of the leather straps beginning to curl. If he had any sense he *would* be on a ship halfway to England, though she had no idea if he was or not. She'd only said that to Harrie so she wouldn't feel guilty about dobbing him in to Bella.

Two days later Sarah received another letter, from, according to the script on the outside of the folded and sealed sheet of paper, the

Office of Captain Francis Rossi, Superintendent of Police and Police Magistrate.

She tore open the seal and read:

> *Dear Mrs Green,*
>
> *It is with great pleasure that I inform you of your Husband's release from Port Macquarie Convict Penitentiary forthwith. I have requested that the Commandant of the penitentiary, Captain Henry Smyth, be kind enough to arrange your Husband's passage back from Port Macquarie to Sydney on the next available ship.*
>
> *Yours Faithfully,*
>
> *Captain F. Rossi*

Feeling light-headed and sick with relief, she crouched on the floor in the centre of the shop, her palms pressed against the tiles for balance, the rest of the post forgotten.

'Sarah? Are you all right?'

She glanced up, her head swimming, to see James standing over her.

'He's coming home, James. I just … I couldn't be better.' And she burst into tears — this was happening to her a lot these days.

James took her elbow and helped her to the stool behind the counter. She sat blindly, wiped at her eyes with her sleeve and thrust the letter at him.

He read it, and nodded. 'I'm very pleased for you both, Sarah, I really am. Decent of them to ship him back.'

'They shouldn't have sent him there in the first place!'

'No, quite. But you should try not to think about that now. He's coming home, that's the main thing.'

'God, are you ever anything *but* sensible?' Sarah said.

'I volunteered to cohabit with you, didn't I?'

Sarah gave a crooked little smile. 'That's true.'

James glanced at the letter again. 'He could be home in four days. Perhaps even three.'

'How do you know that?' Sarah's eyes shone with hope.

'The letter is dated twenty-first of June — four days ago. If Rossi sent the letter of release by sea the same day, it will have arrived by now as I believe it takes, under fair conditions, three days and two nights to make the voyage from Sydney to Port Macquarie. Providing Adam is able to leave Port Macquarie straight away, he should arrive here on ... Wednesday, perhaps?'

'Really?' Sarah was delighted. 'Then I'll go down to the wharf tomorrow. He could be early.'

'Not that early, Sarah,' James said gently.

'Which wharf?' she asked suddenly. 'King's? Campbell's? Pitman's? Bloody Market Wharf? I can't be waiting at them all!'

'I'll make enquiries with the harbourmaster. But he really won't be back tomorrow. Monday at the very earliest, and more likely Tuesday.'

'Monday, then,' Sarah agreed grudgingly. James knew what he was talking about. But she knew the wait would be utter torture.

Monday's weather was atrocious. From the harbourmaster James had discovered that a ship could be arriving from Port Macquarie some time that day or evening — possibly earlier than expected due to the heavy winds tearing down from the north — carrying a cargo of cedar to be unloaded at Campbell's Wharf. At eight o'clock in the morning, a drenched Sarah appeared at the Siren's Arms to collect Friday, who had offered to spend her day off waiting with her.

Not accustomed to hauling herself out of bed so early, Friday nevertheless made a supreme effort for her friend, and together they staggered down to George Street into a vicious wind laced with rain as sharp as needles, hats clamped to their heads and skirts whipping around their legs. Friday was soon as soaked as Sarah.

They found themselves a pair of stools near a low window in a gloomy little pub on George Street, just past the Naval Offices, with a view of Campbell's Wharf and the wildly seething cove. Everything was grey — the sea, the sky, the buildings, the muddy streets.

Friday sipped at her gin.

'A bit early for that, isn't it?' Sarah said.

'I'm cold.'

So was Sarah, though the temperature wasn't anywhere near as freezing as that of London's. She wondered if they'd got used to the warmer weather in Australia, and grown a bit soft.

'You'll be mashed by the time he gets here,' she said.

'No I won't.'

They watched as the wind battered indignant, squawking gulls, raised waves against watermen straining mightily to reach the shore, and hurled rain into the faces of folk dashing past the window in shapeless, dripping hats, coats and cloaks.

'What shitty weather,' Friday remarked.

They had a pie each, Sarah had an ale, and Friday ordered more gin. Closer to midday the pub began to fill, the room grew warmer and smoke from other pipes added to Friday's.

Sarah didn't feel as cold now, though she still shuddered uncontrollably every few minutes — she was getting heartily sick of it. It was her nerves, grabbing her by the neck and shaking her. She should be feeling deliriously happy because her man was coming home, but she wasn't. What if he wasn't on this ship? What if a ship came in tomorrow and he wasn't on that one either? Or the one next week? What if he never came home?

'Cheer up, love,' Friday said. 'It could be worse.' She laughed. 'I said that to Harrie once, in Newgate. She went all bristly, you know the way she does sometimes? And she said, "How could it be worse?" And I said, "Well, you could be swinging."'

'I bet that helped.'

'No, actually, it didn't.' Friday's face sobered. 'You know, I was bloody sure I was for the gallows, that last time I went up in front of the magistrate.'

Sarah nodded; she'd had the same bowel-churning fear, even though her crime was no longer a hanging offence.

'But look at me now,' Friday went on. 'Look at us! This is bloody paradise compared to what we had at home. Well, not today it isn't, it's pissing down. But I'm making tons of chink working for a good boss, you're married to a decent professional man and doing what you love, and Harrie's doing her drawings and dressmaking and being chased by a man who thinks the sun rises and sets on her.'

Sarah stared at her, her face expressionless.

Friday stared back. 'On the other hand, Rachel died, I *hate* my job, Adam isn't actually back yet, Harrie's losing her mind, and we're being blackmailed by a cast-iron bitch. But you can't deny we *are* eating well.'

Sarah smiled slightly. 'That's true. I've put on weight.'

'You *had*. Now you look like a pipe-cleaner again. *I'm* the one with the arse like a beer barrel.'

'A fabulously curvaceous beer barrel, though.'

Friday put her hand on Sarah's clenched fist. 'He'll be home soon. You just have to hold on a little bit longer.'

'I know. Thanks.'

At a little after two o'clock the driving rain eased, though it didn't stop completely, and three ships sailed into the cove, one after the other. Two furled their sails — no easy task in the high wind — and dropped anchor while the third tacked closer to the western shore. By this time Sarah and Friday were standing as close to Campbell's Wharf as they could get, it being private property, holding on to their hats and squinting against the sea spray.

Two watermen swaddled in voluminous oilcloth coats launched a boat from the shore to the ship and a long cable connected to the vessel's capstan was rowed back and attached to the wharf.

The sails on the ship were furled, crewmen heaved against the capstan, and, after what felt to Sarah like hours, the ship was warped in. When the bow was almost touching the wharf, crewmen threw more ropes to waiting lumpers, who threaded them through blocks, heaved mightily and manoeuvred the ship around one hundred and eighty degrees so that at last she came to a restless, creaking halt alongside the wharf, facing out into the cove.

There was a further delay while the ship was more firmly secured, and the gangway locked into place. A man moved onto it; Sarah's heart lurched and goose bumps broke out all over her, but it wasn't Adam. Too tall.

'I'm going up,' she said to Friday.

Friday nodded. 'I'll be here.'

Sarah wrapped her saturated shawl more tightly around her shoulders and, picking her way through the mud, stepped onto the rain-sodden boards of the wharf.

One of the lumpers intercepted her. His hair was plastered to his head and he didn't look pleased to be out working in the rain. 'Sorry, missus, private property, order of Robert Campbell.'

'I know. Has this ship just come from Port Macquarie? I believe my husband is a passenger.'

'Port Macquarie yes. No passengers, but. Just crew.'

'You wouldn't know. This was a last-minute arrangement,' Sarah insisted.

'Here's another one. Bugger off.'

'Bugger off yourself. My husband's on that ship. Will you just —?'

Then Sarah caught sight of him, leaning on the rail at the top of the gangway, staring down at her.

She dodged around the lumper and sprinted along the wharf, her boots thumping on the boards and her bonnet flying off and swooping into the sea.

He met her at the bottom of the gangway and caught her in his arms and, oh God, he was very thin but it was him, it was Adam, she had him back!

Friday watched them from a distance, trying to decide whether she was happy for them, or jealous. Probably happy, given she was dabbing at tears. Or perhaps it was a bit of both. And that was all right, wasn't it?

She moved to the water's edge and poked with her soggy boot at shells washed up by the waves. Torn off the rocks or churned up from the seabed by the rough weather, perhaps? They ponged something terrible, and she wondered if some still contained their occupants, going over now they'd died. Then she noticed something else, a clump of rubbish, bobbing about just beneath the wharf in about three feet of scummy water. She wandered along the beach for a closer look.

The smell got worse, like badly gone-over meat and brine and Billingsgate fish market all mixed up together, and the clump took on a vaguely recognisable shape.

'Sarah,' Adam breathed. 'Oh my bloody God, Sarah.'

She leant back from his embrace. His skin was pale and his eyes sunken and underlined with shadow, but he was smiling.

'Oh, my love, what did they *do* to you?'

'Well, I've certainly eaten better.'

They gazed at each other, oblivious to the rain, then giggled hysterically and hugged again, hard enough to squeeze the life out of themselves.

'I missed you so much, Sarah. I'd almost given up.'

'I missed you, too. Horribly. And I thought you *had* given up. Your letter, it … made me sad. And bloody angry.'

'Five years, Sarah. It's a long time. I didn't want you to feel you had to wait for me.'

'You stupid man,' Sarah said, but she said it gently.

'Are *you* all right? You look exhausted.'

'It's been a hectic couple of months, Adam. Did you get *any* of my letters?'

'Not allowed them. Nearly broke my heart. I knew you would have written.' Adam pushed back his wet hair and wiped the rainwater out of his eyes. 'How did you get me released? The first I knew of it was the commandant telling me he had a letter from Rossi saying my conviction had been quashed. It *was* Gellar who framed me, wasn't it? How did you prove he did it? And where is he? I'll bloody well *kill* him.'

Friday shouted up to one of the lumpers, 'Oi, I think there's a floater down here!'

The man stopped what he was doing. 'What?'

'A corpse. A body, in the water.'

The man swore and fetched a boat hook. 'Show me.'

Friday did.

Wading into the sea up to his knees, the man hooked the body, tugged violently until it detached itself from the barnacle-encrusted pile on which it had become snagged, and dragged it out from beneath the wharf and up onto the wet sand.

Sarah said, 'You'll have to find him first. No one's seen him since Rachel's ghost scared him into confessing he set you up. She was, er, manifesting as a bat at the time.'

'What?' Adam looked horribly confused. 'Sarah, what on earth's been going on?'

So Sarah summarised what had occurred while he'd been away, though she left out the advances Gellar had made towards her; that would only hurt him and he would blame himself.

When she'd finished he pulled her to him and they hugged once more, but this time the embrace was less frantic, and weighted with the knowledge of how close they'd come to losing almost everything that mattered to them.

He pulled back and cupped her cheek with a cold hand. 'Thank you, Sarah. I owe you an enormous debt.'

'You don't owe me anything. I think we're even now, don't you?'

He kissed her forehead. 'Sarah, we've always been even.'

A raucous bellow floated up from the beach: *'Hey, you two lovebirds!'*

'Is that Friday down there?' Adam squinted against the rain.

They walked arm in arm to the edge of the wharf. Below them, on the sand, a small crowd had gathered around a tangled heap of rags and seaweed lying half in and half out of the water.

'What is it?' Adam asked.

Sarah shrugged. Then the wind changed direction slightly and they cursed and covered their noses.

Friday shouted, *'Come and have a look!'*

They did. The corpse was in a dreadful state. Bloated to the extent that buttons on the remaining clothing had burst and seams had ripped, the skin was bleached to a spongy, whitish-green. The corpse's dark hair lay in wet fronds across a pallid forehead and the eyeballs, parts of the lips, eyelids and nose had been nibbled away by hungry crabs and fish. As they watched, a small eel slid out of the mouth.

'Ew,' Friday said, fascinated.

In fact there were two mouths; one where you'd expect, and another gaping slash across the throat. No little sea creature had done that. The smell was appalling, now they'd got it out of the water.

'Anyone recognise him?' someone asked.

Sarah, Friday and Adam said absolutely nothing.

Friday arrived at Argyle Street feeling, and no doubt looking, like a drowned rat, but she knew Mrs H would be eager to hear how the reunion had gone. The girls would be, too. It had been the talk of the brothel. Everyone thought it was so romantic: Sarah, a lone, determined figure, waiting on the wharf in all weather for her beloved to return from exile. No matter that he'd be hopping with lice, four stone underweight and suffering the shits from the rubbish food. That wasn't the point.

She stuck her head into the parlour, noting the presence of Connie, Molly, Vivien and, unfortunately, Lou. The fire was crackling away invitingly and she was very tempted to stand in front of it, damp skirts hoisted, warming the backs of her legs.

'Is he back?' Connie asked excitedly.

Friday nodded.

The girls all clapped and hooted with delight, even Lou.

'Was it lovely? Did you cry?' Vivien demanded.

'I did.'

'Oh, that's so nice,' Connie said, watery-eyed herself. 'A happy ending.'

'Where's Mrs H?' Friday asked.

Molly said, 'Office, I think.'

Friday knocked and let herself in. 'He's back,' she said.

Elizabeth closed her ledger. 'Well, that's wonderful news, isn't it? And not too worse for wear, I hope?'

Friday made a see-saw motion with her hand. 'Nothing a few decent feeds and some time with Sarah won't fix, though. But something else a bit odd happened. When the ship docked at Campbell's it dislodged a body from under the wharf. Quite a rotten one.'

Elizabeth put down her pen. 'Whose, dare I ask? Could you tell?'

'Jared Gellar's.'

'Really?'

'His throat had been cut.'

'I can't say I'm bothered.' Elizabeth poured fine sand from a porcelain sandbox onto the fresh ink in her ledger. 'Serves him right, in fact. Poor Sarah. She was by herself in that house and he was stalking her and wearing her down and thinking he could just help himself. It just isn't right. Who did it, I wonder?'

'I don't know.' Though Friday knew *exactly* who'd killed Gellar.

'It wasn't Sarah, was it?'

'Honestly, Mrs H, what a thing to say.'

'No, you're right. He did push her, though, didn't he? But I don't suppose it matters who murdered him, as long as he's dead. All's well that ends well.'

'I bloody hope it's ended. His stuff's still mouldering on Sarah's porch, so I wouldn't be surprised to see the cops poking round.'

Elizabeth blew the excess sand off her ledger. 'Well, all I can say is bloody good riddance.'

July 1831, Sydney Town

The police did knock on Sarah and Adam's door. Someone had come forward to identify Gellar's body, and to advise them that for the past four months Mr Gellar had been living at the home of his associate Mr Adam Green, a jeweller in George Street, having agreed to manage Mr Green's jewellery business, and supervise his convict wife, while Mr Green was serving time in the penitentiary at Port Macquarie.

Sarah told them that approximately five weeks earlier, after writing a confession to the effect that he had framed her husband, Jared Gellar had left her house and had never returned for his belongings. Yes, she had been extremely shocked by his confession: no, she did not know where he'd gone after that. She had been as horrified as everyone else to learn he'd been fished out of the harbour.

And yes, since Mr Gellar had gone she'd been supervised by Dr James Downey, who had been living with her — in separate quarters, naturally — and she had the papers to prove it. As Captain Rossi — yes, *that* Captain Rossi, superintendent of police and police magistrate — had *personally* arranged for her husband's release from Port Macquarie on the grounds of unlawful conviction as the result of fraud perpetrated by another followed by unlawful imprisonment, Mr Green was now home and Dr Downey had returned to his own residence. Was there anything else she could help with? Only she didn't want Mr Gellar's belongings on her porch any longer. Would they please take them away?

Friday had just finished telling Leo all this when Harrie arrived at his shop with a set of flash she'd recently completed. Angels, this time, with bats' wings, all looking suspiciously like Rachel, and based on the very first sketch she'd done for Leo before he'd hired her. Friday, visiting Leo to begin the outline of a new tattoo to cover the scar on her calf, decided on the spot that was what she wanted.

'In that case, Harrie can draw it,' Leo said.

'On Friday's leg?' Harrie asked, startled.

'Why not?' Leo replied. 'You drew it on paper.'

'I'm not sure I can.'

'Oh, don't be such a lily liver.' Friday lay face down on the bench. 'If you go wrong just rub it off and start again.'

Harrie glanced hesitantly at Leo, who nodded. 'Go on. I have to duck out. Seem to have run out of tobacco.'

'Send Walter,' Harrie said. She could hear him in the other room, scraping dishes and sloshing things about in the washing-up basin.

'He's busy. Back soon,' Leo said cheerfully on his way out the door.

Harrie dithered for a minute, then finally asked, 'Just the outline?'

Friday nodded, her head on her arms.

'Which one?'

'Number three,' Friday said, referring to the numbers on the new series.

Harrie sat on the stool, glanced at the flash once, selected a pen, dipped it into a pot of India ink, and began to draw. To her surprise, drawing directly onto skin was as easy as it was on paper. In no time at all she'd finished. The image extended from just below the back of Friday's knee to about three inches above her ankle, the outstretched wings wrapping around her calf and almost touching on her upper shin.

'It's quite big,' Harrie said. 'But it has to be, to get in all the detail.'

'Good.' Friday sat up.

Harrie warned, 'Don't smudge it.'

Friday lifted her skirt above her knees and extended her leg along the bench, slightly bent, keeping the fresh ink above the cracked and worn leather. 'You're not going to see Matthew soon, are you?'

'Matthew? Why would I visit Matthew?' Harrie tapped the excess ink off the pen's nib and carefully put it down.

'I don't know. But we need him to go to the bank for us.'

'God, it's this Sunday night, isn't it? Do you want me to come with you?' She desperately hoped Friday wouldn't say yes but she had to offer. She didn't like the idea of Friday being all alone with that horrible man.

'Actually, strangely, I *don't* feel like facing Furniss by myself,' Friday said, 'especially not in a stinking graveyard on the stroke of midnight, but there'd be no point you coming. Last time I just handed the money over, he said something smart-arsed about saving for the next lot, and I left. It only took about two minutes. And the graveyard's just up the street from the police office. I can always scream my head off if he tries anything. Very brave of you to offer, though. Sarah offered, too.'

'Are you sure?'

'Positive. Two hundred pounds, though. Fucking Bella. We're going to be left with just about nothing.'

'I know. It's Janie and the babies I feel bad for. They're the ones who are going to miss out.'

Friday scratched her armpit. 'Well, we'll all just have to work even harder, won't we? I don't mind giving more. It's only money.'

'That's easy for you to say. I give just about everything I earn as it is. And I'm happy to do that, I really am, but I can't give what I haven't got.'

'Try not to worry, Harrie.'

'I do try. But sometimes I can't help it, Friday. I really can't.'

Sunday, 10 July 1831, Sydney Town

Friday hurried up George Street, the little bag containing two hundred pounds in English tenners tucked safely inside her jacket. The night was cold and the wind just this side of bitter, though at least it wasn't raining. There was no moon at all, however, and she'd stumbled badly on the uneven footway twice. Insipid light spilt from the occasional house window, lamps shone at the barracks gates and farther up the hill at the gate of the police office, but the market sheds were as black as coal, rearing up to her right and blocking the scatter of stars in the velvet sky. Somewhere not far behind her a dog barked. She had a lantern but dared not light it, not here on the street where someone might follow her into the burial ground, and rob her.

Ha, that would be funny, wouldn't it? Getting robbed of two hundred pounds when she was on her way to hand it over to Amos sodding Furniss?

She would light the lantern, though, once she was behind the high stone wall that bordered the old graveyard. Nothing — *nothing* — would tempt her to wander around in there in the pitch dark.

She ducked down Druitt Street and followed the wall until she came to a gate hanging half off its hinges. Pausing to wrap her woollen scarf around the lower half of her face against the smell, she lifted the gate to one side and stepped inside the abandoned burial ground.

It had been declared full ten years earlier, closed, and thoroughly neglected since. Sydney Town's more recently deceased were now interred in the Devonshire Street cemetery, leaving behind in George Street two thousand corpses gouged into two acres of unyielding clay. Effluvia seeping up through the ground brought with it an appalling stink, especially in summer, as though the dead themselves were protesting their abandonment. Passers-by used the grounds as an open privy, stray animals wandered among the graves, and vandals had smashed headstones and monuments, broken open vaults and tombs, and, according to gossip, robbed them. The old graveyard was a foul place, and nobody went there — unless, it was said, they were up to no good.

Friday crouched in the shelter of the wall and lit her lantern, adjusting the darkened mantle so that only a thin beam escaped, just enough to light her way. God only knew where Furniss would be waiting. The burial ground was huge, particularly in the dark, and she had no desire at *all* to go plunging into some poor, rotting soul's open grave. He would probably sneak up and scare the shit out of her, just for the fun of it. She was starting to wish now that she had brought someone with her. Not Sarah or Harrie — *especially* not Harrie, not here — but perhaps Jack, like last time.

She set off for the centre, picking her way around yawning black holes and sunken troughs in the mean, patchy grass, grey and dead in the lantern light, heading for the outline of a vault, a crumbling black shape against the night sky. Furniss would see her coming; let the bugger come to her.

Feeling a tickle of awareness on the back of her neck, she spun around. Was he behind her? She raised her lantern, but saw no one, only shades of black blending into one another. Prick. He was playing with her. Then, off to her left, she heard a whistle.

'Hey, girlie!'

She turned again and there he was, a shadow materialising from the darkness, his hat pulled low so she could see little more than his leering, gap-toothed smile. But she knew it was him. She could *smell* the arseholery coming off him.

He held out his hand, palm up.

She withdrew the bag containing the money from her jacket and hurled it at him. He caught it and laughed.

'Bastard!' Friday hissed.

'Slag,' he shot back.

'Who told Bella about our money?' Friday demanded. 'It was bloody Lou, wasn't it?'

But Furniss was already turning away.

'Oi!' Friday shouted after him, her voice echoing eerily across the burial ground. '*Oi!*'

He'd gone, dissolved into the darkness again, like pond scum.

Shaking violently, Friday swore and made herself unclench her fists. The handle of the lantern had cut into her palm, and, now that she thought about it, it hurt. She stood very still, her head down, arms slack, and took several deep breaths to calm herself. She couldn't afford to go berserk here — she'd fall into a grave or something and hurt herself.

Slowly and carefully she made her way back to the gate and let herself out. The money was gone and that was that.

She sighed again, a great, ragged heaving in and out of breath, and told herself things could be worse. Adam was back, Gellar was dead and this time they weren't guilty, Harrie was talking to James, and she ... well, she was just the way she always was. Not happy, not sad. Just Friday.

She'd have a few drinks. That would make her feel better.

From his hiding place behind a crooked headstone he watched as she left, her lantern scribbling a skinny beam of light across the ground at her feet. His heart was still thudding madly with a mix of nervous anticipation and raw, simmering rage, and when the bastard had been talking to her he'd wanted to leap out then and there. But he'd made himself wait, because he didn't want to get her into even more trouble. He didn't want to get any of them into trouble, but especially not Harrie.

Now, though, he could do what he liked.

He made a gesture of quiet, made sure the message had been received, and set out after Furniss, darting on fleet, bare feet from stone to stone, ducking behind the ruins of tombs and low vaults, and quickly reached the far wall bordering Bathurst Street. Furniss was almost at the gate, whistling to himself as though he hadn't a care in the world.

Walter slid the knife out of his jacket pocket and stepped up onto a lurching gravestone, his toes gripping the edge like a monkey's.

'Furniss, you rotten bastard.'

Furniss spun around, eyes wide.

Walter launched himself, driving the knife as hard as he could into Furniss's chest. Furniss grunted once, staggered and crashed against the wall, his arms flailing wildly as he fell on his side. Clifford bit into the man's ankle as Walter rolled away, the knife still gripped in his hand, then he leapt to his feet and stabbed again. And again and again and again, until Furniss stopped moving.

'Clifford, drop him.'

The little dog backed off, taking a mouthful of cloth and flesh with her.

Furniss's hat had come off and his eyes were open, but no longer saw anything. His blood, bubbling and oozing out of his chest, looked black. Like his heart. While Walter watched, the filthy flow slowed, then finally stopped altogether.

He hoicked up a good gob and spat on the dead man's face.

Then he wiped his sticky hands on Furniss's trousers, went through his pockets until he found Friday's money, and slipped the little bag into his own pocket.

He hesitated, then bent over and vomited.

Suddenly feeling very shaky, he wrapped his arms around himself.

After a minute he said, 'Come on, Cliffie, let's go.'

Author's Notes

The characters in this story are all fictional, except for the ones already in the history books.

To my knowledge, the real Francis Rossi, police magistrate and superintendent of Sydney's police, never had anything whatsoever to do with any brothels or madams during his time in New South Wales. Also, that Francis Rossi should not be confused with the Francis Rossi in Status Quo.

The subtitles for parts one, two and three of this story come from Henry Wadsworth Longfellow's poem 'Haunted Houses'.

A note on ghosts, as readers might wonder at the gullibility of some of my characters. While the British public's belief in fairies and the like may have faded by the nineteenth century, and witches had in general been downgraded from the devil's handmaidens to wise women, there was still, apparently, an enduring acceptance by a good number that ghosts were real. Perhaps it was because death was ever-present. The infant and child mortality rate was very high, and diseases we don't have to worry about now could take loved ones in a matter of days. The occasional reappearance — real or imagined — of those snatched so suddenly and unfairly from life may have helped to lessen the pain of such loss.

Cultural expressions of death and mourning really took off in the latter half of the eighteenth century, quite some time before the commonly assumed heydey of mourning during Queen Victoria's reign. There were strict social rules (especially for the rich), special clothing, textiles, jewellery, literature, art, complicated burial practices and eventually, in the later nineteenth and early twentieth centuries, even new religions such as spiritualism. With this great emphasis on death, it is no surprise that focus and belief extended beyond the earthly trappings of mourning to the metaphysical world.

For those who subscribed to the existence of heaven and hell there was also purgatory, where the souls of the tormented were trapped, hence tales of unhappy apparitions wandering about on our plane. But for those without the comfort of religious beliefs encompassing an afterlife, the idea of ghosts might have offered tempting relief from the stark and final reality of death.

And as Matthew Cutler says, 'There are more things in heaven and earth.' Or was that William Shakespeare?

Bibliography

One of the good things about writing a historical series is building up a nice little reference library. Particularly useful for this second book, and nearly thumbed to death already, have been FB Smith, *Illness in Colonial Australia* (Australian Scholarly Publishing Pty Ltd, 2011), and Frank Bongiorno, *The Sex Lives of Australians: a history* (Black Inc., 2012). Both are entertainingly written, extensively researched and bursting with fascinating details for writers like me.

For matters concerning nineteenth-century bling, Duncan James, *Antique Jewellery: its manufacture, materials and design* (Shire Publications Ltd, 2007), and Charles Jarvis, *Jewellery Manufacture & Repair* (N.A.G. Press Ltd, 1978) — both with very handy diagrams — were indispensable, and *Georgian Jewellery 1714–1830* (Antique Collector's Club, 2007), by Ginny Redington Dawes with Olivia Collings, provided endless inspiration (and wasted hours drooling over the stunning photographs).

Information on early nineteenth-century European tattoos is a bit thin on the ground, but Steve Gilbert, *Tattoo History: a source book* (Juno Books, 2000) was useful, and *The Japanese Tattoo* (Abbeville Press, 1986), by Sandi Fellman, gave me lots of ideas for Matthew Cutler's arm ink.

Floorcoverings in Australia 1800–1950 (Historic Houses Trust, 1997) is a book I've consulted far more than I thought I would, and a skinny little tome called *The History of Port Macquarie*, written by C.T. Uptin in 1958 and revised in 1983 by the Hastings District Historical Society, which I bought when visiting the excellent Port Macquarie Historical Museum, also turned out to be very handy, especially the plan of the penal settlement in 1830.

This last one isn't actually a book, but a set of notes to accompany a seminar presented by romantic suspense author Bronwyn Parry at 2012's Romance Writers of Australia conference. Bronwyn's subject was 'The most perfect cloth: dress fabrics for Georgian and Regency characters'. It was a fascinating seminar and I've gone back to those notes again and again. Thank you, Bronwyn!

Acknowledgments

In my opinion the best part of writing a book is when you get to collaborate, so thank you once again to the team at HarperCollins Australia, in particular associate publisher Anna Valdinger, dispenser of good ideas, advice and endless enthusiasm. It's been great to work with freelance editor Kate O'Donnell again, too. This series wouldn't be what it is without Kate's input. Thanks also to publishing director Shona Martyn for constantly supporting my work, and to my hard-working agent, Clare Forster.

Another big 'thanks, guys' is due to HarperCollins New Zealand for keeping everything ticking over in Aotearoa, and to my writing group Hunter Romance Writers for answering hundreds of moronic questions about Facebook.

Other people I'd like to acknowledge are my good friend Ngahuia Te Awekotuku, for her advice and guidance regarding tattoo, moko and upoko tuhi; Kim Wallace-Wells, qualified gemmologist at 'Old Technology' at Newcastle's Centenary Antique Centre, for his advice on nineteenth-century jewellery-making techniques and traditions; and Mary and Bridget Nicholls, for 'lending' me their dog Clifford as a model for Walter's dog in this book — though the real Cliffie is a lot nicer (and yes, actually a female).

Finally, thank you to friends and family, and especially my husband Aaron, for making me countless cups of tea. That's two teabags, milk, no sugar.

The Silk Thief

BOOK THREE

Deborah Challinor

1831: Assigned to a good family in Sydney Town and now learning the art of tattoo, convict girl Harrie Clarke is still haunted by the horror of the brutal murder she and friends Friday Woolfe and Sarah Morgan committed the previous year. Powerful and vindictive criminal Bella Jackson continues to demand money in exchange for her silence regarding their crime. And just when it seems that Harrie and her fervent and long-time admirer James Downey might finally be united, an act of pure nastiness severely threatens their chances — and Harrie's life.

When things go from bad to much, much worse for Harrie, everyone who loves her must do their utmost to save her. But Friday, in love at last, is battling demons of her own, and Sarah is forced to lie low for fear of attracting the attention of the police. Who will be the one to rescue Harrie?

Read on for a sneak peek at *The Silk Thief* ...

Early Monday morning, 11 July 1831, Sydney Town

Harrie Clarke hadn't slept at all well during the night. She'd tossed and turned, worry nipping at her like a hungry rat and her dreams becoming as twisted as her sheets, and when Angus the cat had come in he'd selfishly spread himself across half the mattress. And now someone was tapping on her window. Except that was impossible — her room was high up in the attic.

Grateful for the rag rug on the cold floorboards, she crossed to the window and peered down past the shingled slope of the roof. Dawn was still several hours away and there was hardly any moon — she couldn't see a thing. During the day her eyrie at the top of the Barretts' two-storey house afforded her a view of the roofs, privies and dank yards of those who lived below on Harrington Street (and, unfortunately, of the gallows within the walls of Sydney Gaol), of the streets of the town to the south and west, and of Sydney Cove and the governor's enormous private gardens to the east. Now, however, in the velvet darkness, her ears and nose were more use to her than were her eyes. She heard the gentle susurration of small waves on the cove's shore, the strident call of a night bird, and the tuneless singing of a drunk somewhere down near George Street. As always, the stink from nearby cesspits tainted the air even up here, undercut by the sharp reek of yesterday's rendered tallow from the soap- and candleworks in the next street, mixed with wood smoke from hearth fires and the pleasant briny tang of the sea.

But as her eyes adjusted to the night's shifting shadows, she made out the barest outline of a lone figure standing below in the backyard, a pale face turned up towards her. A raised arm drew back and something small and hard bounced off her window, making Harrie flinch. A pebble?

The figure was that of a boy, and she guessed from the way he held himself who he might be — Walter Cobley. But what had gone wrong, to make him rouse her so early on a Monday morning? Had something happened last night to Friday? But why would Walter be here to tell her? He knew nothing about her gruesome midnight errand.

Harrie lit the bedside lamp, keeping the flame low. Angus, awake now, gave a soft meow as she slid her feet into slippers. The air was cool but she didn't bother with a robe. She made her way downstairs, treading gently on the creaky risers so she wouldn't wake anyone, and let herself out through the back door.

He was waiting for her, his lanky form detaching from the solid blackness of the yard wall as though he were made of smoke.

She whispered, 'Is that you, Walter?'

'I need help, Harrie.' His voice cracked and he cleared his throat, the sound close to a sob. 'I've done something bad.'

She lifted the lamp, and almost dropped it. Walter's shirt, jacket, face and hands were splattered with something black.

'Walter! Is that blood? Are you hurt?' She took a step towards him, but his scruffy little dog, Clifford, crouched protectively in front of him, growled menacingly.

'Shut up, Cliffie. It's not mine. It's Amos Furniss's.' Walter swallowed audibly and stared down at his hands — held before him palms up, fingers spread — as though they belonged to someone else. 'I killed him, Harrie.'

Her heart stopped, then lurched into a wild, thumping rhythm. 'Amos Furniss? You've *killed* Amos Furniss?'

Walter nodded.

'But ... where?'

'In the old burial ground.'

Harrie felt dizzy, and sick with dread as the enormity of what he'd done overwhelmed her. And confused, as well — Friday had gone to the cemetery, not Walter. She had the most hideous thought. 'Is Friday all right?'

'I suppose. I dunno.' Walter wiped a trembling hand over his face, smearing tacky blood across his cheek.

'What do you mean?' Desperate to hear about Friday, she wanted to grab his shoulders and shake a useful answer out of him, but he was clearly suffering from shock and she knew it wouldn't do any good. 'What happened, Walter? *Tell* me.'

Walter squatted so suddenly Harrie thought for a second he'd collapsed. But he was only crouching to pat Clifford, his blood-sticky hands running along the dog's hairy back, drawing in comfort stroke by stroke.

'I followed her to the burial ground.'

'Friday? Or Clifford?' she asked. Clifford was actually a bitch despite her masculine name, and Harrie wanted to be very clear about who was who in Walter's story.

'Friday. And I seen Furniss so I hid while she gave him the money. Then when she'd gone I followed him to the Bathurst Street gate and I stabbed him. To death.' He raised his head, his teeth bared in something not even close to a smile. 'And I'm bloody glad I did, Harrie. He deserved it.'

She nodded: the shock of his news had for some reason heightened her sensory perception — she could taste the cold in the air and feel the darkness on her skin, and she fancied she could actually hear the bones in her neck grating together. She shivered. She knew why Walter had wanted to kill Furniss, but to discover he'd actually done it — a twelve-year-old boy stabbing a man to death — was ghastly.

'And I thought I'd feel ... I dunno, happy or something,' Walter said. 'But I don't. I feel funny. I feel sick.'

As if to demonstrate this, he retched and, narrowly missing Clifford, heaved up a little puddle of watery vomit.

Harrie patted his back as he spat out a long string of saliva, and this time Clifford didn't growl at her proximity. This close, Walter smelt like a freshly slaughtered cow and she felt her gorge rise.

'Where's Furniss now?'

'Still at the cemetery.'

Harrie waited until he'd spat some more and wiped his mouth on his sleeve. Then she said, 'Walter, listen to me. Did anyone see you leave? Or on George Street near the burial ground? Is that the way you came here?'

He shook his head. 'I come back along York Street.'

'But did anyone *see* you?'

He shrugged and settled his hand gently onto Clifford's head. She licked his mucky fingers. 'Maybe,' he said. Then he nodded miserably and started to cry.

Harrie dressed hastily, not caring that her shift was on backwards, and wrapped her shawl around her shoulders. She glanced at the rocking chair under the eaves, but it was disappointingly empty. She still felt sick, and a leaden, almost painful, sense of doom had settled in her belly.

She'd despised Amos Furniss herself, but now there'd be *another* dead soul to creep around in her mind and torment her. Liz Parker and Gabriel Keegan, then Jared Gellar and now Furniss. And poor, darling Rachel, of course, though unlike the others she'd been a tremendous comfort since she'd passed. So many folk whose paths she and Sarah and Friday had crossed had died. Was it them? she wondered. Were they somehow responsible for *all* those deaths? Was *she*?

She crept back downstairs. Walter was still there, hunched against the wall in a crouch, head resting on his arms, Clifford at his feet. The dawn was still a good hour or so away. Harrie knew she'd have time to get to Friday's, then Leo's, then back again before the Barretts awoke.

'Come on.' She offered Walter a hand up. 'Let's get you home. Leo will know what to do.'

Walter extended his own hand; in the light of Harrie's lamp they both eyed the blood staining his skin and the rims of his fingernails. He withdrew it, and pushed himself off the cobbles.

'Quickly, love, have a wash.' Harrie indicated the bucket beside the rainwater overflow barrel, and wondered why he hadn't done so already. The shock, probably.

'I lost me hat,' he said forlornly.

'Never mind, we'll get you another, ' Harrie said, as though she were talking to a five-year-old.

Walter splashed his face with cold water and scrubbed at his hands while Clifford helped herself to a noisy drink from the bucket.

'Why did you come here?' Harrie asked as they hurried along Gloucester Street towards the turn into Suffolk Lane. Worried that someone out early would see the state of Walter's clothes, she'd given him her spare shawl to wrap around his shoulders. 'Why didn't you go straight home?'

'Oh.' Walter stopped, dug around inside his jacket and brought out a pouch. 'This is for you.'

Harrie didn't have to look inside to know what it contained. Her heart sank yet again. 'The money?'

He nodded.

'How did you know to follow Friday last night? How did you know who she was meeting?'

'I were listening when you and her were talking about it at Leo's,' Walter confessed. 'When she were getting her new tattoo?'

Oh *God*. Harrie felt as though her insides were turning to water. After all these months, was their secret finally out? What had she and Friday said that day? She really couldn't remember. She was having such trouble remembering all sorts of things lately. 'What, exactly, did you hear?'

'Friday said something about Bella and two hundred quid. And that the money were to be delivered to Furniss at the old George Street burial ground last night. At midnight. And something about a lady called Janie and some babies missing out? You said you haven't got much money to give. So I got it back for you.'

He didn't appear particularly pleased with himself — unsurprisingly he still looked like a boy shocked silly after stabbing a man to death — but Harrie knew him well enough to understand he needed acknowledgment for retrieving the money, whatever other awful thing he'd done. So she said, 'I'm grateful for that, Walter. We all are. Thank you.' Though there would be hell to pay when the blackmail money remained undelivered and Bella discovered that Furniss was dead. She would immediately assume that Friday, Sarah or herself had killed him. Bella already knew, after all, that they were capable of murder. God, why hadn't Walter thought of that? But he was only a boy.

'Walter, when Friday and I were talking, did we say why we were being blackmailed?'

He shook his head.

Harrie allowed herself an inward sigh of relief, and slipped the pouch into her skirt pocket. 'Did you tell Leo what you heard?'

'Hell no. He would've clipped me ears for listening at the door.'

'Oh, love, he's going to do more than clip your ears. Do you not realise how much trouble you're in?'

Harrie thought she might have accepted Leo knowing about the blackmail, if it meant that Leo could then have kept a tight rein on

Walter. Instead Walter had now killed Furniss, a crime for which he would certainly go to the gallows. But she knew that although Walter was young, he wasn't completely naive. He'd have realised that telling Leo what he'd overheard would ruin his plans for revenge.

'He'll tan me hide, won't he?'

'Probably.' Instead of following Suffolk Lane down to George Street, Harrie turned into Harrington Street.

'Where are we going?'

'To make sure Friday got home all right and to tell her what's happened. Then we'll get you back to Leo's.'

It only took them a couple of minutes to arrive at the Siren's Arms, the hotel owned by Friday's boss, Elizabeth Hislop. A lamp burnt outside the pub's front door, but the windows on the upstairs accommodation floor were all dark. Harrie and Walter followed the carriageway around to the stable yard at the back, and stood staring up.

'Which one's Friday's?' Walter asked in a loud whisper.

Harrie wasn't sure; it was hard to tell from outside on a dark night. 'I *think* it's that one,' she said, pointing. 'Throw something. See if we can wake her.'

Walter tossed a small stone towards the mullioned window. It hit the glass with a clack and bounced off.

Nothing happened. He threw another one. And another. Finally the window opened and a tousled head appeared. 'Who the hell's throwing bloody stones?'

'Friday!' Harrie called up as loudly as she dared. 'It's me. Let us in!'

'Harrie?'

'It's me and Walter. We have to talk.'

The window closed. 'Don't worry,' Harrie assured Walter, 'she'll let us in.' And then she realised that Walter wouldn't understand why it was so important she tell Friday what had happened, and that when he did understand he'd feel even worse than he did already. But that couldn't be helped. Not now.

Clifford growled, then a voice behind them said, 'Oi!'

Harrie almost jumped out of her boots and Walter started so wildly he fell to one knee.

'What d'you think you're doing?' It was Jack Wilton, Elizabeth Hislop's coachman and jack of all trades, and he was hefting a wood splitter in one brawny hand.

'Jack, it's me, Harrie Clarke. And Walter, from Leo Dundas's.'

Jack took a step forwards on stockinged feet and squinted. 'Christ, it is, too. What are you doing out here in the middle of the night?' He glanced at Walter. 'And why's he wearing a woman's shawl?'

The back door of the pub opened and Friday Woolfe appeared, a robe thrown over her nightdress, her wild, curly hair unbound and falling almost to her waist. She carried a lamp, its flame illuminating her bare feet. 'Harrie? What's wrong? What's happened?'

'Are you all right?' Harrie demanded.

'Me? I'm fine. Why?'

Harrie glanced at Jack. 'We need to talk. It's important.'

Friday understood immediately. 'Thanks, Jack.'

'Sorry we woke you,' Harrie added.

Jack shrugged, yawned, said, 'I'll get back to me pit then, shall I?' and trudged towards his room above the stables.

'Come upstairs,' Friday said.

Harrie, Walter and Clifford followed Friday back to her room. She locked the door after them, dug around in her dressing table drawer for a small bottle of gin, and said, 'What's going on, Harrie? What's Walter doing here? And why's he wearing your shawl?'

As Walter sat on the chair before the dressing table, Harrie sank onto Friday's bed, relieved beyond words to be sharing the awful predicament caused by his crime. 'Walter overheard us at Leo's the other day and last night he followed you.'

'You sneaky bugger,' Friday said. 'You must have kept your head down. I didn't see you.'

'Weren't meant to,' Walter mumbled.

'He waited until you gave Furniss the money,' Harrie went on, 'then he killed him.'

Friday choked on a mouthful of gin, shooting it out of her nose like a whale's blow and coughing until her face turned puce.

Harrie talked on over the top of her racket. 'And he took the money back.' She removed the pouch from her pocket and dropped it on the bed. 'He thought he was doing the right thing, but now Bella's going to think *we* killed Furniss. So she'll either kill us in revenge, or she'll tell the police what we did and we'll hang.' She heard her own voice rising and was powerless to stop it. 'It's over, Friday. We're going to die and we'll all go to hell for our sins.'

Friday gave one last cough, wiped her mouth on her sleeve and said, 'Calm down, Harrie. Here, have a drink.'

'I don't want one,' Harrie said, her mind darting back to the dreadful episode with the wine in Hyde Park last year.

'Just drink it, will you?' Friday thrust the bottle at her. 'Call it medicinal.'

As Harrie took a tiny hesitant sip, Friday turned to Walter, whose pale, narrow face had gone even whiter, and said, 'Really? You actually killed him?'

Walter nodded miserably. 'But I didn't think ... I'm sorry. I just wanted to make Furniss pay, and get the money back. For Harrie. For all of you.' He swallowed anxiously. 'Why will you hang?'

'Best you don't know, love. Where's Furniss now?'

'In the cemetery.'

'Christ. Does Leo know?' Friday asked Harrie.

'Not yet. We're on our way.'

'Do you want me to come with you? I'll never get back to sleep now.'

'Oh, would you?' Harrie was so grateful. She really hadn't been looking forward to Leo's reaction when he discovered what Walter had done. He was very fond of the boy and would be extremely upset and angry, and would more than likely blame himself.

'Nearly morning anyway.' Friday slipped out of her robe and drew her nightdress up to her waist, revealing long, white legs and a very shapely bare bottom.

'Friday!' Harrie inclined her head towards Walter.

'Oh. Right. Look away, love,' Friday said.

But Walter, utterly exhausted, had nodded off, his chin on his chest, a dangling hand resting on Clifford's head.

Friday tut-tutted. 'Look at him. Twelve years old and a murderer already. What a bloody tragedy. It's all Furniss's bloody fault. The only *real* crime is poor Walter had to top the bastard himself. Someone should have shoved him off his twig long ago.' She pulled her nightdress off over her head and, completely at ease with her own nakedness, stooped to rummage through the pile of clothes she'd left on the floor last night. 'Where the hell are my boots?' she exclaimed, loud enough to startle Walter awake again. He gawped at her nude form for a moment, then quickly looked down at his hands.

'Hurry up and put something on,' Harrie said. 'Was that them at the bottom of the stairs?' She'd noticed an abandoned pair of boots as they'd come up.

Friday sniffed the armpits of yesterday's shift, made a face and put it on anyway. 'Could be. I was in a bit of a state when I got in last night. Had a couple of drinks after the cemetery.' She stepped into her skirt then struggled into the fitted bodice, swearing under her breath as she did up the fiddly little buttons down the front.

Harrie snapped, 'For God's sake, will you *hurry up*!'

'God, I'm not giving you gin again,' Friday muttered.

A sharp knock came at the door — everyone froze.

'Friday? What's going on in there?'

'Shite,' Friday hissed. 'It's Mrs H.'